Forgotten Graves

Wes Markin

David Lynch

Artist, Dreamer, Storyteller

My Inspiration

Thank You

1946–2025

About the Author

Wes Markin is the bestselling author of The Yorkshire Murders, which stars the compassionate and relentless DCI Emma Gardner. He is also the author of Whitby's Forgotten Victims, the DCI Michael Yorke Thrillers set in Salisbury, and the Jake Pettman Thrillers set in New England. Wes lives in Harrogate with his wife, two children, and his cheeky cockapoo, Rosie, close to the crime scenes in The Yorkshire Murders and Whitby's Forgotten Victims.

You can find out more at:
www.wesmarkinauthor.com

facebook.com/wesmarkinauthor

By Wes Markin

DCI Yorke Thrillers

One Last Prayer

The Repenting Serpent

The Silence of Severance

Rise of the Rays

Dance with the Reaper

Christmas with the Conduit

Better the Devil

The Secret Diary of Lacey Ray

A Lesson in Crime

Jake Pettman Thrillers

The Killing Pit

Fire in Bone

Blue Falls

The Rotten Core

Rock and a Hard Place

The Yorkshire Murders

The Viaduct Killings

The Lonely Lake Killings

The Crying Cave Killings

The Graveyard Killings

The Winter Killings

The Black Rock Killings

Whitby's Forgotten Victims

Forgotten Bones

Forgotten Lives

Forgotten Souls

Forgotten Graves

Forgotten Shadows

Forgotten Depths

∼

Details of how to claim your **FREE** DCI Michael Yorke quick read, **A lesson in Crime**, can be found at the end of this book.

This story is a work of fiction. All names, characters, organizations, places, events and incidents are products of the author's imagination or are used fictitiously. Any resemblance to any persons, alive or dead, events or locals is entirely coincidental.

Text copyright © 2025 Wes Markin

First published 2025

ISBN: 9798311165471

Edited by: Candida Bradford

Published by: WFM Publishing Ltd

All rights reserved.

No part of this book should be reproduced in any way without the express permission of the author.

Chapter One

Fog lights cut through the December night.

Kyle Russell clung to the Audi's supple leather steering wheel, whooping with every sharp turn. In the passenger seat, Jason Cleaves was riding a cocaine high, thumping the roof, urging him to push the car faster. However, Kyle had deliberately taken a touch less of the drug and, though his reactions were sharper, he didn't feel invincible.

Ahead, the next bend loomed. A treacherous curve bordered by snow-laden moorland stretching endlessly on either side of the A169.

The view transported Kyle back a decade, to when he was nine years old – wandering the snowy fields of the North York Moors with his father, finding peace and clarity in the pleasant openness. His father's steady presence had been more than guidance through the wilds – it was an education in understanding their place in the world. He so missed tracing those familiar paths with him.

The intensity of the turn brought him back to now. And the sobering reality that those days were gone, buried forever with his father's body.

Kyle glanced over to see Jason tapping cocaine on the back of his hand.

'No sudden moves now, boyo,' Jason insisted. 'Another bump incoming.'

A sharp snort, followed by more pounding on the roof. 'Bump... bump... bump!'

Headlights blazed toward them. Kyle moved further to the side. A car streaked past, horn blaring in protest at their fog lights.

Kyle couldn't resist joining Jason in his laughter, manic though it was. He'd completely embraced the chaos his friend had brought into his life these last six months.

His mother didn't approve, obviously.

But at nineteen, Kyle was done with other people's expectations.

'Another bump, son?' Jason asked.

'In a bit. Let's get into Ruswarp first. Find somewhere quiet. Pull over for a bit.'

'Can't promise there'll be any left.' Jason snorted another line and grinned.

Kyle glanced at him again.

Jason's pupils were blown wide. *'After all, you're in the car with the Bumpa Loompa!'* He launched into a mangled version of the Oompa Loompa song, replacing the words with his new lyrics.

Kyle laughed, turned his attention back to the road, and thundered past the turnoff to Goathland, the engine's roar momentarily drowning Jason's off-key singing. He noticed fresh flakes of snow dancing in his fog lights.

Over the fields, Kyle caught glimpses of sheep huddled against dry stone walls, their wool collecting snow.

Beyond the valley, he could see the lights of Ruswarp.

Then he went back four years – to afternoons at the

Bridge Inn, stealing sips of bitter while his dad pretended not to notice—

The Audi's back end kicked out on black ice.

Kyle yanked the wheel, over-correcting.

Jason's singing immediately transformed into a scream.

He could hear his father's voice – telling him not to hit the brakes, but when fog lights illuminated a weathered-wooden fence, he wished he had.

Splintered posts bounced over the bonnet. Wire mesh shrieked as it tore into the metal.

Then they were airborne, suspended in a moment of terrible weightlessness.

Kyle's stomach lurched.

The Audi's nose dipped, and an impact rattled his bones. Snow sprayed up around them. The steering wheel bucked in his hands. He'd no control, but he could still hear his father's advice, so still he resisted the pedal, not wanting to go into an uncontrollable spin.

Jason continued screaming.

Kyle's eyes widened as a dark shape emerged from the gloom. 'Shit... shit...'

He knew it from his walks.

An old grain silo.

Not massive, but solid enough to kill them both.

Left with no choice, Kyle stamped on the brakes. The car fishtailed, sliding sideways across the frozen ground.

The impact when they hit the silo's base was deafening. With a shudder, the car stopped, its driver's side slamming into the old wood.

Kyle blinked, straining to see through the spider-webbed windscreen.

Jason groaned, shifting in his seat.

An ominous creak echoed from above.

Jason's voice trembled. 'What's that?'

'I don't...' Understanding hit him. It was coming down. 'Get out!'

Kyle barely unfastened his seat belt before a tremendous crash shook the roof.

Heart thrashing, he lunged for the passenger side as Jason pounced from the vehicle, rolling clear.

Another loud crash on the bonnet made him think he was too late.

But then he dived clear too, also rolling over the ice-cold ground.

Up on their feet, they staggered through deep snow, turning and watching as they did so, as the silo collapsed onto the Audi. Wood and dust rained down, pounding and burying the car.

When the destruction finally ceased, they looked back.

'Fuck... did you see that?' Jason asked.

Kyle didn't grace his stupid question with an answer; instead, he watched the dust settle.

To his surprise, the mangled Audi, with steam hissing from the bonnet, was still visible.

Unbelievably, the fog lights continued to function, beacons amidst the destruction.

'Fuck,' Jason said. 'Now what?'

Kyle forced himself to focus. He brushed snow from his sodden clothes. He was shivering, either from adrenaline or the cold. 'Now, we get out of here.'

Jason stared wild-eyed at the chaos. 'Yes... but...' He was shivering. He grabbed Kyle's arm.

Kyle looked him in his wide, wired eyes.

'What about fingerprints and DNA?' Jason said.

Kyle shook his head. Jason wasn't the sharpest tool in the shed. 'Why would they bother with DNA and fingerprints? No one's dead! Besides, are your DNA or fingerprints even in the bloody system?'

He looked as if he was about to throw up. 'I don't know.'

'Well, have you ever been arrested?' Kyle asked.

'No.'

'Then, it's unlikely.'

'Okay... head's buggered, you know?' Jason turned away, shivering, cursing the deep snow.

'We need to move quick. It's fucking freezing,' Kyle said, really shivering now. The cold was seeping into his bones. He wondered if hypothermia was a possibility. He'd seen it in movies before. It didn't look pretty.

As they moved away from the wreck and the Audi fog lights, darkness closed in. Kyle activated his mobile torch to avoid hidden obstacles and suggested Jason do the same.

His friend stopped dead.

Shit, Kyle thought, suspecting what was coming.

Jason frantically patted his pockets before spinning around. 'My phone. My fucking phone!'

'For fuck's sake, Jason.'

Jason turned and pointed back toward the wreckage. 'It was in the glove compartment.'

Kyle suppressed his rising anger. 'And you were worried about DNA?'

'Fuck... I'm sorry... What now?'

'Stay here,' Kyle hissed. 'You're off your head. No point in us both getting buried alive.'

'Let me help.'

'No.' He raised his voice. 'Stay the fuck here.'

Kyle tried to jog back toward the wreck, but it was hard with such deep snow. It was more like a quick trudge. Increasing his heart rate was probably a good idea, though. He still shivered, but it wasn't quite as bad. As he drew closer to the chaos, he looked up at the damaged silo. It was about five metres high. Half its wooden exterior had now given way, lying on or around the vehicle. Inside, he could see a metal ladder leading up to an exposed, narrower floor. Miraculously, the rectangular silo still stood, though its ramshackle roof sagged dangerously and wouldn't hold for long. Bags and debris hung over the edge of the second floor.

Praying nothing else would fall, he reached through the open door of the Audi, his heart hammering as the wood creaked overhead.

Almost there...

The glove compartment opened with a thud.

Jason's phone was there, the screen glowing.

As Kyle's fingers closed around it, there was another thud onto the roof above. Not as loud as last time, but certainly enough to nearly stop his heart dead. 'Bollocks!'

He backed out, his eyes regarding the covered roof.

'Fuck... no...'

It couldn't be.

He turned his torch onto it.

It was.

A curved spine.

'God!' He choked back a scream, staggering backwards.

'What is it?' Jason's voice came from behind him.

'Stay back,' Kyle warned, hand raised. 'It's a body.'

But the warning only drew Jason closer.

They stood together, torch beams playing over the skeleton curled in a foetal position.

Hollow eye sockets stared up from a grinning skull.

'Fucking hell,' Jason gagged. 'That's messed up. Now what?'

Kyle had no answer. He took several steps back, light still shining on the skeleton.

Distant sirens wailed.

'We need to go!' Jason said.

Kyle thought of his father again – how that loss had changed him forever, his mother's constant reminders that he'd never been the same.

Now here he was, staring at a decomposed body lying on a stolen, demolished car in the ice-cold, gloomy arsehole of nowhere.

He wondered if this night would mark another point of no return – another moment from which he'd never recover.

'I'm staying,' Kyle said. 'It's the right thing to do.'

Chapter Two

DCI Frank Black was adjusting his tie in his bathroom mirror for the fourth time. *Bloody hell,* he thought, *you can't polish a turd.*

He heard the chime of his doorbell, flinched, and his fingers fumbled the knot. 'Balls.'

Frank took off the tie and crammed it into his pocket before undoing his top button. He regarded himself as the doorbell sounded again and sighed. Then he headed toward the front door, reassuring himself that it didn't matter too much. This wasn't a date, of course, just the coming together of two close friends. The suit, twenty years old and fresh from the dry cleaners, felt like a straitjacket. Still, at least he could fit back into it. Just. A year back, it'd be hanging off him in shreds by now.

Passing the kitchen, he glanced in at the set table, his eyes lingering on the bottle of San Pellegrino centred between the plates.

Bloody hell, right now, the craving for something stronger was something else! These were the moments that tested his resolve – the social niceties, the friendly gatherings.

The not-dates.

Because, no matter what Gerry believed, that's exactly what it was. The doorbell went for a third time, and this time his stomach lurched. Christ, he thought, I'm keeping her waiting in the cold.

And she wasn't well!

He checked his breath. Fine. He hadn't smoked a roll-up in over an hour and had used mouthwash twice.

He yanked the door open.

Janet Wainwright stood on his doorstep, bundled up in a thick coat and earmuffs, hopping from foot to foot.

'How do? Come in...' Frank said, stepping back.

Janet shook her head. 'No, I'm under strict instructions not to stay.' She stepped aside to reveal her mother, Evelyn, settled in her wheelchair at the foot of the steps. She wore an elegant navy dress under a cream wool coat, a bouquet of yellow daffodils brightening her lap.

'Even if it is freezing,' Janet continued. 'And a cup of tea may be the only thing standing between me and pneumonia.'

'Always the drama queen,' Evelyn said. 'You can't catch anything from cold weather.'

'No,' Janet said. 'Try telling that to great uncle Paul.'

'Paul was hit by a car, dear,' Evelyn said.

'Yes, after it skidded on the ice. Then he caught that superbug in the hospital. So technically, it counts.'

'Give over.' Evelyn's tone was sharpening.

Frank shifted awkwardly in the doorway, his eyes flicking between mother and daughter, wondering if this was just normal banter, or if there was some real tension between them.

Janet looked at him. 'Charming, isn't she?'

He smiled weakly.

'What time shall I collect her?'

He found the question odd, and it triggered memories of him dropping Maddie at birthday parties when she was a child. 'About seven?'

'Three hours?' Janet raised an eyebrow. 'You can put up with her for that long?' She laughed.

'You see what I have to put up with, Frank?' Evelyn said.

Frank laughed, but it surely didn't sound real.

Janet shot Frank a sympathetic look and stepped behind her mother's wheelchair. She attempted to tilt it up onto the step, but the height proved too much.

'Wait a moment...' Frank moved to help. 'Allow me.'

Janet stepped aside. 'It's a bit too high, I think.'

'Damn thing's old-fashioned...' Frank said. 'Who needs a step? I've been planning to get it removed,' he lied. He gripped the chair handles, his back protesting as he tilted it back. 'Nothing to it,' he lied again, teeth clenched.

Evelyn craned her neck to look up at him, scepticism clear on her face.

'On three?' Frank bent his knees, ignoring the warning twinge in his lower back. 'One... two...'

The wheels refused to go up over the step. Sweat beaded on Frank's forehead.

'Frank.' Evelyn's voice cut through his struggle. 'Stop this instant, before you hurt yourself.'

He lowered the chair back down, trying to hide his laboured breathing. 'Just... need... a different angle, that's all.' He repositioned himself.

'You'll do no such thing!'

Her tone reminded him so much of Mary, it carried that same mix of authority and concern. It squeezed his heart.

Without ceremony, Evelyn handed the flowers to Janet

and gripped the arms of her wheelchair. 'I may be in this bloody chair, but I'm not made of sodding china!'

Open-mouthed, Frank watched her push herself to standing. Janet moved smoothly to support her mother, and together they made their way inside, leaving Frank to fold up the wheelchair and trudge behind them with what remained of his dignity.

Up on the step that had caused the issues, a flutter of movement off to Frank's right caught his attention. Henrietta Timber, his neighbour, watched him from her window.

He wasn't surprised. Her nosiness was as predictable as the sunrise.

He aimed his usual scowl in her direction, though these days it was tinged with some affection. After all, she'd been there that terrible night when he'd discovered his daughter Maddie had visited while he was out. She'd sat with him until dawn, brewing endless cups of tea and letting him pour out his grief.

They'd grown closer since then, their decades-old animosity softening into something like friendship.

Still, traditions had to be maintained, so he tried to keep that scowl as authentic as possible. And she did the same.

'Nosy old bat,' he growled, but a smile crept onto his face once he was through the door and out of sight.

Chapter Three

DI GERRY CARVER needed three plates for her dinner.

One for the steamed cod, another for the quinoa, and a final one for the sautéed vegetables.

As well as respecting the boundaries between each separate food type, she'd also carefully measured out the portions.

Across the table from Gerry, Tom Foley made do with one plate. Foods touching didn't bother him in the slightest. If not for being her boyfriend, the concept of food separation would be completely alien to him, but he was used to it now.

Both were relatively quiet eaters, so apart from the gentlest clink of cutlery, the sound of Rylan's steady breathing was the only other sound intruding on the silence. Gerry was comfortable in silence, but she knew many people weren't. Tom was one such person. She regarded the familiar tension in Tom's rigid posture, born from his growing feeling of discomfort.

Since she'd established clear boundaries about dinner conversation – no work talk (right at the top of the list), no discussion of her parents' deaths, and absolutely no mention of his own family – dinner times had become somewhat strained. Every night, without fail, he'd manage only five minutes or so, before he cleared his throat and said, 'Anything bothering you, Gerry?'

'No. I'm fine. Are you okay?'

'Yes... but what are you thinking about?'

'I'm thinking about Frank having dinner with Evelyn.'

Tom's fork paused halfway to his mouth. 'Really? Isn't that the widow of the man who'd had an affair with Frank's late wife?'

'Yes.'

Tom lowered his fork. 'Controversial. And they're dating?'

'He says not.'

Tom nodded. 'And do you believe him?'

'He's offered no facts to the contrary as yet.'

'Okay... I can see why you're distracted. You must be worried about him.'

'Not him, as such. I think I'm worried about the food.' She studied her segregated plates.

'Sorry?'

'He's cooking exactly the same dish. Steamed cod, quinoa and sautéed vegetables. I talked him through it several times, but he never sounded too confident in relaying the process back to me.'

'Ah.' Tom's hand drifted toward the salt grinder. 'I'm sure he'll be fine. He's a grown man.' He laughed.

Why was that funny? Gerry thought, regarding him. 'He's had very little cooking experience.'

'True, but looking at him, I'd say he's eaten a lot of food – he'll know how it should taste!' He began liberally grinding salt over his meal.

Gerry watched the white crystals fall. 'You don't know how it should taste.'

'Come again?'

'You don't know how food should taste. There's enough salt in this dish. You'll mask all the subtle flavours.'

He set the grinder down. 'Frank on a date. Crazy.'

'Just dinner.' She repeated his exact words.

Tom shrugged. 'It sounds like a date.'

'Frank just needs more social interaction. At the moment, I'm the only person he talks to. Someone closer to his age might help.'

'So, he's doing it because you asked him to?'

'No, he wanted to do it. I just encouraged him.'

'Do you think he wants a new relationship?'

Gerry's fork paused in midair. The slowness of his comprehension confused her this evening. 'It's not a date. Just dinner.'

'Okay... do you think he wants companionship?'

'He needs it.'

Tom smiled. 'Yes, everyone needs it. You needed it.'

'I don't think so. With me, it's different.' She smiled. 'I just grew to like it.' The distinction was important to her.

'I like that you care about Frank,' Tom said. 'It's nice.'

Tom glanced at Rylan, who sat at attention, his gaze fixed on every movement. The Lab's unwavering stare while he ate dinner had been a source of tension since day one. Initially, he couldn't cope with being watched while eating, but he'd adjusted to a point. 'Strange how he still does that. I've never given him food or anything.'

'It's not about food any more.'

'Okay... what's it about then?'

'Maybe he just enjoys watching you? Or maybe he's wary of you because you're ever-present in his life at the moment. I don't know the reason. I can't interpret his exact thoughts.'

'I wish he'd stop.'

Gerry felt irritated. Tom knew that Rylan's presence wasn't up for negotiating. Still, she tried to be polite. 'I'm sorry. His social norms are different. He doesn't understand that staring at you while you eat is inappropriate.'

Tom's laugh carried a hint of nervousness. 'I think he's worried about me choking. Maybe I should see him as a guardian angel. After all, he might spring up and do the Heimlich manoeuvre.'

Gerry's expression remained serious, her eyes tracking the salt grinder as he reached for it again. 'With the amount of salt you use, a heart attack or stroke is more likely than choking.'

Chapter Four

FRANK TRIED to serve the food exactly as Gerry had explained to him. Steamed cod, on a bed of quinoa, alongside some sautéed vegetables.

He was concerned about the small amount of seasoning he was told to use.

Gerry had assured him that the food would be tasty enough, and that it was important to adjust to a lower sodium content, anyway. She also added that Evelyn, following her stroke, would appreciate these efforts.

In his marriage, Frank had always left the cooking to Mary. Not because he was lazy, but because he'd always been so busy. If it'd been left to him during those seventy-hour weeks, he'd have functioned on takeaways. Frank regarded Evelyn, the widow of Nigel Wainwright—the man his late wife had an affair with. They'd become friends for the sole reason that their spouses had been killed together in a car accident. Evelyn believed their friendship could help heal some of the guilt and pain, and Frank had come around to the idea.

He smiled at her. 'Ready?'

She grinned. 'Yes.' Frank seized the dishes from the work surface and presented them to Evelyn. She clapped her hands. 'Look at that!'

'Well...' Frank said, 'Let's give it a whirl first. Sorry if it's too bland, like.' He lowered himself into his chair, joints protesting. 'I'm cutting down on salt and other shi—' He caught himself mid-word. 'Rubbish.'

'Wise. You should think about your health.'

'Truth is, I don't. At least, I didn't. My colleague, Gerry, does that for me... you know, thinks about my health. I just do as I'm told.' He laughed.

'Sounds like she's got your back,' Evelyn said, reaching for her knife and fork.

'Aye. Or rather, she's on my back all the time.'

Evelyn laughed. 'It's good to have friends who care about you.'

Frank managed a small smile, the words hitting closer to home than he'd expected. 'So, I hear. Never done so well in that regard.'

'Maybe you're making up for lost time?'

Frank nodded reluctantly. After Mary's death, and Maddie's disappearance, he'd convinced himself he was alone. Now he had to admit that wasn't completely true any more.

'Anyway, it looks very wholesome,' Evelyn said, cutting the cod.

'Aye, wholesome.' He prodded the quinoa without enthusiasm.

'Tell me about Gerry,' she said, just before taking a mouthful.

'Nice lass, Gerry. Cracking brain.' He tapped his temple. 'Like a whirlwind up there. Everything presents itself as a puzzle which she can solve' – he clicked his fingers – 'like that. Knows a lot too. I struggle to remember what I did yesterday. She can remember everything she ever read.' A fond chuckle escaped him. 'It can be too much. Overwhelming sometimes.'

'You told me before that she was autistic.'

'Aye. She's this therapy dog, Rylan. Keeps her grounded. When her head runs away with her, you know? Rylan brings her back to earth. Everyone's head runs away from them, sometimes, I know, but Gerry has more triggers, you see. The way the world works doesn't always cater for her. That's how she explained it to me anyway. It can be isolating... and Rylan. Well, he's great. Bailed us out a few times. Clever dog, you know? Never really realised.' He took a mouthful of food and winced over the blandness.

'Sounds like you value both of them.'

He swallowed, reluctantly. Then he nodded, pushing the food around his plate, wondering if he could actually eat this. 'Aye... at least I did till she made me chuck out all my condiments. Sauces – the lot. Doesn't trust me not to season everything to within an inch of its life.' He attempted a conspiratorial wink. 'I could rustle up some salt though... you know... if you fancy it?'

Evelyn chewed thoughtfully. 'I'll leave it, thank you. I like it. The food is gentle... not overpowering.'

'That's a diplomatic way of putting it.' *It tastes like cardboard to me*, Frank thought, resisting the urge to unearth his secret stash of salt, determined not to put temptation in Evelyn's way.

They lapsed into comfortable silence, broken only by the gentle fizz of their soda water. Frank gestured at their glasses with a self-deprecating smile. 'Water, too! Bloody hell, I certainly know how to get a party started!'

Evelyn's laugh was warm and genuine. 'Having dinner with you is anything but boring, Frank Black!'

He blushed, uncertain how to handle the compliment.

'Who needs brown sauce?' she added lightly.

'HP. Has to be HP.'

She laughed.

Suddenly concerned he'd been overly impolite regarding his closest friend, he said, 'Jokes aside, though... since Gerry... and her rather, what's the word – draconian? Yeah, draconian, ways... I've been feeling better.'

She nodded over to the pouch of tobacco visible on the counter behind Frank. 'You're still smoking, though?'

'Aye.' He shifted uncomfortably. 'One step at a time.' He nodded, more to convince himself than her. 'Look, if I give that up, you might as well bury me now!'

The words hung heavy in the air. Too late. Reflections on burial and loss weren't the best dinner conversation for two widowers. His face fell. 'Christ, I'm sorry. That was thoughtless.'

'It's all right.' Evelyn's voice was gentle. She met his eyes with a smile that reached her own. 'It was five years back. I've lightened up a bit since then.'

Frank nodded. 'Still, best to be tactful and—'

'In fact,' Evelyn said, cutting him off. 'This is the lightest I've felt in five years. Started when I bumped into you, actually, Frank.'

Frank felt heat rise in his cheeks. 'What, that day at the cemetery?'

She laughed. 'Well, maybe not when I first bumped into you. When you visited me in hospital with those Bulgarian flowers. Grief shouldn't make people enemies, Frank. We both lost something... dear... regardless of the circumstances.'

He nodded. She hadn't been wrong. Together over the last weeks, their determination to understand the people they'd lost, and their secrets, by sharing their grief, had brought them some understanding.

It wasn't just Evelyn feeling lighter.

'Sometimes I forget,' Frank admitted, his fork tracing patterns in the quinoa. 'How far we've come, I mean. From wanting to throttle each other to... this.'

'Breaking bread together?' Evelyn's eyes sparkled with humour. 'Although I use the term bread loosely.'

'Aye, well, God, I wish I had some bread now.' He grimaced. 'I could crumble some on this bloody fish. Although Gerry would have my guts for garters.'

The conversation flowed. Evelyn spoke about her recovery, her frustrations with Janet's constant hovering. 'She won't have gone home, you know,' she said with fond exasperation. 'She'll be parked up around the corner, ready to swoop in at the first sign of trouble.'

Frank set down his fork, plate empty despite his complaints. 'Aye. I can see how that's irritating. But, you know, having someone love you that much, can't be too bad...' The words escaped before he could stop them. 'There was a time when...'

He trailed off, memories flooding back: Mary and young Maddie, excited whenever he made it home early. Those rare, precious moments of cuddles... laughs... kisses...

Their absence suddenly felt like a physical presence at the table.

Evelyn's expression softened with understanding, so like Mary's that it made his chest ache.

'Any word on Maddie?' she asked softly.

He shook his head.

His daughter Maddie had disappeared years before

Mary's death. She'd been lost to a haze of homelessness and heroin. Recently, she'd returned, and he'd helped her through withdrawal – after, there'd been a brief, beautiful moment when he'd thought he might get his daughter back. But then he'd gone and cocked it up, hadn't he? Hiding her phone, lying about it being lost, all to keep those bastards who'd dragged her down from getting their claws back in. He hadn't counted on her young homeless friend dying, on Maddie being cut off from saying goodbye because of Frank's deceit. She'd disappeared again after that.

There'd been whispers from Leeds – a contact in the force keeping his ear to the ground – but nothing concrete. Then she'd used her key while he was out, coming back for that bloody backpack. He'd checked it himself, been certain it was empty. Now it haunted him, that mystery. What had been so important she'd risk coming home?

'I'm sorry,' Evelyn said.

Frank nodded.

He took a deep breath, ready to share more of his feelings about Maddie, but the weight of emotion was unexpected. He stood. 'I need the loo.'

'Of course.'

'Sorry.'

'Don't be.'

He pushed back from the table, seeking escape from the memories pressing in around him, needing space to breathe, to remember how.

Chapter Five

After dinner, Gerry and Tom sat on the couch, watching an animal documentary. Tom's interest in animals and documentaries suited her. She couldn't handle fiction. If it wasn't real, what was the point of her giving time to it?

Gerry reached out and took Tom's hand.

While for Gerry, an unexpected touch could be overwhelming, a touch she initiated could be pleasurable.

They then embraced and lay beside one another. These moments of intimacy might feel orchestrated for some, but to her, it helped her connection to a world where Rylan was often her only anchor.

Heightened sensitivity to touch also allowed her to pick up the subtlest changes. She detected that Tom's palms were slightly clammier than usual, and he was adjusting his position more regularly against her. His restlessness was made even more peculiar because they were watching a documentary on extinction that Tom should be completely consumed by.

Before she could question him, he sat up, pulling his

hand from hers and reaching for the television remote to pause the programme.

His abrupt movement drew Rylan from his corner. Intrigued and tense, he stood close to them.

Tom looked at Gerry. His nervousness prevented him from saying what he clearly wanted to. He chewed his bottom lip.

'It's fine,' she said, keeping her voice steady while studying his face. 'Take your time if you've something to say.'

Tom leaned forward and kissed her.

She touched her lips afterward, processing the unexpected gesture.

Then, he slid off the couch onto his knees.

Too much unpredictability had her internal warning system at the ready.

Rylan shifted closer.

Tom glanced at him before looking back at Gerry. He reached over and fumbled under a small cushion that had been in the small of his back. 'Sorry... I...' Face creased, he slipped his hand in the crevice between the main cushion and the arm of the sofa, and fumbled around. 'Shit... wait—'

'What're you doing, Tom?' she asked.

His face scrunched in concentration as he continued his search.

'Got it... here...' He yanked out a small box.

She saw a familiar jeweller's symbol. 'Are you going to ask me to marry you?'

Colour flooded his cheeks, but he seized the moment. He opened the box, revealing a gold ring with a diamond set in it. 'Gerry Carver, will you marry me?'

This was unexpected.

Completely.

'Gerry?'

She looked at his wide eyes, realising she'd just spiralled off for a moment.

She opened her mouth, searching out the most logical thing she could think of. 'When?'

His face lit up. Had he taken this as an acceptance? 'Soon... as soon as... if you want... or we can go slow... wait a bit... up to you.'

'I see.'

'I love you.' He took a deep breath and shuffled closer.

Gerry looked away.

'Gerry? What're you feeling? What're you thinking?'

She decided to answer the questions and looked back at him. 'Well, I'm feeling surprised,' she said. 'And I'm thinking it's unexpected.'

'Are you unhappy?'

'No.'

'Happy then?'

She bit back her initial response. *I'm not sure.*

'I love you, Gerry, and I want to spend the rest of my life with you.'

She managed a smile. After all, Gerry understood these were culturally significant statements in marriage proposals.

Deep down, though, she knew that all words – whether lies or truths – required careful evaluation.

Love?

Rest of life?

Yes, these required very careful evaluation.

Rylan went over and licked Tom's face.

Tom laughed warmly. 'I know, I know... you come as a package deal. I love you and want to spend my life with you, too. We can all be together. A happy family.' He reached out to stroke Rylan.

There it was again.

Rest of life.

He went to sit beside her and put his hand on her leg. This was one such instance when touch caused her discomfort. She shuffled away. 'Sorry.'

'What's wrong?'

He was waving the ring at her now, but she'd not really looked at it yet. He wanted to put it on her finger, but that didn't feel right in the moment. In fact, it made her feel rather cold and unsettled.

'Gerry, you need to talk to me, tell me what's going through your head,' he said.

She was having a lot of thoughts now. A barrage of them. But she was trying to hold them down. Frank often advised her on restraining potentially offensive thoughts.

'Please, Gerry... tell me exactly what you're thinking.'

Stop pushing, she thought. *You might not like it—*

'Gerry? What?'

'I'm thinking that the last time I checked, 42 per cent of marriages end in divorce. They end unhappily and...'

She imagined Frank's disappointed stare. 'Aye,' she imagined him saying. 'That'll do it.'

The silence that followed confirmed this.

Now what? 'It was kind of you to ask, though,' she added. 'I'll give it careful consideration.'

Tom stood, closing the box. 'Forty-two per cent of people aren't right for each other. I thought we were.'

Gerry bit back her thoughts. *Based on what? I concluded we were right for each other to date. I never evaluated us with marriage as a factor.*

'Look,' Tom said, sitting back down. He took her hand. She resisted the urge to pull it away and nodded. She felt Rylan pressing against her legs.

'We complement each other,' Tom said. 'You help me be more organised, more precise, less all over the place. You put things in perspective. Growing up with my parents I had no sodding perspective. Then, I met you. You try new things, even if they're small things, and we have fun... and the sex is great.'

She thought about this. He made some good points.

'And I'm not saying sex is the be all and end all. We've more than that. So much more.'

She nodded, beginning to process the possibility.

'Your parents were happy, weren't they?'

A complex memory surfaced. 'Yes... but after I showed up, their marriage was focused on me most of the time. They had to work hard to maintain their relationship while meeting that commitment.'

'And if we ever have something else, then we'll work through it too.'

'But I wasn't planning for children. I understand how consuming my own needs are. It always seemed... like a selfish thing.'

'Nonsense, you'd be a great mum.'

Her thoughts accelerated, overwhelming her. Rylan pressed harder against her leg, and her hand dropped to his fur.

'Sorry... this is my fault... too much, too soon...' Tom said. 'When you stood up for me with my parents, Gerry, I fell head over heels...'

He pulled his hand away. She reached over and grabbed it. 'No... you're right. Thanks for asking. It's sweet. Can I just have some time to consider the pros and cons?' She met his eyes directly. 'Does that sound offensive?'

'It doesn't.'

She studied his expression. 'You're lying.'

'A little, maybe, but I understand you. That's how I know I love you.'

She nodded.

'Take all the time you need to think about it.'

'Thank you,' she replied.

He leaned in for a kiss.

They kissed for a short time, then, seeking the comfort of routine, desperate for it, she picked up the remote, sat back and resumed the documentary.

Chapter Six

In the bathroom mirror, Frank studied his reflection with the same analytical eye he reserved for suspects. He'd been critical of himself earlier, before Evelyn had arrived. But he was being hard on himself. The dark circles that had shadowed his eyes since Mary's death had softened since he'd quit drinking. His face, while still heavier than it should be, had lost its bloated, unhealthy pallor.

He considered the rolling tobacco in the kitchen. The last vice. His fingers twitched with a familiar craving. Maybe it was time to vanquish that demon, too?

Who says you can't polish a turd? he thought and winked.

He had a lot to be thankful to Gerry for. He thought of Evelyn in his kitchen, and realised that she, too, was part of his healing. She'd allowed him to understand his loss. Process it.

Even Henrietta could take some credit. On that night, he'd poured out his grief to her, and she'd shared stories of her own estranged son. It had made him feel less alone in his heartache for a short time.

Was that the secret to happiness?

Learning to let other people in, even when it terrifies you?

Frank had initially left the kitchen for the toilet because of his emotions over Maddie. Having calmed himself, he thought of Mary on his way back to the kitchen and felt another rush of emotion.

He gripped the edge of the hallway table, his breath coming in shallow gasps, and he feared a panic attack.

He turned and headed into the living room, intending to get control of his breathing, before returning to Evelyn. There he stood behind the half-closed door, regarding his sad looking plastic Christmas tree by the window. It looked withered, and the baubles had lost their sparkle. At least he'd got it out, though. It must have been the first time in five years.

Now, feeling more centred, he looked at Mary's photograph on the mantelpiece. It was from about fifteen years ago. She was smiling, caught in a moment of amusement because of Frank.

Not because of any joke, he most certainly wasn't that funny, but because he'd been attempting to juggle oranges and failing.

Maddie had taken the photograph.

He went close to the picture and stroked her face. 'We're just friends, love,' he mouthed. 'She's helping, I promise.'

As he was leaving, he heard Mary whisper in his memory. 'It's okay, love. And remember, Maddie will come back, Frank, when she's ready.'

Chapter Seven

Later that night, Gerry lay beside Tom, unable to stop herself from reflecting on their scheduled intercourse. He'd not approached it with his usual enthusiasm. It'd been rather mechanical.

It was clear she had sapped his usual warmth with her reaction earlier.

She felt some distress about hurting him and reasoned this was a good thing. It was significant evidence that she cared for him immensely.

But that didn't solve the problem, did it?

Solutions for her had never been straightforward though. Her mind operated on its unique wavelength – a fact her parents had understood, her doctors had confirmed, and Tom was still learning to navigate.

She couldn't imagine processing his proposal any differently—it would require rewiring her entire nervous system! After all, her lifestyle was rigid – not out of self-centredness, but self-preservation.

She waited ten more minutes – she didn't need a clock; she could measure time without one – and then reached for a melatonin tablet. It helped settle her mind whenever her thoughts raced.

Twenty minutes later, she had her last conscious thought before sleeping.

Sometimes statistics and facts alone couldn't provide solutions.

It was a terrifying thought.

Chapter Eight

THE PHONE CALL from Constable Donald Oxley came just as Frank was finishing his third roll-up of the morning.

He looked out the window as he listened. Two young lads pelted each other with snowballs, their laughter carrying through the glass.

Lucky buggers, he thought. *School's out.*

There was no such luck for him. He had a body to see.

Donald gave him the location.

'Bloody hell,' he said, his joints already aching at trudging through the snow.

He didn't have to be told that he needed decent footwear. Donald told him anyway.

I'm sure he still considers me incompetent, even after working with him for several decades. Bertha, his faithful yellow Volvo, had seen far better days. She was far too long in the tooth to weather these treacherous conditions. Also, her heater had been throwing tantrums lately, and the mechanism controlling the wipers had started jamming.

We share that in common, lass, he thought. *Both of us hate the cold.*

Ten years ago, he might have tackled the two-mile walk to the scene. But he was a lot heavier now. One slip on that ice could put him out of commission for weeks.

Frank rummaged through his closet, unearthing an old pair of hiking boots that were stiff but serviceable. He added his winter jacket, and – with a pang of melancholy – Mary's old fur-lined leather gloves. Months ago, he'd lost his own pair and never got around to replacing them. He completed his get-up with a beanie hat.

It took four phone calls to find a taxi driver willing to brave the conditions.

When he was finally en route, the cab's heating blasted at full force, turning the interior into a mobile sauna. Frank stripped off some of his layers in the back. At least the driver was silent. Chatty cabbies, especially first thing, ranked right up there with leaf-blowers on his list of pet peeves.

Through the windscreen, the snow-blanketed landscape stretched endlessly along the A169.

He sighed, thinking about the two joyriders who had raced down this stretch at breakneck speed last night. Frank had been young once, and he'd experienced the pull of adrenaline himself, but driving at that speed in these conditions. It was just suicidal, making their survival nothing short of miraculous.

He didn't need directions to the scene – police vehicles and vans lined the road. Other than that, the road was quiet. The weather was keeping most indoors. Good. A steady stream of traffic down here would have been a pain in the arse.

After paying the driver – with a generous tip for his blessed silence – Frank wrapped up tight again, and stepped out into the biting cold, and light snowfall. The morning sun blazed off the snow, forcing him to push his prescription sunglasses from his forehead down over his nose.

Only one police car had their lights flashing. It provided a surreal blue heartbeat in the quiet, white expanse.

At the broken fence line, a fresh-faced constable manned the log-in point. Orange tape fluttered in the bitter wind. He doubted he'd have to keep any pedestrians away. Who in their right mind would be here in these conditions other than them?

'Morning, sir!' The young officer's face split into an eager grin. 'You okay?'

Frank suppressed a groan. When had over-enthusiasm become a job requirement? 'Aye... thanks... How do?'

'Good. You look much better than last time.'

Frank frowned. 'Eh?'

'Do you remember me, sir?'

Frank's memory banks came up empty. 'Sorry, son... I'm a man of certain years.'

'PC Thompson, sir. That mess outside the Rusty Anchor a few months back.'

Ah. That explained the comment about looking better. He'd been sporting several shades of purple after searching for Maddie that night. Frank nodded. 'I remember, aye. I wasn't looking my best then... a couple of black eyes after a nasty fall.'

'It's a privilege to see you again, sir.'

Christ on a bike! Was this the universe's punishment for dodging the chatty taxi driver? 'Thank you. I must get on—'

'And that wasn't what I meant, about looking better. The bruises, I mean. You look healthier. You've lost weight. And there's more of a glow about you.'

Frank shifted uncomfortably. Was this conversation really happening? It felt like a surreal dream.

In his day, men didn't discuss such things. The observation felt oddly intimate, even if well-meant. He wasn't very good at reciprocal pleasantry, but he gave it a whirl. 'Aye, well... you're looking more confident yourself. Growing into the uniform, son.'

The constable beamed.

Enthusiastic that he'd managed it, he added, 'Like a baby finding its feet.'

The constable's face suggested that was a little too much.

Ah well. His tolerance for small talk was exhausted now. He gestured toward the crime scene. 'Right then, laddie... onwards.'

Chapter Nine

Onwards was a bloody nightmare.

The waterproofing on his old hiking boots was completely shot. And after two minutes of crunching through metre-high snow, icy water was seeping through to his socks.

He thought back to Donald's warning about decent footwear.

He's right... I'm bloody incompetent.

As his toes burned with the cold and every step made his joints flare, he couldn't help but think, *Sixty-five and still not retired! I need my head read!*

Still, as was the norm whenever the retirement question popped up, the image of a smiling and relieved Donald Oxley crept into his mind...

He clenched his teeth and trudged with purpose.

The thought of Donald celebrating his retirement always had him feeling resolved to continue until he dropped dead.

By the time Frank reached the crash site, his feet were blocks of ice.

Still, the scene before him quickly drove all of his own discomforts from mind.

The old wooden silo had been a familiar sight on these moors for as long as anyone could remember. Now destroyed, it'd have to be removed. Half of its wooden exterior was scattered across the snow. The Audi jutted from beneath the wreckage - now a wreck itself. White-suited SOCOs moved around the scene. In their white oversuits, they looked like arctic explorers, their forms barely distinguishable against the snowy backdrop.

Frank caught sight of John Spears, the forensic photographer, circling the wreckage, snapping away. Above them, a drone swooped back and forth in the air, a mechanical insect capturing a more impressive view of the chaotic scene.

The modern bloody world, Frank thought. He couldn't have less of a desire to keep up with it.

'Morning boss!' DS Reggie Moyes approached, hand raised.

Now here was an old man embracing everything the modern world had to offer.

Starting with relentless exercise.

He hadn't seen Reggie in well over a month, and his white over suit did nothing to hide his newly bulked-up frame. He'd been banging on about 'upping the weights' in early November. Seems it hadn't been hot air.

As if running marathons in his late fifties wasn't enough? *Ridiculous.*

A small, traitorous part of his mind whispered that his derision masked envy.

He hated that part of his mind, although he should probably concede that it was right.

Reggie drew closer, moving gracefully through the snow, forcing Frank to reflect on his own sluggish limp.

He inwardly sighed, suppressing, as he always had to, his irritation. After all, despite Reggie's self-professed reputation as a ladies' man, shameless discussion of his exercise routines, and tendency towards workplace inappropriateness, Reggie was one of Frank's most reliable detectives. And, on very rare occasions – emphasis on rare – even a friend.

But then he saw what was on Reggie's face, and Frank realised there were limits on what he could tolerate. Frank pointed at Reggie's shaggy new moustache. 'What the bloody hell is that?'

'Sorry, boss?'

'On your top lip.'

'Oh yeah...'

'*Oh yeah...* That chuffin' caterpillar?'

'Caterpillar?' Reggie touched his moustache defensively, a frown creasing his forehead.

'Caterpillar, aye. And not just a scrawny one either, it's like, something huge, and bulbous... from a rainforest somewhere.'

'It's just a moustache.'

'One that isn't working. You don't look like Tom Selleck. It's the wrong shape, and colour.'

'It's for Movember boss.' Reggie stroked the questionable facial hair proudly.

'It's December, Reggie, and that thing won't fill anyone with Christmas spirit.'.

'It's all the rage at the moment. It's back in.'

'What next? A mullet?' Frank rolled his eyes.

'They're making a comeback.' Reggie puffed out his

chest, speaking with the confidence of a man who'd read one too many men's lifestyle magazines.

'With the bloody kids, Reggie!'

'You're never too old,' Reggie said.

'You are.' Frank exhaled heavily, wondering how many years of these conversations he had left to endure.. 'Now, update me.'

He noticed Gerry now. She was over on the other side of the wreckage, lost in her methodical examination of the scene.

'All I know is that the joyriders, Kyle Russell and Jason Cleaves, are being checked over in the hospital. It was a wonder they weren't killed.'

'Let's hope the scrotes have learned their lesson.'

Reggie nodded. 'Well, at least something good has come out of it.'

'Like what?'

'They unearthed a body.'

'Bloody hell, Reggie, give them a medal. Have you seen the crime scene? Have they left any evidence intact?'

He sighed. Still, Reggie had a point. Without them this body would have remained hidden for God knows how long. On top of however bloody long it'd been lost here.

He trudged over to Gerry, photographing the scene with her phone, her movements precise and measured as she documented every angle. Between shots, she took notes on her phone.

'Want me to take a photo with you in it?' he offered.

She frowned, the joke having fallen flat against her unwavering focus.

'Never mind. Are you able to tell me more than Reggie?'

It was a ridiculous question, really. She'd have more,

and then some. Without looking up from her phone, she said, 'This silo hasn't been operational for decades.' She tilted her head as she examined a close-up of a metal ladder inside. 'Grain. It was part of a working farm that ceased operations almost fifty years back.'

'And the farm?' Frank said, looking around. 'Where is it?'

'Gone.'

'They saw fit to close down a farm, but not its god-awful silo?'

'It has status as a local landmark.'

'It's a bloody eyesore.'

'It's popular with hikers, and forms a destination on many walking guides.'

'Are you serious?'

'Yes. Why wouldn't I be?'

Frank swallowed his retort. 'I can't believe they leave these things up. It's a bloody deathtrap waiting to happen. Reggie was right. The bloody joyriders have done us a favour in more ways than one. So, do we let the hikers know they'll need to update their guidebooks?'

'That's not up to us, sir.'

His attempt at levity was pointless. Also, when you considered how many tourists had snapped photos here, unaware of what lay hidden within, it was probably in poor taste.

Gallows humour could help at a crime scene, but only with the right audience.

Gerry looked at a photo, then pointed upwards to the exposed upper level. 'The impact caused structural failure. The body fell from that elevated space, which you reach by that metal ladder. Fortunately, it'd been wrapped in some insulation material which cushioned the fall and, although the material split on impact, the body remains intact.'

Frank nodded. Another secret dragged into the light.

'Right then, let's go and see what this old silo has been hiding.'

Chapter Ten

After suiting up, Frank and Gerry approached the black mat beside the crumpled Audi. Dr Nasreen Quereshi was kneeling beside the skeleton. Frank was glad to see her. He trusted her methodical approach and sharp eye for detail.

His breath fogged in the cold air as he looked at the remains. They lay in a tight foetal position, arms and legs drawn close to the torso in an unnatural pose that made Frank's chest tighten. Yellowed bones jutted through tattered remnants of fabric, the synthetic material clinging like dark cobwebs to the skeletal frame. The scene carried an eerie stillness, as if the very air held its breath around this grim discovery.

'The position suggests binding.' Nasreen's gloved fingers traced the curve of the spine, then the arms. 'Wrists were likely secured behind the back, ankles bound. There're indentations on the bones where they were tightly bound by ropes.'

'How long does it take rope to decompose?' Frank asked.

'Depends on the elements.' She looked up. 'There would've been some protection from the wooden silo walls, I guess. Natural fibre would be long gone after ten years. Synthetic ropes have been known to last as long as fifty years plus if well protected from the elements. If it was synthetic, we'll find some traces. It may help us date the remains.'

Frank knelt beside her, his joints creaking. His feet were already ice cold, but now he could feel it seeping through his protective suit.

He fixed his attention on the vulnerable form.

The skeleton seemed to shrink further into its defensive curl.

What horror had brought this individual here?
What monster had done this?

'Female,' Nasreen said, pointing out features of the pelvis and skull. 'Wider sciatic notch, more gracile skull features. Young too... Late teens, early twenties would be my initial estimate based on bone fusion and dental wear, but a very initial estimate, mind.'

After decades on the job, he knew this moment well. The transformation of anonymous bones to someone.

And young female victims really hit Frank hard. Keeping his thoughts from Maddie had always been impossible. He took a deep breath, closed his eyes, and sighed.

He let the familiar weight of responsibility settle over him like a heavy coat and then he opened his eyes.

Now he really saw the victim, rather than old bones.

He could hear whispering on the wind – the beginnings of someone's story.

As always, his eyes found their way to the empty sockets, trying to imagine the face they once held, the light they once carried, and what terrors they'd witnessed in those last moments before that light was taken. 'Cause of death?'

'Tricky at this stage,' Nasreen said, showing the damaged bone on the rear of the skull. 'Perimortem? Or from last night's fall from there?' She nodded up at the exposed floor of the silo. 'Impossible to say definitively at this stage. Also...' she continued, running her gloved fingers along a section of dark, degraded fabric. 'The clothing. Synthetic, so some remains – although decomposing. I think she's been here a while. Fifteen years at the least, probably longer, potentially much longer. 'Sorry, that's as precise as I can be for now.'

Gerry knelt beside him. She pointed at the remaining fabric on the victim's legs. 'These are jodhpurs.'

Frank glanced up. 'How can you tell?'

'The cut is distinctive.' Gerry's fingers hovered over the fabric without touching it, tracing the patterns with practiced expertise. 'Despite the rotting, you can see that there were reinforced seams here – you can still see a pattern. And also...' She indicated a darker patch nearer the centre of the leg. 'That's a suede knee patch.'

She pointed at the waist. 'Can you see if there's a label, please?'

With a delicate touch, Nasreen used tweezers to pull the clothing back.

Gerry took a photograph, but also summoned John Spears with a raised hand.

Gerry zoomed in on her photo, eyes narrowed. 'Caldene...'

'Sorry?' Frank asked.

'Caldene. A high-end British manufacturer. These particular style features...' She traced the distinctive seam pattern on her phone screen. 'They stopped producing this design in the early nineties.'

Outstanding.

'Is there anything you don't know?'

'Of course. No one can know everything.'

'So horse riding is just one of your specialities?' Frank asked.

'I used to ride, a lot, before I took up sailing with my parents.' There was an unusual softness to her voice. Over two years ago, her parents had died in a sailing accident. Gerry had been there, instructed by her father to jump before their yacht crashed into the rocks.

Frank nodded. 'Is there a riding school around here?'

'I don't know,' Gerry said.

He looked at Nasreen, who shrugged.

'Best find out then, hadn't we?'

Frank looked at the victim again. The morning sun caught the bones at an angle that made them gleam like fragile glass.

Jodhpurs.

At least it was something. After all, when he'd first seen the carnage, he'd expected nothing.

He stood, his knees cracking. 'Did you ever own a pair of these, Gerry?'

'No, they were very expensive.'

'Top of the range, eh?' Reggie said, coming up alongside them. 'Someone with money, perhaps?'

'Let's not get ahead of ourselves, Selleck.'

The strengthening sun caught the bones, making them gleam against the black mat like polished ivory. So stark, so final. Yet this ending was also a beginning.

There was a story to find. And no truth should be allowed to dissolve into nothing.

Let's find out who you were, lass, he thought. *And not just your name.*

A name was important, of course. It'd be a start. Identity was an absolute must in any investigation. But looking at those bones gleaming in the morning light, Frank saw more than just remains. He saw someone's daughter. Someone's friend. Potentially someone's mother.

I want to know the real you, he thought, his resolve hardening. *Without that, there's nothing.*

Chapter Eleven

FRANK FELT the sting of snowfall on his face.

Their boots crunched through fresh powder as they trudged toward the car, shoulders hunched against the bitter wind.

Reggie had agreed to give Frank and Gerry a lift back to HQ. It went without saying that he'd have to pick up Rylan on the way.

Gerry focused on her phone as she walked, researching riding schools with characteristic focus.

He'd be arse over tit if he attempted that!

A familiar voice cut through the swirling snow. Helen Taylor, chief forensic officer and Mary, his late wife's, best friend, was hurrying toward them, her white suit nearly invisible against the landscape. 'You two go on,' Frank said. 'I'll catch up.'

Reggie snorted under his breath. 'Catch up?'

'Eh? What was that, DS?'

'Nothing boss... a noisy blast of wind.'

'It'd better have been.'

'We'll go slow, boss,' Gerry said, matter-of-factly. 'Your

core temperature appears to be dropping. In fact, your lips show signs of cyanosis.'

Bloody hell! It was far worse when comments like that came with no sarcasm. 'I'll be fine, thank you. *Both of you.*'

He turned and regarded Helen. She threw back her white hood and did a double take. Her eyes widened with pleased surprise. 'As I live and breathe, you're looking trim, old man.'

'Jesus, am I really viewed as a lumbering, incapable old fogey? Can I not be continually defined by my good looks rather than my age and weight?'

Helen laughed.

'At least I know you well enough to take a compliment from you, Hel. Not sure I appreciated the schoolkid, PC Thompson on the fence over there assessing my dietary successes.' Frank huffed a laugh, watching his breath fogging in the chilly air. 'Anyway, it's only a few pounds.'

Helen laughed, circling him like a fight promoter assessing new talent. 'When did you last weigh yourself?'

'Eh? Weigh myself? Why would I do that? I'd have to buy a set of scales for a start.'

'It can be motivational. Tracking your progress.'

'How's that motivating? Sounds like hard work. Torture, even! If the weight is coming off, it's coming off, I don't need chuffin' graphs and charts.'

'Well, I'd say it was more than a few pounds. If I didn't know better, I'd say Evelyn Wainwright was having quite the influence.' She winked.

Frank felt heat rising in his face that had nothing to do with exercise or the weather. He didn't know which was more nauseating, the wink, which implied something sordid between him and Evelyn, or her tone, which conveyed her smug satisfaction at initiating their blossoming friendship.

He rolled his eyes. 'She's nothing to do with this.' He pointed at his body with an awkward gesture as if he was suddenly the leading man in a Marvel movie, rather than a fat man that had lost a couple of inches off his gut, which again, made him feel ridiculous. 'This is down to your little axis of evil with Gerry, ganging up constantly, and bullying me into a... what did you call it...' He made exaggerated quotation marks with his fingers. '"A better version of myself"?'

Helen snorted. 'First, let's rewind. Axis of evil? Even for the king of melodrama, that's dramatic.'

'Is it? Comparing notes behind my back, trying to strong-arm me into things I don't want to do, never wanted to do, never thought I would do...' He shook his head. He was in no mood to give her the satisfaction and admit, as he'd done to Evelyn, that he was secretly grateful.

Helen's expression softened into something that looked dangerously like affection. 'It's helping though, isn't it? You must be the doctor's new best friend. You're our success story.'

'Self-praise is no praise,' Frank said.

'I also heard you're seeing a psychiatrist.'

The cold suddenly felt sharper. 'Bloody hell, is nothing sacred? Not with you two, apparently. Not yet. I'm on a waiting list with a head doctor.'

'All steps forward, Frank. Good steps.' She touched his arm gently. 'Mary would be proud.'

'Aye, well, best not get ahead of ourselves. I'm still the same miserable old sod I always was. I'm only doing this because I like you both.'

'Jesus, finally, a compliment?'

'You know I love you Helen... anyway, what's that you're holding?'

She held up a small plastic evidence bag. Inside was a small, corroded metal object.

'A pin?' Frank squinted through his glasses.

'Found it tangled in Jane Doe's blouse remnants. Took some careful work to extract it intact. Give my team time to clean it up, and we might find something distinctive.'

'Great work.'

'You really look well though... apart from the blue lips and impending hypothermia.'

He shivered. 'Best let me get warm then.'

'Frank?' she called as was walking away.

He paused and looked over his shoulder. 'Aye?'

'Good to see you.'

'You too.'

Frank trudged after his colleagues, marvelling at life's strange turns. Five years ago, after Mary died, he'd believed himself utterly alone – no friends, no family save Maddie, lost to addiction's undertow.

Now he'd Gerry with her razor-sharp mind and unwavering loyalty, Helen playing both brilliant forensic scientist and determined cheerleader, even Reggie, despite that unfortunate moustache. And Evelyn... Frank still wasn't sure what to make of that development. The widow of the man who'd destroyed his world was becoming a fixture in his life.

A fixture? What did that even mean? A friend? The answers remained elusive. A year ago, he'd have laughed – or thrown a punch – at the suggestion he'd willingly share a meal with Evelyn Wainwright.

Yet here he was – trimmer, healthier, and loathe as he was to admit it, perhaps marginally happier. He wondered if a psychiatrist would help further, though guilt over Maddie's unknown whereabouts still gnawed at him. But he clung to that quiet hope he'd heard in Mary's voice the previous night: *Maddie will come back, Frank, when she's ready.*

As predicted by Reggie, Frank couldn't catch up. When he arrived at the car, it was already running, exhaust pluming white in the frigid air. Gerry sat in the back, still absorbed in her phone.

Frank settled into the passenger seat with a groan.

'There's a riding school in Ruswarp. Meadowside Riding Academy, established 1952.'

Frank glanced between his colleagues, feeling the familiar surge of anticipation that came with a fresh lead. Tensed, poised, and ready. 'Well, we all know what that means.'

'And what's that, boss?' Reggie asked, his hand hovering over the gear stick.

Frank clicked his seat belt home, the sound sharp and definitive in the quiet car. He allowed himself a grim smile. 'It means the starter gun just fired. Time to run this race.'

Chapter Twelve

Through the thickening snow, the bridge over the River Esk emerged like a ghostly arc. Frank watched as it faded in and out of view while Reggie guided the car through Ruswarp.

The Bridge Inn's windows glowed with Christmas tinsel and warm welcome, stirring memories in Frank of several afternoons spent there with Mary – pints by the hearth, her laugh carrying over the murmur of regulars.

A handful of people braved the weather, heads bowed against the snow and wind. Steam fogged the butcher's windows, while the primary school stood silent, its playground a pristine blanket of white.

'Can't remember them ever closing school when I was a kid,' Frank said.

'They announced the closure of all schools in Whitby and the surrounding areas at 6.47 this morning,' Gerry said, still not looking up from her phone.

'Very precise,' Frank remarked.

'I've an app that delivers local announcements. I always check it as part of my morning routine.'

'Why not just use notifications?' Reggie asked.

'They're intrusive,' Gerry said. 'I prefer to look when I'm scheduled to look, rather than having them interfere with other aspects of my morning routine.'

Reggie looked at Gerry. 'I get that.'

'Aye... good,' Frank said. 'But Reggie, didn't I already tell you to stay focused on the road?'

'Yes, you—'

'So, why am I saying it again?'

They turned onto a narrow lane that wound its way uphill, passing between hedgerows laden with snow. The trees formed a white tunnel, their branches meeting overhead. After about half a mile, a wooden sign emerged from the gloom: 'Meadowside Riding Academy – Est. 1952'.

The complex sprawled across impressive acreage – clear evidence of seventy prosperous years, no doubt. A vast indoor arena dominated, its metal roof rising above meticulously maintained paddocks. Outbuildings clustered nearby, and snow-covered fields stretched to the treeline.

'Nice set-up.' Reggie pulled into the car park. There were only three other vehicles, each one covered by a blanket of snow. 'Best not take too long... don't want to get snowed in.'

'You stay here, Reggie. Keep the engine ticking over. That's not an excuse to sit here and daydream to ABBA's greatest hits though. Get your phone out and start researching.'

'Researching what?'

Frank pushed the door open slightly. 'Sure you'll figure something out. Small price to pay to keep your feet dry.' He stepped out.

'They're already wet—'

He shut the door before Reggie could reply, feeling the

snow soak into his hiking boots once again. 'Join the bloody club.'

Gerry came up alongside him. It was only at this point that he clocked her Wellington boots.

'Good thinking,' he said, nodding down.

'I didn't really think about it. It seemed the obvious thing to do.'

'Good thinking is an expression like "good idea".'

She shook her head. 'Wasn't really an idea, either.'

He sighed. 'It was just a compliment. Forget it... Just enjoy your dry feet,' he muttered, lowering his prescription sunglasses onto his nose. He groaned because it was too dark for them now. *I need sunglasses that automatically adjust to the sun's brightness..* He put the glasses back onto his forehead.

Chapter Thirteen

FRANK FORCED down the craving for a roll-up as they passed a row of stables extending along one side of the arena. Too much wood about, and he didn't want to cause a fire. He was already feeling like a disaster zone this morning – what with the footwear and sunglasses.

Through an open stable door, a chestnut mare watched them, steam curling from her nostrils in the frigid air.

Frank paused, meeting the horse's gaze.

'Sir?' Gerry prompted.

'A chestnut mare.' His voice softened.

'You know your horses?'

'Ha. No. My daughter learned to ride on one when she was twelve.'

The mare tossed her head, her coat gleaming like polished copper in the weak winter light.

Frank's mind drifted back to those precious Saturday mornings, watching Maddie transform in the saddle. He remembered her face lit up with pure joy, the way she'd chatter non-stop about the horses on the drive home, her bedroom walls slowly filling with rosettes and ribbons. In less than a year, those awkward, uncertain movements became fluid grace. Her tentative touches turned to confident handling. The stables had become their special place, a refuge from the growing tensions at home. For a time, horse riding had made Maddie whole.

Gerry's voice cut through the memory. 'Are you okay, sir?'

'Aye... just remembering, you know? Like you do.'

There was a pause before Gerry asked, appropriately, 'Would you like to talk about it, sir?'

Gerry was clearly practicing her empathetic responses. Although, on this occasion, he was certain he detected a hint of genuine concern buried beneath the rigid delivery.

'Not now, thanks,' Frank said. 'Let's just crack on.'

Nodding, Gerry turned and continued toward the reception area.

The converted stone farmhouse loomed before them, its weathered walls testament to decades of Yorkshire winters. Inside, the temperature rose sharply. He wiped at his damp face with Mary's old gloves while Gerry stomped snow from her boots. His own feet were beyond saving, already soaked through to the bone.

Over in the corner was a real Christmas tree that put Frank's to shame. It must have been over seven feet, and looked so glorious that it didn't need many decorations.

He thought of his drab plastic one back home.

Two women who could have been mirror images of each other looked up from behind a counter. Both had steel-grey hair and weather-beaten faces. Their matching padded gilets bore the Meadowside Academy logo.

'Morning... can we help?' the slightly taller one asked, her accent a curious blend of Yorkshire and finishing-school polish.

Frank slid his sunglasses down, momentarily forgetting again, but quickly pushed them back up. He showed his ID. 'DCI Frank Black, and this is DI Carver. Are the owners available?'

The women exchanged glances. 'That'll be us. I'm Chelsea Winters,' said the taller one. 'This is Lorraine, my sister.'

Frank caught Gerry's subtle nod – she'd already checked the ownership records.

'Is everything okay?' Chelsea asked.

'We're just making inquiries regarding a discovery earlier. 1952, eh? You've been around a while?'

'Yes. Our parents started the business,' Chelsea said. 'We took over in the late nineties when they passed. A year apart.' Her matter-of-fact tone held a trace of old grief. 'Sorry, DCI Black, what's the discovery?'

Frank cleared his throat. 'I appreciate your discretion until we make an official announcement,' he said, his eyes sweeping the empty reception area and settling on the door they'd come through. 'Maybe we could lock reception just in case...'

'No need,' Lorraine said. 'Anyone comes close to reception, a sensor picks them up and sounds an alert.' She pointed to a small black device mounted above the door frame.

She gestured to a door behind her. 'We live back there. In fact, if someone even drives into the car park the sensor chimes three times. You see, we're always on site because of animals, and are always aware of who's on our property.'

'Anyone else back there now?' Frank asked, nodding at the door she pointed out.

'Only ever us two,' Chelsea said.

'Okay.' Frank leaned forward. 'This morning, human

remains were recovered near the A169. They were inside the old silo. You know the one, I'm sure.' Frank observed their faces as they nodded. Their surprise looked genuine. 'We believe that the body has been there a good while. Decades, potentially. Now, we're here because the deceased was wearing riding clothes.' He looked at Gerry.

'Caldene jodhpurs,' Gerry said. 'The specific design places them in the late eighties, early nineties. The quality would suggest someone who took riding seriously.'

Frank noticed the colour draining from their faces. Probably just news of a fellow rider's demise, but he made a mental note anyway.

Chelsea took a deep breath and sat up straighter, her spine suddenly rigid as a fence post. 'Many people around here take riding seriously.'

'I imagine. It's the reason you were our first port of call... Are you able to tell us of any female riding students who may have disappeared around then? Young woman. Late teens, early twenties, perhaps?'

The sisters shared a look and Lorraine said, 'In the early 1990s?'

'Or the late eighties. Sorry to be vague.'

'It is vague, DCI Black,' Chelsea said. 'We've had thousands of students over the years. Some stay, some leave the area. And not just from Ruswarp either. Some come from Scarborough... In fact, they come from all over North Yorkshire.'

'Aye,' Frank said. 'It is a long shot. But sometimes long shots pay off. Anything set an alarm bell ringing – any disappearances?'

Chelsea placed her weathered hands on the counter as she spoke. 'A student suddenly going missing? Not that I recall. I'm sure there're many students that may have gone missing over the years outside of Ruswarp. But in Ruswarp, well, nothing is grabbing at me...' Her voice trailed off as she caught her sister's expression. 'Lorraine? What is it?'

'Sarah,' Lorraine said. 'Sarah disappeared.'

Chelsea's eyes widened, but then she thought about it, and shook her head. Her hands fidgeted with a pen on the counter. 'But she wasn't a student then; she was a former student.'

Lorraine's face had gone pale, her fingers gripping the edge of the desk.

Frank felt that familiar tingle at the base of his skull – the first thread of a lead unravelling. 'That doesn't matter. There was nothing linking her specifically to Meadowside. Who's Sarah? Was she local?'

'Yes. Sarah Matthews,' Chelsea said. 'It was 1988.'

'1989,' Lorraine corrected.

'And she was definitely your former student?' Frank asked.

'One moment.' Chelsea turned her attention to her desktop. 'When we upgraded, I went back and put all the former records into the system. It wasn't necessary to go all the way back to '52, but we did it anyway. We liked the idea of having everything documented. Every student that ever walked through our door. When you have a family business, you can get sentimental like that.'

Sarah Matthews, Frank thought.

He recalled the eye sockets earlier... thought again of the light they'd once carried...

I want to know the real you.

'Here,' Chelsea said. 'Sarah Matthews became our student on 14 November 1981 when she was fourteen years old. She was with us until the end of August 1985. She was eighteen then.'

Frank saw Gerry making notes alongside him.

'Date of birth was 2 February 1967,' Chelsea continued.

'Do you have a picture?' Gerry asked.

Chelsea shook her head. 'These are old, vague records. I only typed them in for sentimental reasons. A complete overview of everybody who walked through our door. There's an address... but I can tell you that address doesn't exist any more. That road was on the outskirts, just past where the old post office used to be, and has been replaced with a service station, the Morrisons local, and a small supermarket.'

Frank jotted the address down anyway.

'Mother really enjoyed teaching her,' Lorraine said. 'I remember because everyone was surprised she'd natural ability. No one thought she'd be as good as she was. She'd never been near a horse before and had had a rather troubled childhood. Some trouble with the police for stealing, had an older boyfriend... her father was in jail, too. In fact, he died there. She didn't jump to mind when you first came in because, well, she didn't disappear while she was taking lessons. That came later.'

'How did she disappear?'

'Well, not so much disappear,' Chelsea said, looking up. 'The consensus was that she'd run off with an older man. The police put a notice out. Someone last saw her with an older man entering a red... red...'

'Fiesta,' Lorraine finished.

'That's it,' Chelsea said. 'Outside the Bridge Inn. The investigation petered out, and most people assumed she'd gone off with this man. She'd always been edgy... and she'd that history of being in trouble with the law.'

'Who saw her getting into this Fiesta?' Gerry asked.

'I'm not sure we were ever told,' Lorraine said. 'To be honest, I haven't thought about Sarah since then. I just can't imagine her being the girl. She seemed to have a lot of fight in her... couldn't imagine her being anyone's victim.'

Frank, on the other hand, could imagine it.

Victims didn't fit neat stereotypes. The quiet ones, the loud ones, the troublemakers – murder didn't discriminate.

'It seems like a long shot that it's her,' Chelsea admitted, a note of desperation creeping into her voice. 'I really hope not. Be nice to think she found whatever she was looking for in life.'

'We'll look into it,' Frank said. 'Anyone else you can think of?'

They drew a blank.

Frank pointed at the computer. 'Is it okay if we get copies of that file with Sarah Matthews?'

'Of course,' Chelsea said. 'Do you want me to print it?'

Frank handed over his card. 'Just email if you could please.'

Chapter Fourteen

Gerry had already started researching as they exited reception and journeyed back towards the car.

'Sarah Matthews, twenty-two, reported missing October 12, 1989,' Gerry said. 'She'd been living with her boyfriend, Tommy Reid, twenty-five, in Ruswarp. She went out walking around 8 p.m. after an argument with Tommy and was last seen outside the Bridge Inn by a regular, Malcolm Hargreaves. He witnessed her climbing into a red Fiesta but claimed he didn't see who with and said he didn't think to remember the licence plate. Malcolm passed in 2002, so we won't be able to follow that up.'

Frank nodded, eyes fixed on the ground, so he could keep his footing in the thick snow.

'A lot of attention was given to rumours,' Gerry continued. 'Mostly from locals who'd never spoken up during the original investigation, that she'd been spending time with an older man. There isn't much else in the public record.'

'Sounds like a rather flat investigation.'

Gerry pulled her coat tighter against the wind.

'Assuming this is our victim is quite a leap at this stage and—'

'I've a feeling.' Frank cut her off.

They walked in silence through the thickening snowfall for a minute or two. 'Aren't you going to ask me where this feeling comes from?' Frank asked.

'No,' Gerry said. 'We've no evidence.'

'Sometimes you have to buy into feelings, Gerry.' He hesitated before adding, 'Did you see the looks on Chelsea's and Lorraine's faces? I think they had the same feeling.'

'Even if they did, the gut instinct of three people isn't evidential.'

'When someone goes missing from a small place like this, Gerry, you can be certain secrets are simmering. I saw it in their eyes. And if there's one thing I've learned over the years is that when there's smoke, there's fire... that's evidence based.'

'No, it's an analogy, sir, used to trick someone into taking something at face value.'

'When there's fire, I don't ignore it. To do so is dangerous.' He knew the extension of the analogy would irritate her.

The familiar outline of the stable, which they had passed on their way to reception, loomed ahead. Because of his earlier memories of Maddie, he felt drawn to it.

He went inside. The stable block was warmer than he'd anticipated and there was a thick smell of hay and horses enveloping them. The first two stalls were empty, but in the third, a young girl of around twelve was grooming the chestnut mare they'd seen earlier. Her movements were confident and practiced, her riding clothes immaculate – jodhpurs and a padded navy jacket, blonde hair tied back in a neat plait.

The mare's coat gleamed under the brush strokes. Steam rose from its nostrils as it regarded them with one liquid eye.

The girl startled at their approach. She stopped brushing.

'Sorry.' Frank held his hand out. 'I didn't mean to startle you.'

She nodded warily.

'What's her name?'

She hesitated, eyeing them with suspicion.

Frank showed his ID. 'We're police detectives. Nothing to worry about. We've just spoken to Chelsea and Lorraine and, well, I saw this beautiful mare...'

'Chelsea and Lorraine are my great-aunts.'

Frank smiled. 'I'll leave you to the grooming. I'm sorry to disturb you, dear.'

'Kate,' the girl said.

'Sorry to disturb you, Kate.'

A smile broke out on her face. 'No, this is.' She stroked the mare. 'I'm Alice.'

'Two very nice names.' Frank nodded. 'How long have you been riding, Alice?'

'Four years, since I was eight.' She patted the mare's neck.

'Is Kate yours?'

'She's no one's,' Alice said. 'But she lets me ride her when I'm here. She's my best friend.'

He stroked the mare. 'Fantastic. You're your own person aren't you, Kate? Promise me you'll keep at the riding, eh, Alice?'

'I will.' Alice smiled again.

Frank left. He glanced back at her to wave as he left, but Alice was back at it with single-minded focus.

The warmth of the stables fell away as they stepped back into the biting cold. They walked back to the car in silence. The thickening snow clung to Frank's eyelashes and shoulders, while the wind drove it sideways, reducing visibility. Frank's throat felt tight and he didn't know what to say, but he could feel Gerry's questioning glances.

He knew her analytical mind was in overdrive trying to explain his behaviour.

On the outskirts of the car park, he stopped. 'Go on, ask...'

'Why did you tell her to promise to keep at it? Is it because of Maddie?'

'Aye. Some things you never forget as a father, no matter how worn down you get with age. My daughter's smile while she guided her mare through precise figures of eight is one moment...' The memory caught in his throat.

He kept the last part to himself – *Maddie's face, once alight with joy, her movements once so sure and confident.*

They carried on towards the car.

'I'm not sure how that explains why you asked her to promise,' Gerry said.

Frank paused and closed his eyes. More images of Maddie shot through him – horrendous ones. The hollow eyes... the track marks on her arms...

He took a deep breath and opened his eyes. 'Because if Maddie had kept at it, if she'd held onto something that made her happy... who knows... maybe I'd know where she is now.'

He turned away. *But if I did, would it make any difference? Is the daughter I knew back then already gone?*

Of course she was.

That version of Maddie had been laid to rest a long time ago.

It was a hard truth.

But that doesn't mean I should forget her. And damn anyone who tries to forget who Sarah Matthews was, just because of who she became.

All graves existed for a reason.

To remember to honour who they were, not just how they ended.

And if it was Sarah Matthews in that old grave, which he genuinely felt it was, now it was the time to remember.

And someone knew. Someone always knew.

Chapter Fifteen

They crawled through Ruswarp's narrow streets while the windscreen wipers pounded back and forth, struggling against the relentless snow.

Frank caught sight of the Bridge Inn again as it loomed through a white haze. Frank stared at its windows, imagining Malcolm Hargreaves peering out of one of them on an autumn evening, watching Sarah Matthews climb into a red Fiesta and vanish into history. He had no real picture of either of them in his mind, and still no concrete proof the bones belonged to Sarah. But the certainty sat deep in his gut, as immovable as the ancient stones that went into building up Ruswarp itself.

Even if I'm wrong, he thought, *at least I'm paying some attention to that poor young woman again.*

I mean how long did it take them to dismiss it? Write it off to a troublesome young woman running off with a sugar daddy?

It was too soon to say, but he'd experienced small communities who'd had little patience for such behaviour, before. He wasn't naïve to some people's beliefs that stepping out of line somehow justified whatever fate befell you.

Maddie had been, and God willing that she was alive, troublesome.

He wouldn't be turning his back on her. Or Sarah Matthews either.

Through the passenger window, St Bartholomew's Church emerged from the swirling snow. The medieval building had endured countless Yorkshire winters, its weathered stone carrying the weight of centuries. Now it seemed to watch him with the same hollow intensity as the victim's eyes had watched him. Frank glanced into the back seat where Gerry was absorbed in her phone, no doubt uncovering details others would miss. She hadn't yet asked about his dinner with Evelyn – the steamed fish and quinoa experiment, the careful dance of conversation between two people carrying so much shared history.

With everything going on, there hadn't been a chance.

He was sure it would come.

'This is bloody ridiculous,' Frank said as they crept past the ghostly primary school again at a snail's pace. 'We're not getting to Scarborough in this.'

Reggie nodded.

'We need to do what everyone else has done and get ourselves home.'

'Rain is forecast all night,' Gerry said from the back seat. 'There's a high chance it'll clear most of the snow for the morning.'

'I bloody hope so. Okay, Gerry, access the Sarah Matthews files from home. Once you've done that, feed back to me and then you can research all the missing people from that era, okay?'

'Meanwhile I'll try to expedite identification of the

body against Sarah's dental and medical records,' he continued, watching snowflakes build up on the windscreen. 'Probably sod all chance. Still, we can hope Nasreen made it back to her office before it started piling up again.'

'Office?' Reggie looked at Frank and grinned. 'You mean morgue?'

'Eyes on the road, Reggie, or at least the parts still visible *otherwise* we'll be in the fucking morgue.'

'Never crashed in my life, sir.'

'Jesus wept.' Frank leaned back in his seat, exhaling heavily. 'I'm not a superstitious man, never have been... but please don't tempt fate with such bravado in my presence.'

'Sorry, sir.' Reggie hunched forward, peering through the thickening snow.

Frank rubbed condensation from his window with Mary's old glove. 'And if you want to be Tom Selleck, remember he takes better care of his tash than that.'

He turned in his seat, catching Gerry's eye in the back. 'Gerry, keep us in the loop. We'll set up a call tomorrow to go over everything.'

A gust of wind buffeted the car, cutting off his words. He gave it a moment and then said, 'Let's just focus on getting home in one piece.'

So, the rest of the journey passed in contemplative silence. Frank's mind drifted back to Alice in the stable, so confident with Kate the mare. Just like Maddie had been with horses, once. Before whatever darkness had taken root in her soul had bloomed into something unstoppable. Had something similar happened to Sarah Matthews? Had she too lost her anchor, and been dragged down beneath the ocean's surface?

Chapter Sixteen

Courtesy of floor-to-ceiling windows, Stephen Walker could see the snow blanket the harbour below. Because of the elevated position of his property, a slight turn of his head presented him with the brooding silhouette of Whitby Abbey looming on the opposite cliffs.

The view had cost him, but it had been worth every penny.

He had to ensure he enjoyed his remaining years. After all, he was seventy-five now, so he had to be realistic about how close the finishing line was.

He ran his fingers through his daughter's hair. She rested against his shoulder. A familiar and comforting weight against him. Thirty-two, and Christie still adored him in the same way she'd adored him in childhood.

He really was blessed.

'What if the kids see straight through me?' Christie asked.

'To what, flower?'

'An entitled, rich bitch telling them what to do.'

'Since when were you entitled?'

'So, I'm a bitch?'

'Ha. You know that you're not.'

'Well, we're rich. And they'll know that.'

'Yes.' He stroked her hair. 'But if they know that, then they'll probably know we weren't always.'

'I guess.'

'Which in a way is inspiration is it not? They too can achieve. I think with all this in mind you're fine telling them what to do.'

'I can be as bossy as I like?'

Stephen laughed. 'No comment, flower.' He adjusted his daughter's head and leaned quite far forward, reaching for a mint from the crystal dish on the coffee table. He'd upped his yoga sessions of late, and it really was showing. He hadn't felt this limber since his twenties. He settled back in his chair. 'Now listen, flower... enough of all this. Your students will see exactly what I see – a capable, intelligent young woman who was born to teach.' He threw the mint in his mouth.

'Does the fact that you're my father make you biased in any way?'

'Of course it does, but...' He prodded the mint to the corner of his mouth. 'Employing teachers is something I know a great deal about. More than most if you can believe it.'

'Dad. That was a long time ago. Things change.'

'I only retired twelve years ago!'

Christie's voice carried that gentle teasing tone she'd perfected over years of managing her father's ego. 'Twelve years is a long time.'

'Behave! You're still young, Christie. At my age, twelve years is the blink of an eye.'

'Still... things are different now. Teaching is different.'

Milo, his eldest, strode into the room with characteristic precision. He was dressed in his usual tailored suit, despite being stranded here by the snow. He stopped by the seven-foot real Christmas tree, tapping away on his phone, smiling.

'Closing another deal?' Stephen asked.

'Something like that.'

Stephen laughed. 'The difference between my two children is that one tells me everything, and the other, well, the other tells me nothing.'

Milo sat down, still smiling. 'Dad, trust me, it wouldn't interest you.'

'Banking?'

Milo arched an eyebrow. 'Eh? Banking. It's more than that.'

'So enlighten us then?' Stephen asked.

'Another time,' Milo said and snorted.

'What's so funny?'

Milo shook his head. 'Well... it's hard to explain. You wouldn't get it.'

'You see, this is what happens when I put my children up on a pedestal,' Stephen said. 'The pedestal grows and grows until they start looking down on me from a great height.'

Christie hit his arm.

'Okay, maybe just the one child,' Stephen said.

Milo didn't respond; he'd tuned out.

'Bloody snow days,' Christie said. 'I could be getting day one over and done with, putting the nerves to bed.'

'Look at it another way, flower. Another day to keep the excitement going.'

'Excitement! Following in your footsteps at Riverside

College... Everyone there still talks about you, Dad. The legendary Mr Walker. The super head from another world.'

A familiar warmth spread through his chest at her words. He had, indeed, cultivated a rather impressive reputation. Having such a legacy really did keep him content in these twilight years.

From the opposite end of the sofa, Milo laughed. 'Legendary! Well, it's better than being known as the dragon lady who terrorised the maths department for thirty years.'

'Your mother was firm but fair,' Stephen said. Memories of Caroline in her sharp suits and clicking heels slid through his mind like old photographs. 'She was also a genius.'

Was a genius.

He flinched.

Just this morning, she'd wandered into the kitchen wearing mismatched slippers, confused about whether it was breakfast or lunch. '*Is* a genius,' he corrected firmly.

Milo looked up from his phone at his father for the first time. Stephen saw the sadness in his eyes. He gave him a nod, reassuring him that it was good to talk about her – that they shouldn't gloss over it now she was deteriorating rapidly.

There was a lingering silence, until Christie, God bless her skills at managing the mood in a room, giggled suddenly. 'She was only a dragon lady to you, Milo, because she caught you smoking behind the bike sheds in sixth form.'

'Piss off,' Milo said.

'Language!' Stephen said.

'A detention in your own mother's classroom,' she continued. 'The shame!'

Milo glared at her, smoothed his already immaculate tie, and returned to his phone.

Caroline appeared in the doorway, holding a bottle of prosecco. She was dressed in an elegant nightgown with perfectly styled silver hair. For a moment, you could be fooled into thinking everything was okay. But then she approached their small cocktail bar, and it was clear something was off-kilter in her movements, like a clock with its gears slightly misaligned.

'I thought you could all use a nightcap,' she said, lining up four glasses on the bar with trembling hands.

It was early afternoon.

Christie sat up straighter. 'Mum, I'm okay thank you. I want to keep my head clear for tomorrow.'

'Nonsense,' Stephen said. 'This is the perfect opportunity to celebrate your new position.'

Stephen rose and went over to help his struggling wife. 'Please, dear, allow me.'

Caroline smiled and went to sit down next to Christie.

After he'd poured the drinks, he joined them. He could see the pain in his children's eyes.

Caroline took Christie's hand. 'How are you feeling, honey?'

'Can't wait.'

'Nervous?'

Christie kissed her mother's forehead. 'Not at all.'

'So happy to hear that.' Caroline beamed.

Stephen smiled over his daughter's compassion.

Stephen turned and gazed through his window again. There was a brief moment of bright sunshine over the harbour. He tried to freeze this moment of closeness with his family in his ageing memory. The life he'd built for them all was solid, and despite the inevitability of cracks appearing, and the finishing line looming close, he'd do well to remember that.

Later, sitting alone in his office, with the door closed and locked, Stephen retrieved his much-loved photo albums from the safe beneath his desk.

Since retirement, he often revisited the photo albums, especially when feeling emotional.

After all, this had been a special time in his life.

A time filled with creativity and hope.

It was only in these last years that he'd taken more time for reflection. Since retiring twelve years ago, he had carefully built a fortune through stocks and shares, cultivating a position in the Conservative Party with the same precision he once applied to his teaching career. He was respected around town and invited to many openings and gatherings. But he too was winding down now. And sometimes, it became necessary to lose yourself in fond memories.

It was, however, strange how frequently he'd been revisiting these souvenirs of late. Since Caroline's diagnosis, he'd been back to these albums twice a week. Now, since her mind had really started to unravel, he was maybe in them daily.

However, did it not make sense?

After all, with his world fracturing around him, did it not seem apt to revisit the more solid nature of perfect, wonderful times?

He flipped the pages.

Then, he started smiling. Trying to and *almost* feeling the same happiness he'd felt then during those special, special times.

Cassie. Sandy. Kayleigh. His breath caught as he turned the next page. And then – Sarah. He stroked her face, closed his eyes and sighed.

When he opened his eyes, a tear ran down his face.

Despite the happiness, there was a deep gnawing hunger for times gone by.

Times when he'd felt truly alive.

Chapter Seventeen

Even though it was only three in the afternoon, the weak winter sun had already started its descent.

Unfortunately, as the sky darkened, the gaudy, bloody Christmas lights from 21 Sycamore Close irritated Peter Watson even more with their strobing effect.

Peter massaged his temples with his arthritic fingers and then pushed himself up from his armchair, wincing as his bad hip gave him a tentative warning about sudden movements.

He closed the living room curtains, not wishing to have a migraine in the name of the Christmas spirit.

It made little difference.

Bursts of red, green, blue and white continued to dance through the curtains.

'Tacky bastards,' he said.

He went into the kitchen and switched on the light. The bulb flickered as he filled the kettle. He'd replaced the bloody thing only last week!

Must be the wiring, he reasoned. *On its last legs.*

He patted his hip. A bitter smile crossed his weathered face. *Just like me.*

As he waited for the kettle to boil, he glanced at the digital thermostat that Donna had insisted on, a month before she went and bloody died on him. Nineteen degrees. Usually, he'd go over and knock it down to eighteen and pull his beanie hat further down onto his head.

No sense burning money just to peel off clothing. However, as he didn't plan to be around for the next set of bills, there was no point in worrying.

Might as well die in warmth.

He couldn't give a hoot what they did with his house. He'd no will, but he suspected his money-grabbing half-brother might appear for the first time in over ten years.

His gaze returned to the flickering bulb. *Let that dickhead fix the wiring.* He glanced at the thermostat a second time. *And pay the bills.*

As he finished making his cup of tea, his gaze fell to Bryan's water bowl. It was getting low again.

'Daft old fool,' he chided himself, picking it up and refilling it. The metal bowl felt cold against his fingers as he topped it up. A month since Bryan had gone, and here he was, still filling his water bowl.

Still, now that Bryan was gone, it meant that he could take his early exit.

Every cloud and all that.

He looked down at the bowl and sighed. Although the memory of Bryan curled up at his feet, combined with the bloody fact that he'd never do so again, felt anything but silver.

Tea in hand, he returned to his sofa. He placed it on the side table next to the bowl filled with over two hundred paracetamol tablets. He picked up the remote control and turned the television on. The ancient machine crackled reluctantly to life, its picture tube taking an age to warm up, just like his joints these days. 'Give over... you're not that old,' he told the television. 'Try being in your seventies.'

His gaze landed on the bowl. One handful would be enough, but he'd gathered two hundred to be sure. No point in botching this like he'd botched so many other things in his life.

He nodded at Donna, who was smiling from a picture on the mantelpiece, and then turned his attention back to the television.

One more afternoon quiz show.

One more *Deal or No Deal*—

The sudden thumping of the bass made him jump. Hip be damned, he was out of his chair like a bullet. He looked at his wall – he couldn't actually see it vibrating, but he knew damned well it was. 'Does he ever bloody learn?'

He slipped on his boots and yanked open his front door. He stomped next door, brushing snowflakes from his face as the cold air bit through his jacket.

It took five knocks to get the pillock to the door, although, in fairness, he didn't leave a great deal of time between each pounding. A cloud of marijuana smoke billowed out.

No wonder the dickhead can't get a job, Peter thought. *The bastard must spend most of the day horizontal.*

Jake Rimes, the twenty-something layabout, had his long hair tied back in a messy bun. His eyes were red and unfocused. 'Hello... Mr Watson?'

Peter waved the billows of smoke from his face. 'Bloody hell... you partying with a hippie commune in there?'

Jake grinned. 'It's medicinal.'

'Ah, I see. I guess it's treatment for your ears then.'

Jake frowned, confused. He pointed at his ears. 'Eh?'

'Well, I'm assuming you can't hear a bloody thing... not if you have to have the music up that loud.'

It took a moment for realisation to dawn on Jake's face. 'Ah...'

Peter's eyes narrowed. 'Ah... yes... the music.' *You fuckwit.*

'Sorry, I just keep forgetting.'

Peter made a smoking gesture. 'I'm not surprised.'

Jake called over his shoulder, 'Lou! Turn it down!'

A female voice, presumably Lou, called back, 'Really? You sure?'

Peter nodded at Jake, who nodded too, and repeated, 'Really! I'm sure.'

The music went down.

Thankfully.

'Shit. It's not that miserable old bastard from next door again?' Lou called in.

Jake smiled and said, 'The door's still open, Lou!'

'I'm not miserable.' Peter rubbed his temples. 'I've just got a headache from your sodding music.'

'No,' Jake said, nodding. 'You're not miserable.'

Peter scowled. 'I'm happy enough.'

'I agree,' Jake said. 'Merry Christmas.'

'Merry Christmas.' Peter turned away.

As he walked away, Peter thought, *Get a proper job, you layabout.*

He'd barely made it halfway home when a Bentley SUV was pulling into his driveway just behind his car. He stopped dead and regarded the fool behind the wheel.

Desmond Chapman from number 11.

He was already out of his car, sporting a designer coat and Kashmir scarf.

What an absolute clown!

'Oi... Des!'

Desmond turned around. His face sagged. He looked at his car and then back at Peter. 'Just two minutes, Peter. I promise. Two minutes. Just picking up Sophie...'

'So, park on your ex-wife's driveway?'

'I can't. Her new fella parks there.'

'Doesn't look like he's there now.'

Desmond looked. 'Yeah... but he could be back any moment.' He looked back. 'Best not to piss the ex off... you know how it is.'

Peter shook his head. 'Not really, no. I suggest you piss your ex-wife off rather than me, though. I'm totally blocked in!'

'You're not going anywhere, are you?'

'Aren't I?'

'Are you?'

'I don't know. It seems you've decided I'm not.'

Desmond nodded and opened his mouth to respond. But then he realised he didn't know what to say. So, he closed it again.

'Could you move your car, Desmond?' Peter said.

'It's two minutes, Peter. Two minutes.'

Peter looked at his watch. 'Actually, it's getting on for three now.'

Desmond looked exasperated. Good. Teach him a lesson.

'Are you scared of your ex-wife?'

'No... well... yes. Please?'

'No... move it, or visitation rights will be the least of your problems...'

'Sounds like a threat.'

'It was.' Peter marched to his own car. A modest old Volvo

but built like a tank. He hoisted out his keys and opened the doors. 'I'm a doddering old man who's about to reverse off my drive. Unfortunately, I didn't see you parked there. My eyesight isn't what it once was. And look at this bloody weather. Tsk.' *Plus, thirty minutes from now I'll have gone bye bye, so what do I bloody care?* he thought. He climbed in and started the engine.

He watched, smiling, as Desmond, palm in the air, rushed back to his gleaming Bentley. 'Okay! Okay!' he said loudly. 'You've made your fucking point.'

For a brief moment, Peter considered doing it anyway. But then, after a few deep breaths, he killed the engine.

After Desmond had moved, Peter climbed from his Volvo.

As he marched to his home, he looked back at Desmond, glowering at him from his wife's driveway. 'You know what, second thoughts, the weather's shite... best stay indoors. Merry Christmas.'

Peter caught Desmond's response before he closed his door.

It was fairly predictable.

'Fuck you.'

~

Having missed a chunk of the show, he decided to forgo *Deal or No Deal* and just get on with it.

His neighbours had soured his mood. Before that, he'd felt more positive than usual.

He turned off the television and plucked Donna's photograph from the mantlepiece and sat on his chair.

He looked at his wife. His fingers traced the familiar curves of her face through the glass. 'I'm surrounded by cretins, Don. The world has moved on and there's no place for me in it, I can tell you.'

He could almost hear her gentle reply, the way she'd so often soothed his temper with infinite patience. 'There's always an easier way of managing it, Pete, remember, count to ten...'

A sad smile tugged at his lips. 'No, that was always your way! No one had patience like you. So, without you here, what bloody chance do I have? Plus, you know, without you, and now without Bryan, too, it just gets duller and duller... So...' He placed the photograph on the side and scooped up a fistful of paracetamol from the bowl. 'Here or the bedroom...?'

A pounding out the back made him jump. The pills cascaded from his fingers and scattered on the floor.

'Bollocks!'

It was the bloody back gate again. Sometimes the postman came through the back and left it unlatched.

He slammed the bowl down and stood, heart hammering against his ribs.

'Idiots!'

In the kitchen, he flicked on the light and looked through the window. Sure enough, his wooden gate was swinging in the wind.

He slipped on some Wellington boots he kept by the back door and headed out. He could see the parcel on the ground, poking from a mound of snow. 'Ridiculous.'

His garden was small and hemmed in by a large wooden fence. The door was banging open and closed harder now. He crunched through the snow, quickly, grumbling, fearing it was going to come off his hinges.

He'd already made his mind up to complain to the post

office when his foot caught on something buried in the snow. He stumbled forward. 'Shit—'

The gate swung violently in the wind. There was a flash of movement, a crack of wood against his forehead, and then searing pain.

As he fell backwards into the snow, everything went black.

Chapter Eighteen

From his father's bedroom window, Lewis White watched snowflakes dance in the amber glow of Victorian streetlamps.

He pressed his hands against the cold glass, desperate to feel the moment.

The mindfulness had been helping lately.

Yes, he'd scoffed over the offer at first, argued that breathing exercises wouldn't help a man who'd fractured someone's skull against a urinal, but he was glad he'd given it the time of day.

The anger was still there, glowing within him, but at least he could see it now, and in time, he'd get control of it.

Today, however, was posing a significant challenge to his growing calm.

After all, mindfulness required living in the present, whereas being here now was dragging him relentlessly back into the past.

And memories could sometimes be lead weights. They really could. Especially when they reminded you so painfully of the ones you'd lost. And it was hard not to revisit them at this time of the year.

He found himself in a memory of his seventh Christmas, four decades back, throwing snowballs at his mother in the back garden while she ducked and dived behind the snowman they'd made together. She caught one in the chest and collapsed to the floor, playing dead.

In the here and now, he rolled up his sleeve, and looked down at her name, Elizabeth, tattooed in elegant copperplate script, each letter a permanent reminder of the mother he'd adored and lost.

Then he was back in his memory. At the moment, Felix, his ten-year-old brother, crept up behind him and delivered a snowball to the back of his neck. A sudden icy burn, followed by Felix's wild laughter.

He rolled up his other sleeve.

Felix.

Another name, another significant loss, inked into his skin.

Lewis turned from the window and regarded his father, John White.

He moved towards his bed, his fingers curling into fists.

'Where were you in that memory, John?'

Of course, John wouldn't answer back.

He merely issued another rattling breath.

He hadn't even opened his eyes since Lewis had arrived.

'Too busy, eh? Story of your life. Always too busy.'

He stopped at his father's bedside.

John White – once a lion of property development, jetting around the globe for deals – was now a withering shell beneath expensive cotton sheets. Lewis touched them, saw from a label that they were Egyptian cotton. Of course they were – nothing but the best for John White.

He wondered if his father would ever hear or speak again. He'd love to know his father could hear him, would love it even more if the old bastard could try, weakly, to justify his behaviour.

'We tried enjoying ourselves that Christmas without you there. I often wondered if you enjoyed that Christmas wherever you were. That one, and the others, many others, you missed. In fact, thinking about it now, how many Christmases did Felix have left at that point? Two... three... Were you there for any of them?'

It'd been over twenty years since he'd last seen his father.

It'd been over thirty years since he'd last called him Dad, sometime around his fifteenth birthday, when the police had caught him joy-riding a stolen Mercedes, and it took him several hours to pick him up from the station. He'd expected an almighty bollocking – would have preferred that, showed that he truly cared – instead he simply took him back to his mother, telling him that you reap what you sow in life, and fucking off back here, to this place he'd lived alone since the early nineties.

'You look like shit, John.'

And it was true. His skin had taken on the sallow hue of old parchment, stretched tight across handsome cheekbones that had once made him quite eligible to other women – that and the bank balance, of course.

Ironically, now his impressive cheekbones only emphasised the skull beneath, a visual representation of death claiming its latest subject inch by yellowed inch.

Mark Bridges, his father's nurse, came into the bedroom. Mark was trained to within an inch of his life to present a jovial, spritely attitude while administering palliative care.

It was impressive to Lewis. Not a single twitch or mumble, just a breeziness that made death seem like the norm – which, Lewis supposed, it was. He recalled the professionals who'd dealt with him during his three years in prison. They'd been full of mumbles and twitches – their anxieties as obvious as their cheap polyester uniforms – and even those that taught him mindfulness had been stoic, and officious. No jovial, spritely attitudes to lighten the mood there. Ever.

But only the best for John White.

He was, after all, a very wealthy man.

'Apparently rain is on the way,' Mark said, moving through the room as if he were hosting a dinner party. 'Hopefully we won't need to start shovelling after all.' He smiled and looked between father and son. 'How we doing?'

Lewis flashed him a look that surely revealed what he was thinking... *Well, he's dying, and I'm bitter and pissed off.*

Still, if Mark, the well of happiness and contentment, clocked it, he wasn't about to acknowledge it in his carefully curated environment.

'Fantastic,' Mark said, either immune to tension or trained very well in ignoring it. He went over to John, checked the drip, and tapped a button on the machine. 'Just a touch more morphine for the afternoon, Mr White.'

Mark took a few vitals and scribbled them on a clipboard.

He looked up at Lewis. 'He was looking forward to you coming.'

Lewis felt a familiar heat rising in his chest. He took a deep breath and tried to force it down, because it was the same heat that had ended with Gregg Ince's blood on his knuckles, and the poor bastard's head bouncing off the urinal.

Mark smiled and continued, 'He really hoped he'd be awake.'

'You've just dosed him again... Is he unlikely to wake again now?'

Mark held onto his smile. 'Yes, I'm sorry... the morphine is important, though, Mr White. It makes it more peaceful.' Mark turned his smile down to Lewis. 'Doesn't it, Mr White?' Mark touched John's skeletal hand, affectionately, and left the room.

Mark's relentless showmanship was grating against his nerves.

It'd been Mark who'd tracked him down, phoned him and begged him to come and say goodbye to his father. His father had asked, apparently.

Maybe it wasn't theatre, then? Maybe Mark had genuine compassion for the old man? After all, cold-calling a convicted violent offender wasn't in a nurse's job description.

That idea of genuine compassion made his stomach turn.

Lewis exhaled, then took another deep breath. He was, at least, getting better at calming himself. It was almost four years since he'd beaten someone half to death because of anger. He was working hard to ensure that never happened again.

Lewis wondered, and not for the first time, what the hell he was doing here.

It couldn't be sympathy. It must be a good riddance?

Or, maybe just to prove I'm not you – running away when family needs me most?

John's skeletal hand twitched on the covers. Lewis did

have some early memories of that hand – holding his tiny fingers, teaching him to throw a ball. They were, of course, vague, though. And, had they actually happened? After all, he'd read somewhere that there was a fair amount of fiction in memory. But one thing he was crystal clear on was this. John hadn't been holding Felix's hand when meningitis took him at twelve. In fact, John had been nowhere near the hospital. He was in Dubai, closing a deal while his son closed his eyes for the last time.

'You made it back for the funeral, though, didn't you?' Lewis said. 'First class? God bless you, John.'

Lewis stood in silence, haunted by the memory of Felix's cold, empty hand. At least their mother had been holding the other.

'She was there for us, John. Always. Not like you.'

This was all Lewis could bear.

He circled the bed for the door. He turned before exiting. He clapped. 'Well done, John. What a legacy, eh? Built on broken promises, affairs, neglect and the misery of others. All that money... yet you can't even take it with you... was it all really worth it?'

He turned to leave—

Behind him, he heard a weak voice. 'Don't...'

Lewis froze.

'Please...'

Lewis looked back over his shoulder, his blood running cold. His father's eyes were open.

'Stay...'

Bile rose in Lewis's throat. He didn't know what to say. In fact, he didn't even know what he was feeling.

But then came that usual, default surge of anger.

How dare you ask that?

How dare you need me now!

'No!' he said, moving swiftly through the door. He flew down the stairs. Mark was at the bottom. He kept his eyes fixed on the floor – he was in no mood for the nurse's compassion.

'Mr White—'

'No!' he repeated, slipping on his jacket and boots and heading through the front door.

The icy blast of air was sobering.

He trudged up the snow-covered path.

Don't...

He felt the ink spelling his mother's name burning on his arm.

Please...

He saw his brother's cold, empty hand.

Stay...

He looked back at the house, its windows glowing warm against the gathering darkness.

He thought now about Gregg Ince, the man he'd put in hospital during that pub fight, skull fractured against a urinal. He'd written him letters. Tried to apologise but had received nothing back.

Never really expected to. But...

Where were the answers?

To all of this?

Him?

His father?

'Fuck,' Lewis whispered, his breath clouding in the frigid air.

He turned back towards the house.

Chapter Nineteen

AFTER BEING DROPPED off home by Reggie, Frank had stormed into his kitchen with cold feet and thrown his hiking boots away in disgust.

Then, he'd taken a shower, during which he could almost hear Mary's laugh: 'About bloody time, love!'

Mary had always called him a hoarder and used to laugh when unusable camera film and leaking batteries from decades earlier showed up at the back of old drawers.

Following his shower, he took a nap and woke up feeling rather proud of himself for ditching the hiking boots. It was a sign that he wasn't settling for shite any more. Another step forward, like giving up the drink and eating Gerry's rabbit food.

And why not? Who wants to be a walking Yorkshire stereotype?

However, five minutes ago, he'd come into the kitchen for a glass of water, and the sight of the bin had triggered something in him.

He was currently resisting the urge to retrieve the boots—

A sharp knock at the door made him jump. 'God help us...'

He opened the door. The darkness surprised him at first. His nap had obviously been more than a nap!

Henrietta stood shivering on the doorstep, her smart wool coat no match for the cold, a Tupperware container clutched to her chest. She looked good. She'd styled her silver hair in soft waves that framed her face, and she'd applied makeup.

'You off out, Henrietta?' he asked.

'No... why?'

'You look...' He bit his tongue before the word 'nice' could escape. *What impression would that give? Also what was appropriate in this day and age?* He'd lost track. 'Like you made an effort?'

His cheeks burned. That was probably worse.

Bloody hell, between Henrietta and Evelyn, I feel like a teenager again, fumbling in conversations!

'No more than usual.' She smiled.

Relieved she hadn't asked, 'Why, what do I usually look like?', he exhaled.

'I noticed you got back earlier. I was glad. The snow was too awful to be out.' She pressed the container into his hands. 'Thought you'd appreciate this.'

He took it. 'Thanks.'

'And if you don't mind me saying, Frank, you look like you've been neglecting your food lately.'

The unexpected comment took him aback. 'Is that a compliment?' He looked down at himself. 'It was kind of the idea. Neglect was part of the process.'

'Yes... I get that... but a man like you needs flesh on his bones.' The gesture was somewhere between motherly and something else entirely. He wasn't sure which he'd prefer. 'Full-faced and hardy,' she continued.

Full-faced and hardy?

'So,' she said, 'lasagna.'

He opened the container and looked down. Steam rose from the pasta, carrying the rich scent of tomatoes and herbs. 'Thanks. I love lasagna. And it's a big wedge so that will certainly add fullness to my face.'

She laughed. 'My speciality. Once upon a time, my kids used to love it. Ian, in particular.' Her voice caught slightly on 'Ian' – she hadn't spoken to him in a couple of years for reasons unknown. It was the shared pain of estranged children that had finally bridged their decades-old animosity that night after Maddie's clandestine visit.

Frank nodded. 'And it certainly beats the shite – sorry, junk – I had in the fridge.'

'Yes.' She glowed, clearly revelling in his gratitude.

The warm container in his hands suddenly felt like more than just a gift of food.

He'd seen in films that people often brought food round when people died. No one had ever done that with him. Not when Mary died, not when his world collapsed. Henrietta had been next door when Mary had passed but hadn't brought so much as a sympathy card. Yet here she was. Five years late. Commenting on his figure, styling her hair, and wearing perfume that could knock out a horse.

With women, he'd never been the brightest spark, but he wasn't a complete imbecile.

'You really didn't have to,' Frank said, concluding it'd be better if she just went now, before he felt any more uncomfortable.

'Well, I did. So are you going to invite me in?'

Seems she wasn't going anywhere.

He stepped aside. 'Would you like a cup of tea?'

At least the house was presentable enough after yesterday morning's cleaning frenzy for the meal with Evelyn.

He showed her through to his living room with his unimpressive Christmas tree, and then he went to put the kettle on.

When he returned, he found Henrietta looking at Mary's photograph. His stomach clenched. He coughed and she turned, looking rather uncomfortable. 'Sorry...'

He waved it off. 'It's okay.'

'She really was beautiful.'

He handed her a cup of tea. 'Aye, she was.'

She sat down, took a mouthful, put her cup down, and patted the sofa alongside her.

He sat as close to the left arm of the sofa as he could, not wanting to invade her personal space, then wondered if that was exactly what she'd been hoping for. He shook his head and inwardly cursed himself for letting his imagination run away with him. He blew on his tea. 'Hope it's not too strong.' He took a mouthful. 'Folk often say I make it too strong.'

'Tea can never be too strong.'

'Aye... that's what I always tell them.'

She smiled. 'Anyway, I'll be away for Christmas.'

He swallowed. 'Nice...' He wondered why this was important. She'd never told him she was going away for Christmas before. In fact, until recently, they'd barely spoken!

'Nigel's,' she said. 'In Norfolk. You know, the one son who talks to me.'

He didn't know what she was drawing attention to here, so he went for the positive angle. 'Sounds lovely...

the Norfolk Broads, eh? I'll keep an eye on the house for you.'

She nodded. 'I'd be grateful for that.'

The silence stretched between them, filled with the ghost of her other son – who'd been referred to twice now since she'd appeared on his doorstep.

Frank decided it was best not to go there.

'And you... where are you going?' she asked.

'Me?' he asked. 'Same as every year. Here. I'll be fine.'

'You've got no one to spend it with.'

He waved his hand. 'Christmas is for the kids, anyway.'

He expected her to retort with, 'It's for family,' but it seemed she was savvy enough not to refer to something he didn't have.

'You know,' Henrietta said. 'I could always ask Nigel. They've got a blooming big house... and—'

He held up his hand. 'Thanks Henrietta, but I can't be away. You know. Just in case... well... just in case.'

'Maddie gets in touch.'

'Aye.'

This was the truth. Not that he'd have accepted her invitation anyway. He made a habit of rejecting all of them.

Even Gerry had asked him to join her for Christmas. And although he'd declined – rather rudely, now he looked back on it – he doubted that would be the last he heard of it.

He'd like to say that Gerry wouldn't be able to badger him into it, but so far, her track record of wearing him down and getting her own way stood at a solid 100 per cent.

There was a moment of silence, and Frank detected something serious was coming.

Eventually, Henrietta asked, 'How was dinner?'

'Sorry?'

'Yesterday.'

'Yesterday?'

'Evening...? You had company.'

Frank felt his heart racing. 'Ah... aye...'

'Who was that?'

'Evelyn.'

'Who?'

'Evelyn. I told you about her.'

'Did you?'

Actually, he wasn't sure he had. 'Sorry... I thought I had. Just a friend.'

'I didn't know you had any.'

Charming! True, maybe... but still, did it need announcing?

'You told me about Gerry. Although, you didn't say she was your friend. You told me she was your life instructor.'

'Did I?' He must have been feeling grumpy at the time. 'She's both.'

'Anyway, Evelyn? You two close?'

'As close as friends usually are.'

'I see. Where did you meet?'

His chest tightened as he explained she was the widow of Nigel Wainwright, the man Mary had died in a car accident with.

'The wife of the man who shat on your life?' Her eyebrow arched like an accusation.

'Aye... I guess you could put it like that...'

'Interesting.'

'I know... Just before we go any further... I've made peace with that.'

'You're surprisingly forgiving, Frank.'

'Can't say I've heard that one before!'

'It's true.'

'Well, it wasn't actually her that did anything... so, forgiving Evelyn wasn't really necessary.'

'But you must have been pissed off?'

'For a while, aye, but I made my peace with it.'

'How?'

Frank sighed. 'We talked. About the past. About understanding the people we lost.'

Henrietta drank her tea in silence for a moment.

Frank tried to convince himself that she was merely contemplating this, but it was clear that disappointment was radiating off her.

'Sometimes it's better to move forward,' Henrietta eventually said. 'And sometimes you need to understand the past to move forward.'

It was a good point, but he was desperate to change the subject. 'Aye... so anyway, when do you get off to Norfolk?'

She started to reply, but Frank's phone cut her off.

'Sorry.' He hoisted it out. 'Might be work.'

His heart kicked at the sight of Evelyn's name on the screen.

Henrietta saw and nodded. 'Take it.'

'You sure? I could call her back.'

'Take it, Frank.'

'Okay.' He stood. 'I'll just...' He pointed at the door.

Henrietta nodded.

He went into the kitchen, closed the door, and answered. 'Evelyn?'

'It's Janet.'

His stomach plunged. 'What... is she okay?'

'Yes, fine Frank, nothing to worry about. Well, there was, but now there isn't. She came over faint earlier. It passed, but I insisted on bringing her in to be looked at. After the last stroke, well, I didn't want to take any chances.

She wanted me to phone you and tell you everything is fine, in case you found out she was in hospital.'

'Okay.' He took a deep breath, but it didn't help too much with the anxiety. 'Can I speak to her?'

'She'll phone you later. I just want her to rest now.'

'Okay.'

'She'll tell you it was a complete overreaction.'

'Better to be safe,' Frank said.

'Overprotective daughter syndrome. You think that's a thing?'

'Aye,' he said, forcing a laugh, but the joke hurt. His daughter wanted nothing to do with him. 'You think I should come—'

'Rather you didn't,' she interrupted. 'I want her to rest. And no point in you risking yourself in this weather.'

'Aye. Thanks for telling me.'

'You're welcome.'

He hung up and automatically glanced at the fridge, feeling the old familiar pull. When he realised that his ale-drinking days were behind him, for fear of Gerry's death stare, he took three long deep breaths instead and left the room.

'Sorry about that, I—' He stopped. Henrietta was gone, leaving only the lingering trace of her perfume.

He saw her, through the window, walking outside his house, back to her own.

He went and put the kettle on again, and then sat, listening to his central heating thumping through the pipes.

Why does it always feel so bloody cold in this house?

He looked up at Mary, seeing her smile.

It was like regarding a fossil preserved in amber while the world moved on.

His mind turned to the backpack that Maddie had come

back for a couple of months ago. Why had she come back for it? It'd seemed a rather desperate move.

He thought of Henrietta heading to Norfolk, and Evelyn in hospital being doted on by Janet. He also thought of Gerry spending Christmas with Tom, finally finding happiness.

All these connections, these threads of care and concern, felt just out of reach to him.

Then, he closed his eyes and glimpsed empty eye sockets.

I want to know the real you.

He opened his eyes.

Sarah.

Poor lass won't be spending another Christmas forgotten in that silo.

Whoever did that to you is going to pay.

He stood and looked out into the darkness. The snow continued to spiral under streetlights.

Then, something nagged at him.

He tried to work out what until he was feeling rather hot and flustered, but remained clueless.

And then he realised. He'd some old dubbin somewhere. No point wasting perfectly good shoes when they just needed waterproofing.

With a sigh, he opened the bin and fished out his boots.

You can take the man out of Yorkshire, but you can't take Yorkshire out of the man, he thought.

Though of course this made no bloody sense as he was still here and probably would be until they carried him out feet first.

Chapter Twenty

GERRY WATCHED from her living room window as the first drops of rain began. According to the weather forecast, it would go to work on the snow that had brought Whitby to an almost complete standstill.

She reviewed her research so far – a comprehensive profile of Sarah Matthews in preparation for the upcoming briefing.

She'd been over the entire missing person's investigation and yes, granted, there were some interesting angles. The suspicious boyfriend, the aggressive father who'd died in prison, the potential older man, the red Fiesta seen by Malcolm Hargreaves on the night she disappeared, the records for shoplifting... there'd been complexity in Sarah's life, and many angles to explore but, regardless of what Frank believed, physical identification was the starting gun. And they didn't have that yet.

Dental records would be good, but Nasreen was at home now, while the body remained in the morgue.

She'd contacted seventeen riding schools across North Yorkshire, methodically documenting each conversation.

She'd prepared a list of other missing young horse riders that fit the criteria. All living within reasonable distance, who'd gone missing around the late eighties and early nineties.

But, admittedly, none had yielded anything as promising as the Sarah Matthews lead.

Especially considering Sarah was actually from Ruswarp – where the remains had been discovered.

Even without physical evidence, it seemed more and more likely that Frank's instincts were correct.

She had been working quickly, methodically organising facts into neat columns and bullet points. But now, she'd hit a brick wall – and her personal concerns began to creep in.

Rylan's cold nose pressed against her hand. After looking into his concerned brown eyes, she sank her fingers into the fur just behind his ears. 'I know...'

The marriage proposal had been sitting in her mind like a complex equation waiting to be solved – calling to her for careful consideration.

'I've an idea now of how to approach it.'

Rylan tilted his head, encouraging her to continue.

She opened a new document, fingers hovering over the keys.

'I'm aware that marriage is about love, Rylan – but if I neglect the practical considerations, then, what? You know this is important.'

The Lab's tail thumped once against the floor.

She nodded and her fingers began to move:

MARRIAGE CONSIDERATIONS – INITIAL DRAFT
   1. Living Arrangements
  Rylan's sleeping location maintained (left side of bed)

> Designated quiet hours for work (0200-0600 must remain undisturbed)
>
> Personal space requirements must be satisfied when Tom's relatives visit (half a metre minimum, and visits limited to once a year)

She paused, and moved her fingers through Rylan's fur, finding comfort in the familiar texture.

He nuzzled her and she continued typing.

She'd already determined that each point was a safeguard, a way to maintain order in what could easily become chaos.

It took her a while to manage '3. Finances.' The numbers were comforting – concrete, measurable things she could control. But she realised it was necessary to keep separate accounts – too much blurring of their identities would be disorientating. A joint account was fine for emergencies, but they must be equally weighted based on salaries.

She scratched behind Rylan's ears, and her fingers vibrated as he gave a pleasurable growl.

She added another couple to her list.

If either of them was late for work, they should make every effort to eat on the way home to avoid disrupting anyone else's mealtime. She also documented her preferred times for yoga and brisk walking.

Rylan pressed closer, laying his head in her lap.

It wasn't long before she reached point 7.

7. Holiday Protocol

- Quiet individual yoga retreat for Gerry twice a year

- Arrangements for Rylan if they shared a holiday must be five stars
- Holidays, away from Rylan, would be limited to four days

The list then evolved at speed.

At point 80 – bathroom scheduling protocols – she sighed, concerned that she'd barely scratched the surface. And by point 105, acceptable noise levels, she realised she was going to need much longer than an afternoon. By point 125 (acceptable dinner time conversations), the real complexity of marriage was becoming apparent to her, and the anxiety started to return—

Her phone's ringtone cut through her concentration. Frank's name appeared on the screen. She answered. 'Hello.'

'How do?'

'Busy...'

'On...?'

She glanced at her marriage consideration list. She'd still not shared the news with Frank.

'I'm planning to get married.'

The phone went silent for a time.

'Sir?'

'Eh? Say that again... Sorry, that's not what I was expecting. But did I hear you right? You're planning to get married?'

'Yes, sir.'

'Well... wow... planning... Does Tom know?'

'Of course, sir. He proposed last night.'

'Of course he did. And you're planning the big day already? Well, I guess it is quite exciting...'

'No sir... I'm not planning the wedding, I'm planning

the marriage.' She glanced at the cursor blink beside point 126 on her list. It was long and would get longer. 'Actually, I may be doing this in order to decide whether to actually go ahead.'

She heard Frank draw a long breath. 'Okay. I see. Well, congratulations... maybe... you probably just need some processing time.'

She used the mouse slider to wheel through about ten pages. That was an understatement.

'What's on the plan?' Frank asked.

'Just the basics at the moment.'

'Like? Give me an example?' Frank pushed.

'Sleep disruption?'

'You only have four hours a night. You already disrupt your own.'

'It's optimal... for me.'

'That's a bit pointless anyway. I think you can still fit in four hours when married.'

'True.' The logic of his statement settled something in her mind. 'Maybe I'm being too thorough. Sir?'

'Aye?'

'You know marriage statistics aren't good.'

He snorted. 'Ignore them. Best thing I ever did, Gerry. Statistics mean nothing.'

'But Mary had an affair—' She broke off and put her hand to her mouth. She was impulsive, and often thoughtless, but she should have caught that one in time.

Silence.

'I'm sorry, sir.'

Still silent.

'Sir... I'm—'

He cut her off with a sigh. 'Pack it in, Gerry. A bolt of

the truth never hurt anyone. Look, the affair was my fault. But still, maybe you're right; keep your stats in mind.'

Gerry failed to see how it was his fault being that he wasn't the actual person cheating, but this time she did clamp her hand over her mouth again, quick smart.

Frank must have heard his own bitterness, because his tone suddenly shifted. 'Actually, scratch that! We would never have split, Gerry. Ever. I would've fixed it. We defied those statistics, and my advice? You defy them too – if you decide to say yes.'

'What was the reason you were phoning, sir?'

'Big news. Nasreen is grounded at home, but all is not lost... Helen made it to the lab. That pin we recovered... she cleaned up. It was a pin for reaching first place in the Yorkshire Dales Cross Country horse riding Championship in 1984. Take a look at the past winners.'

Gerry's hands flew over the keyboard. She found the website for the competition and scrolled through the list of past winners.

1984. Sarah Matthews.

'You were right, Frank.'

'A proud moment for the lass, I imagine. She'd have been seventeen. I can see why she still wore that pin. What've you got for me?'

She fed back everything on Sarah's background. Education, family, work history... right through to her tearaway boyfriend, and eventual disappearance. Then, they discussed the investigation, which had been rather too brief for Frank's liking.

'A lot of the investigation hinged around Malcolm Hargreaves' witness statements, and the inconsistency of them. The original investigating officer noted that Malcolm Hargreaves changed his story about the time he actually saw

Sarah three times during initial questioning, although he remained consistent on the red Fiesta.'

'So, he was pissed as a fart...'

'I also compiled that list of other potential victims for you as well.'

'You did all that in a short afternoon.'

'Yes, sir.' *As well as a draft of my marriage considerations,* she thought, *though that still feels grossly incomplete.*

'I'll call the briefing for five-thirty...' She listened as he provided details of what he needed her to talk through. Then, he told her the next steps that he felt were appropriate. 'Sound in order to you?'

'Yes.'

He didn't know why he bothered asking; she'd let him know if she wasn't happy with anything.

'Okay... I'll see you on Zoom. I'll leave you to your marriage document.'

'Do you think it's a bad idea?'

'I won't lie, it threw me, but then, I didn't know you like I know you now. And if there's one thing I've learned over this last year is that your overly methodical approach – even making lists like this – usually leads you to the right approach.'

'Which is?'

He paused. 'I'm sure you'll figure it out – like you always do.'

Chapter Twenty-One

Despite knowing, deep down, that he couldn't unfreeze people on Zoom with brute force, Frank walloped the side of his laptop anyway.

When technology was involved, Frank had little patience... or skill.

He hit it again, releasing more of his frustration.

Then, he took a time out for a glass of water, because if he released all of the frustration Zoom was causing him, he'd owe his department for a new laptop.

When he returned, Gerry was unfrozen.

'Bloody machines,' he said.

Because Gerry was looking directly at her laptop – and therefore the camera—she seemed to be staring right at him. It felt like continuous eye contact and was unusual for Gerry. He assumed she'd probably minimised him to prevent feeling overwhelmed.

'I can't hear you, Gerry.'

'Because I've said nothing, sir. I'm just opening the lobby so I can allow everyone in. Have you updated your internet service like I told you to?'

He recalled her badgering him to do so several weeks back, along with the many other things she pestered him about. 'To optical fibro?'

'Fibre optics.'

'Ah yes. Fibro optical. I've emailed like you said. But I've been waiting on a callback.'

'They're usually prompt with upgrading services and charging more.'

Frank thought of the countless unanswered calls over the last couple of days – simply because he didn't recognise the number. And the countless voicemails from the provider, who he'd been too lazy to call back.

The screen froze again. Frank exhaled sharply. 'Give me strength.'

He picked it up from the kitchen table, carried it to the lounge, and sat closer to the window. That seemed to help. He also noticed that the rest of his team was now on the chat.

'Can you all hear me?'

'Yes, sir. We can hear and see you clearly,' Reggie said. 'Although your camera angle suggests you're holding the laptop at an odd elevation. Perhaps place it on your desk?'

'I can't. Internet is crap. Seems to work up by the window.'

Gerry said, 'It's nothing to do with being close to the window. Are you closer to your router now?'

'The black box thingy?'

'Yes.'

'Aye.'

'That'll be the reason,' Gerry said.

'Oh...' he said, feeling his cheeks redden. He sat on the sofa with the laptop on his knees.

Outside, the rain hammered against the windows with growing intensity and would help to wash away the snow.

Good. He didn't want to be cooped up in here too much longer.

He scanned the faces of the *odd bunch*. He meant the nickname as a term of endearment rather than a criticism, but he never said it aloud, fearing a negative reaction.

Gerry aside, who was obscenely talented and was being hunted by every department in North Yorkshire these days, Donald could never fathom why Frank kept requesting these particular officers for his team.

But it was hard not to ask for them when they were on such a roll.

Again, aside from Gerry, they might lack great reputations or skill sets, but their compassion was paramount – and in cases like this, where the bones were cold and lives forgotten, passion often mattered more than polish.

Still, with this lot, he had to be on his guard. And a Zoom call was not the best place to get them on the straight and narrow.

Unable to cope with that bloody moustache, he minimised Reggie's box. He did the same to DC Sean Groves, who was lounging about in a jogging suit. However, he left DC Sharon Miller, smartly dressed, up there. He couldn't understand why Sharon wasn't in demand. She could be fierce and principled, and he liked that. Sean, on the other hand, always looked five minutes away from falling asleep. But, as long as he didn't have to get up off his arse, he could really come up trumps with research. Clara, their data analyst, was a newer addition, and the jury was still out on her, but she seemed competent enough. Clara had chosen a virtual background that erased her surroundings, making her look more like a computer-generated avatar than a real person.

That was the odd bunch.

His odd bunch.

A smile tugged at his lips as he remembered Donald Oxley's smug expression when he'd first assigned them to Frank – intended as punishment, delivered as a gift. He clearly hadn't realised he was giving Frank exactly what he needed – people with something to prove.

'Right then,' Frank began, 'let's crack on. Gerry, if you would. Sarah Matthews.'

Sarah Matthews smiled at them from the photo, dressed in a crisp nursing uniform. Her sandy hair was tied back neatly, her eyes bright with purpose.

Frank's chest went tight as he recalled her skeleton in a tight foetal position, arms and legs drawn close to the torso in an unnatural pose.

'Sarah was twenty-two when she went missing on October 12 1989,' Gerry said. 'She was a student paediatric nurse, and this is a photograph taken in January 1989 during her first and only nursing placement with Dr Hannah Wright, a child psychiatrist. The practice was situated just beyond Ruswarp, a farmhouse surrounded by open fields.'

'Let that sink in,' Frank said. 'A paediatric nurse who wanted to help children, helped children I expect. We've already heard some negativity surrounding Sarah, but this suggests to me she was a force for good.'

Gerry's tone carried its usual analytical certainty as she went through her information. 'Despite the significant behavioural issues in her youth, Sarah successfully completed her Levels at Riverside College between 1983 and 1985, and then got a nursing degree from Middlesbrough over the following three years. So, she began working for Dr Hannah Wright when her course ended in 1988.'

Frank leaned closer to the image of Sarah on his screen and hoped his team was doing the same. Not just seeing another woman, but a life interrupted, a story unfinished. 'This version of Sarah is important,' he said. 'Remember it. This is who Sarah became, not who people seem to suggest she was as a youngster. She tried to make something of herself. Help others. Five years of intense education before becoming registered as a nurse to help children, and obtaining a placement with a reputable doctor. And even before that, we've positivity... Gerry?'

Gerry clicked through to a series of earlier photographs – Sarah on horseback, beaming with pride, holding various ribbons. There was a picture of her holding the trophy for first place in the Yorkshire Dales Cross Country Championship in 1984 Frank described the pin that had been found near the remains. 'So, a keen love of horse riding marked Sarah's teen years. Before this, there're reports of significant behavioural challenges during her time at secondary school.'

'Having read these reports,' Gerry cut in, 'she would've benefitted from further investigation into neurodivergence.'

'Unfortunately,' Frank said, 'such investigations were a rarity back then. Especially for girls whose struggles were dismissed as mere defiance.'

He noticed Gerry stroking Ryan. She was clearly feeling discontent over the system's failure to recognise potential needs in Sarah.

'Yes,' Gerry said. 'Any diagnosis was rare for girls exhibiting "difficult" behaviour. Still, at fourteen, in 1981, Dr Hannah Wright, during some routine observations in the local school, had noticed her struggling. Hannah offered to help her.'

'Hannah? This is the doctor Sarah worked for after training to be a nurse?' Reggie asked.

'Yes,' Gerry said. 'It was also Hannah who funded the university course at Middlesbrough, on the condition that she'd return to do her placement with her.'

'We'll come back to the placement,' Frank said. 'Let's not get too ahead of ourselves. Gerry, tell us about the treatment, please.'

'Hannah Wright's approaches were unconventional in that era,' Gerry said. 'But they aren't really that controversial. In fact, these days, such recommendations from psychiatrists are commonplace. She really pushed the therapeutic value of natural activities such as outdoor walking, running, caring for a dog and, in Sarah's case, horse riding. A lot of these ideas and therapies are in play today, with mindfulness and so forth. And she seemed very skilled at horse riding... possessing a natural talent,' Gerry added, displaying competition results. 'As we pointed out, Sarah won first place in the Yorkshire Dales Cross Country Championship in 1984, and her teacher at Meadowside, Sylvia Winters, had considered her remarkable – according to her daughters, Chelsea and Lorraine Winters, who now run the school.'

'However,' Gerry continued. 'Before this happier period of her life, she experienced great turbulence, which seemed to peak when she was thirteen and she started a sexual relationship with a boy.'

Frank sighed. *A tale as old as time.* His mind drifted briefly to Maddie and her own troubled teenage years.

'Tommy Reid was sixteen. Another child with behavioural issues. He spent more time out of school than in it.

When Sarah's father, Rory Matthews, discovered them in bed in 1980 together, he severely assaulted Tommy. They sentenced him to a lengthy prison term.'

'Jesus,' Reggie said. 'Jail? His daughter was thirteen... I mean, who wouldn't see red?'

'Assaulting someone is against the law,' Gerry said. 'Whatever the motive.'

Frank expanded Reggie's video window and watched him stroke his moustache, deep in thought. 'Still... I've some sympathy—'

'Reggie,' Frank interjected. His voice carried the sharp edge his team knew meant no argument. 'Severely... that's the key word here. This wasn't a slap around the chops. A bruise on the arm to buck up ideas. This was a fractured skull, coma and dance with the reaper.'

'Okay,' Reggie nodded, paling.

Frank's methods of clarification weren't always gentle, but they were effective.

He did immediately feel a little guilty, though. If that had been Maddie, would he have done the same?

He'd like to think he'd stop at a warning blow, but honestly, could he rule it out?

'Well, I guess he learned to keep his hands to himself,' Reggie said.

'He did little learning,' Frank said. 'Someone murdered him in jail. A brawl in the canteen. He hit his head on a table.'

'Christ,' Reggie muttered.

'Idiot attacked a prison officer,' Frank added, before Reggie could start casting Rory as some kind of tragic hero. 'That's what started the brawl. Another prisoner saw him off. All this did, at least, end the relationship with Tommy.'

Gerry continued, 'It was at that point that Dr Hannah

Wright approached and offered to help Sarah. She'd read about the case in the newspaper. Going to the school, Dr Hannah Wright saw Sarah's disaffection and subsequently approached her mother, Margaret, to offer help. She was clearly very wealthy and believed in Sarah's potential. She not only paid for the horse riding but also, as mentioned before, financed her university education – on the condition that Sarah would return to work for her.'

Frank leaned forward, his face dominating the screen as the rain drummed harder against the window. 'But things went badly wrong again in 1989 when she rekindled her relationship with Tommy Reid.'

'Christ,' Reggie said. 'Why?'

'Love, I guess,' Frank said. 'He'd a job at this point. A mechanic. A little more stability. He was twenty-four, she was twenty-one, I guess the age difference didn't seem so controversial any more. She actually moved in with him and his mother. From what we gather from the missing persons investigation in late 1989, Hannah wasn't best pleased with the nurse she'd rescued, trained and given a job to going to live with Tommy. Sarah stopped working with Hannah in March 1989.'

'Sacked?' Sharon asked. It was the first time she'd spoken, and you could hear the outrage in her voice.

'Well, put on leave... although, she would've been welcome to come back if the relationship ended.'

'Sounds like blackmail!' Sharon said. 'In what world is that even allowed?'

'Ours, it seems. Although none of this was ever in writing, of course...' Frank said. 'Sounds more like an argument that escalated to Sarah walking away with Hannah's blessing. She said she'd keep the job open if she saw sense.'

'Flushing her life away over an idiot,' Reggie said.

'Well, no one should be blackmailed!' Sharon said. 'It's outrageous.'

'Aye,' Frank said. 'I agree with both of you. Tommy Reid has been in trouble a fair number of times. Doesn't seem like the law-abiding type. Moral of the story... beware of the scrotes... there's a lot about, and they can ruin your life. Gerry, can we see the timeline please on the day she disappeared?'

Another slide appeared and Frank went through it. 'Tommy Reid claimed Sarah left his mother's home on Thursday October 12, 1989, following an argument. Apparently, she was upset that he'd been late to work several times this week, and they were threatening to sack him. This, of course, concerned her, as money would be tight while she wasn't working.

'Malcolm Hargreaves then saw Sarah outside the Bridge Inn in Ruswarp. He said she climbed into a red Fiesta. Unfortunately, Malcolm Hargreaves's timeline was inconsistent across three separate interviews. At first, he said, he saw her at around 8.15 p.m. The next time, he'd shifted it up to 8.45, and on the third occasion, he moved it down to 7.45. He also reported the person driving as an older man on two occasions, but on one occasion, he said he hadn't even seen them properly! Now, the police never got to the bottom of who was driving the red Fiesta, or if it even existed because, as you can probably tell, Malcolm wasn't the most reliable of witnesses. Drunk as a skunk most of the time, apparently. Gerry, would you like to continue?'

'The investigation leaned heavily towards the wayward Tommy Reid. But Tommy's mother, Honey, stood by him, and provided an alibi. She'd recently had an operation and was bed bound. He was helping her as much as he could. Actually, that ended up being the reason he'd been late to work frequently over the last weeks. When Sarah had stormed out on him, she'd mentioned meeting a friend for drinks, but she never said who, but no friend ever came forward, and all her known friends denied any planned meetings.'

'So the investigators went hard at Tommy,' Frank interjected. 'But struggled to break through this alibi.'

A yellow hand appeared on Clara's box, indicating that she wanted to ask a question.

'Clara?'

'I'm finding witness statements regarding an older man,' Clara said, her dark eyes intense behind her glasses.

'Aye,' Frank nodded. 'We've got them too.'

Gerry said, 'There were three separate sightings of Sarah with an older man on recent days. One in the Pannett Park, one in Church Street car park. There was also a report of an older man coming to watch her at Meadowside several times. But all these were descriptions given during the investigation varied so widely they couldn't generate a useful composite. Ultimately, they came to nothing.'

'Okay... Gerry and I have chatted at length, and tomorrow,' Frank continued, 'weather permitting, we'll interview Sarah's mother, Margaret Matthews. She still lives in Ruswarp. She's almost eighty.' He paused, his expression grave.

'Good lord,' Reggie said.

'Aye, I know,' Frank said. 'So, hopefully, by then, we'll have some confirmation from Nasreen regarding dental and medical records. Look, I'm 99 per cent sure, but it's always good to be crystal clear.'

'Reggie and Sharon,' Frank continued, 'I'd like you to interview Tommy Reid. He's still living with his mother, Honey, in Ruswarp.'

'Still with his mum?' Reggie's eyebrows rose. 'At his age?'

'Aye. Still under maternal supervision. Make of that what you will. And she's also pushing eighty.'

He heard Sharon sighing.

Sean's yellow hand now appeared again in his video window. 'And Dr Hannah Wright?'

Frank smiled. 'Glad to see you paying attention, Sean. I was getting to that. This one is for you.'

'You want me to interview her?' There wasn't much excitement in his voice.

'No need for you to go anywhere, Sean.'

'Sorry?' He sounded confused.

'She died on March 2, 1991,' Frank confirmed. 'There was a gas explosion at her home, killing her and another man. A gardener, Clive Morton. According to the report, which I've only glanced at, they were close to the site of the explosion, and it was concluded that Clive had been trying to find the leak.'

'Jesus,' Reggie said. 'Probably would have been best if they'd just stayed outside and contacted someone.'

'You'd have thought. On my brief glance, there doesn't seem to be anything suspicious, but if you could take a closer look, Sean?'

'Be happy to.' He sounded enthused this time.

'And while you're at it,' Frank added, 'Dr Hannah Wright developed innovative but sometimes controversial methods for treating troubled children. Might be worth you looking into any other young patients she treated around the same period. Are there any connections there, perhaps? Any complaints worth digging into, etc.'

'Okay.'

Frank took a deep breath. 'Okay, we'll reconvene in

person tomorrow afternoon after our assignments, unless the weather reverts to form – in which case, we could go back on this bloody Zoom. Oh, one last thing Gerry, could you pop that image of Sarah up again, please? Thank you. Remember, keep in mind what I said earlier. Whatever anyone says about Sarah Matthews, she was someone who fought past her difficulties to build a life helping others. You can refocus yourself with that at any point because it's the truth. If that doesn't do it for you, just remember she was someone's daughter, someone's future mother. Think about where she was left, and how she was left.'

He put the screen on gallery mode so he could see all their faces – Reggie with his ridiculous moustache, Sharon, Sean, Gerry and Clara.

His odd bunch.

'Let's do right by her.'

After they signed off, Frank sat back, watching the rain. He willed it to keep falling, to wash away the snow – and maybe, just maybe, reveal the truth hidden in the darkness of the past.

Chapter Twenty-Two

Tom's presence on the sofa surprised Gerry as she emerged from the bathroom. She expected him to still be in the kitchen.

Their evening routine was precise – dishes first, television after.

Unease prickling beneath her skin, she peered into the kitchen and saw he'd already made quick work of the dishes – the dishwasher was humming away.

She sat by him and noticed he was watching a nature documentary on penguins. She waited a couple of minutes for him to launch into an explanation of mating rituals and migration patterns. Tom loved sharing facts she already knew. So she'd always pretended to learn for his benefit.

When the explanation didn't come, she observed him and saw that he was rather pale.

His stony stillness was unusual.

'Is anything wrong?' she asked.

'No.' He pointed at the television. 'Just watching.'

Rylan wandered over. He paused between the legs of

the sofa's two occupants, looking both ways, unsure where to deliver his attention.

'Do you want to tell me what I missed?' She pointed at the television.

'You've seen it before.' He sighed. 'And you know everything already, anyway.'

Rylan chose Tom's knee and rested his head there. Tom didn't stroke the Lab.

Gerry surveyed the room and regarded her open laptop on the coffee table. The display had gone dark. A cold realisation settled over her.

She'd no screen lock enabled.

She regarded him again. His pallor was that of someone who'd just received a shock. He'd seen the marriage considerations document.

Noting the tension crackling between them, the Lab opted to shuffle away.

'You saw what was on my laptop.'

Tom stood abruptly, the movement jarring enough to make Rylan's ears prick up. 'I'm going to bed.'

'It's still early...' Too early. They'd a routine.

'But I'm tired.'

She nodded. 'It'd be nice for us to watch television, or we could pause it and discuss what you saw before?'

'And then, afterwards, we could go upstairs and have sex?'

Gerry could hear the bitterness in Tom's voice.

'That's the usual way of things, isn't it?' Tom continued.

She frowned. 'You're unhappy? I thought this was a pattern you liked.'

He turned away. 'Sometimes, but spontaneity would be nice, too, occasionally.'

Gerry scrunched her brow. 'This is the first time you've mentioned it.'

'Okay... does that make it any less important?'

'No, but you need to mention it in order for it to be considered. Shall we talk?'

'I'm too annoyed.'

At least he'd now admitted it.

'It's irrational to be annoyed when you haven't voiced a concern,' Gerry said.

'For pity's sake, not everything needs to be analysed, Gerry.' His voice carried an edge she'd never heard from him before.

'Shall we talk tomorrow instead?'

'Maybe. You know sometimes other people need space, too, not just you.'

'I accept that.'

He seemed to consider this for a moment, then shook his head as if reaching a different decision entirely. 'Good. So you'll understand why I'm heading home.'

She watched him collect his coat, snatching it from the hook with deliberate force, each movement exaggerated and sharp – the kind of theatrical display designed to emphasise his hurt and disappointment.

After he'd left, she went over and sat at her laptop.

It was unfortunate, but he would've had to see it eventually, anyway... although, maybe not in its first draft.

She considered the point he'd tried to make about their routine.

Maybe there was some logic to what he was saying?

She added a bullet point to the document.

126. Some planning of spontaneous behaviour.

She paused. The contradiction between 'planning' and 'spontaneous' made her feel twitchy.

She deleted 'planning of', so it merely read:

126. Some spontaneous behaviour.

She then added:

(To be discussed with Tom when emotional equilibrium is restored.)

She was about to close the laptop when she thought of something else.

127. Complete honesty required.

She added a couple of notes, which included:

No reading private documents without explicit permission.

Rylan padded over and rested his head on her leg. Then she spent the next hour focused on the documentary, trying to impose order on a world that suddenly felt anything but orderly.

Chapter Twenty-Three

Frank sat on Maddie's bed, staring at her wardrobe.

Why had she come back six weeks earlier?

He stood and opened the wardrobe and looked down at the empty space on the floor next to a pile of scuffed trainers and old shoes. The gap where the backpack had been mocked him. She wouldn't have made all that effort to sneak back in just for a backpack. There must have been something of great significance within it.

And this was what really bugged Frank.

After she'd disappeared months back, he'd checked everything, including that bag– over and over.

It'd been empty, or at least, he could have sworn it'd been empty.

Had he missed something obvious? Something that might have led him to wherever she was?

A secret compartment, perhaps, that he'd failed to notice? Or a discreet cut in the lining? Something light, maybe, a document, secretly stashed inside?

It couldn't have been heroin. She'd gone cold turkey in

this bloody room... No one did that in the presence of a bag of heroin!

He groaned. *You're a fool, Frank Black, you should have been more diligent.*

There could have been something significant to her whereabouts.

Despite knowing it was futile; he'd searched the rest of her belongings every day since.

He'd not changed the front door lock either. This was her home, too. If she ever returned, he wanted her to know that, and not turn away in disgust, to disappear yet again.

Then, his eyes drifted to a photograph on the bedside table – all three of them together. Fingerprints smudged the glass from constant handling. In the picture, Maddie had been twelve. She still had that look of innocence in her eyes before she'd gone off the rails.

He regarded Mary. 'What did she come back for, love? What've I missed?'

Frank ran his hands over his face, exhaustion settling into his bones. He realised it'd been almost a week since he'd last visited Mary's grave – the weather had deterred him. But now, the urge to stand beside her headstone, to pour out his fears and doubts, was overwhelming.

But he couldn't go. The roads were still treacherous. Bertha, in her golden years, wouldn't stand a chance.

He looked at his phone. *Nothing.* He'd hoped for a message from Evelyn.

Her stay in the hospital worried him, and he'd the urge to phone her, to check on her, but he didn't want to risk irritating Janet, who'd done right by him in letting him know what had happened.

Janet had requested time for her mother to rest, and it was better that he respect that.

Restlessness drove him to the fridge. It hummed as he opened it. He regarded the empty spaces where beer bottles once stood, sadly, then reached for a bottle of Perrier – bloody overpriced fizzy water. He'd only bought it because the bottle looked nice, and he'd not wanted to look like a complete tight arse to Evelyn.

Mind you, he was positively flush these days, what with the money he was saving on not boozing in the pub.

He went through to the lounge and looked out the window.

He remembered the Ford Cortina that had been stalking him a couple of months back. It'd turned out to be a scrote driving Maddie back and forth, waiting for his absence. He really hoped they returned.

The Cortina made him think of that red Fiesta, and it turned his mind back to Sarah Matthews.

I want to know the real you, Sarah.

Right now, he hoped that most of what the drunken witness, Malcolm Hargreaves, had said had been true.

Because when it came down to it, that's all Frank and his team really had.

All he had to stop Sarah being completely forgotten.

Somewhere out there, someone was holding onto more than just memories. The truth of how she ended up in that unsavoury wooden grave.

Someone, perhaps, who'd been driving a red Fiesta, or at least knew who had been on October 12, 1989, when Sarah Matthews had disappeared forever into history.

Chapter Twenty-Four

Stephen Walker remained vigilant as he drove his daughter to Riverside College. Last night's downpour had shifted a lot of snow, but piles of slush dotted the sides of the roads. There was also a heavy fog clinging to the morning.

Regardless, people were out again, getting on with life.

It was Christmas, after all.

He stopped his Mercedes GLS near the entrance gates and looked up at his old school, trying not to be overwhelmed with nostalgia. Still, he'd served an excellent headship here, one which had earned him an OBE for services to education. It was so difficult not to lose himself in the wonderful memories.

He smiled at Christie in the passenger seat. 'Do you want me to accompany you?'

'We've already discussed this, Dad...'

'I know, but—'

'But nothing. You promised. Remember?'

'Remember?' He frowned. 'I—'

'Stop winding me up!'

'Force of habit, flower.' He winked. 'It's your first day at school, after all.'

'As an adult... not as an eleven-year-old...'

'Have you forgotten that I drove you to college at sixteen?'

'How could I? You remind me periodically.'

Stephen laughed. He felt a moment of genuine contentedness. Christie always had a way of drawing that out of him. Even in these darker days, while Caroline was slipping away from him.

He gazed up longingly at the Victorian buildings.

Still, it would've been nice to go in there again...

But Christie had, indeed, made her feelings very clear on this. 'You'll steal my thunder.'

'Twelve years! The younger folk in that place won't know who I am, and the older ones will have long forgotten me.'

He recalled Christie rolling her eyes.

Stephen's protests had ended there, of course. This had never been about him. This had always been about his most precious flower.

She got out of the car.

He watched her out of the windscreen. She looked just like her mother had done way back then. With a smoothing motion, she adjusted her skirt.

Then she came around the other side of the vehicle and knocked on the window. He wound it down. She leaned in and kissed him on the head.

'I thought you'd forgotten,' Stephen said.

'Love you, Dad.'

'Good luck, flower,' Stephen said. 'Knock 'em dead!'

She went around to the boot and grabbed her bag.

He watched his daughter go through the school gates.

She'd forbidden him from leaving the car. As if legions of adoring fans might accost him! 'I'm not the fifth Beatle, flower,' he'd insisted last night.

Still, he was poor at keeping promises, so he exited the car, leaned on the bonnet and watched her disappear through the gates.

He half-expected her to turn and wave, and to catch him in his betrayal! Fortunately, she didn't. She was too busy being sucked into the current of her new teaching career, and before the day was through, she'd be swept away in the waves of a breathless world.

It was so tempting to head to the gates himself...

His recent yoga bouts had done wonders for his joints, and at seventy-five, he was moving with the grace of a much younger man. In fact, he thought to himself, I could walk through those gates and have that entire place ship-shape again before the day was through.

Not that he'd heard it'd gone to the dogs, because it hadn't. But he couldn't help but assume it wasn't as good without him steering the ship.

'Mr Walker!'

A young man in his late twenties, possibly early thirties, jogged toward them, his face splitting into a broad grin. 'Mr Walker, sir! I can't believe it!'

Stephen smiled. He didn't have a clue who it was. There'd been so many faces over the years.

'Michael Barnes, sir. Class of 2008.' He thrust out his hand.

'Nice to see you, Michael,' Stephen said, a feeling of recognition coming over him. 'Dropping a youngster off, are you?'

'No, sir—'

'Stephen, please.'

'No, sir... sorry, Stephen. I work here now. Geography teacher. Head of Geography, actually!'

A flutter of pride stirred in Stephen's chest – Geography had been his specialism, too. 'Now, well done, lad!'

'Yes... I was inspired by the best.' He winked.

Stephen waved away the praise, though he hoarded it like treasure. 'Don't be silly. An honourable vocation, Michael. Well done.'

'Look, sorry, I have to run – don't want to be late for first period – but I had to say hello. I knew you'd be here!' He winked again. 'Everyone is excited about your daughter starting!'

'Well, take good care of her on her first day, will you?'

'Judging by what I heard regarding the interview, she'll be taking good care of us before long!'

That's my girl! The thought came with fierce pride – Christie was everything he'd wanted in a daughter, everything he'd tried to shape in others.

He smiled. 'Sounds like her, all right!' Stephen clasped the young man's hand. 'Take care.'

He watched Michael jog toward the main building, his youthful enthusiasm stirring memories.

He took a deep breath, and nostalgia suddenly overwhelmed him. Within that building, he'd found a happiness that could never be re-created.

He recalled his photo album. Cassie... Sandy... Kayleigh... Sarah...

The ones who'd whispered such glorious words.

His special ones.

The familiar sounds of a school awakening drifted into his reverie – slamming car doors and scattered laughter.

Each sound was another echo of those precious moments when he'd been king of this small domain.

A sleek BMW screeched to a halt behind his SUV. Considering the weather, it'd been going far too quickly.

A young lad exited the car and darted over the street towards the gates.

He caught the eyes of the female driver, who still had her engine running.

Her stony expression made his skin prickle. He tried smiling at her, but that did nothing to break her glare.

Maybe she wanted to get a move on, and he was in her way?

He sidled along his Mercedes to get back in—

She killed the BMW engine. Her car lights went dark, too.

Hand on his own door handle, he glanced at her.

She'd already dropped her son off, so why—

The woman, likely in her fifties and noticeably overweight for her short frame, got out of the car and strode toward him. Her movements were sharp with barely contained energy. Something about her was familiar.

He took a deep breath.

'Morning, Stephen,' she said, her face losing none of its severity.

Her voice stirred something inside him. Something uncomfortable. He tried to push the feeling away. 'Do I know you?'

'You don't recognise me?'

He opened his mouth to tell her that he didn't. After all, judging by her age, if she was an ex-student, it could have been forty years since he'd last seen her.

'Figures,' she hissed.

That tone of voice, filled with bitterness, intensified the sense of recognition.

A chill ran down his spine.

Georgina Prince.

He stopped himself short of saying her name.

It couldn't be, could it?

But everything about this woman was suddenly familiar.

He could feel his stomach turning over, and decided it was best to just get away. 'I'm sorry, I'm seventy-five now, and my memory isn't what it was.' He turned away from her hostile expression. 'If you'll excuse me. Sorry to offend you!' He opened the door.

'Why are you back here?'

Ignoring the question, he eased himself into his car seat.

'Of course... Christine Walker. On my son's timetable. English. Fuck. I didn't think. She a relative of yours – granddaughter?'

'Daughter.' He pulled at the door handle. 'I have to go.'

'It's me, Georgina Prince,' she said, holding the door open.

His chest was tightening. The situation was inconceivable. 'I don't know who you are... now let go of my door.' He looked at her and truly recognised her now.

She gave him a wide smile.

He tried to pull the door closed, but despite his newfound flexibility, she surpassed him in strength and looked to weigh considerably more than him.

'Does your daughter know who you really are?'

'Let go of my door.'

'Her dirty old man of a father.' Bitterness dripped from every word.

He started the engine and edged the SUV forward. 'Let go, or I'll put my foot down and take your hand off!'

She let go of the door. He seized the opportunity to slam it.

As he drove away, he glanced in the rear-view mirror at Georgina watching him. She stood, motionless, staring in his direction. He focused on his breathing, the way his yoga instructor had taught him. In through the nose, out through the mouth.

It didn't help.

But how could it?

That was the first time he'd seen Georgina Prince in forty years!

Chapter Twenty-Five

Peter Watson probed the edge of the head wound with his fingers and winced. At least it was scabbing over. It had bled long into the night and could probably have done with some stitches.

He turned in profile to the bathroom mirror. Quite the lump!

Bloody back gate. Sodding postman.

And how typical that he'd survived!

Many a man his age would have been killed by a tumble like that.

Would have saved me the sodding hassle of doing it myself. Just my luck. He replaced the bandage. *Well, fingers crossed for a bleed on the brain and a surprise exit before the morning is through...*

His bandage looked like a small child had tied it. The adhesive tape crossed at odd angles, refusing to lie flat. The sight of the bandage would have horrified Donna. His late wife had been an A&E nurse for almost forty years. She'd have had it sorted in seconds, then frogmarched him to the hospital for an x-ray.

'Sorry, Don, love, but best to save your former colleagues the bother. Unforeseen circumstances last night, but this evening will be as good a time as any.'

As he turned from the mirror, he recalled coming to in the snow, head throbbing, before stumbling back inside. He'd almost slipped again on the water spilled from Bryan's overturned water bowl and realised someone had seized the opportunity to go into his house while he was out like a light. Such was the nature of the area. Some were inclined to rob you rather than help you.

The bastard hadn't stayed long. It didn't look as if they'd made it upstairs, and Don's jewellery and other special things remained beneath the bed.

It seemed that they were only interested in the Volvo. They'd grabbed the keys from the kitchen and made off with it. He hadn't bothered calling the police. That was the last thing he needed. No sense having them poking around, potentially identifying him as a suicide risk... forcing him to go to the hospital. *No thanks.*

He moved through to the lounge and caught a glance of Donna's picture. 'Don't sweat it, love. I feel fine.' He nodded at the bowl of paracetamol. 'They're taking the edge off the throbbing.'

A flash of movement drew his eye to the lounge window. He noticed a removal van parked two doors down, next to number 5, one of the social houses. It was blocking half the road. A battered Vauxhall Corsa trundled up into the driveway.

Here we go again. Another bloody bunch of layabouts to drag the neighbourhood down.

The last bunch had been a disgrace! Bins overflowing outside, crap blowing down the street on a windy day... constant shouting and arguing.

He'd told them once to at least close the front door while they were kicking off.

As if Jake next door, at 7, with his music and his conveyer belt of girlfriends, wasn't bad enough!

Well, at least I won't be around to watch another family festering in filth.

He turned and went into the kitchen to make a cup of tea. His head throbbed with each step. He'd lied to Donna's picture – in truth, the painkillers weren't cutting it.

Maybe he should just get on with it now?

Still, he always worried about people coming over during the day, interrupting him, potentially calling in someone to pull him back from the brink.

Better in the evening, when nobody ever came knocking.

Just the thieves, he thought with a snort.

When he returned to the lounge with his tea, curiosity drew him back to the window. The movers were wheeling belongings into number 5.

To his surprise, a smartly dressed woman who looked to be in her mid-thirties was engaged in a discussion with a girl in her mid-teens, both wearing neat clothes that wouldn't have looked out of place in Marks & Spencer. The girl was bouncing a baby against her shoulder – her younger sibling, no doubt.

Well, that made a change from the usual tracksuited rabble. Still, where did they get the money from for nice clothing? Sucking the taxpayers dry, no doubt.

He noticed a lad, probably the teen girl's older brother, sprawled across the bonnet of the Corsa, head nodding to whatever racket was pouring through his headphones.

Ridiculous. He should get stuck into the unpacking!

Thank God he'd be gone before this street became a

complete slum. He looked at his watch. Two hours since his last dose of paracetamol.

Why was he even bloody timing it? His liver would soon be an irrelevance. Yes, he was on the donor list, but come on, who wanted a seventy-four-year-old's liver that had been pickled with alcohol?

He sat down, finished his tea, closed his eyes and took a nap.

In his dreams, Christmas lights sparkled overhead as he walked through snow-covered Whitby streets, holding Don's hand—

The sound of a revving engine woke him with a start.

'God love us!' He stood and marched to the window.

The Vauxhall Corsa shot down the street at an unbelievable speed, its exhaust rattling like machine gun fire. The delivery van was already gone.

'Fucking lunatic.' The words escaped through clenched teeth. Peter might be ready to shuffle off this mortal coil, but he'd be damned if he was letting some little prick put lives at risk while he was still on watch.

He slipped on his boots and grabbed his jacket.

Though most of the snow had washed away, some ice patches remained, so he looked down while marching. His head throbbed with each step, and it seemed the second dose hadn't done enough. He jabbed the doorbell of number 5 harder than necessary.

The woman in her mid-thirties answered, holding the baby. Dark circles shadowed her eyes, and she'd that harried look common to new mothers. She wore a neat skirt and blouse – more office worker than benefit scrounger – although, ironically, probably paid for by benefits.

'Hello,' she said, gently. 'Can I help?'

He nodded. 'Aye...' He took a step back and regarded

her. 'That lad of yours...' He thumbed over his shoulder. 'He can't be driving around here like that.'

She nodded.

'Like a bloody maniac,' he said, emphasising his point.

She nodded again. 'I know.'

You know? Peter thought. He rose an eyebrow. 'So, tell him?'

She sighed. 'I tell him all the time. And I'll tell him again when he comes home.'

'So, he's not listening?' Peter said. His tone was one of disbelief.

'I'm sorry.'

'Don't be sorry.' Peter shook his head. 'Just stop him.'

'I'll try.'

'Try, for Christ's sake, try?'

She nodded. 'Yes... I'll try.'

The baby looked at Peter, chuckled, and spat out their dummy.

Peter narrowed his eyes.

'Is your head okay?' she asked.

He reeled a little, surprised by the question. 'Aye... fine... yes... don't worry about it...' *Back to the issue at hand, Peter.* 'Why not just stop your son driving the car?'

'It's not mine to stop him,' she said.

'You're his mother.'

'Yes, but Reece's father left it to him when he died last year.'

Peter reeled again. He knew what it was like to lose those closest to him. He suddenly felt that familiar ache in his new neighbour. He softened his own tone. 'I'm sorry to hear that.'

'Thank you.'

But he wanted a resolution.

His forehead suddenly itched beneath the bandage. It was away from the wound, so he reached up to scratch it. 'There're younger and older folk around here. It'd be awful if he ended up in an accident. Maybe... take the keys off Reece for a bit?'

The woman smiled.

'Something funny? I—'

'Yes... sorry... do you have children?'

He flinched. 'No.'

'Well, it's just, disciplining an eighteen-year-old is like banging my head against a brick wall.'

'I remember my dad giving me the slipper at nineteen because I stumbled in drunk and smashed a vase.'

She laughed.

At first, he narrowed his eyes, annoyed at being laughed at. He hadn't intended to be funny. But then he saw how it could have sounded amusing. The world was a very different place these days, after all.

'Would you like me to have a word?'

She laughed again.

'Why's that funny?'

'Well, I really don't think that would do much good. Reece doesn't respond well to... how do I put this... the blunt approach?'

He nodded. 'Well, it needs addressing.'

'Okay, I'll mention it, again, as soon as he's home. I'll tell him you're upset. But I can't get too abrupt. He'll just move out and live with his mates again.'

Good riddance, Peter thought.

'And that didn't end too well last time,' she continued. 'I'd rather avoid that. I'm Lucy, by the way. Lucy Coombes.' She held out her hand.

Peter puffed out his cheeks. She seemed decent enough,

even if she was as soft as butter with discipline. He shook her hand. 'I'm—'

The baby interrupted him with a sudden wail. Lucy looked at the baby and then called back into the house, 'Mia! Grab another dummy.'

Peter looked down at the fallen dummy, appreciating the fact that she hadn't just picked that one up and shoved it back into the poor tyke's mouth. He'd seen that happen many times before. Vile.

He gave a swift nod of approval and then finished introducing himself, raising his voice slightly so he could be heard over the crying. 'My name's Peter... I live at number 9.'

She nodded. 'Nice to meet you, Peter. The first neighbour I've met.' She smiled.

'She's beautiful,' Peter said, smiling at the crying child.

'Sophie,' Lucy said.

He gazed at Sophie's reddening face, and took a deep, pleasant breath. 'So cute.' He felt something stir inside him which was rather uncomfortable, and turned his eyes back to Lucy.

'Do you live alone, Peter?'

'No. Sorry... yes...' He shook his head. 'Why is that relevant?'

'Just wondering who to ask round for dinner when we're settled...'

He shook his head. 'No... no... that won't be necessary.'

He didn't do friendship. *Besides, I'll be long gone by then*, he thought.

The girl in her mid-teens appeared at Lucy's side, holding a dummy. He assumed this to be Mia.

Lucy confirmed it.

Mia looked him up and down, gave him a nod, said, 'Hello,' and then slipped a dummy into Sophie's mouth.

Kids these days, he thought. *Mind you, at least she said hello. Most of them simply look at me like I'm wasting the air in their world before sidestepping me.*

'Sophie looked like she needed that,' Peter said with a smile.

Mia now gave him a wary look that suggested he was wasting the air in their world.

Whatever, he thought. *This isn't my world. Thankfully.*

Mia held out her arms toward her mother. 'Sophie... come to Mummy.'

The words hit him like a second wooden gate to the head. He looked at Mia. 'You're the mother?' As soon as the words had left his mouth, he acknowledged that he probably shouldn't have said them. At least not with that tone.

'Yeah, why?' Predictably, her response sounded abrasive. She took hold of her child.

He looked apologetically between all three of them. 'Sorry... I... well, I assumed—'

'Yeah, well, you assumed wrong,' Mia hissed, bouncing Sophie up and down.

Peter felt his cheeks burning. 'You just looked very young... I'm sorry.'

'I'm fifteen.'

Yes, very young, he thought. 'I'm sure you're an excellent mother,' he said, trying to smooth things over.

'Eh?' Mia hissed.

'Mia,' Lucy said, placing a hand on her daughter's shoulder.

'What?' Mia look at her mother with a face like thunder. 'Who is this old fart?'

Old fart! Christ, it was getting worse.

'Don't be rude, Mia...'

'Mum! He's at our door talking shit about Reece and me.'

'It's not like that. I think a lot has been taken out of context,' Lucy said. She smiled at him. 'Isn't that right, Peter?'

'Yes, but...' He really tried to hold back. After all, maybe he'd overstepped some boundaries, but come on... how was calling him an old fart acceptable? He felt a rise of anger, supplanting any embarrassment. 'Your daughter was quite rude. She shouldn't speak to me like that... anyone like that... Does she speak to you like that?'

Lucy, for the first time, looked flustered. 'No.' She puffed up her chest. 'Just the nosy ones,' she said.

Peter took a step back. 'Just trying to help. Stop your boy ending up wrapped around a lamppost, or in jail...' He waved his hand. 'Whatever. Merry—'

The door was already closed before he could finish the sarcasm.

He marched away, grumbling.

Really, he thought. *Why do I bother?*

Is this all being socially minded gets you? Abuse?

Well, let all these layabouts sort themselves out... They'll get a shock when I'm no longer here and it all goes to ruin!

The door to number 5 suddenly opened behind him.

'Help!'

It made him jump, and he turned.

'Help!' Lucy was in the doorway alone, beckoning frantically. 'Please help!'

Chapter Twenty-Six

L*EWIS W*HITE WAS ELEVEN AGAIN.

Cross-legged on the living room carpet. Wrapping paper scattered around him. Snow pressing against the windows. Twinkling Christmas tree lights casting coloured shadows across his mother's face.

Her skin was as pale as milk, dark circles haunting her eyes.

Smiling.

God, how she tried to keep smiling.

'Another one, sweetheart.' Elizabeth passed him a perfectly wrapped package. Her hands trembled slightly. 'This one's special. It's from Felix.'

His brother's name bit deep.

He almost asked how he could have bought him a present, but wasn't the answer obvious? His mother was how.

She'd die before she'd let Felix's presence leave this house completely.

Lewis peeled back the paper, revealing a bright red Ferrari model kit. Felix had loved these, spending countless hours at the dining room table, assembling intricate models with painstaking care.

Had this present originally been for Felix?

Bought, potentially wrapped, before the meningitis took him?

'Thanks,' Lewis said, looking at his mother. 'I'll build it today.'

Her eyes were filling. She nodded toward the last present, almost as if rushing to finish before her composure cracked.

He read the card.

Love Mum and Dad xx

He wondered if his father even knew what this was as he unwrapped it.

A Nintendo Entertainment System.

Lewis's stomach clenched.

He could still see the two circles around the same item in the Argos catalogue – his in blue pen, Felix's in black. A shared dream, now half-empty.

'Thank you.' Lewis set it aside without opening the box.

His mother lowered to her knees and embraced him. He waited for her to crumble –for her tears to soak his shoulder, as they'd done many times before – but when she lifted back her head, she still had it together.

'One more,' she said, smiling. 'For your brother.'

Together, they unwrapped the present under the tree addressed to Felix.

A Middlesbrough FC football shirt.

Lewis held the fabric between his fingers, a memory rising. Their father had taken him twice before to the Riverside and had promised to do so again.

Of course, that would never happen now.

The phone's shrill ring cut through a heavy silence. His mother went to the kitchen to answer it.

'John?'

Still holding the Middlesbrough kit, Lewis tried to listen, but his mother's voice was unclear.

When she returned to the room, she pulled her shoulders back like armour, her brittle smile fixed in place. 'Your father wants to wish you Merry Christmas, love.'

He went to the kitchen and took the receiver, pressing it to his ear, stretching the coiled cord that connected it to the telephone on the wall. 'Hello, Dad.'

'Lewis!' John White's voice boomed. 'Merry Christmas, son.'

'Merry Christmas.'

'How's that console? I can't wait to grab a go on it with you.'

Every word felt hollow. His mother's happiness had sounded forced since Felix died. His father's? It had always sounded that way.

Lewis thought of the unopened Nintendo. Two brothers' dreams reduced to one unwanted gift.

He was no longer really listening to what his father was saying.

Lewis waited for a break from his chatter and said, 'Goodbye.'

He set the phone down and headed for the stairs.

His mother's voice followed him up. 'Do you want me to help you set up the console?'

'Not yet,' he said. He'd no intention of touching that console. Not today.

Not ever.

The memory slipped away, melting like snow in rain. Lewis woke. His neck ached from sleeping in the chair.

His father lay before him, breath rattling like dead leaves in his chest.

Mark came into the room with the usual carefully cultivated cheerfulness. 'Good morning.' He moved to check the monitors.

'Why didn't you wake me?' Lewis asked.

Mark jotted something in his notebook, his face carefully neutral. 'Sorry, you didn't ask me to.'

'Did you come in during the night?'

Mark nodded. 'Yes, regularly.'

Lewis sighed. 'I really wish you'd woken me.'

'I'm sorry,' Mark said. 'If I'd known, I would've done. Still, I'm sure he appreciated you staying.'

Lewis shot him a bitter look because he couldn't care less what his father appreciated.

Mark was fiddling with the morphine controls, and something occurred to Lewis. '*Don't.*'

Mark recoiled at the command.

'Don't give him any,' Lewis insisted.

Mark's face was creased with concern as he looked over at Lewis. 'I have to... It doesn't really work like that.'

'It does. Today, don't give him any.'

'He'll be in pain.' He pleaded with his eyes.

'But awake?'

'Maybe. But not necessarily lucid and—'

'I'll take that chance.'

Mark shook his head. 'I just can't. Your father consented to this. He doesn't wish to suffer. I can show you the—'

'I don't give a fuck about his consent,' Lewis said, rising from the chair.

Mark's eyes widened, and Lewis recognised the look – he'd seen it in Gregg Ince's eyes. Fear.

'Hold off on the morphine this morning, at least,' Lewis said, narrowing his eyes. 'I want to speak to him... at least once.'

Mark looked as if he was going to throw up. His professional mask slipped as he looked between the monitor and Lewis. 'Please...'

'I'm not giving you the choice,' Lewis said, purposefully adding menace to his tone.

'Mr White, you're putting me in such a difficult position.'

Lewis leaned towards Mark over the bed. He felt as if he was in the prison yard again, standing his ground. 'I want to talk to him.'

'Such pain...' Mark pleaded, stepping back.

'Once I've spoken to him, you can give him morphine.'

Mark sidled toward the door, his cheerful demeanour completely shattered now. 'I'll... I'll have to speak to someone. It's not my decision.'

He glared at him. 'I rather you didn't.'

'Be reasonable...'

'Look, you be reasonable... If you give me this time, one conversation, I'll stay right here with him until the end, night and day. What's the price of that to him, do you imagine? Definitely worth the cost of a little pain. Let him have one more moment of clarity, and you give him the best ending. Or you could take that opportunity from him.'

Mark looked torn. He was pale. His eyes darted from side to side. 'I don't know.' He turned and exited the room in haste.

Lewis didn't know if he'd got through to him. He'd tried everything – threats, emotional blackmail. All he could do now was hope that he wouldn't call his superiors, cause trouble.

And if he didn't. Well...

Lewis settled back into his chair, leaning close to his father's wasted face.

Finally, we might get some truth around here.

'Time to wake up, John.'

Lewis's fingers traced the tattoos on each of his arms. Elizabeth. Felix.

He thought about the Nintendo.

Still in its box, gathering dust somewhere in his mother's belongings stored away in the attic.

A shrine to dead childhood dreams.

Chapter Twenty-Seven

ALONE, Frank drove to Ruswarp in the morning fog.

Because he hadn't driven to HQ in Scarborough first and checked out a vehicle, he was heading to Margaret Matthews's home in Bertha. At the crack of dawn, Nasreen had headed in, and using dental records, had confirmed the body belonged to Sarah.

Gerry refused to step foot in his battered yellow Volvo.

'You're an acquired taste, old girl.' Frank patted the steering wheel.

As if in response, Bertha's heater wheezed asthmatically.

Gerry hadn't minded going on foot. 'The snow has kept Rylan from a proper walk for days.'

He saw her standing ramrod straight at their meeting point, Rylan poised beside her, his breath fogging in the cold morning air. Frank pulled up, Bertha's brakes squealing in protest.

He parked up and, now that his old Volvo was stationary, she was happy to climb in. Panting, Rylan jumped into the back.

Frank had chosen not to ring ahead and tell Margaret. Death notifications were delicate things which could cause extreme distress. Margaret was almost eighty, living alone, and the news he carried would more than likely shatter her world. This was the most humane approach. He'd made the mistake of calling ahead in a previous investigation and had worried relentlessly about that particular mother again – he liked to think he was learning from his errors even in his twilight years.

Because this was an unannounced visit, Rylan didn't have permission to go into the house. Gerry would wait with Rylan in the car for Margaret's approval, if such approval was forthcoming. Gerry had come equipped with her laptop, in case the decision regarding Rylan didn't go how they hoped. She'd positioned her laptop perfectly on her knees, the screen's glow illuminating her face in the grey morning light.

He left Bertha, Gerry and Rylan, and as he approached the house, he realised how tired he was. He'd lain awake most of the night, playing it out in his head, focusing on every single detail.

His biggest concerns were around describing how the poor girl's wrists had been bound and the fact that her grave was a crumbling, wooden wreck.

Still, in the morning, after a restless night, he realised how pointless his ruminations had been.

After all, if someone had been delivering the news about Maddie, he'd want to know every detail. God help anyone that tried to keep anything from him.

So, he knew he owed Margaret the same.

Chapter Twenty-Eight

Margaret Matthews stood barely five feet tall in her slippers, her frame bird-like beneath a carefully pressed blouse and skirt. Her delicate frame and translucent skin gave her the look of someone who might suddenly melt away like morning mist, and he realised that he'd made the right decision in coming in person. News like this couldn't be delivered over the phone.

A tiny Yorkshire Terrier darted out between her feet. It had neatly trimmed silvery grey fur. The dog yapped excitedly, circling Frank's ankles with incredible speed.

'Jasper,' Margaret said. 'Spare the poor man's shoes!' He was pleased to hear a depth and strength in her voice that was lacking in her appearance.

Jasper ignored her, continuing to dance around Frank's feet, his collar jingling cheerfully. It was a sound that made Frank's heart ache. The cheer of the morning was about to shatter.

Frank showed his warrant card. 'DCI Frank Black. I'm sorry to disturb you so early.'

She smiled. 'Behave... who am I to complain about being disturbed by a handsome young man at my age?'

Frank shifted uncomfortably. He'd never been good with flattery, and especially not in these kinds of circumstances. 'Been a few years since I heard young, and I don't think I ever heard handsome.'

'Well, you've heard both today.' She smiled.

Frank felt the weight of his news pressing down harder. Under different circumstances, he might have enjoyed this gentle banter, but now it only made what he had to say more difficult.

'Aye, thank you.' He forced himself to maintain his professional demeanour. 'Can I come in and talk with you please, Mrs Matthews?' He offered a more serious expression.

'What's it concerning?'

Frank took a deep breath, steadying himself. In his mind, he saw Maddie's face again – the constant fear of bad news that had haunted him during her absences. He'd want directness. He felt he owed Margaret that same directness.

'It's about your daughter, Mrs Matthews. I'm so sorry, but we've discovered her remains.'

Chapter Twenty-Nine

Before mentioning Gerry and Rylan, Frank sat her down in the lounge and broke the news to Margaret.

She sat in silence for a couple of minutes, stroking Jasper.

Frank had witnessed countless reactions to death notifications – screaming, fainting, denial, rage. Quiet dignity was always the hardest to witness – it left you with nothing to manage, no way to help. You merely had to wait, watching as they processed, with great pain, a sudden change in their world. A few tears appeared, but her composure was astonishing.

Eventually, concerned that her long silence might show she was going into shock, he asked her if she'd like him to make a drink.

She shook her head, and Jasper curled tight against her. 'I just need another minute, please.'

As Margaret's fingers trembled through Jasper's fur, he looked around. Evidence of a carefully maintained life filled the room—photos arranged just so, cushions precisely aligned, everything in its proper place. Was this the order that comes from having too much time alone with memories? Frank certainly didn't have time like this. Maybe that wasn't such a bad thing.

He passed her the tissue box from the coffee table. She took one, dabbing at her eyes for another minute. Eventually, she nodded. 'Of course, I knew this day would come.'

'I'm so sorry,' Frank said.

'Don't be... it's fitting you got me this news now, before I...' She looked down and stroked Jasper, who reached up and licked the salty tears from her chin. 'Well, I'm dying, you see. Doctor says another year or two at the most. It's in my bones now. The cancer.' She gestured at Jasper, who'd settled his chin on her knee, dark eyes watching her face intently. 'It's Jasper I worry about. He's still young. Sylvia next door has agreed to take him in when I no longer can, but... he'll miss me.' She winked at Frank. 'He gets more treats than any dog has business having.' She looked down and then up again, her face greying further. 'How did Sarah...' She broke off.

Frank met her gaze, recalling his promise – complete honesty, no matter how painful. He looked down, then up again. 'We can't say for certain, but there's some head trauma, and her neck, well, it's broken. But it really is hard to say at this stage. It was so long ago, and damage could have been caused to the remains when they were discovered.'

She narrowed her eyes. 'That silo. I mean... who'd put her in there? It's a horrible old thing. Such an eyesore. All these years I've walked past it, other people have walked past it... never knowing...' Her voice cracked. 'I heard it came down yesterday... I didn't realise there was a body inside.'

'Nobody does,' Frank said. 'There hasn't been a press release yet.'

Margaret straightened in her chair, one hand still buried in Jasper's fur, the other clenched in her lap. She fixed Frank with a stare and smiled. 'You know, in some ways, her disappearance, it still feels like yesterday.'

Frank felt the familiar weight settle in his chest – the same weight over Maddie. The not knowing. And the potential of never knowing. Followed by the endless possibilities of what could have happened – each option worse than the last. At least he still had hope, he guessed. Margaret's hope was now buried forever.

'You know, I always thought, hoped rather, as the police seemed to think, that she might have just run away... started again... a whole new life, you know? A settled one. A peaceful one. She never seemed to find that here. Apart from when she had the horse riding, maybe.'

Frank watched as Margaret's eyes drifted to a photograph on the wall – Sarah laughing, young and full of life, holding the halter of her horse. The contrast between that vibrant image and what they had found twisted something deep in his chest.

'They talked about an older man. I tried to imagine her with a gentleman. A kind gentleman. It gave me some hope. After all, anything was better than that foul-mouthed fool, Tommy Reid.'

He stopped himself short of asking about Tommy just yet. He wanted, if possible, to get Gerry in the house first. There was one more thing he wanted to tell her first, though, before making this request.

Frank glanced at a timeline of Sarah's life on the mantelpiece – school photos, riding competitions, her nursing graduation... She was always laughing in this silent biography, presenting a happier narrative than was perhaps true.

He inwardly sighed.

'There's evidence that she was bound... tied up.'

Margaret shook her head. 'Good lord...'

There was a lingering silence before she eventually looked up, and said, 'As if leaving her all alone in a fucking silo wasn't cruel enough?'

Chapter Thirty

Sharon and Reggie arrived to find Tommy Reid's door ajar.

Reggie knocked, and the door crept open further. Tobacco smoke billowed out, and Sharon waved her hand in front of her face.

She exchanged a look with Reggie. He mouthed, 'Disgusting.'

'Who is it?' It was an older female voice, which was reminiscent of gravel being crushed.

Sharon suspected this was Honey Reid. She held her breath and leaned in. 'Mrs Reid? It's the police. We're here to speak to your son, Tommy, if he's available.'

A violent fit of coughing obliterated the response.

'Maybe we should give this one a miss?' Reggie asked with a raised eyebrow.

Sharon wished he wasn't joking.

When she eventually stopped coughing, Honey shouted, 'What you waiting for, then? Come in!'

They entered the house. Normally, Sharon would remove her shoes, but the bare, stained floorboards – testament to decades of cigarette burns and spilled tea – deterred her.

They followed the sound of coughing through to the lounge, brushing smoke out of their way.

They arrived in time to witness Honey Reid, leaning over the side of her wheelchair and expelling what sounded like a significant chunk of her lung into a bucket.

Sharon felt a wave of nausea.

Reggie was holding out his warrant card. 'Mrs Reid. Detective Constable Miller and Detective Sergeant Moyes.'

'What do you want?'

'To speak to Tommy.'

'Ha.' She fumbled a cigarette to her lips with nicotine-stained fingers and lit it, drawing deeply as if her life depended on it.

Sharon expected coughing again.

Instead, Honey exhaled, patted her chest and said, 'That's better.'

'Police? For my son?' She smiled, revealing teeth the colour of old tea. 'Nothing new there. Drink?'

Sharon willed herself not to gag over the thought of Honey making her a drink.

'No thanks,' Reggie said. 'Do you know where Tommy is?'

She laughed again. 'He's behind you!'

Reggie shook his head. 'This is a serious visit—'

'I didn't say it wasn't. I'm serious. He's fucking behind you.'

Sharon spun around, adrenaline flooding her system.

'Can I help you?' Tommy asked.

The man who stood before them bore little resemblance to any photograph they'd seen so far. He was sixty-one now and certainly hadn't aged well. His bulk strained against a stained T-shirt, greasy hair clinging to his scalp. A patchy beard did little to hide his jaundiced skin. His bloodshot eyes peered over the rim of his mug. The stains suggested it hadn't seen soap since Sarah disappeared.

'Good morning, Mr Reid,' Reggie said. 'We could do with talking to you about Sarah Matthews.'

Tommy squinted at them like they were aliens. Then he frowned. 'Eh?'

'Sarah Matthews. Your girlfriend in 1989, you were living—'

'I know who she is. Why are you here? Fuck. Have you found her or something?'

Reggie and Sharon exchanged a glance.

Reggie nodded.

'Dead, then?' Honey said from behind.

Sharon looked back. 'I'm afraid so, Mrs Reid, but what makes you say that?'

'Ha! By the fact she disappeared, and she was an unhinged maniac.' Her entire face creased up. Honey's laugh turned into a wheezing cough as she blew out a plume of smoke.

'Shut the fuck up, Mam,' Tommy said.

The sound of Honey's phlegm hitting the bucket punctuated the tension.

'But if you think it's owt to do with either of us two,' Honey croaked, 'then you'd be best fucking off right now, because it ain't.'

'Can we sit for a moment?' Reggie asked.

'You not listening DC Dickhead?'

Reggie was about to warn her when Tommy jumped in first. 'Shut it, Mam. How did she die?' Tommy asked.

Sharon saw something crack in his expression – shock, grief, something real. 'Let's sit first, shall we?'

'Whatever.' Honey patted the sofa next to her with a yellow-nailed hand. 'Who's next to me, then? How about you dear... you've a nice figure... reminds me of mine once upon a year.' She winked. 'I don't fucking like the look of DC Dickhead.' She nodded at Reggie.

Irritated, Reggie glared at her. 'DS Moyes, and—'

'Let's sit, sir,' Sharon said, staring at him, trying to communicate that it was in their best interests not to let this escalate.

Sitting next to Honey Reid was the last thing Sharon wanted to do, but she did it for the sake of putting an end to her little show.

Tommy and Reggie sat on the other sofa.

Sharon swept her eyes over the living room. Nicotine stains crept up the walls like dying vines. Ash dusted every surface.

Jesus, Sharon thought, *was it like this when Sarah lived here?*

A framed photograph caught her eye, perched atop an old television. It showed a different Tommy Reid – leather jacket, mirrored shades, long hair and trimmed beard. The casual rebellion that might catch any young woman's eye, especially an unsettled one – the kind looking for an escape from the mundane and the orderly, perhaps.

The man sitting opposite her now didn't even seem an echo of that image. Rather than the cool, nonchalant attitude, he looked wounded and anxious. His fingers worried at his nails as his feet tapped an endless rhythm against the floor.

Was he hiding something or had the many years of living with his mother in this hell ground him down?

'So,' Tommy said. 'How did she die?'

Reggie turned side on to Tommy, and leaned forward,

keeping his voice steady and professional despite the escalating frosty atmosphere. 'We found her remains in the old grain silo near Ruswarp. They were discovered when the structure collapsed yesterday. She'd been tied up, although the cause of death remains ambiguous.'

Tommy's eyes dropped to the floor, and for a moment Sharon saw that genuine grief, again – until his mother's hacking cough shattered the moment like breaking glass.

She spat into her bucket with practiced aim and lit another cigarette from the dying ember of her last, the movements as natural as breathing. After she reset her lungs with another drag, she said, 'That one? Bound to end up dead. Always was a disaster waiting to happen.'

Tommy's fist hit the table hard enough to rattle the empty mugs. 'Just shut the fuck up, Mam!'

Sharon flinched. Reggie was back on his feet. 'We need you to calm down, Mr Reid.'

'Ha!' Honey said. 'Fat chance of that happening.'

Tommy rose to his feet. 'I'm fucking warning you Mam...' He pointed down at her.

Sharon's mind raced. *How the hell do I get Honey out of the way before this blows up?*

Chapter Thirty-One

Margaret was more than happy to accommodate Rylan.

At first, Jasper saw the Lab as a source of fun and the Yorkshire Terrier scurried around him, nudging him, trying to get him to play.

Of course, nothing was further from Rylan's style. Not only was he well-trained, but he was a dog tuned into the emotions of others – so could keep his own emotions secondary.

Sure, if the situation, and Gerry allowed it, he might enjoy the occasional sprint around the park cavorting with other dogs, but he knew, clearly, how he was supposed to behave in this very moment.

There was also great sadness in the room, which Jasper wasn't picking up on yet.

Rylan felt the sadness, respected it and attended to it. He spent most of the interview at Gerry's feet, but every now and again, padded over to Margaret, offering her his solid presence.

Margaret stroked Rylan in exactly the same way as she'd

stroked Jasper before he'd become giddy over the Lab's arrival – with gentle and precise movements.

There seemed to be a real rhythm to the strokes. It reminded Frank of someone counting sheep to fall sleep.

They'd been talking for over twenty minutes about Sarah's childhood while Gerry and Frank took notes, when she suddenly paused. She was already pale but seemed to come over even whiter. Frank instinctively leaned forward, ready to spring and catch her if she suddenly fainted and fell forward off her chair.

'I want to see her,' Margaret said.

Frank took a deep breath, caught her eyes, preparing to respond.

But Gerry got there first. 'It's permitted. Although, it's been a long time, and the remains have been decaying. We really don't advise it.'

Margaret's eyes widened as she stared at Gerry.

Frank touched Gerry's arm gently, showing she should leave it there. Clinical precision had its place, but not here. He'd learned the hard way that grief followed no logical path. If the bereaved wanted to see their children, if this was the closure Margaret's mind craved, then it shouldn't be extensively questioned.

'I'll arrange it,' he said with a gentle nod.

Margaret returned the nod. It seemed to bring some colour back to her cheeks. 'I'm aware she won't look like Sarah any more. But I'll know, won't I? That it's her. That it's my daughter. I'll know. For me, that's enough.'

'I completely understand,' Frank said.

'And there's something I need to apologise to her about... Something I've never had the chance to apologise for.'

'Can I ask what that is?'

She lowered her head. The delay intrigued Frank. Eventually, she looked back up and said, 'For failing her. For allowing her to become lost in life. No mother should do that.'

To Frank, this sounded vague. He wondered if she was sitting on something a little more specific.

Still, he guessed there was genuine truth in her sense of failure. How many times had he apologised to Maddie's empty room? To Mary's photograph?

They returned to discussing Sarah's early childhood in the seventies. Her voice grew stronger as she spoke of happier times. It almost hid the shadow beneath the words. Almost. Everyone in the room knew something darker was coming to the surface.

'But Rory could never handle her spirited behaviour. In his mind, everything had to be controlled, you see. He wanted everything on his terms. When Sarah refused to be so obedient, around ten years of age, he'd get angry. Furious... and...' Her words trailed off as Rylan pressed against her legs.

Frank felt bubbles of anger forming in his stomach. 'Did he abuse Sarah?'

She sighed and nodded. 'Hit her. Sometimes left marks.' Margaret's voice cracked on the word 'marks', her fingers unconsciously touching her own arm as if remembering something. Her face had taken on an ashen quality.

'Do you need a glass of water?' Gerry asked.

Margaret shook her head. 'No, dear. Best to keep going now I've started. Anyway, I tried to reason with Rory. He always promised to control his temper in the future...' She looked off and sighed. 'But there was always another time. You can surely see why I've a lot to apologise for.' Her eyes were filling with tears. 'What must you think of me? Well, I know... because I know what I think of myself.'

'I don't know everything about the situation,' Frank said, which was true, although he was struggling inside with the idea of her remaining complicit in the physical abuse.

'Often when a child is abused the other parent is, too,' Gerry said. 'It creates a culture of being trapped.'

Margaret looked at Gerry as if she understood what she was getting at. She nodded and stood. 'I want to show you something.'

She went over to a cabinet, opened a drawer, and pulled out a photo album. Returning to her seat, she leaned forward, placing it on the coffee table for all to see. She flicked through it, revealing Sarah at various ages, explaining them as she went. Sarah in leg warmers and a ra-ra skirt, posing with friends outside the Wimpy; a school disco, Sarah with enormous, back-combed hair; Sarah, on her first day in college, nursing textbooks clutched to her chest.

'She looked like she had many happy times,' Frank said, thinking of his own collection of photographs at home – Maddie grinning with ice cream on her chin, Maddie on her first bicycle, Maddie before the darkness crept in.

But Frank knew, all too personally, that you could learn little from a collection of images.

Because demons were always hiding in the dark moments between every click of the camera, every carefully chosen recording.

Margaret reached a photo of Rory Matthews. He stared out from the photograph. His face was set in the time's fashion – careful moustache, collar-length hair, a pastel Miami Vice-style jacket. But his eyes were hard and at odds with his wide smile and trendiness.

'It quickly got worse. The smallest things set him off,' Margaret said. 'If she was late home, if her room wasn't tidy enough, if she talked back... He couldn't handle it. His father had been similar. Worse, even. A mean-spirited man. He used to pummel him and his brother, relentlessly, for the slightest thing!

'This isn't an excuse for Rory. He had a problem... an awful problem. And it became too much when she was twelve, and she became more fiery.' He pushed her so hard, she banged her head on the skirting board, and I'd to take her for an x-ray. She was okay, but they asked questions... and we all lied.' She shook her head. 'Shame on me. Shame on me.'

Frank looked down. He knew that anybody was capable of anything when they lived in fear, but not doing something about the plight of a twelve-year-old? He'd struggle to make peace with that, even though he could genuinely tell that this woman had adored her daughter.

'Sometimes, despite everything, I found myself sympathising with him.' She traced the edge of the photograph with trembling fingers. 'His father had knocked nearly everything out of him, but there was still some compassion there. I saw it in the despair and the pain he felt over his actions. It was like light through a crack in the curtain on a dreary winter day. He claimed to be getting help from the doctors, so I *always* gave him another chance. But they were always just quick flashes of promise.' She sighed, turned the page, and her fingers traced a photo of young Sarah, grinning despite a grazed knee. 'He drank too much, and he hit both of us, and I was a coward... I should have left him sooner. I should have protected her better.'

Frank's fingernails dug into his palms. Abuse of this nature was always difficult for Frank. He'd seen it many times in his career and seen the damage it led to in that young person's life. It also mixed, viciously, with a moment that often visited him in the dead of night – a moment that filled him with guilt and regret.

When Maddie had been younger, Frank had once slapped her hand very hard for going into his office and playing with his lighter. She'd cried for over an hour, and he'd felt dreadful. He justified it to Mary because lighters were dangerous. But there was no justification, really. Seeing that flash of hatred and betrayal in his daughter's eyes had torn him to pieces. To this day, the event still revisited him, waking him late at night.

Margaret turned another page, revealing Sarah in a school uniform. At first, she smiled, warmed by a memory, but then it quickly dimmed. 'At thirteen, a teacher phoned because she'd forgotten her homework. When Rory challenged her on it, she argued back. Looking back, it's hard not to admire her fight, her willingness to express opinions, even if it got her into trouble. Rory didn't hit her on this occasion, but he did something far worse. He went into her room and tore her diary to pieces. The diary she'd been keeping for over two years.'

Frank felt his heart sinking even further as he made a note.

Margaret rubbed her temples. 'He said she spent too much time daydreaming and writing in it... such an awful shame... I saw genuine despair in her face. She cried all night. And then she didn't have a diary again, at least not one that I know about.'

'What happened after he destroyed it?' Gerry asked.

'She became even more secretive. Hiding more things.' Margaret drummed her fingers on the armrest.

Gerry nodded. 'Was Rory ever spoken to by social services, or the police?'

Margaret shook her head. 'No... but after he assaulted Tommy Reid, they were all over him. If they hadn't locked him up, they'd probably have taken her into care.'

'Sarah was thirteen when she started a relationship with Tommy, wasn't she?' Frank asked.

Margaret nodded. 'Yes... and he was sixteen. Disgusting. It was brief. At least, I think it was. We only found out about it when Rory caught them together... in bed... well, you know what came next. Sometimes, I wonder if Sarah did the whole thing on purpose, you know, to get her father out of her life. I know, stupid, eh? More than likely she did it because of how badly she was being treated – she was looking for happiness, and kindness elsewhere perhaps. I'm sure Tommy Reid was offering this, or rather deceitfully promising this, in spades!'

'We'll get to Tommy in a moment, Margaret,' Frank said, 'but could you tell me what Sarah experienced after they imprisoned Rory?'

She nodded, staring off into the distance, her face brightening. 'Ah... this is where the story gets better. Dr Hannah Wright was the best thing that ever happened to my daughter. An absolute angel. Talk about finding heaven after hell... So sad what happened to her in that fire. A day doesn't go past when I don't think about Hannah and what she did for Sarah.' She trailed off into silence.

'Talk us through it please, Margaret,' Frank said.

'Hannah was visiting the school for research, when she heard the story of what happened to Rory and Sarah from the headteacher. Interested, Hannah asked to observe her, and talk to the teachers. Apparently, she saw several teachers speaking to Sarah in a dismissive, critical way, despite her horrendous experiences. Hannah explained to the head that continually reprimanding Sarah for her behaviour was making things worse. The headteacher was defensive when Hannah told her that Sarah wouldn't become the best version of herself with their approach. She was right, of course. Not that the school was prepared to change anything.

'So then, Hannah came to me and offered to help Sarah for free. She'd fund it as a research project. At first, I was sceptical – why would anybody do anything for free – but realising I'd such few options, I said yes, and then...' She paused, lost in memory for a moment while Rylan pressed his head against one knee, and Jasper the other. 'The most wonderful thing. I couldn't believe it! Over the months, I got my happy, smiling daughter back... the one I remembered before Rory went completely off the rails...'

Her eyes filled up, and Frank passed her another tissue.

'I once asked Hannah what she'd seen in my daughter that day that'd so captivated her... made her want to help... She told me that Sarah was a star, an enigmatic, unique star. And was completely misunderstood.'

Frank and Gerry waited while Margaret pressed the tissue to her eyes for a couple of minutes.

Eventually, she dropped the tissue and said, 'Like I said, Dr Hannah Wright was an angel. She saved my daughter.' She flicked forward a couple of pages of the album. There was Sarah on horseback. 'Sarah needed an outlet, something to channel her energy into. This is what Hannah offered and, you know, paid for, too! With that research fund. And oh, how my baby took to it.' Margaret glowed again, years suddenly falling from her face. 'It was almost overnight! She was alive again. Shining again.'

Margaret showed them another photograph – Sarah

beaming with pride, holding a trophy in one hand, and the pin that had been recovered at the silo in the other. 'First place in the Yorkshire Dales Cross Country Championship. Happiest day of my life, watching her up there. She was so proud...' Her voice caught.

She took a couple of deep breaths.

'When you're ready,' Frank said.

'Rory was dead by this point, but earlier in her treatment when she was fifteen, I gave him pictures of her riding while visiting him in prison, and he seemed interested and proud. You may not believe me, but he had a heart. He wasn't drinking at this point either, and he was a different man, vowing to be a better person when he got out. Even though I'd fallen for it before, it was hard not to believe him when he looked healthier, and more settled because of kicking the alcohol.'

She paused, nodding and reflecting. 'You know, it was surprising when he started a fight with a prison guard and got himself killed. To me, he really seemed to be improving, getting control of his temperament. But what do I know, eh? You already know my shameful track record! Is it awful that I sometimes think it was probably a good job he died and never got out, because he probably would have begun the cycle all over again?'

'That's understandable,' Frank said. 'When Sarah turned sixteen, she attended Riverside College – how was that?'

'Interesting. She discovered a passion for writing. In fact, I'd like to show you something upstairs, in her room, after this conversation. Is that okay?'

'Of course.'

'Okay... so after college, Hannah sponsored her training at university to become a nurse in paediatrics.'

'Middlesbrough?'

'Yes,' Margaret replied. 'It meant that she'd then work for her for five years afterwards. But in itself, that was also fantastic. After all, a guaranteed job?'

'Aye,' Frank said. *Not to be sniffed at*, he thought.

Margaret's face darkened. 'Problem was that boy again. Tommy Reid. He's no good, DCI Black. He's always been no fucking good.'

Frank considered that was only the second time he'd heard her swear. Her distaste for Tommy was deep.

'Sarah had made a real go of her life. Thanks to Hannah. The horse riding, the nursing qualification, a career... what more could you ask for?' She narrowed her eyes. 'And then she just threw it all away for that fool. He's a spider... and she walked straight into his web again. Twenty-two – how could she not know better? Twenty-two, saved by that angel, and she pressed the self-destruct button again. Moves out of here and goes to live with him. And the mother, too! Don't get me started on her. She's an animal. Smoking and drinking every minute of every day. I heard that she was still alive! How is that possible? It's unbelievable.'

Frank made some notes. 'Did you try to talk her out of living there at the time?'

'Of course,' Margaret said. 'Relentlessly. But that just seemed to make her more determined to go. He cast a spell over my girl, and I don't know why. Hannah did what she could... but it wasn't enough.'

'And what was that?' Gerry asked.

'Well, she told her straight that she couldn't work there while living with Tommy. Maybe she shouldn't have said that, but she told me later that she was just trying to deter Sarah – make her see sense before it got out of hand. But calling her bluff didn't work... and then... well...' She sighed. 'Friday Oct 13, 1989, I went round to their house to speak to my daughter. Honey was laid up following an operation, but she was vile as always, telling me how much of a terrible mother I was, trying to sabotage a loving relationship of two people meant to be together. And if anybody was risky business, it was Sarah, and not her reliable son! I confronted Tommy, and he told me they'd argued the previous night, left and hadn't come back – that she was probably staying at a friend's. On Friday night, he came around, panicking, saying he'd not heard from her. He looked devastated, but I didn't buy it... and don't to this day. The man is a spider, as I've already said. He told me she wasn't home yet, and he was worried.'

She rubbed her temples. 'On the Saturday, I contacted the police. They came and asked their questions, and by Monday, everybody was talking about a red Fiesta and an older man. Malcolm Hargreaves had seen her.'

'And what're your views on that?' Frank asked.

'At the time, it seemed crucial. But now, it's hard to take it at face value, especially after I found out his story kept changing. Malcolm was an old drunk, after all. What do you think?' She looked between the two of them. 'Do you think the red Fiesta is a thing?'

'I can't say,' Frank said, but he always believed that anything 'was a thing' if it kept coming up and demanding attention. 'What about the older man? There were sightings from different areas, although the descriptions never seemed to match...'

'Look, I told you earlier, I believed there was a man, maybe he was older. It's been so much easier to believe that for all this time. A nice, older man, who'd taken her away from Tommy Reid, and this world she'd really struggled to settle in. But these varying descriptions just added fuel to the fire, and fuelled the rumour mill. People, in their usual pig-ignorance, started speculating on her having many affairs, because my daughter was bad through and through – a nasty influence, despite everything she'd accomplished after her father was finally out of her life. In fact, many came to the side of Tommy, claiming him to be an unsettled lad with a negligent mother, who'd a good heart, really, just never got the opportunities. They believed he just needed to meet the right person to settle down. Some people were even angry with Sarah for leaving him – saying that he'd never been better and had been getting his life on track.' She snorted. 'I'm glad that things have changed for the better. A girl that had made mistakes back then got little but sneering, and never seemed to be able to earn forgiveness.'

Frank nodded, thinking of how often he'd seen it, especially in his early career – female victims dismissed because they didn't fit society's idea of 'good girls'. How many cases had prejudice botched?

After another period of questions, Margaret put the album away and stood. 'Can I show you that thing I mentioned before?'

'Of course,' Frank said.

'Would you like me to stay here?' Gerry asked. 'With Rylan?'

'Of course not. We're going to my daughter's room. She loved animals... especially horses...' A ghost of a smile touched her lips as Rylan's tail thumped gently against the floor. 'And dogs.'

Chapter Thirty-Two

TOMMY WAS STANDING, glaring down at Honey, having taken offence at her disparaging remarks about Sarah.

Sharon suspected this was as good a time as any to get him away from his mother. 'Would it be possible to speak to you alone, Tommy?'

He glanced at Sharon before turning back to Honey, who gave a swift shake of her head.

To Sharon's surprise, Tommy sat back down and said, 'Anything that you need to say to me, you can say in front of my mother.'

So that's how it is, then, Sharon thought. *Honey really is in charge, and she doesn't trust you to speak for yourself.*

'Tommy,' Reggie said from beside him. 'Do you know anything about Sarah's death?'

He shook his head and lowered it. 'I loved her, okay? We loved each other.'

'Are you surprised about her death?' Sharon asked.

'Not really. I always knew. I get many people thought she'd done a runner with someone... someone old... but nah, not me. She'd have come back. She would never have been able to stay away. Me and her were soul mates.'

Honey's laugh rattled around the room, before she coughed and spat into her bin.

Sharon noticed Tommy seemed to deflate, sinking back into the sofa. 'But I hoped...' He muttered under his breath. 'For many years... I hoped.'

Sharon waited until he looked up before fixing him with a steady gaze. 'It concerns us how young Sarah was when you started your relationship with her,' Sharon said. 'I know you were made aware it was illegal after you were assaulted by her father.'

'It was only three years,' Tommy said.

'But you were sixteen, and she was thirteen' Sharon pressed.

'And now I'm sixty-one!'

'What's your point?' Reggie said. 'Just because it was a long time ago doesn't make you innocent of the crime.'

'Just saying. What's the point of this conversation now?'

'The point is that we now know she's dead,' Reggie said.

'But she didn't die when she was thirteen!'

Sharon and Reggie exchanged a glance. He was clearly missing the point.

'They never pursued a case of statutory rape,' Sharon said. 'Seems that Sarah had your back. She denied you ever had sex?'

'There you go then,' he said, almost triumphantly.

'Yet, her father caught you.'

His face contorted, a flash of that old violence breaking through a rather defeated exterior. 'Look – what the hell does this matter? Are you not listening? We loved each other. Age? What the fuck does age matter? Love doesn't recognise age!' He tried to sound profound, like he was a romantic poet asserting a pure ideal.

'The law recognises age,' Sharon said, trying to sound professional and hold back her anger. 'They may not convict you, but it reflects poorly on your character, especially given that we now know she was murdered.'

'Bloody hell, love,' Honey said. 'Give it a rest. He's almost sixty. He was a twat then. In fact, he's still a twat now... just less of one.'

'Thanks Mam,' Tommy said and sneered.

'Okay, let's talk about that relationship when you were both young and in love,' Reggie said.

Sharon caught her superior's sneer.

As Tommy spoke, his hands never stopped moving – picking at loose threads on his shirt, drumming against his thighs, clenching and unclenching. His eyes darted between Sharon and his mother, like a cornered animal searching for escape. The constant movement made him appear younger somehow, more like the teenage boy who'd first met Sarah than the sixty-one-year-old he'd become.

Tommy answered questions while Sharon and Reggie took notes. When they reached the part about Rory beating him half to death and putting him into a coma, they both stared at him. His account was brutal. The beating could have killed him.

He pointed at his head. 'He damaged me in here.'

'Not half,' Honey said. 'And no compensation either. I've been left to pick up the fucking pieces,' Honey growled, causing herself to cough again. It ended with the now-familiar wet clang of phlegm hitting metal.

Sharon guided him through an explanation of how they rekindled their romance in 1988. 'For years, she wouldn't come near me... I tried, I always tried, but she didn't want to know. Then, one day, she just shows up.' He clicked his fingers. 'Like that. Out of the blue. Told me she was bored.'

'With what?' Reggie asked.

'Everything.' Tommy shrugged. 'Her life, I guess.'

'That girl was wild,' Honey said. 'Always was. There's only so long someone with a nature like that can keep it in check.'

'Leave it, Mam.' Tommy's voice cracked. 'I know what you're saying, but we've been through this. She missed me. She was bored without me.'

'And I've told you, it was bollocks,' Honey said. 'She'd have moved on to the next adventure. The next bit of excitement. Which we were pretty sure she'd done. A wild animal, she was. With an even wilder heart. She was never any good for you.'

'Ha! And now what do I have, Mam? Almost sixty-one! Where's the better option you said would always come along?' He leaned forward, pointing at the floor. 'We were happy. For a while. When we got back together, we were happy.'

'Never seemed that way,' Honey said before breaking into a cough.

'Will you shut up, Mam!' He rubbed his temples and shook his head as Honey continued to cough. 'You know that this was your fault. She would've been happy here without you talking to her like she was shit on her shoe... telling her what to do all the time... like a fucking servant...'

Honey was still coughing. She lit and puffed on another cigarette, rubbing her chest as it settled. 'Look at the job she gave up for God's sake. Who in their right fucking mind gives up a job like that?'

Tommy glared at his mother. 'Someone in love. And that bitch, Hannah... that horrible bitch put too much on her... Telling her who she could and couldn't love?' He raised his hands in the air. 'She was a fucking dictator! I told her she was best getting shot.'

'And then she did as you suggested. Chucked a nice earner,' Honey said. 'Thick as pig shit, the both of you! If someone had given me an opportunity like that, I'd have done what I was told.'

Although it was frustrating, Sharon realised that the argument taking place in front of them was informative.

'She could have gone back to that job any time,' Tommy said. 'Sarah knew it was a bluff. She was sure they'd ask her back once things settled.'

'It was settled before it ever got unsettled,' Honey said, taking another drag. 'You know, that girl was earning more than you'll ever earn in your life, Tommy... She was stupid, and so were you, although I don't so much blame you.' She tapped her head. 'It isn't all your fault... but that bastard got his just desserts, didn't he?'

'You referring to Rory Matthews?' Reggie asked.

'I don't see any other bastard who almost took away my only child, do you? Seems he did a good job of getting himself a taste of his own medicine. I heard someone fractured his skull too.'

Sharon noticed Tommy grinning and nodding. She made a note to have another look into Rory's death in prison.

'What happened the last time you saw Sarah?' Sharon asked.

'We argued.' His knee bounced up and down, the tension coiling tighter inside him. 'The worst fight we ever had.'

'The last fight!' Honey tapped ash into her bucket with theatrical precision.

'But I didn't hit her,' Tommy said, jabbing his finger at Sharon like a man desperate to be believed. 'Okay? Not like her father did. I never hit her.' He looked to his side at Reggie.

'What was the argument about?' Sharon asked.

'The devil in a bottle!' Honey's laugh dissolved into yet another rattling cough.

Tommy said, 'Her father drank, see? A lot. And look what he did. He was a violent, evil bastard. I wasn't like that – never raised a hand to her. But I get awful anxiety, because of what he did to me, and how cloudy it gets up here' – he pointed to his head – 'and sometimes only the drinking shuts it off... but she said...' His voice trailed off, Adam's apple bobbing as he fought for control.

'Go on?' Reggie prompted.

'Said if she'd given up her job for me, I could give up the drink for her.'

'And then she smashed my favourite fucking teapot!' Honey said.

'And it was replaced!' Tommy hissed. He looked at Sharon. 'And nobody was hurt. I loved her. She loved me.'

'Come on,' Honey said. 'She loved them all I bet. Including the one she fucked off with. The older one that probably ended up killing her!'

The temperature in the room seemed to drop as mother and son faced each other. Tommy's shoulders hunched forward, his breathing becoming shallow and rapid. The vein in his temple pulsed visibly, and Sharon noticed his hands had stopped their restless movement, instead curling into tight fists at his sides. He hit the table again and he pointed at his mum. 'If you say that again, I'll throttle you, Mam.'

'Ha... do me a favour... put me out of my fucking misery. You know it's true.'

He stood. 'Sarah made him up. He doesn't exist. Just shut your fucking mouth!'

The sudden escalation was concerning but this radical new thread in the narrative was intriguing. Reggie was standing to warn Tommy he needed to sit, but Sharon got there with a question first. 'So Sarah talked about an older man? Who?'

'It was all made up!' Tommy said, eyes wide. 'Now look what you've fucking done, Mam!'

'Who, Tommy?' Sharon insisted.

Tommy slumped back down, bloodshot eyes pleading. Sharon watched Tommy's face carefully, noting how his expression shifted from defiance to something more uncertain.

'She wanted me to know that she'd other options. That she could walk away from me if I didn't get my act together. An older friend. It was bullshit just to scare me into giving up the bottle.'

'Except she was seen with an older man the night she disappeared,' Honey said.

'Strange coincidence, eh?' Reggie said.

'Even if this man was real – which he wasn't,' Tommy said. 'She told me it wasn't like that anyway. They were just friends. That he was married.'

'Ha! When did that ever stop them?' Honey asked. 'What other interest would an older man have had in a twenty-two-year-old? Wake up and smell the fucking coffee, boy!'

Sharon leaned forward slightly. 'Did she give you his name?'

'No.'

'His location?'

'No. Look, he's not real,' Tommy insisted.

'Do you have anything other than what you just told me?'

He shook his head with the fervour of someone who'd convinced himself of something he needed to believe. 'No. Just that she'd other options if I didn't stop the booze. That he was older and married... She told me she loved him, but not in the way that she loved me... that it wasn't like that.' He glared at his mother. 'She wanted me to think she could up and leave. She still wanted to make it clear she'd eyes for no one else – she just wanted me to stop drinking.'

'Did she ever say how they met?' Sharon asked.

'No! Because it was all nonsense. She spoke about him like he was some kind of guardian angel, for God's sake. Who has guardian angels who swoop down to help?'

'The ones that want something!' Honey sneered.

'She'd never have cheated on me.'

'Anything else?' Sharon said. 'Think, please.'

Tommy shook his head for a couple of seconds, screwing up his face. He then stopped and shrugged. 'One time, Sarah said, "if not for him, I'd have been banged up by now – I owe him everything."'

'What did she mean by that?' Reggie asked.

'You tell me! For God's sake... can you not see how it all sounds like bollocks?'

'And that's my son, ladies and gentlemen.' Honey's voice dripped with venom. 'Any other man would have tracked this lecherous bastard down and made him pay... Your father wouldn't have stood for it, Tommy, as well you know.'

'So, you often tell me, Mam,' he sneered. 'Often before you tell me what a bastard he was.'

'Well, he'd many faults, yes, but that was one of his qualities. Expecting the truth. And maybe, if you had done, you'd be able to tell these two here who the killer was!'

'A lie is what it was. It was a story that came from nowhere ... and each time she mentioned it, it sounded more and more odd... If anything, it sounded like she considered him her best friend, nothing more. An imaginary friend. That's what it was.'

'You're cuckoo, son. Why would she paint stories for you? And since when could men ever be friends with young women?'

Sharon's jaw tightened at Honey's words – decades of casual misogyny disguised as motherly concern.

'You got played,' Honey continued. 'And you should have found that man, and cut off his fucking balls.'

'Okay, Tommy,' Reggie said, leaning forward and looking at him from the side. 'After she left on October 12, 1989, where did you go?'

Tommy's head snapped around, his eyes suddenly sharp with anger. 'You know this. We said at the time. I was here.' He nodded at his mother 'With her!.'

'Who you referring to? The cat's mother?' Honey hissed.

Sharon looked at Honey. 'You still maintain that's the truth? He was here with you?'

'Ha! Really?' Honey drew herself up in her chair, smoke curling around her. 'I'll say now what I said back then. I spent half my life with one bastard before he did us all a blessing by connecting a hose to his exhaust pipe. I wasn't about to write off the second half of my life to another bastard. Tommy is a lot of things, thick as pig shit, gullible, brain damaged, and offers very little to our home life, but he's not a bastard. Somewhere under those layers of grease and fat is a heart. He didn't kill that wild animal and that's the truth. He was here with me after a major operation on my bowels. He was there to hold me over the fucking toilet. So, yes, the dipshit does have a heart. That's the truth.'

'But are you telling the truth?' Reggie asked.

'Smart arse. I was right about you,' Honey said, her voice carrying fierce pride. 'If I was ten years younger, I'd fuck some sense into you for good measure.' She grinned.

'Mam, for God's sake,' Tommy said.

'I don't lie, DC Dickhead.' She stroked her tongue over her lips. 'If you look back through your records, you'll see how serious that operation was. If my son had gone out to kill her, he'd have left me swimming in my own shite. Use your common fucking sense. The only thing my son was doing that night was wiping my arse and picking up the remains of my fucking teapot.'

Sharon had heard enough. The whole interaction was becoming stomach-churning. She checked her list of considerations she'd prepped beforehand. One left. 'You know about the red Fiesta outside the Bridge Inn, Tommy?'

Honey laughed. 'We know about Malcolm's drink problem. Man used to sing his heart out on the way home drunk seven nights a week. Been far quieter since he died.'

'I asked Tommy,' Sharon said.

'You're fiery, dear!'

No... just desperate to leave, she thought. *I can feel my bloody clothes absorbing this acrid smell with each passing second.*

'What my man said,' Tommy added. 'Malcolm was always pissed.'

Reggie asked a few more questions, while Honey's coughing and spitting became more frequent, each episode punctuating their questions like grim percussion. Sharon wondered if she was doing it purposefully to get shot of them.

It was working.

Tommy seemed to retreat into himself as the interview wore on, his gaze growing distant as if watching memories play out on the nicotine-stained walls.

'Are you okay, Tommy?' Sharon asked, near the end.

'I miss that life inside her. I miss it so much. I don't think I can ever stop being addicted to it—'

'Poppycock,' Honey muttered. 'Only thing you've ever been hooked on is alcohol. Eaten you up inside it has.'

Sharon fought the urge to point out the irony of a woman who treated her lungs like an ashtray lecturing anyone about addiction.

The relief of fresh air hit Sharon like a physical force as they stepped outside. She breathed the winter wind deeply, trying to clear her lungs.

Reggie looked like he was about to throw up.

'You okay?'

'That smoke was awful. I feel like I've just smoked two packets. I can barely breathe. I've a marathon in two weeks!'

'Surely sir, you must have been knocking around when passive smoking was the norm. Have your natural defences not kicked in?'

He shook his head. 'I stayed out of the pubs.' He coughed again, the sound carrying a worrying rattle. 'In there – it was so intense.'

'Shall we contact Frank now?' Sharon asked.

'Later. He'll expect us to run straight with that lead. The older, married man, who kept her from being banged up.'

'She'd a few brushes with the law,' Sharon said, raising an eyebrow. 'Shoplifting. Let's start there.'

'Okay, can we drive with the window open?' Reggie asked.

'Why?'

'In case I bring something up... I refuse to use a bucket.'

'Disgusting. I hope you're bloody joking.'

As they walked back to their car, Sharon couldn't shake the image of Tommy Reid's face when he'd talked about Sarah and the mysterious older man.

He had so desperately wanted to believe it was a lie.

But behind his aggressive protestations, she'd sensed his realisation.

Deep down, he knew – his mother had been right all along.

Chapter Thirty-Three

This wasn't the first time that Frank had been into a preserved room.

Keeping such rooms was a coping mechanism for many. Some kept them as shrines to lost loved ones, while others simply couldn't move on and left them frozen in time. There was also that small group that awaited the return of the occupant.

This seemed like one such room – pregnant with the promise of a return.

Posters of Madonna, George Michael, and The Cure adorned the walls, edges curling slightly with age. A Walkman with tangled headphone cords sat on a pile of yellowing *Smash Hits* magazines. A cork board above displayed polaroid photos of Sarah with friends. Competition trophies were neatly arranged on a shelf, alongside some well-thumbed paperbacks.

Biographies of Willie Carson, Bob Champion, and Lester Piggott sat alongside a collection of well-worn poetry books: Sylvia Plath, Philip Larkin, and several volumes of Wordsworth. He noticed an interesting horse figurine on Sarah's windowsill. Although a chunk of it was missing, she had clearly treasured it enough to keep it there.

'Lift up the mattress, DCI Black,' Margaret said. 'And you'll find a folder there.'

'No... let me,' Gerry said, kneeling first, then lifting and reaching in..

Frank felt his cheeks flush.

'It's nice to have people who care,' Margaret said.

Good point, Frank thought, spoken by someone whose tone suggested they had little left in their life. It made him feel momentarily sad, and rather guilty for always moaning about people's compassion towards him.

Why did he always feel so compelled to resist?

To push back?

Gerry handed the folder to Margaret and she sat on the bed. The detectives sat alongside her, while Jasper and Rylan curled up by their feet.

'Poems.' Margaret opened the folder. 'She'd always kept these hidden from me... but I found them not long after she'd gone. Of course, she'd shown me some of them before, back when she was in her late teens, but I never knew the extent to how many she'd actually written. She was a deep thinker, my Sarah; for the life of me, I don't know where she got it from!'

Margaret selected a poem. Her voice trembled as she read:

'Closed hall. Why does a closed hall not hear? There're so many voices. Shouting, screaming into shadows. Yet no one actually listens. Words with weight and worth, sink into the depths. Perhaps when we drown out the noise, the words will finally be heard?'

Frank had never been a reader of poetry, so he didn't

really know what the best approach was regarding critique. He tried regardless with a positive. 'Emotive.'

'Yes,' Margaret said. 'A deep thinker, see? There always was a lot of emotion when Sarah was around.' She chuckled, but the laughter quickly died, and she sighed instead.

'Did you ever think of sending these to anyone?' Frank said. 'You know, to be considered for publishing or something?'

'Well, I doubt it'd be that easy. Plus, what if she'd have come back? Oh, my... her outrage would have been terrible! Maybe now I should consider it?'

She looked at Frank for a response, but he didn't know what the best advice regarding that would be. 'Maybe, aye.'

'Can I look, please?' Gerry asked, reaching for the folder. She flipped through the sheets while Frank observed.

So many poems, he thought.

And shit, what do I know about poems?

He'd read so few in his life. Mind you, he loved Bob Dylan, and many considered him a poet. Maybe he knew more than he realised.

Gerry read a few. 'These seem to suggest she feels lost... unheard.'

Margaret nodded. 'I felt the same when I read them.'

'Have you read them all?' Frank asked.

'Oh yes... many times... I adore them,' Margaret said. 'They're sad, yes, but sometimes, they make me feel closer to her, you know?'

Frank nodded.

Gerry said, 'This one ends – Now you hear me. Thank you for you. Do you have any idea who she might be referring to Mrs Matthews? It's dated November 1984. That would make her seventeen, yes?'

'Oh yes... she told me about that one. It was a thank you for someone special to her.'

'Hannah?' Frank asked.

'No...' Margaret shook her head. 'Stephen Walker. Headteacher at Riverside College. He started a poetry writing group at his school around that time. She was grateful. Until that point, she'd had no confidence in writing anything like that.'

Frank glanced over at Gerry and saw that she was taking a note of the man's name.

Stephen Walker.

'Do you recall if they stayed in touch after she left college?'

'I believe so. Maybe to let him know how she was getting on. She was very grateful to him. He was a delightful man.'

'I guess he'll have retired by now?'

'Oh yes... he worked for the Conservative Party for a time. People here respect him highly. I'm sure he'll be happy to talk to you.'

And I'll be happy to talk to him too, Frank thought.

Chapter Thirty-Four

Teaching her first ever lesson at Riverside College, Christie Walker was a bag of nerves.

She had never been so acutely aware of her surroundings.

Of the students that widened their eyes with enthusiasm, of those that had them half-closed with fatigue, and, of an irritating few, who'd the audacity to roll them.

Overwhelming, to say the least.

Her father would have been horrified if he'd still been headteacher here, and had walked into this classroom. Standards must certainly have slipped since his day. She'd have to have serious words with a few of them at the end of the lesson.

She was introducing one of her favourite Shakespeare plays: *Othello*. She wanted to draw them in, make them crave this unit.

'Has anyone ever questioned their relationships based on something said by someone else... something that turned out to be false?'

At least half the class raised their hands.

Good.

She recalled her mentor's maxim: 'Make it relevant and they will come.'

She swooped on the most relevant thing to young people these days – social media! 'Who here has felt jealous over something posted by someone else... feeling like the grass is greener...?'

Two-thirds of the class – *even better!*

Some may have already read *Othello*, keen to get a head start. 'Has anyone who's read it want to share why it's still relevant today?'

A hand shot up. A young man, his shirt pristinely pressed and tie perfectly knotted, stood out from some of his dishevelled classmates – particularly those with rolling eyes.

She looked at her seating plan she'd devised so she could learn their names – identifying the solo volunteer. 'Jamie?'

'Jealousy,' Jamie said without hesitation. 'Manipulation. People can manipulate others into doubting their deepest convictions. In Othello's case, Iago manipulates him into doubting Desdemona's innocence.'

Christie nodded, impressed. 'Perfect.'

Jamie glowed.

And that was what she'd needed.

The nerves seemed to fade away into the background, and a confidence surged through her. 'So never believe everything you're told. Even those closest to us can be deceptive and manipulative—'

A sharp knock cut through her words.

'Excuse me.' Christie opened the classroom door to find a woman standing there. She appeared to be in her midfifties and wore very casual clothing. Her face was flushed. Christie assumed, by how the school receptionist, Maisie

Lindon, hovered anxiously close by, holding a walkie-talkie, that this was an angry woman who'd not taken no for an answer.

'Mrs Prince,' Maisie stammered. 'I must insist that you return—'

'I want my son,' Mrs Prince cut in. 'Now.'

She thought of her seating plan. *Jamie?* The boy who'd actually tried!

Christie glanced back at Jamie in the classroom, who'd shrunk in his seat. His face was as red as his mother's now, but for entirely different reasons.

'I don't understand,' Christie said. And she really didn't!

There was a burst of static from Maisie's walkie-talkie and then she edged forward. 'Unless you return to reception now and sign in correctly, someone will come and remove—'

'Not without my son... not without Jamie.' Mrs Prince clicked her fingers in front of Christie's face. 'Now, please.'

She did it so instinctually that Christie couldn't help but feel Mrs Prince was used to getting her own way.

Poor Jamie.

'Mrs Prince.' Christie tried to keep her voice steady, professional. 'Is there an emergency? Has something happened?'

'Not yet. Which is why I'm here.' She leaned closer to the room, but Christie blocked the doorway.

Christie wouldn't be surprised if she ended up getting pushed, but she wasn't moving willingly. Come hell or high water!

'I don't know what this is about, I really don't, but let me assure you, Jamie's settling in wonderfully. He's already contributing brilliantly to the discussion. Maybe we could all sit down and discuss this after the lesson—'

'That bracelet.' Mrs Prince's eyes widened. She pointed at Christie's wrist. 'That fucking bracelet.'

Taken aback, Christie looked down at the silver, engraved bracelet. She then looked up at the erratic mother.

'Reach for the stars?' Mrs Prince's lip curled.

Christie looked down; the engraved side was on the underside of the wrist – how had this woman read that? She frowned. 'How did—'

'Your father gave it to you, didn't he?'

Christie nodded. She felt very nauseous. 'What's this about?' She clutched her bracelet. 'How do you know about this?'

'Because I've seen them before.' Mrs Prince snorted. 'Four times, in fact. That's the fifth.'

'That's impossible. It's bespoke. My father had it made for me when I was sixteen.'

'He had it made for four other children, too.'

The nausea intensified. She couldn't comprehend what was happening here. It felt like some kind of sick joke.

'Do you have one?' Christie asked.

Mrs Prince's eyes narrowed. 'No... not me... I wasn't one of the fabulous four.'

All the strength had fallen from Christie now, and Mrs Prince could push past her into the classroom. 'Jamie, we're leaving... now.'

Jamie had already gathered his belongings. He looked close to tears.

Christie felt bad for him, but she was stumbling headlong into her own panic attack in this moment.

Head down, shoulders hunched, Jamie walked out, past Christie, past his mother, past Maisie and off down the corridor.

Mrs Prince came closer to Christie. She could smell her

body odour, no doubt caused by her fury and charge to the door. 'I won't have a Walker anywhere near my son.' She turned and glared at Maisie. 'And I'm not sitting around waiting to discuss it. Your father... God, what a man, eh? You know what they say – the apple doesn't fall far from the tree.' Her eyelids flickered with something unreadable. 'And I won't have my son tempted by poison apples if you catch my drift. My son will be educated elsewhere.'

She stormed off. Maisie hurried after her, surely relieved she was finally heading for the exit.

Christie went back into the stunned classroom. There wasn't a great deal of variation between the faces of her students now. All were wide eyed and pale.

She took a deep breath. 'Give me a moment.'

She took a second deep breath, and perched on edge of her desk.

A poison apple.

The way she'd said it... it was almost accusatory... defamatory... like Christie had some kind of intention towards a sixteen-year-old boy!

Why? What had her father done to this woman when she was younger?

She put a hand to her mouth. Her father?

No. That just isn't possible.

'Miss?' A quiet female voice penetrated the fog. 'Are you okay?'

'Just another minute, please...'

Who was she kidding? She needed more than a fucking minute. A lot bloody more!

Her carefully prepared lesson on *Othello* was in ruins.

She looked at the bracelet – her father's gift. It suddenly felt unbearably heavy. She unclipped it without really thinking and pushed it into her suit pocket.

'Just open the play and start reading.' She looked between their stunned faces, forcing the tears back. 'Please.'

They all nodded and opened their plays.

Well, that was one way to take charge of a classroom, she thought, staring up at the clock, wondering if she could last twenty minutes without throwing up.

Chapter Thirty-Five

Following Lucy's cry for help, Peter sprinted to the door, the sound of rushing water meeting him before he even stepped inside.

He followed Lucy inside, where water rolled out from the kitchen, soaking into the hallway carpet. 'Where's the stopcock?'

'What's that?' Lucy asked, glancing at Mia, who stood frozen on the bottom step, clutching a bewildered Sophie.

Peter turned and hurried back outside, cursing under his breath. At the front, he pried open the metal cover. His arthritic fingers fumbled with the valve before he managed to twist it shut.

'It's stopping!' Lucy called from inside.

Peter rubbed his forehead and winced. 'Shit!' He'd forgotten about the gash there.

He rose to his feet, his joints suddenly feeling stiff.

He made his way back to the house, unable to rush a second time like he had the first. His bad hip twinged with each step.

'Oh God... oh God,' Lucy was saying, her hands pressed against her cheeks in distress. 'Look at it.'

Catching his breath, Peter assessed the damage. In his fifty-odd years of home ownership, he'd seen far worse, but it still wasn't pretty. Water covered the solid kitchen floor. The hallway carpet was wet, but it hadn't spread too far. It would've been much worse if he hadn't got to the stopcock when he did.

'You need towels and lots of them,' Peter said. 'Dry the kitchen floor first, then attend to the carpet. A dehumidifier will help.'

Lucy looked at him in horror.

He smiled. 'I've got one you can borrow.'

She turned towards the lounge and then turned back. 'The towels are all bloody packed!'

'Find what you can,' Peter said, nodding. 'I can help with that.'

While Lucy and Mia rustled around, he made his way back home, trying to ignore the protest in his joints. In his airing cupboard, he found Donna's old collection of towels – she'd always insisted on keeping extras.

He filled a bin liner with them and hauled it back over to number 5.

~

After helping dry the kitchen floor, Peter lowered himself carefully to examine the pipes under the sink. He traced several pipes until he found the rotten one that had burst. 'That must have been eager to go for a good while now,' he said. 'You should call a plumber to come and replace it.'

She didn't respond.

'In fact, to be honest, I'd get the entire thing looked at.'

Still silence.

He looked back at her. Her face had fallen.

'Are you okay?'

'I'm not sure I can afford a plumber.'

'This is council property. Won't they pay?'

'Yeah... but how long do you think it'll take for them to sort it? I've got a baby here.' Lucy's face tightened. 'Look... I've a part-time job in a supermarket... I've some savings. Do you know anyone I can call just to get it patched up for now?'

He bent and took another look. 'This isn't a patch-up job. Besides, I don't know anyone. I always did this stuff myself.'

From the stairs, Mia said, 'There'll be YouTube videos, Mum.'

'I don't know,' Peter said, careful to rub the back of his head now.

'Call Reece,' Mia said. 'If he wants to act like the man of the house, he can prove it for once.'

Peter couldn't help but smile. That layabout who drove like a nutcase would never have the brains and patience for this job. Peter checked the valve to the burst pipe one final time, his fingers moving with the certainty that came from years of home maintenance. He nodded, rubbing the back of his head. *Aye. I've got this.*

He pushed himself up from his knees, trying to hide his wince as his back protested.

He dusted off his hands and regarded the mother, daughter and granddaughter. 'I'll grab the dehumidifier and then get to work.'

Lucy and Mia exchanged a glance.

'You what?' Mia said.

'You heard,' Peter said with a wink. 'This old fart might as well do something useful.'

Mia scowled and looked away, red faced.

'We can't let you do that,' Lucy said.

'Ah, whatever.' He waved. 'Just make me a cup of tea.'

'We can't,' Lucy said. 'Seriously.'

'Ha... well, in case you hadn't noticed, I can be a serious man too.'

Lucy and Mia exchanged another glance.

'I'm so sorry we got off on the wrong foot,' Lucy said.

'It's okay... was just worried about your kid... and him having an accident... I say the wrong thing. I'd love to blame my age, but I've always been like this. Vocal. So, sorry.'

Lucy looked at Mia, who was looking down. 'Mia, now you.'

Mia shook her head.

'Mia, say sorry!' Lucy's tone was sharp.

Mia sighed.

Peter waved it off. 'Seriously... look, it's okay... everyone loses their temper. I'll just crack on.'

'Sorry, okay?' Mia said, without looking up.

Sophie chose that moment to spit out her dummy and gurgle.

Peter smiled at the girl. 'No need for you to say anything... you weren't involved.'

Lucy laughed. Mia didn't.

'Okay, so now peace is established, I'll get equipped,' he said.

'I'm going to get Reece back to help,' Lucy said.

Peter didn't like the sound of that. 'Best not, eh? I work alone. Delicate work. No offence.'

'None taken. You sure?'

'Yes.'

'You don't have any plans, do you?' Lucy asked.

Well, actually, aye, I do, he thought. *But the pills can wait if needs be.*

Ten minutes later, he was back with his trusty toolbox – the one Donna had given him on their twentieth anniversary – and the dehumidifier. The familiar weight of the tools in his hands put a swagger in his step.

'Would you like that cup of tea?' Lucy offered.

'Not yet. Just some quiet would be good, just so I can work some things out... I'm going to need Reece after all, though. I need him to do me a favour.'

While she went to contact him, Peter settled into the familiar routine of measuring and calculating, his mind focused on the task rather than the darkness that had been consuming him lately.

After writing a list of what he needed, he returned to Lucy and Mia, still working on the carpet. Their earlier hostility seemed almost forgotten in the shared crisis. Even Mia was looking more cheerful and was actually making eye contact with him again.

Sophie slept peacefully upstairs, oblivious to the drama below.

He proffered the list. 'Get Reece to pick up that stuff from that address, please. His name is Ralph Braintree. Good bloke. He knows me. Just tell him to whack it on my tab... I'll settle it up. Let me know when you have it.'

'I couldn't possibly,' she said, taking the note. 'I've got some money. How much?'

'No need.' He waved her off. 'He owes me anyhow,' he lied.

Aware of a sudden spring in his step, he turned and wandered back to the kitchen. He couldn't remember the last time anyone had needed him.

Forgotten Graves

Maybe I'm not a waste of the air in the world after all?

Chapter Thirty-Six

JOHN WHITE's eyelids fluttered and then opened. His unfocused eyes darted around the room like a trapped bird.

His lips parted and he issued a weak groan as his withered hands clutched at the sheets.

He was so far now from the commanding presence that Lewis remembered from his childhood.

Lewis had expected satisfaction – but instead, all he felt was a strange, hollow weight in his chest. He looked away, stunned, and took a deep breath.

When he looked back, John's eyes had found him. 'Son...'

Lewis swallowed. For the previous hour, he'd rehearsed this moment. Practiced the accusations he'd hurl – the demands he'd make.

But now, faced with his father's fragility, his mind felt emptier than ever before.

'Son...'

John's hand inched across the crisp sheets, seeking comfort – he was in so much pain. The movement was vulnerable and childlike – a contrast to everything he remembered about him.

'Please...'

He was desperate for his son's hand.

'No,' Lewis hissed. He hadn't meant the word to come out so hard. He thought he saw his father flinch.

Then he cursed himself for the guilt creeping in.

Gritting his teeth, he stood abruptly, turned and marched to the window. Outside, the rain was washing away the last traces of snow. He closed his eyes and tried to focus on his breaths – take a few moments of mindfulness to centre himself – summon up the strength to confront his dad.

It wasn't possible. His father's moans drilled into his skull.

And then he was in the past, in another hospital room, by another deathbed.

He imagined Felix whimpering while the meningitis ravaged him. His mother holding one hand while the other lay empty, waiting for his father.

'Lewis...' his father said from behind him.

Lewis blinked furiously, angry at the tears in his eyes. He turned and marched back to the bed. His father's eyes suddenly looked more focused, but whether this was a projection of his own rush of adrenaline, he wasn't sure.

'It's time, John, time for you to tell me what was so fucking important to you – that you had to abandon your family.' Even as he said it, he realised how ridiculous the request was. How could this bastard possibly articulate almost five decades of abandoning Lewis? Of not being there for his other dying son? Of leaving Caroline, such a wonderful woman and mother, to wither away, broken?

'Need... water...' he rasped.

Lewis hesitated. He considered withholding this small mercy, to demand the answers first. But cruelty, he realised, wasn't something he needed to feel, or want. That wouldn't fill the void. If anything, it'd only make him more like the man he despised.

He reached for the cup. With surprising gentleness, he held the straw to his father's lips, supporting his head. His silver hair felt as brittle as straw. John sipped weakly, water dribbling down his chin.

Lewis lowered his father's head back to the pillow.

'Thanks...'

Movement at the door caught his attention – Mark hovering uncertainly.

Lewis glared at him. *Give me longer, damn you.*

Mark seemed to get the message and turned.

He'd linger close, and would be back soon though.

I'll be lucky to get five minutes.

'Son... I'm... dying...'

Lewis nodded. *I know.* The anger bubbled away, but he felt that pity too, looming ever closer.

He didn't want that pity – not yet. For so long, there'd been anger. Its presence felt wrong... destructive, threatening to unravel his sense of self.

'Thanks... for coming...' John broke off in a cough. To Lewis, it sounded weak, but it still shook his entire fragile frame. Each cough painted his expression with fresh agony.

After, Lewis gave him another sip.

'Felix? Where... is... he?'

Lewis felt his father's fingers brushing against his own. The touch burned him in the same way ice would. He yanked his hand away. 'Dead. 1987, John. Twelve years old. And you weren't there.'

John closed his eyes, wheezing. 'I...' His face seemed to

crumple further. The sound that escaped his father's throat was neither sob nor moan, but something more primitive.

Lewis looked down at those reaching fingers. 'Meningitis while you were overseas – at least, we think you were overseas... making some kind of deal. Is that even true? You didn't make it back in time to say goodbye.'

'I...' John's eyes remained closed; a tear ran down his face. 'Remember.'

Lewis touched his own face, surprised to find it wet. 'Do you feel guilty?'

'Always...' John's eyes opened, glassy with tears.

Lewis took a step back. 'I don't know if I can do this... I don't know if I can stand here and do this.'

John looked at him. 'Longer... please...'

Lewis darted in closer, so he was inches from him. He was close enough to smell the impending death on his father's breath. 'Felix... your son... my brother. He died when you weren't there.'

Mark appeared again, his face tight with professional concern. Lewis lifted his head clear and said to the nurse. 'A couple more minutes... okay? A couple more.'

Mark nodded. 'Two minutes.' He looked back at his father. Tears tracked down the dying man's cheeks.

'I'm sorry...'

Apologies felt like a hammer. 'No... no... It's too late to plead... too late for apologies, for guilt... I just want to know why you did it. Did you not love us?'

'It was... complicated.' His father's voice, barely more than a rasp, held a whisper of old strength.

'Tell me why, then. Tell me why your life was so fucking complicated that you couldn't be there for your family.'

John's eyes widened, desperately fighting the pain to get words out. 'Someone... else...'

'Other women? Oh, I know. I heard. You disgust me.'

He tried to shake his head. 'No... not that...' John's eyes fluttered closed.

'John? John?' He grabbed his father's hand. 'Wake up.'

Lewis felt the lightest of grips. John's eyes opened slowly.

'Tell me,' Lewis said, tightening his own grip. 'Why we weren't enough?'

His breathing was shallow now, his face contorting and twisting. 'Love you...' John said. 'All... of you.' His eyes were closed again.

'I almost killed someone. Where were you? Where have you been?'

Mark appeared again. He looked genuinely distressed. 'I'm sorry Mr White, it's time. He's suffering immensely.' He approached the machine that controlled the morphine pump.

'A little longer!' Lewis shouted, spitting tears.

'I'm sorry.' Mark's fingers hovered over the controls.

Lewis leaned over his father's bed, tears suddenly flowing. 'Why? Why weren't we enough? Who did you love really? Who?'

But his eyes were closed.

He moved even closer. 'What was so fucking complicated?'

The eyelids stirred. His eyes opened again.

'Love you all. You, Felix... and...'

Lewis gasped between sobs, his father's eyes locked onto his with an intensity that seemed to transcend the pain.

'Who?'

His father's eyes rolled.

'Don't...' He pointed at Mark, while patting his father's eyes to bring his attention back to him.

'Too late... I'm sorry,' Mark said. 'It's going in...'

'Your...' John's voice grew fainter, peace starting to replace pain on his weathered features.

'Your?' Lewis prompted, but it was too late.

Lewis collapsed forward, his head coming to rest on his father's chest. He'd failed to learn anything.

He heard a whisper. 'Your...'

Lewis lifted his head and watched John's lips move with desperate purpose – he was fighting the morphine. He leaned close enough to feel John's breath on his ear.

'*Your... sister.*'

The words hit like a lightning strike.

'Sister?'

But every muscle in John's face eased, as he succumbed, finally, to the drug.

Lewis staggered back, the room spinning around him. He glared at Mark. 'No... stop giving him that shit... I need to know... I need to know.'

The nurse's face was a mask of professional sympathy. 'Mr White... I'm sorry. I understand the trauma. But you saw how weak he was, how much pain there was.'

'Take that line out of his arm! No fucking more.'

'If I do that again, it may kill him.'

'I don't care.'

'You need to calm down.'

'Then I'll pull it out.'

'And if he dies... well... then, you'll be in trouble, and I wouldn't want that.'

'He's dying, anyway!'

He spun, rubbing his temples. Sister? Sister? The word was like a constantly ringing bell in his mind.

He clutched his head, as if he could physically stop his world from spinning.

He stared at Mark. 'He said I have a sister. Did you hear that?'

Mark's silence was heavy. He was pale and clearly very traumatised himself.

'Did you hear him? Talk to me? Or am I fucking imagining it, man? Did he say I have a sister?'

Mark nodded.

Lewis collapsed into the chair, emotional exhaustion hitting him like a physical blow. The tears came again. This time, hot and unstoppable.

'You bastard…' The words came between sobs. 'You tell me that… now what? Is that all you give me? Even in death, you tear out my fucking heart, John.'

Chapter Thirty-Seven

FRANK AND GERRY had only just stepped out of Margaret Matthews' home when his phone started ringing. It was Chelsea Winters at Meadowside Academy.

'Are you available today, DCI Black?' Chelsea said. Her voice was tight with urgency.

'Aye, of course,' Frank said. 'I'm close by, actually. Is everything okay?'

'I'm not sure... it might be something, might be nothing, but I think you need to see it.'

'Okay. Give me ten minutes.'

As expected, Gerry refused to get into Bertha. Instead, she hailed a taxi to HQ and promised to meet him there later.

After parking at the academy and starting the walk to reception, Frank couldn't shake the words in Sarah's poem, *Closed Hall*, from his head. He heard parts of it, replaying again and again on a loop, in Margaret's voice.

No one actually listens. Words with weight...

Through the mist, Frank caught sight of Alice, the

young girl from yesterday, guiding Kate, the chestnut mare, around the paddock. Her movements flowed with the grace that comes from complete trust between rider and horse. Each turn, each transition, was precise yet effortless, like a dance choreographed through instinct rather than instruction.

Everyone finds their voice differently, Frank thought. *Is this how you were heard, Sarah? Finally listened to? Through the grace and power of riding? Was each ribbon, each trophy, a declaration of your worth?*

Or was it the poetry, Sarah, that unlocked you?

But if it was, what role did Stephen Walker play in that?

His motives may have seemed innocent, Sarah, but someone put you in that silo...

Someone deceived you.

Alice guided the mare through another series of movements.

'Words with weight and worth, sink into the depths.'

But they hadn't sunk, had they? Like a message in a bottle, they'd survived in that folder beneath her mattress, waiting.

The Winters sisters were waiting in their office, faces drawn. Lorraine's eyes were red-rimmed, as if she'd been crying.

'Is everything okay?'

'Yes,' Chelsea said. 'We've just been going through Mum's old things – it's left us rather emotional. Anyway...' With reverent care, Lorraine picked up a leather-bound album. 'We were looking through the pictures in some of her albums dated in the early eighties. There were so many of Sarah. I recall Mum taking a shine to her, but I never realised quite how much. There're many photographs here and she always seemed to do well in competitions.' Lorraine turned the pages. Sarah's face smiled up at them from countless photographs – receiving ribbons, mounted on various horses, beaming with pride beside the Winters sisters' mother.

'Did you know Hannah paid for everything?' Chelsea asked. 'The lessons, the competition fees, even leased horses for her.'

Frank nodded. 'Yes, I've heard. For research initially, but it was clearly a lot more than that. From the age of fourteen, eh? Free counselling and all these fees here... plus, that university course, and a job... That's certainly an act of great charity.'

Lorraine nodded. 'It seems my mother wasn't the only one who took a real shine to this girl.'

An expensive shine from Hannah though, Frank thought. The kind that raised more questions than it answered. He'd be interested to hear how Sean was progressing in that research – Hannah Wright was becoming more than just a peripheral figure in this dark story.

'This caught our attention,' Chelsea said, her fingers trembling slightly as she turned another page. The photograph showed a gathering at what appeared to be a prestigious competition, the kind where reputation and money mingled freely. She pointed to a woman who stood out even in the well-heeled crowd – elegant features, expensive clothes, radiating the confidence that came from power.

'That's Hannah Wright,' Lorraine said.

Frank regarded her for the first time and, he felt deep down, certainly not the last.

'Smart... She looks wealthy,' Frank said.

'Do you see this man?' Chelsea asked, showing a similarly well-groomed figure. Everything about him spoke of careful cultivation – the tailored suit, the artfully styled hair, the professional smile that didn't quite reach his eyes.

'Yes, he also looks wealthy. Who is he?'

'We don't know,' Chelsea said. She turned another page with delicate care. 'But there he is again.' The man stood alongside Hannah, both watching Sarah navigate a complex jump. Their attention seemed focused entirely on the young rider, their stance suggesting more than casual interest. 'And again...' She flipped another couple of pages.

Four photographs in total. Four photographs. Four glimpses of a man lurking at the edges of Sarah's success like a shadow. Frank's mind raced. 'It's not Stephen Walker, is it?' he asked. 'The headteacher from Riverside?'

Chelsea scrunched her brow. 'Stephen Walker? No, definitely not. Everyone knows Stephen Walker around here. He was a local politician following retirement from the school.'

Frank leaned closer to the photographs, his trained eye catching details others might miss. There was something about the man's stance, the calculated casualness of his positioning – close enough to be part of the group, but somehow separate. Professional, yet intimate. Was he perhaps a predator trying to blend in with the herd?

'What year were these photos?'

'Between 1981 and 1983. At least, that's what it says on the front of the album.'

He did the mental calculation. Her fourteenth, fifteenth and sixteenth year.

'Any more?'

'Unfortunately, we couldn't find an album for the year

after. The next we found was 1988. She isn't in any of those photos.'

'Do you know if she continued riding while she was away studying to be a nurse between 1985 and 1988?' Frank asked.

'I'm sorry... I don't know that.'

'And there're no more photos of this man that you can see?'

Chelsea shook her head. 'We'd a good look. But these are the last of Hannah, and the last of this man.'

'What do you know about Hannah Wright's death?'

'No more than the next person, I suppose,' Chelsea said. 'Died in a gas explosion – her and the gardener, Clive Morton, who was trying to find the source of the leak? Seems strange to me. If I thought there was a leak, I'd be straight out of the house.'

'Aye,' Frank said. 'I guess he must have thought he was a jack of all trades.'

'Maybe they didn't recognise the leak until they got up close?' Lorraine asked.

'The gardener's widow still lives around here – Becky Morton,' Chelsea said. 'Not too well. Quite a religious zealot these days, I believe.'

'Could we keep these?' Frank gestured to the photo albums. 'We'll be careful with them.'

Chelsea nodded. 'Of course.'

Outside, Frank paused again to watch Alice work with the chestnut mare. Their movements were poetry in motion, each stride speaking of trust earned through patience and understanding. The kind of relationship that couldn't be bought or forced, only built through mutual respect.

'Now you hear me. Thank you for you.'

Stephen Walker wasn't in these photos, but that didn't mean they didn't hold the truth.

Somewhere in these albums, in these frozen moments of triumph and connection, could lie the answer. The truth about why a young woman with so much promise ended up in that lonely, forgotten grave.

Chapter Thirty-Eight

Stephen leaned against the doorframe, feeling his age.

His body stiffened, years of yoga practice offering little relief.

The sunset, through his floor-to-ceiling windows, highlighted every crease in Christie's dishevelled professional attire, and every tear which tracked on her face.

How quickly everything could unravel.

'Your mother is sleeping. Hearing you shouting exhausted her!'

'How dare you!' Christie narrowed her eyes.

Stephen observed her, unsure of how to proceed. The familiar impulse to comfort her felt wrong. It wouldn't work. For the first time in her life, he was the source of her pain rather than the one offering solace.

She was sitting on the sofa, and he considered sitting beside her. The space between them, even across the room, pulsed with unspoken tension. He stepped into the room, wincing. His joints were a mess. He made his way over to the opposite sofa and lowered himself.

'But she'll be okay...' Stephen said. 'Because she loves us and knows that misunderstandings happen in families. Just too much excitement, you know?'

'Excitement?' Christie's head snapped up, her tear-stained face twisting with disbelief.

And there it was again – the look he'd seen twenty minutes earlier when she'd burst through their front door. The hurt and the confusion. 'Have you not been listening to what I'm saying?'

'Of course, flower, but I think it's important we all calm—'

'Poison apples.' Her eyes blazed. 'That's what your former student, Georgina Prince, called us. Poison apples. Why would she say that?'

'I don't know...'

'Well, for a man so good with words, I'm surprised you don't have a fucking opinion on that expression!'

The venom in her voice made him flinch. Until today, she hadn't raised her voice to him since childhood. He was finding it hard to weather. 'Christie, please... your mother! And your language. You know better. Never resort to bad language during temper and argument – that's not how you make a point. That's not how you get through to people—'

'Piss off, Dad, not now. Not one of your lessons.'

He shook his head. Christie never swore. The shock of it unsettled him.

'A random woman just stormed into my classroom and pulled her son out because of you. Because I'm your daughter.' A bitter laugh escaped her. 'And you're concerned about coarse language?'

Stephen pressed his fingers to his temples and closed his eyes. 'I'm getting a migraine, flower.'

'Georgina hates you. Absolutely despises you. Enough

to take her son from the college without a second thought. And you don't have a clue?'

He continued massaging his temples. 'That doesn't make sense.'

'Rubbish. You need to think!'

He kept his eyes closed, but removed his fingers from his temples, and spread his hands in a gesture of helplessness. 'All I can say, honey, is that sometimes they hold grudges... ex-students... a suspension, here, or even a couple of detentions can do it. Years after the fact! You'll learn this in time—'

'Bollocks! This wasn't a detention or a suspension. This woman felt seriously aggrieved.'

He sank deeper into his armchair, feeling the weight of old secrets. 'Yes, it's strange. I'll look into it. This is wholly inappropriate.' He opened his eyes, the threat of a migraine subsiding slightly. 'I promise I'll get to the bottom of it, but I'm confident that it'll turn out to be nothing. In the meantime, you need to focus on your classes... and your career and—'

'I can't go back there.' She jumped to her feet and started pacing. 'I completely melted down in front of those kids. My first day, and I fell apart. It's ruined my career before it's even started. You've ruined my career by... by... whatever it is you've done.'

'Stop being so dramatic, Christie!' He only realised he'd raised his voice, for the first time, when he reached her name.

She whirled to face him, her finger jabbing the air like an accusation. 'Dramatic... excitable? Jesus, Dad... this is normal, and I want the truth.'

'I promise there isn't any!'

In one fluid motion, she yanked at the silver bracelet on

her wrist. The catch snapped. She hurled it onto the coffee table.

Stephen stared at the bracelet, his heart sinking.

Reach for the stars.

His stomach clenched as past, and present, blurred. 'I gave you that for your eighteenth birthday.'

'Why?' Her laugh was hollow. 'Did you just have a spare lying around?'

'You're being immature.' He glared at her now.

'Georgina had seen that bracelet before. Four times, she said. You told me it was original. Bespoke. Just for me.'

'It was. This is a lie. The woman is disturbed. You shouldn't listen to her!'

'But it was underneath my wrist!' Christie's voice rose to fill the room. 'The engraving! There's no way she could have read it! How would she have known?'

'I really can't answer that!'

A sound from the doorway made them both turn. Caroline stood there in her nightdress, grey-faced and swaying as if caught in an unseen wind. Tears carved paths down her cheeks. She whispered, 'It's happening again, isn't it?'

Stephen felt his insides turn to ice. Caroline's expression held more than confusion. The weight of old wounds reopening. She was going to make the situation worse.

He stood and moved towards her—

But Christie was there first with outstretched arms. 'Mum, please, I—'

Caroline recoiled and pushed their daughter harder than he thought possible. Christie stumbled backwards, catching the side of her head on the coffee table.

He felt his insides lurch.

'Christie!' He gasped, diving towards her.

His daughter rolled aside, clutching her head.

'Vicious girl!' Caroline's voice wavered with a fury Stephen hadn't heard in decades. 'Vicious, vicious girl!' She lurched forward, jabbing her finger at her injured daughter like a weapon. 'You won't destroy us. You won't keep hurting us again! Did you not learn?'

Christie pushed herself up with one hand, while holding her head with the other. Her father was putting his arm around her. 'Get off me!'

Stephen obliged, standing with his palms out.

'Mum?' Christie said from the floor. 'I don't understand.'

Caroline's entire face was trembling with fury. 'Get out of our fucking house!' She advanced, her movements jerky... unpredictable...

'It's me. It's me, Christie!' Blood oozed from her forehead.

Stephen could see that Caroline's eyes had glazed over. Her focus, fortunately, had moved somewhere else.

Stephen approached slowly, hands raised, ready to embrace her like his daughter had tried to. 'Honey, listen, it's me, Stephen. You need to lie down. Christie's hurt now and—'

The slap caught him with force, snapping his head to the side.

He stumbled backwards. It was another surprising display of strength.

'What've you done?' She inched forward, raising her hand, her eyes focused again. He let himself fall onto the sofa, holding his hands up to shield himself.

'This is all your fault!' Spittle flew from her lips.

She turned and ran from the room.

He listened carefully, worried he might hear the opening and closing of the front door, and was relieved, only momentarily, when he heard her feet on the stairs.

Christie staggered to her feet, clutching her head, which was bleeding.

Stephen stood again and held out his hands. 'Oh my dear, please I—'

'Stay back,' she cut him off, pointing at him with a bloody finger. Her face was as hard as stone. 'I'm going to find out who this Georgina Prince is...'

And then she was walking away.

This time, he heard the front door opening and closing.

Stephen pressed his fingers to his stinging cheek and closed his eyes. The present dissolved; he was back in Riverside College, decades melting away like snow.

He opened the door to a fierce knocking.

Georgina Prince stood there, her face contorted in fury.

'You can't be knocking so aggressively...'

She barged past him. It was totally unexpected. He was fortunate that he was holding the door still, so he could absorb the force, or he may have just fallen onto his back.

Georgina went over to Sarah, who was sitting on his office sofa, twirling her new bracelet, which caught the light of the dying sun through his office windows.

Georgina was shaking her head as she looked between them. 'Liars!' Georgina screamed. 'You're both fucking liars!'

Georgina ran, her footsteps thundering down the corridor, screaming, 'Fucking liars,' over and over.

He closed his door and sat beside Sarah and sighed. He watched her fiddle with the new bracelet he'd given her only moments before. She looked sad.

He put his arm around her and pulled her close.

The memory dissolved, and Stephen opened his eyes to his present reality. Christie's bracelet lay on the coffee table, catching the dying sunlight just as Sarah's had done all those years ago.

Yes, it said the same thing, but it didn't make it any less special, any less meaningful.

They had all been special. Each one, meaningful in their own way.

Chapter Thirty-Nine

Peter set to work on the pipes.

It'd been a long time, but his hands remembered.

He rolled back the years, measuring, cutting and fitting as if it was only yesterday.

Not that he didn't physically feel it...

His joints were stiff, and his back and forehead throbbed, but he didn't allow that to get in the way of the satisfaction.

Near the end, he paused for a cup of tea which Lucy had brought him ten minutes earlier. It was lukewarm, but he still drank it, admiring his handiwork, while catching his breath, praising himself on always being good at putting things back together again.

Well, most things...

A flash of memory ambushed him. He staggered to the sink, so he could put the mug down into it before he dropped it. He leaned into the work surface, taking deep breaths as the vision swept across his mind like a dark tide: shattered glass glinting like diamonds, twisted metal groaning, thick black smoke reaching toward heaven. He shut his eyes, forcing himself to breathe, just as his therapist had taught him. But the sounds still came – he could never silence those. The screams. The crying. His own voice raised in despair.

No. Such visceral memories were here to stay.

'Are you okay?'

It was the jolt he needed to really bring him back. He startled, and turned to find Mia watching from the doorway, her baby sleeping against her shoulder.

'Aye... just tired, that's all.'

'You sure?' She looked concerned.

He forced a smile that didn't quite reach his eyes. 'Aye, of course. Just not a spring chicken any more! How's the little lass?'

'Sleeping... she seems to do more of that during the daytime than at night at the moment...'

He nodded, smiling. 'It'll get easier, I'm sure...' He turned, his smile falling away. 'Best get on, though.' He looked out the window at the sunset. 'The day's getting away from us.'

Peter finished the job over the next hour and tightened the last fitting with perhaps more force than necessary.

He piled up the corroded pipes.

He popped outside, turned on the stopcock, returned and tested it.

All in working order.

Turning, he saw Mia had returned, this time without Sophie. He knew already that Lucy had left to do a shift at the supermarket. 'Where's Reece?'

'PlayStation, probably.'

Bloody layabout. 'Well, he's got a man's job down here. All of this needs taking to the tip.' He looked at his watch. 'He should catch it if he goes soon.' With a nod down at his work, he said, 'I also could do with showing him what I've done in case you've any teething errors.'

'A man's job!' Mia repeated, rasing an eyebrow.

Peter felt heat creep up his neck. 'Sorry... aye... old habits die hard, like. I get it's a different world now. And rightly so!'

'Rise of the women and all that?' Mia grinned..

His embarrassment deepened, but something about her teasing put him at ease. 'Truth be told,' he said. 'I did always think women were more capable than men. I was married to a very capable one for most of my life. She was more bloody capable than I'd ever be.'

'What was her name?'

'Donna. Aye.' He stood, stretching out. 'Very capable, lass, she was.' He touched his head, avoiding his injury. 'Understood things in here, too, better than I ever did. Better than most, to be honest. And, don't tell anyone.' He put his hand to his mouth and pretended to whisper. 'She'd still have sorted those pipes faster than I did.'

Mia laughed. 'Can you tell my brother that we're the greater sex then?'

A genuine laugh escaped him – when was the last time he'd laughed like that? This girl reminded him so much of her. His eagle. 'He'll know already. All men know, really. Just don't admit it.' He attempted a conspiratorial wink. 'The only person I ever admitted it to was Donna, because you know – there was no pulling the wool over her eyes. But in the interests of being cool, just her, like... Your brother will keep his thoughts secret for the same reason.'

'I don't know, maybe you should chat with him,' Mia said. 'He needs something in his life.'

'An old man like me – not sure he'll want to talk to me.'

'I don't know.' She smiled. 'You seem interesting enough, actually.'

'Bloody hell, we're coming on leaps and bounds here!' He whooped.

She laughed again. 'You're nuts... Anyway, you should see Reece's mates! Trust me, there isn't an interesting one amongst them.'

Peter stretched, wincing at the familiar pop of vertebrae. 'Well, I can guarantee I won't be competing with his playbox.'

She laughed. 'PlayStation.'

'Aye... that...' He gestured her over with weathered hands. 'So, now we know that you're the real man of the house – come over here.'

She approached, and he walked her through the new fittings, his explanation precise and methodical.

'Sounds a piece of piss.'

'Language... and don't you be belittling my hard work!'

She mimed zipping her lips.

He winked. 'But yeah, it is easy. Well, I'll get out of your hair.'

He was almost at the front door when Mia's voice stopped him. 'Mr Watson?'

'Peter, please. We've lived through a catastrophe together now.' He turned.

Mia was emerging from the living room, having just collected Sophie.

He shook his head. 'Nah... now—'

'That's a shame.'

He nodded. 'Let me know if there're any problems over the next twenty-four hours... any leaking, hit that stopcock, remember?'

'I will. Sorry for earlier. I think you're funny...'

Peter grinned. He felt his cheeks redden slightly. 'You know, I don't think I've heard that in a very long time.'

'You're misunderstood.'

He waved a finger at her. 'That's the word. Maybe you should tell my other neighbours that. Jake, at 7, would disagree.'

'Sounds like an idiot,' she said.

'No comment,' he said, smiling.

She turned Sophie around, the baby now awake and alert, her eyes bright with innocent curiosity.

Something drew Peter forward, despite every instinct screaming at him to leave. Reaching out, his calloused finger gently touched Sophie's cheek, then he pulled a face, and her giggle pierced straight through to his heart.

Inhaling deeply, he caught that unique baby smell.

After another giggle, he closed his eyes, drifting unintentionally towards a warm memory.

'Peter?'

He snapped back to the present, blinking rapidly. 'Sorry... don't know what went on there... worn me out...'

'Would you like to hold her?'

'Eh?' He took a step back.

'Sophie?'

He shook his head. 'No.' He backed away some more. 'I couldn't, possibly.'

'Why not?'

He held out his hands, watching them tremble. 'These old things for a start. Wouldn't be safe.'

'You just fixed our kitchen. I think they can handle Sophie. She doesn't wriggle that much. Go on...'

He could feel a cold sensation in his chest. 'No thanks.' He turned. 'Must—'

'Go on... She'd love—'

'No.' He only realised after that the word had exploded from him. He turned back, his eyes wild with decades-old pain.

Mia flinched, taking a protective step backward with Sophie. Her face shifted from concern to alarm.

He could see the damage his outburst had done. 'Sorry...'

Sophie's face screwed up and she cried.

She glared at Peter. 'Look what you did.'

Peter felt shame wash over him like a wave. 'Why don't you just bloody listen, then?' He exited the house, trudging away. At the end of the path, he realised how out of order he'd been. He turned back, meaning to apologise, but the door was already closed.

I'm sorry, okay... just... you know... he began in his head.

He started to edge back down the path, determined to ring the doorbell, but froze mid-way.

Really?

What was the point?

The damage was done.

Feeling remarkably low again, he sighed and went home.

He'd things to be getting on with.

Like doing himself, and the world, a fucking favour.

Chapter Forty

Your sister.

The words rang in Lewis's head as he wandered his father's house, each step heavier than the last.

Your sister.

He drifted through cold, unfamiliar rooms - a stranger in a house he'd rarely been inside. The phrase hammered in his skull: *What sister? How could there be a sister?*

His mind reeled. Not once in all these years had there been any hint, any whisper...

He moved through the house as if through a maze of secrets, each room holding potential clues in its drawers, cupboards, and wardrobes. His search began in the pristine living room - leather sofa, glass coffee table, abstract art. Expensive.ABlifeless.

The space felt as sterile as a museum display - all costly furnishings but devoid of life or warmth. No family photos, no personal touches, nothing to suggest anyone had ever truly lived here. Even the neat stacks of financial and car magazines appeared untouched, like props in a carefully staged scene.

After searching room after room and finding nothing but expensive order, and a lack of soul, he collapsed on the bed in one of the spare rooms, exhausted.

'Who is she, John?' His voice sounded hollow in the emptiness, like it belonged to someone else.

Was this even a truth?

Or had John's morphine-addled mind crafted one last lie?

His eyes fixed on the wardrobe door opposite. He realised he hadn't searched it yet.

With sudden determination, he was up and yanking open the door. Inside was a set of drawers. His hands shook as he pulled them open, rifling through meticulously folded clothing. Everything spoke of careful control – shirts arranged by colour, ties rolled with geometric precision, cufflinks nestled in velvet boxes like precious artefacts. He'd had countless failings. Most notably in parenthood. But no one could ever accuse his father of disorganisation.

A top shelf sat above head height, over a rack of expensive suits. American movies flashed through his mind – those inevitable scenes where characters discovered shoeboxes full of guns or cash. Given his father's life of secrecy, neither would have surprised him.

He reached up and latched onto a plastic container. It came down with surprising weight, dust dancing in the afternoon light.

When he removed the lid, the distinctive smell of chemical processing and trapped time hit him.

He upended the box onto the carpet, old photographs cascading. Frozen moments. So many. His chest constricted.

He began sorting through them with trembling hands, each image a punch to the gut: baby photos of him and

Felix. School plays. Birthday parties. Each one bore his father's precise handwriting, labelled with a curator's cold efficiency: Lewis, age six, Christmas 1983, admiring Millennium Falcon. Felix, age five, first bike, Christmas 1980. Scarborough beach, August 1981.

Felix's last Christmas, 1986.

Then, there were photos he surely couldn't have taken, like his graduation photo from university in 1999.

His father hadn't been present for many of these moments, but he'd collected them, preserved them, labelled them with an accountant's attention to detail. How many nights had John sat here in his final years, dying by inches, poring over these captured moments of a life he'd chosen to watch from a distance?

Had he regretted it? Trading family for money, women and success – watching them evolve, then fall apart, from a distance?

He felt himself welling up again, and the vulnerability of it made him angry. Angry at feeling anything for a man who'd documented their lives like a distant observer rather than a father. He swept his arm through the remaining pile, as a tear ran down his face.

The photos scattered.

He froze.

Among the scattered photos, one caught his eye. A woman he didn't recognise.

The woman had dazzling blue eyes, and carried a smile, filled with a lightness he'd not seen in his own mother again after Felix died... a lightness he couldn't ever remember feeling himself.

With trembling hands, he turned the photograph over, preparing for the truth.

Faded ink carried his father's familiar handwriting – not the precise documentation of family moments, but something hastier, more urgent.

A phone number.

Chapter Forty-One

They'd had the relentless snow, the heavy rains, the thick mists, and now, the icing on the cake – a brutal wind.

The incident room window rattled, and Frank looked into the darkness, which pressed against the glass like a living thing.

There he saw those forgotten remains festering. Year after year. In every season. In every conceivable weather.

He turned to his team, glad to have them in the flesh. 'Feels good. When I first started this job and the fax machine was playing up, I was told never to rely on technology. The same applies now.'

'The technology is reliable, sir,' Gerry said. 'If you update to fibre optics, as I recommend, you can cut out any issues.'

How many times?

'Thanks again Gerry.'

'Fibro optical, wasn't it, Gerry?' Reggie said.

Only Reggie and Sean laughed. Sharon and Clara knew better, and the sarcasm wouldn't interest Gerry.

Frank narrowed his eyes. Reggie gulped. 'Just a joke, boss.'

'And what a funny one it was, too. Well, as soon as technology becomes reliable, Reggie, you'll be the first to know... and the first to go.' He smiled. 'Somehow, I think I'd prefer a cleanly shaven robot.'

'I think you'll find artificial intelligence is already powerful enough to replace DS Moyes,' Sharon said.

A ripple of laughter went around the room. Clara, usually focused intently on her screen, even took a break for a chuckle.

'Whatever,' Reggie said and snorted. He seemed to take it in good humour. Although, the obscene mistaken moustache that jiggled on his top lip certainly took away Frank's remaining modicum of humour.

'Let's crack on. Margaret Matthews.' He paused, gathering his thoughts, and took a deep breath. 'She's dying. Bone cancer. One to two years, most she reckons. I'd like to think we can give her the answers she deserves before... you know. That's on us. I'm not shelving this case like the last lot.' He thumbed over his shoulder. 'So let's get to work on that board behind me – which is looking too bloody bare for my liking.' Outside, the wind howled. 'And listening to that, we probably don't want to be leaving too late.'

'More snow coming apparently,' Reggie said.

For fuck's sake, he thought, and then went through Margaret Matthews's interview.

At its conclusion, he announced, 'Gerry has been reading through the poetry and has picked up on a few things. She asked my opinion on it, but I'm not, despite popular belief, much of a poet... Gerry?'

Gerry straightened in her chair. Rylan lifted himself attentively and stood by her feet. 'There're a lot of references to secrecy and truth,' Gerry began. 'For example, in this one – "Truth lies beneath the surface, like stones beneath ice – waiting for the crack." Then, in another passage, there's a suggestion that she can trust someone, but not others – "In darkness, one light burns steady, unchanging, while others flicker and fade." But, the one, so far, that really stood out, was this: "Some gifts come with strings attached, pulling tighter, day by day, until you can barely breathe." Did someone make her feel special and take advantage of her?'

Rylan's tail thumped against the floor in approval as his handler finished speaking.

'There's more... a lot more... but those are the three that Gerry thought were the most important.' Frank said. 'The idea of someone taking advantage? It's hard not to think of this head teacher, Stephen Walker... It seems he made her feel special in this creative writing group, according to Margaret... and if so, what're these strings that were attached? Stephen Walker would have been forty when she disappeared. So, is he the older man in the red Fiesta? Is he one of the older men that she was observed with in the weeks before her death?'

'Stephen Walker's reputation is exceptional. He's an OBE for services to education,' Gerry said. 'He took on the headship in his early thirties. That's young, but under his leadership, the school saw a 37 per cent increase in students achieving top grades, which was fairly consistent throughout his entire leadership. He implemented many programmes for struggling students, particularly focusing on creative outlets. I spoke to a Yasmin Howes from the board of governors – they still reference his tenure as their "golden era". And his daughter, Christie Walker, has just started teaching English there.'

Frank moved to the window and looked out into the darkness again. 'It's a shame she didn't date the poems; tracking her state of mind while she wrote them might have been possible – allowed us to join more dots.'

'Yes,' Gerry said. 'There're definitely differences tonally and thematically between the poems. I could group them? Maybe that could give us an idea of her varying state of mind, possibly establish a timeline? It may be very vague, subjective even, but it may offer something – I detected a range of potential groups on first read.'

Gerry's mind always fascinated Frank. Where others saw chaos, Gerry found patterns. Detailed, explosive patterns.

'That would be fantastic, Gerry, but our priority, first thing tomorrow, is to pay a visit to Stephen Walker. Look at the man who turned around the youth of Ruswarp.' He realised his tone was sarcastic, and he was running before he could walk regarding this suspect – he could easily turn out to be the pillar of the community he was touted as.

'I'll look at the poetry again this evening, sir,' Gerry said.

He knew she would. 'Thank you, Gerry... now, let's get on to the infamous Tommy Reid.'

Sharon exchanged a glance with Reggie before speaking. Frank was already aware of the grisly experience that they'd spent together in that smoke-infested house. He needed it recapped, in detail, for Sean, Clara, and Gerry, though. Sharon did a fantastic job.

They all listened as Reggie explained the mysterious older friend, who was married.

'Why did Tommy not think to mention this during the first investigation?' Clara asked.

'Probably because Tommy thought it was a lie,' Sharon said. 'He thought she was inventing him to keep him on tenterhooks – make him believe she'd another option if he didn't knock the booze on the head.'

'The mother, though, Honey...' Reggie said, 'Now she thought he was very real. She made it clear she thought Sarah and this man were at it.'

'At it?' Sharon said with a raised eyebrow. 'Did you really just say that, sir?'

'In sexual relations,' he hissed, rolling his eyes. 'Anyway, Tommy told us that Sarah had insisted this man had stopped her from being banged up. So we'd another look into her criminal history. We know already that she was collared twice for shoplifting. Once in 1980, just after her father had gone to prison. A portable radio from Woolworths. Then, in 1981, when she was fourteen, she lifted a Walkman in Dixon's. This is where we caught a break. We caught up with the retired security guard who'd collared her. Roger Grip. He remembered the incident well. Mainly because, two months later, he'd changed jobs to WHSmith. A much bigger store. Here, he saw her again – except he wasn't the one who nabbed her. A colleague got to her first.'

'And yet there were only two recorded incidences?' Clara asked, seeking clarification to update HOLMES with the information.

'Yes. This time she stole a book—'

'A book?' Sean said, curling his lip. 'On what?'

'Horse riding,' Reggie said.

Frank noticed Gerry sitting up to attention. It was a compliment to Sharon and Reggie. They'd pulled on one hell of a thread here.

'This other security guard, much to the annoyance of Roger, let her go,' Reggie continued. 'Roger pointed out that he'd caught her before – that she'd a record. The other security guard said this was the point. It was more of a reason to let her go – because she could end up banged up in a juvenile centre. He didn't want her life ruined over a book on horse riding. He was not apologetic – but assured Roger that Sarah would never steal again. Guaranteed it, in fact.'

'Eh? But how can you guarantee that?' Sean asked, his face still creased from his last expression of surprise.

'Don't know,' Reggie said. 'But he was adamant. I can't say for certain she never shoplifted again, but there're no more records. So, he either stopped her somehow, or she got better at it! The security guard lost his job, as you'd expect. Roger never stayed in touch with him, so he couldn't confirm or deny that he'd helped her on the straight and narrow. However,' – he smiled to himself – 'he does remember this other security guard's name.'

'Bingo, you two...' Frank said. 'Bingo... Tell us about him.'

'Peter Watson. After losing this job, he set up his own security business, fitting alarms and locks and what not... His wife, Donna, worked as a paediatric nurse at Scarborough General. She died recently, in fact... last year... so he's living alone.'

The wind stilled for a moment as Reggie continued detailing Peter Watson. It was ominous and created a rather eerie atmosphere as he described an unspeakable tragedy.

Frank had already heard it, but the impact was barely reduced on the second listen. 'Good lord.' The words barely made it past the tightness in his throat.

Frank looked up and watched as Gerry's hand found Rylan's fur, seeking comfort in the familiar texture. The Lab pressed closer, sensing clear distress.

'It was a long time ago,' Reggie said.

Frank shook his head. 'There's no amount of time, Reggie, carrying that... no amount of time...' Frank paused for a deep breath, realising he'd witnessed too much human suffering in his life. As he exhaled, he said, 'Okay, so Sharon and Reggie will speak to Peter tomorrow while we're with Stephen. Should be interesting folks, as neither person was spoken to in the last investigation. So, let's think about this... Aside from the red Fiesta report, there were three other sightings of Sarah with an older man, remember? All three descriptions differed. Just throwing this out there... completely hypothetical of course... what if one was Stephen and another was Peter?'

'Then that would leave us with a third?' Reggie said.

'Your maths, DS, has come on leaps and bounds.' Frank went around the room, handing out a bundle of photocopied images. They were the four photographs of the mysterious man at the horse shows provided by the Winters sisters.

'Maybe this is him with Hannah Wright? The third older man. He seemed to take a keen interest in Sarah between 1981 and 1984.' He explained how he'd come across the images.

'He could have just been dating Hannah at the time? There may have been no actual connection to Sarah?'

'Maybe, Reggie, maybe.' Frank sighed. 'But I want to know who he is. Then, we can make a judgement call on that. Let's show this image to as many folk as possible.'

He turned to Sean. 'Run us through what you've found out about Hannah Wright, Sean.'

Sean sat up straight. 'Dr Hannah Wright was born in Ilkley. She was from old money – landed gentry with significant property holdings across Yorkshire.' He flipped through his notes. 'First educated at Roedean, then Oxford. First in Psychology before specialising in child psychiatry. Published extensively. Four textbooks on child psychology, focusing on alternative therapies. "Beyond Traditional Boundaries" became required reading in several universities. But it's her case studies that are interesting.' He pulled out a well-thumbed copy. 'She mentions a "Sandra" throughout. Pseudonym for Sarah, perhaps? After all, she claimed she was funding Sarah's treatment for research. I'll give you a quote – "Sandra's inherent connection with horses provided an emotional outlet previously denied by traditional therapeutic approaches. Through this connection, we witnessed not just healing, but transformation. The child who'd been labelled 'troubled' and 'unwilling to adapt' revealed herself to be extraordinarily gifted, and of profound emotional intelligence when given the right environment to flourish."'

'Sounds like our lass. Nicely written, too,' Reggie observed, stroking his moustache, making Frank wince.

'Gerry looked through some of it earlier with me,' Sean said, flipping pages. 'Gerry was drawn to this quotation – "Sandra represents the failure of conventional therapeutic approaches. Her perceived behavioural issues masked a deeper truth – a desperate need to be truly seen. Through our work together, I discovered that what others labelled as defiance was actually a fierce determination to be heard."'

'It sounded very personal,' Gerry added. 'It's formally written for a textbook, but I sense a deep fondness and adoration for Sandra.'

'Sarah?' Frank asked.

'I would agree,' Gerry added.

Frank moved back to the window, watching his reflection ghost against the dark glass. 'When were these published?'

'The first two books came out in '83 and '85. The last

one...' Sean checked his notes. 'Published posthumously in 1991, just after she died in the gas explosion.'

'Tell us about that.' Frank's voice carried an edge of anticipation.

'Only what we've covered so far. According to the fire investigator's report, the blast patterns were consistent with a gas explosion. The structural damage indicated the explosion originated in the cellar, where the gas main entered the property.' A sudden howl of wind interrupted Sean. For a second, Frank expected the double-glazed window to implode.

After a moment, Sean continued. 'Enough of Clive Morton was recovered for identification. Hannah's remains were more badly damaged, and identification was trickier. They could go as far as gender, and approximate age, but no further.'

Frank sighed. 'There always has to be a bloody question mark, eh? If not Hannah, then who? Well, let's keep the question mark, but run with Hannah for now – I can't see her abandoning her life's work... also, where did all her money go?'

'No living relatives. All her money went to a charitable trust. She didn't stand to gain much from faking her death then... But still,' Frank mused, 'something really bothers me about Hannah. A saint, a saviour, an angel... all these accolades... Maybe she was genuinely that altruistic... Pays for her education, her riding lessons. Writes books about their special connection. But then suddenly cuts all ties when Sarah returns to Tommy Reid. Some would argue she was enticing her to see sense, but what if there was something more? What if adoration had turned to hate... what if it later turned to murder?' Frank took a deep breath. 'I'm getting ahead of myself here, but such ruminations show how up against it we are! How about this Clive Morton?'

'I've something there,' Clara said. 'Once upon a time, he'd been a groundskeeper at Riverside College.'

Frank spun from the window. 'Really? When?'

'1986. Eight months.'

'Why did he leave?' Frank asked.

'Mutual agreement.'

'Eh? Why?'

'Sorry, no more details.' Clara said.

'Sarah went to university in Sept 1985, so her path didn't cross Clive's at Riverside... but they'd have crossed at Hannah's. She started there in 1988, right?'

'Yes... Clive started there in December 1987.'

'I see. So, add Clive to our list. We need to keep digging... bloody hell.' Frank pressed his fingers to his temples. 'Maybe he's the third man? "Mutual agreement"!' he snorted. 'My arse! God, how many sodding suspects do we need? They're tumbling out of the sky. Sean and Gerry, excellent work, can you speak to the governors at Riverside regarding this "mutual agreement" and find out as much as you can about this Clive character? Also, contact Becky Morton, Clive's widow, by phone. I heard she's on her last legs, so let's mine that bloody information, before we lose another witness to the great beyond. And everyone, remember the bloke in these pictures?' He tapped the photos with his finger on the table.

After everyone had left, Frank updated the board and then sat alone for a while, preparing some roll-ups to smoke on his way home.

He looked up at the picture of Sarah Matthews. Around her now, were pictures of different men, and Dr

Hannah Wright, all with lines, moving back and forth from Sarah, explaining their connection.

Peter Watson. That unspeakable tragedy. Did it turn you into someone compassionate, desperate to help put some light back in the world no matter the cost?

Or did it do the opposite? Take you down an even darker path?

Stephen Walker. An idol. An inspiration. Revered by a young student. That was nothing new. But those poems? If they were about him, was that really acceptable? How close could you really become to someone who you'd a duty of care to?

Clive Morton. A "mutual agreement" to walk away from a school where Sarah went, before getting a job where Sarah had one? Coincidence? Planned?

And mystery man in your pressed suit, with your expensive haircut – who were you really at the races for? Hannah? Or that poor young woman destroyed in a rotten old silo?

The night pressed against the windows.

And the biggest question of all: was Sarah's killer out there? Still alive? Walking free?

He stayed for a while, staring at the darkness into the forgotten stories of one girl, and so many others.

And then Frank Black desperately craved the light.

Chapter Forty-Two

Peter stared down at his armchair, the evening shadows lengthening around it like accusing fingers. He'd attempted to sit there three times tonight, but each time his restlessness had driven him back to his feet, wearing paths in the carpet with his pacing.

How could he have spoken to that poor girl like that?

He'd seen fear in her eyes.

Poor little Sophie had even started crying!

The urge to go over there and apologise was strong... but how could he apologise?

What could he say?

How do you tell a fifteen-year-old mother that sometimes the past reaches out with icy fingers, grabs you by the throat, and bounces you off the wall like a bloody football?

Her life would be anything but easy! What were the problems of some 'old fart' to her?

He sighed as he looked at Donna's photograph, her smile unchanged by time or dust. He could see her shaking her head. As she always did when Peter's temper got the better of him.

'I know, Don, love... I know...'

The bowl of paracetamol caught his eye on the coffee table, and he sighed a second time.

In a way, tonight, as he'd planned, was the perfect time for this.

Before he caused any more bloody damage!

Still, deep down, he knew he wouldn't go through with it this evening.

It may have been completely irrational to think so, but he didn't feel like he could check out without making things right with Mia.

Could he really stomach offending that child as his last act on earth?

Mending those pipes would have been a perfect swansong.

Oh, Don, why did I have to fuck it up—

A knock at the door startled him.

Now what?

It was the same issue as yesterday – whoever came to his door at this bloody time?

He looked out through the window. Lucy in her supermarket uniform, holding something beneath a tea towel. Her stunt car driver of a son, Reece, was beside her. The lad had his hands deep in the pockets of his baggy tracksuit bottoms, and his shoulders were hunched. The perpetual earphones were also gone, leaving him looking oddly vulnerable.

Hopefully, she'd finally had him on the end of a good bollocking.

The wind was strong tonight, so it whipped their jackets up and around them.

They hadn't spotted him watching, so he slipped back into his solitude.

He really didn't like guests. Okay, Lucy, he could handle now. She'd been much nicer than he'd expected. Although, if she knew about his altercation with Mia, he too might be about to get a bollocking! *But the lad... no way was he coming in here. No bloody way!*

Plus, he'd prefer to maintain the peace and quiet.

He looked around the lounge where he'd spent the last couple of hours pacing, and almost laughed out loud.

What peace and quiet, old man? You'd have to be knocked unconscious again to sit still!

He headed to the front door, sighed and opened it. He could feel the wind. 'Blowing a gale tonight, eh?'

'Yes.' Lucy smiled, hopping from foot to foot, and raising her eyebrows. 'You haven't given me a chance to thank you! The work you did... well... it's fantastic!'

'There's no need,' he said. 'It was my pleasure.'

Obviously, you haven't spoken to Mia yet, he thought.

'Are you okay?' Lucy asked, squinting.

'Yeah... why?'

'You look pale...' She pointed at his head. 'Do you want me to look at that?'

'It's fine. It's just a bump. Yesterday, I banged it on the mantelpiece, bending over and picking something up.'

'Go on.' She inched forward. 'Let me check it. Mum is a nurse.'

'Aye, so was Donna, my wife. I know what to look for.'

She looked disappointed. 'Okay, if you're sure?'

'I am. Just tired. In fact, it was my pleasure, but I'm beat now. That's probably why I'm pale. So—'

She cut him off. 'How much do I owe you?'

How many bloody times!

'Think nothing of it... a housewarming gift. Now, if—'

'Please, let me give you something. Just a little bit.'

'No need. I told you I got the parts for free,' he said, repeating his lie from earlier.

'And the labour?'

'Well, I wasn't doing anything else, and I'm retired, so my time costs nowt.'

Lucy smiled. 'Well, thank you, that's one mega housewarming present! I doubt I'll get any more, but if I do, it won't be a patch on yours.'

'You're welcome. Now, I'm quite tired.' *And I need to figure out what to say to your daughter tomorrow when she's cooled down.*

Lucy thrust whatever she had wrapped in the tea towel toward him. Steam escaped from beneath the cloth, carrying the rich aroma of tomatoes and herbs. 'Well, I've tested out my improved kitchen – made spag bol. So, here's your portion.'

That made him feel quite ashamed of his clear desperation to get rid of them. When was the last time someone had cooked for him? 'Thanks, but you don't need to be this generous.'

'Take it or I'll be paying for the kitchen.'

He accepted the bundle, feeling its warmth against his palms. The heat seemed to travel up his cold arms.

'Also...' Lucy gave Reece a meaningful prod between the shoulder blades. 'Reece wants to say something.'

Even though Reece had gone out earlier to collect the parts, he'd avoided all contact with Peter when he'd got home with them – leaving them at the foot of the stairs and disappearing straight to his room to hit the computer games, apparently. This was the first time Peter had been this close to the lad. There wasn't much to the lanky streak of piss, to be honest. Eighteen, but he could just have easily been fifteen.

Reece shuffled his feet, looking down at his trainers, the bravado of the street swagger he'd seen yesterday very much replaced by teenage awkwardness. 'Sorry about the driving, earlier.'

'Reckless,' Peter said, crossing his arms. 'One day, your squealing tyres are the last thing some poor bugger is going to hear!'

He waited for Reece to respond. It took a while. 'I promise not to drive like a dickhead again.'

He inwardly sighed, feeling a moment of sympathy. The poor lad didn't have a father to point some basics out to him. He gave him a break. 'It takes a real man to apologise...'

He caught Lucy's frown and recalled Mia calling him out on his old-fashioned sexism earlier.

'A real character...' he corrected himself.

'Sorry, again,' Reece said and looked at Lucy. 'Can I crack on with the car now, Mum?'

She nodded.

'See ya,' he said, nodding at Peter, before turning and running back towards their home, the wind pulling his jacket up behind him like a superhero's cloak.

'What's wrong with his deathtrap?' Peter asked.

'Struggling to start.'

'Probably a good thing, eh?'

Lucy laughed.

'Let me know if he can't get it going,' he said.

'You've done enough.' Realising he was holding the food, and he had a nice person on his doorstep, he felt a pang of guilt for not inviting her in. Donna would have had his head for it. 'You want to come in? Tea?'

'I can't stop... but if you let me look at that head, I'll be grateful. And a minute out of this bloody wind would be nice!'

He nodded and allowed her in.

A couple of minutes later, he was in the armchair, having his wound cleaned and bandaged properly. She checked that he'd been to the hospital.

'Aye, all good,' he lied.

'And they didn't want to give you stitches?'

'No need, they said.'

She shook her head. 'These days, eh? No time for anyone. I doubt this will close up in a hurry on its own.'

'I'll give it another day or two.'

She regarded his bowl of paracetamol on the side table. 'Funny way to store your pain killers?'

He felt his blood run cold. 'Eh?' He looked over at it, trying to give the impression that he didn't know what she meant. 'I've always done that. Popped them from the blister packet, save space.'

'I suppose if you don't have children around.'

'Aye.'

She stood. 'Anyway, I best get back to the madhouse.'

He followed her to the hall.

'Once again, I'm so grateful. Enjoy the spag bol.'

'Listen, I was sharp earlier, with Mia. I think I scared her. She asked me to hold Sophie and I didn't want to. I was tired, like.'

Lucy nodded. 'Mia can be intense sometimes. Overwhelming. With people she likes. She obviously likes you.'

'I think this was more my fault – I'll come and apologise tomorrow if that's all right.'

'I'm sure it won't be necessary.'

'It is,' he said.

She turned around in the front door and smiled. 'Well...' Her eyes drifted over his shoulder and she noticed something. She looked intrigued. He followed her line of sight to the clothes peg. To two pink jackets side by side. A larger one, Donna's, and a smaller, child's one. When he looked back, Lucy's mouth was opening to ask an obvious question, but something in his expression must have dissuaded her.

'Well, thanks for the food,' he said, quickly retreating behind his door. 'And the bandage. Night then.'

'Night.'

He closed the door.

He turned, stroked the small coat, sighed, and went to eat the spag bol.

'It was almost as good as yours,' he told Donna's photograph after. 'Almost.'

He finally settled down and spent a while thinking about Mia, and how she'd made him laugh before they fell out.

No wonder she'd reminded him of his eagle earlier. They, too, had had a tempestuous relationship, especially towards the end.

Fierce independence and personality had always captivated him, but so often, he realised, it came with costs.

Mia was so like her. The way she carried herself, that determination to be heard…

His feet carried him there before he could stop himself, his hands moving with the weight of memory as he opened the drawer and pulled out the thank-you card.

He regarded the picture of the soaring eagle on the front.

After reading the poem, he smiled, nudged a tear away, replaced the poem in the drawer, and closed it.

Another ghost.

Among many.

He turned to head up to bed, looking forward to the morning when he could see Mia again. To apologise, of course.

Chapter Forty-Three

The wine bottle hadn't been full when Christie started it, but there'd been well over half, and now it was empty.

At least the alcohol numbed the throbbing in her head from slamming into her parents' coffee table.

She closed her eyes and thought of her confused, angry mother.

Vicious, vicious girl!

Georgina's words about poison apples clung to her like a stain she couldn't scrub off.

Where the hell had this day come from?

She'd hoped that the alcohol would steady the storm in her mind. It hadn't. If anything, it'd stirred it up, and it now joined in with the gale outside, sounding like some fucking tempest.

Still, she had no choice but to chase the storm. She grabbed her laptop, which was sitting alongside some lined-up Christmas cards from family.

With a deep breath, she opened her laptop and started digging.

Over time, her fingers struck the laptop keys with increasing force, but she could find nothing but glowing praise for her father, Stephen Walker.

He had an untouchable legacy in educational circles.

The tributes seemed to mock her paranoia from the screen: improving test scores, innovative programmes for troubled students, glowing testimonials from former pupils.

'Stephen Walker OBE represents the very best of British education.' The words of Sir Geoffrey Pembroke MP burned into her wine-blurred vision.

Tireless dedication...

Commitment to troubled youth...

Focus on the arts and creativity in those less fortunate...

A national treasure.

Nothing about *poison apples*.

Her mother's confrontation raged hard in her memory again. *You won't keep hurting us again! Did you not learn?*

Who'd she been referring to? Georgina Prince? Or one of the other four girls with that bracelet?

Reach for the stars.

She recalled her mother turning on her father. *What've you done? This is all your fault.*

The answer was starting to feel too obvious.

Too painfully obvious.

Had her father – beloved headmaster, dedicated educator, recipient of countless accolades – really abused—

'No!' she said out loud.

She wasn't ready to go there yet. She just couldn't.

He'd been the most important person in her life. Her inspiration. If he fell from that pedestal, then she'd surely fall with him.

Two poison apples falling together.

'So who are you Georgina Prince? And why have you set fire to our lives?'

Her fingers flashed over the keys.

The LinkedIn profile for Georgina Prince glowed accusingly on her screen. Marketing Manager at some firm in Scarborough. A mobile telephone number listed at the bottom of the profile.

Christie's fingers hovered over her phone. The wine urged her forward, past hesitation, past fear. She dialled before she could lose her nerve.

One ring. Two. Three.

'Hello – yes?' Georgina's voice was sharp, and so very familiar from earlier at the college.

'It's Christie Walker... today, you—'

'I know who you are.' A harsh intake of breath. 'You shouldn't be calling. This is my business phone, which the college doesn't have. So I guess you've been looking me up?'

The wine surged in Christie's blood, turning fear into anger. 'How can I not after what you said to me today?'

'I think I made it very clear who you should speak to.'

'I need to know the truth!'

Georgina snorted. 'You've come to the wrong place then, love. You know where to go...'

Christie narrowed her eyes. She may have been pushed into a corner earlier, but she had alcohol fuelling her now. 'Your suggestions bring up nothing online. Now, how can that be if you're not lying? For all your talk of poison, and a multitude of bracelets, I can find nothing but praise for my father—'

'Because there never was an investigation.' Georgina's interruption cracked like a whip.

'You said four girls.'

'There were four bracelets… that's not a lie.'

'Four girls are enough for an investigation…'

'Speak to them about it, then? Or your father? Only he knows the truth of why nobody spoke.'

'It seemed to have everything to do with you today.'

'I don't want your father near my son knowing what I know. You're a connection. That's enough for me. A Walker. Let's leave it at that.'

'No.' Christie's voice found an even harder edge she didn't know she possessed. 'You can fucking well talk to me. You've opened this can of worms.'

'A can of worms! Ha.'

'What else do you call it?'

Silence crackled between them. Christie could hear her own heartbeat in her ears, feel the wine burning through her veins.

Georgina didn't hang up.

Did she want to speak?

Was she happy to be pushed?

Maybe, she should try appealing to her ego. 'Look, Mrs Prince… Sorry for getting wound up,' Christie continued, pressing her advantage. 'I'm a good person, not poison, and I can tell you mean well… If you help me understand, you'll see that like you, I'm kind, I care.'

There was another period of silence before Georgina sighed. 'Maybe I was over the top with you, Christie. I shouldn't have called you those things… the sins of the father aren't the sins of the daughter and all that. But you'd understand it if you were in my shoes.' Georgina sounded more distant and haunting than angry. 'After everything that happened, I've built a life. A good life. It's not my place to change the outcome on what happened, and all I can do is keep my son away. It is all I can offer.'

'How could it be such a good life?' Christie pressed the phone harder against her ear. 'If you're still angry enough to humiliate a stranger in front of her students. There's bitterness.'

'Maybe... but if I hadn't seen that bracelet, I'd have held it together better.'

Christie's free hand went to her wrist where the bracelet had been, the skin there feeling naked, exposed. 'What does that mean?'

'I can't speak about the other three girls. I never spoke to them. But ask him about Sarah Matthews.' Georgina's voice dropped to a whisper.

The whisper seemed to freeze the air in Christie's lungs, but she managed to speak. 'So, this Sarah was part of the writing group?'

'Oh yes – very much so.'

'Maybe I should speak to her.'

'You can't.' A breath. Then softer, almost a whisper. 'She disappeared many, many years ago.'

Christie's grip on the phone tightened, her pulse hammering in her ears. 'Who was she?'

'My best friend. Or at least she was. She stole my poems, okay? My fucking poems. Great. It got her into that creative writing club but look how that turned out for her, eh? I'd be thanking her if I knew where she'd bloody run off too – sparing me that trauma. Look, leave it at that... I've said too much... Ask him about Sarah Matthews and leave me alone. We're done.'

The line went dead, leaving Christie alone with the spinning room and her spiralling thoughts. Her hands trembled as she typed 'Sarah Matthews' into her laptop.

The first headline hit her hard.

It was from the beginning of 1990.

Margaret Matthews giving up hope over her missing daughter, Sarah.

She put her hand to her mouth.

Chapter Forty-Four

Lewis watched the steady rise and fall of his father's chest.

It seemed impossible that this peaceful figure was the same man who'd been writhing in agony merely hours ago.

The photograph he'd found felt heavy in Lewis's hands, its edges worn smooth from his constant handling. He couldn't take his eyes from the woman with piercing blue eyes and an enigmatic smile.

Like a ritual he couldn't break, Lewis turned the picture over and looked at the familiar phone number. There was little point. He'd already memorised it. How could he not? His eyes burned from studying every detail, every shadow.

01483.

Guildford.

The location sparked possibilities that made his chest tight. An affluent area. Had his father owned a place there? He'd enough financial success to fund another home. Or had someone important to him lived there?

Another life?

He closed his eyes and imagined Felix. Memories of

him were his go-to in turbulent times. His brother had died at twelve, yet he remained frozen in time – always older, always a role model. His wonderful guide had been there to help him when he'd beaten Gregg Inch into a coma and spent years inside, advising him to take up mindfulness, to work on his anger, to let go of the past and his demons.

Always, when he went to his brother Felix, it was in that memory when he taught him how to skateboard. His brother had been so full of patience and encouragement that day. He'd made Lewis feel special, although he'd kept falling and falling.

'Watch this, little brother!' Felix would execute a perfect kick flip, desperate to inspire him.

Even now, decades later, Lewis could still hear the pride in his brother's voice when he finally mastered it.

But it wasn't this memory his mind was interested in now.

It was another one.

A darker one. One he'd not gone to for many years.

One that had been truly buried.

Two weeks before he died of meningitis, Felix came home crying. He'd followed their father on his skateboard to work, only to see him meet a woman for coffee at the train station.

'I saw her,' Felix whispered. 'It's not right, Lewis. I saw them kissing. And she... God, she was so beautiful... those incredible blue eyes...'

Lewis snapped back to the present, focusing again on the woman in the photograph - her striking gaze the same vivid blue as the one Felix had described. *Was this the beautiful woman his brother had been talking about?*

She was certainly beautiful.

Back in those turbulent years, this wasn't the first time

Lewis and Felix had had to confront their father's deceit. Their aunt had often made veiled references to John's indiscretions, much to their mother's fury, who was fearful they'd picked up on it.

Which they had done, of course.

'Not in front of the boys,' Caroline would snap at her sister, but the damage had already been done, and you could be sure she'd be back to cause more.

The chances were, on that day in the train station, Felix had only seen one of his father's many women.

But still – what if it'd been this woman in the photograph?

Could she be the mother of their sister? A half-sister he'd never known?

The possibility made his hands shake. The way incidences linked and connected through time. And it took only a minute before he became absolutely convinced that Felix had glimpsed their father's other life at the train station that day before carrying the truth all the way to his grave the following month.

But not before leaving the seed to gestate in his younger brother.

Lewis's heart pounded against his ribs. He was ready.

His fingers trembled as he took out his mobile and dialled. Each ring seemed to last an eternity. The sound echoed in the quiet room like a countdown. On the fifth, a woman answered. An older woman with a gravelly voice. 'Hello, can I help you?'

His mouth went dry, tongue sticking to the roof. He hadn't planned what to say, hadn't thought beyond needing to know. The words tumbled out before he could stop them. 'Who are you? Who am I speaking to?'

A pause stretched between them, before, 'Actually, maybe you should tell me who you are?'

Fair response. He sighed. *I've nothing to lose.*

'I'm Lewis White.'

The silence that followed felt thick enough to choke on.

If the name meant nothing, wouldn't she have responded immediately? He pressed his advantage. 'My father is John White. I thought you may know him.'

He waited, desperately wanting her to crumble under the weight of the surprise. Wanting so badly for her to spill the truth.

'I can't help you,' she said.

'So, you don't know him?'

'No, so I'm afraid I can't help.'

Frustration tightened his throat, making his throat crack. 'He's dying, you know. Here, right in front of me, dying of cancer. He can't have long left. Days. Hours. Who knows?'

Another weighted silence.

Why are you so quiet? Is there something personal there?

Are you the woman in the photograph? The blue-eyed lover Felix saw at the train station?

Finally, she spoke. 'I'm sorry to hear that. It is an unforgiving part of life – to see your parents die. I hope your father is at peace, I really do. But I don't understand why you've contacted me. How did you get this number?'

He explained about the photograph, his father's laboured breathing filling the silence. 'You... were obviously very special to him.'

Again, silence lingered, pregnant with possibility.

'I'm really sorry. I can't help you. Our phone line must have reused an old landline number... you know how that can happen when you change companies.'

It was very plausible.

'I really hope your father isn't suffering,' she added. Something in her tone made his skin prickle. Did he detect a sadness there, perhaps, that transcended mere sympathy for someone unknown to them?

'He wanted to tell me the truth about something.' Until we drugged him senseless again, he thought bitterly, watching the morphine drip its steady rhythm. 'I don't think he can rest until...'

'I see... I'm so sorry I can't help.'

Desperation clawed at his throat. 'He said I'd a sister?' His pulse roared in his ears.

She sighed. 'I'm sorry...' she said. 'You've made a mistake.'

'Please,' he said.

'I'm going now, Lewis.' The words echoed, then settled like a heavy stone in his chest. 'I'm sorry for your loss.' The line went dead.

He stared at the phone.

I'm going now, Lewis.

She'd sounded as if she knew him.

Fingers shaking, he tried calling back immediately but got an engaged tone. He kept trying throughout the night, watching his father sleep while the busy signal repeatedly mocked him.

His father's words echoed in his mind: *Your sister.*

His brother's: *I saw her.*

Hers: *I'm going now, Lewis.*

With all these voices, he felt like his head was going to split in two. While outside, the winds battered the windows, and somewhere in Guildford, a phone remained stubbornly engaged.

Chapter Forty-Five

Gerry sat cross-legged on her living room floor, with Sarah Matthews' poetry spread out in careful arcs around her. Rylan lay nearby, watching her, but perfectly at ease.

Tonight, she could feel the tiredness creeping up on her – it'd been a weighty day, heavy with emotion, but she had stumbled onto something significant and she wanted to focus a short while longer.

Sometimes, if she felt tiredness like this in Rylan's presence, she could close her eyes for a couple of minutes and listen to his steady panting. If she followed along in her mind, she could often slip into a tranquil state for fifteen minutes, which left her feeling contented, refreshed, and ready to go again.

Most of Sarah's poems pulsed with unprocessed emotion and were raw, direct, and honest. She could sort these poems easily into four groups: 'anger/confusion'; 'relief/understanding'; 'gratitude/connection'; and 'despair'.

However, there were six poems which differed wildly from the others and didn't really fit into one of the four groups. She called this pile 'anomalies'.

Interestingly, two of these six poems had 'submission?' written across the top. Someone had struck a line through the word on one, but not the other. Had this been submitted to a publisher?

She reread this one. It was called 'The Beginning'.

Childhood dreams, dandelion seeds.
Scattered.
Floating on air and precious.
Dance, innocence, dance.
Winter's wisdom is coming.

Calculated and controlled poetry. It didn't fit with everything they knew about Sarah Matthews so far in their investigation. These weren't the words of a troubled teenager finding her voice – they weren't primal screams; they were the work of someone who already knew exactly what they wanted to say – crafted and polished.

In that moment, she was sure – someone else had written the 'anomalies'.

The mystery thickened.

Next, she had a go at trying to establish a timeline with the poems. Not in the order they were written, because poems were reflections, but on how they married up with what they knew about her life so far.

It was difficult, but she quite enjoyed the task.

On top of her 'Anger/Confusion' pile, she had a Post-it note that said:

Childhood to 13 (1980). Rory's drinking, abusive behaviour, sexual relationship with Tommy, Rory imprisonment and death, shoplifting, poor behaviour at school.

She moved to the next pile, 'Relief/Understanding'.

14-15 (1981-82). Dr Hannah Wright – free counselling/horse riding. Peter Watson supporting her regarding criminal behaviour? Man accompanying Hannah to watch Sarah ride (4 times)?

The third pile. 'Gratitude/connection'.

16-21 (1983-8). Developing bond with headteacher Stephen Walker? Discovering poetry as an expression? Further development of a relationship with Peter Watson? Dr Hannah Wright? (Nursing qualification paid for, job taken). Was the man from the photos still about? Did she get to know Clive Morton while he was the gardener for Hannah?

The final pile: 'Despair'.

22 (1989). Tumultuous relationship with Tommy. Hannah's anger and ultimatum. Unemployed. Despair over loss of connections?. Sightings with older men – Stephen? Peter? Clive? Man in earlier image? Red Fiesta?

She traced the arc of poems in her mind, leading them to the silo. To bones hidden behind rotting wood.

Then, the aftermath. A gas explosion in 1991 which killed gardener Clive Morton and Dr Hannah Wright, although there was a question mark over her remains, due to them being so badly destroyed.

With this organisation, she planned questions to ask Peter and Stephen. She'd send some over to Sharon and

Reggie for Peter, and they could choose whether to use them. She'd run the Stephen Walker questions by Frank in the car in the morning. He'd already checked out a decent car from HQ and taken that home, so he was picking her up around eight.

For another hour, she continued to read the poems, trying to jar loose other insights. A single verse, or even a single word, might hold the key to understanding what had really happened to Sarah Matthews.

She checked her phone again – no messages from Tom. This would be the first evening in months he'd made no contact whatsoever. The memory of his face when he'd discovered her marriage considerations list created an uncomfortable sensation in her stomach.

She attempted to meditate for fifteen minutes, tuning herself to Rylan's breathing, but it didn't work. Her thoughts refused to align themselves with their usual neat patterns.

Have I been that unreasonable?

She'd meant to discuss it with Frank, knowing he'd offer his particular brand of gruff wisdom. She could almost hear his voice: 'Ditch the list, lass. Marriage isn't about rules and regulations.'

Words of wisdom to the neurotypical, perhaps. But they didn't work for her.

She remembered Frank once telling her how it'd taken Mary ten years to get used to him. 'We'd to learn how to dance without knowing the steps... and even then, she could barely put up with me.'

Many would have laughed at such a comment – she knew that.

It was sarcasm and Frank, unlike her, was exceptional at it.

Still, the joke had stuck out like a mathematical error she couldn't resolve.

But if she wanted a shot at a future, with a man that she was nearly 90 per cent sure she loved, she needed to do what she hated doing above all else.

She said the word out loud, hoping it might reduce its harshness. 'Compromise.'

The word felt foreign on her tongue, like an equation she couldn't solve.

She texted Tom.

> Can we meet tomorrow after work? I'd like to discuss things properly.

Her phone remained silent as the evening deepened, but Rylan stayed close, his presence a reminder that some connections did transcend the need for rules and regulations. Some things, like his unwavering loyalty, couldn't be captured in a spreadsheet or reduced to a list of requirements.

She poured herself a glass of water and tried to go to bed.

Even some melatonin couldn't help her sleep.

Was it Tom's silence that kept her awake?

Or the knowledge that, by morning, she might be face to face with a killer?

Chapter Forty-Six

With flowers in hand, Frank stepped into Evelyn's hospital room.

Evelyn's face brightened when she saw him, though fatigue shadowed her eyes. She looked small against the starched hospital sheets. 'What a surprise...'

'Aye, Frank and flowers – what more could you want?' His attempt at lightness felt clumsy, but he pressed on. 'Hope this is okay? Janet phoned me and said you were staying in another night – she asked me to pop in, cheer you up.' He placed the flowers where she could see them and settled in the chair beside her bed. 'I said I could pop in, couldn't guarantee the cheering up, though.'

'Nonsense, you already have done,' Evelyn said as Frank took a seat. The plastic creaked beneath his weight, making him feel rather embarrassed.

'So how are you feeling?' he asked.

'Oh, fine... but listen, I know it's the pot calling the kettle black, but you look exhausted.'

'Ha! Don't you worry about me. This is default. Always

walking around half-comatose. Imagine the damage I could do if I was actually awake?'

She laughed. 'I guess you can experience being completely awake again when you retire.'

'I'll give it careful thought.'

Being wide awake with nothing to do sounded like a one-way ticket to self-pity hell. All day to consider everything he'd lost in his life, and countless other failings...

'What've you been doing?' Frank asked.

'Apart from lying here?'

He smirked. 'Aye.'

'Watching *Celebrity MasterChef.*'

He dropped his spectacles over his eyes and looked up at the mounted television. Somebody was showcasing a cheesecake. 'They're celebrities?'

'Yes... you don't recognise him?'

Frank squinted. Then shook his head. 'Not unless it's Eric Clapton or Roger Waters... What does that fella do?'

'He's a social influencer.'

'A what?'

'Someone who makes a lot of videos for people to watch.'

'Ah... like *You've Been Framed*?'

'Are you serious?'

He shook his head. 'Nah. I've heard of these YouTube celebs. Sounds ridiculous. I did like *You've Been Framed* though. At least to start with. Got a bit tedious later on, like.'

She pointed up at the screen. 'Mind if I watch this part? Just want to see who wins.'

'Of course, aye...' Frank kept his eyes on the screen, feigning interest.

Within seconds, words were echoing in his mind: *Some*

gifts come with strings attached, pulling tighter, day by day, until you can barely breathe.

Before he knew it, he was on that tragic rollercoaster of Sarah Matthews' short life again—

'Earth to Frank?'

He blinked and noticed the credits were rolling on *Celebrity MasterChef*. 'Bloody hell. Sorry. Away with the fairies. Although forget fairies. There's nothing magical about where I've just been away to.'

'Where's that, then?'

'You'd rather not know.'

'Maybe I would.' She turned the television off with her remote.

'Good job I'm not allowed to tell you about it then.'

She sighed. 'Fair enough. Is there something other than the case weighing on you?'

He sighed. 'Nothing in particular.'

'Doesn't sound like it.'

He met her gaze with uncertainty. 'No... I'm fine...'

'Go on. One thing on your mind and then I'll leave off, promise.'

He looked at her for a moment, working out how to change the subject, when he noticed something in Evelyn's eyes. Something familiar.

It was a similar look to the one Mary used to give to him when he shut himself off. A look that could draw a splinter from a wound.

'It's just all these investigations... well, they always seem to connect back to me. Or rather, they make me reflect on my own life... and... oh, I don't know, maybe it's just getting old and being filled with regret. Bloody hell, forget me, this all sounds foolish and you're tired, and the one in hospital—'

'Behave. I'm interested. Tell me what the connection is?'

'The usual, I guess...' The words stuck in his throat for a moment before breaking free. 'Parenting... I spent my entire career dealing with it – neglect, abuse, the way it echoes down through generations. The damage it does.' He shook his head. 'I thought I knew better. But when I look back, I wonder – was I really any different?'

'I bet you were.'

'I wish. Nah. I was a poor father – work obsessed. I wasn't there enough for her. Wasn't sensitive enough when she needed me. Not hearing... I mean really hearing... when she needed me to listen.'

He looked down, studying his hands. How had he failed so spectacularly in holding on to the things that mattered most?

'Look Frank, I know people change, but knowing you as I do now, I just can't see you being as bad as you're making out. I think we can always look back and see things in new ways – those new ways don't always feel good. But things change in the world all the time. I imagine you were busy... you're a police officer, after all... and think about how many people you've helped. You loved your daughter. She would have known that – felt it – even if you weren't always there. Love isn't just in words.'

'Then why have I lost her?'

'Isn't it possible that the reason isn't you? Life, sometimes, just... happens? With or without parental approval and guidance.'

He didn't want a get-out clause. Yes, parenthood over the ages was an interesting concept. It ebbed and flowed with the times. Still, the core remained. Love. The expression of love. That could, and should, never change. He should have expressed it more. 'The problem is, I've always been this angry. Probably because my father never showed me any attention either. And when he did, it was physical. Aggressive... He was a big drinker. Lacked emotion. Always angry. What do they say about apples falling from trees?'

Evelyn shook her head. 'I don't think you're angry.'

'Really? Come and speak to my colleagues.'

She continued to shake her head. 'I see a man who makes himself unapproachable, but I don't see a man living in fury.'

'Similar though?'

She reached for his hand, her touch surprisingly warm. 'No, Frank. Anger burns everything it touches. What you do – keeping people at arm's length – that's not anger. That's fear. Fear of being hurt again, of failing again. You're not your father, Frank – try not to compare yourself to him.'

He took a deep breath and steered the conversation to Evelyn, and what she planned to do for the rest of the week. It was Christmas Eve at the weekend, so they planned to meet the day before. He almost offered to pick her up, but then remembered it'd be in Bertha, and she was in no fit state to bounce around the interior of his banger.

He'd miss Bertha, but his new year's resolution had to be to get a new car... make things easier with Gerry, and his new friends, like Evelyn.

Before he left, Frank squeezed her hand gently. 'Get some rest.'

'You too. And whatever this case is – don't let it swallow you whole.' She caught his eye. 'You're a better man than you give yourself credit for.'

Outside in the car park, Frank checked his phone – he'd had it off in the hospital. One missed call from Henrietta. She'd left a voicemail.

'Frank, someone came to your door about twenty minutes ago. Youngish, looked nervous. I don't think it was the lad who came with your daughter last time, but I can't be sure.'

Bloody hell, he thought, *not again!*

'Anyway, I took a photo through my window, then opened my door and asked who he was. Sorry, he ran off. Thought you should know.'

His heart lurched as he opened the attached photo. As was often the case these days, the lad wore a hoodie pulled low over his face. It told him nothing.

Bollocks!

He got into the Audi he'd taken out from the carpool and let out a string of obscenities.

Why can't I catch a break with my daughter? Be here, when her, or one of these scrotes – of which there seemed to be an endless supply – shows up?

As he drove back, he wondered if this particular scrote had paid a visit of his own accord. After all, he'd not changed his locks since Maddie had come in with the spare key, so if he'd come on behalf of his daughter, he'd have been able to get in.

He wondered briefly whether he should change the locks, but then decided against it. He couldn't risk locking her out. What if she came back, desperate to see him, and he wasn't home?

Yes, he'd probably end up robbed, but it was a small price to pay for the peace of mind.

Besides, what did he really have? He'd carefully hidden anything sentimental of Mary's.

The drive home passed in a blur of streetlights and possibilities.

But by the time he pulled up, the street was empty save

for Henrietta standing at her gate, wrapped in a cardigan against the evening chill.

'You all right?' she called.

'Fine,' he managed. 'If it was to do with Maddie, and he wanted to speak to me... he'll be back. I'm going to be positive.'

'I agree. You want to come in for a drink?'

'No thanks... I'm beat.'

'You were working until this late?'

'Yes.' He wondered why he'd lied. Was he trying to avoid hurting her feelings over the fact he'd been with Evelyn these last hours? He chided himself for his paranoia. Why was he assuming Henrietta had a thing for him? Because she'd been friendly, recently?

'You should take better care of yourself,' she said and returned to her house.

Theme of the day, he thought, recalling Evelyn's comment about his exhaustion.

After he went inside, the house felt emptier than usual. He stared out the window for a long time, watching the street for that scrote in the hoodie.

Maddie, are you reaching out?

Are you okay?

Safe?

The darkness beyond the glass offered no answers, only the reflection of a tired man waiting for ghosts.

Chapter Forty-Seven

Frank collected Gerry in the Audi. Gerry's neighbour was off work, so he'd agreed to take care of Rylan while they were interviewing a major suspect.

Gerry ran through her findings regarding the poetry and suggested some questions to ask. Frank made a mental note.

Stephen Walker's Victorian townhouse dominated the corner plot, its windows gleaming in the morning sun like watchful eyes.

'Ready to see what's beneath all that polish, eh?' Frank asked Gerry and rang the doorbell.

An elderly man, presumably Stephen Walker, answered the door. He was dressed in pressed slacks and a cashmere sweater that undoubtedly cost more than Frank's entire wardrobe.

'Mr Walker?'

He nodded. 'Yes. It's early. So I assume it's important?'

'It is.'

'In that case, can I help?' Despite his seventy-five years,

Stephen carried himself with the precise authority that came from decades of commanding respect.

'I'm DCI Black.' Frank showed his warrant card. 'This is DI Carver.'

'Sorry DCI Black, but I can't see your ID without my glasses.' The former headteacher had a cultured accent, but the Yorkshire twang shone through.

'We can wait,' Frank said. 'If you want to get your glasses.'

Minutes crawled by.

'You think he's doing this on purpose?' he grumbled to Gerry.

Stephen suddenly returned, giving her no time to answer. After he'd checked their identification, he asked, 'This is very official. I appreciate that. But can you tell me first what it's concerning?'

'It'd be better for us to come in and discuss it, sir,' Gerry said.

Stephen's expression tightened. 'It might be better for you... but maybe not so much for me and my wife. You see, she's resting upstairs... she's not well.'

'We're sorry to hear that, sir—'

'Dementia,' he said, fixing Frank with a stare that had probably quelled generations of unruly students. 'It's important to keep her away from stress.'

Frank nodded. 'We could have this discussion at the station?'

'The station... really?' He didn't look too enamoured with the idea.

Older men were stubborn. Frank knew – he was one of them. 'It's about a former student of yours, Mr Walker. Can we come in?'

'You know I've a lot of former students, DCI—'

'Sarah Matthews,' Frank said, cutting him off.

Stephen's reaction was subtle – a slight tightening around the eyes, a barely perceptible intake of breath – but Frank caught it.

'It's very important. So, here or the station, Mr Walker?' Frank asked.

Stephen took a step back. 'Here... is she dead?'

Frank nodded as they entered. 'We'll try to keep our voices down...'

'Yes, of course, thank you.' He turned away, his movements suddenly less commanding and precise, and led them to the lounge.

Their suspect was visibly shaken.

Chapter Forty-Eight

Peter watched Reece fumble with the distributor cap.

'No, lad, like this,' Peter said. He took the screwdriver and showed the correct technique. 'See how the contacts are corroded? That's why she's struggling to start.'

Peter's arthritic fingers ached as he worked, but the pain was worth it. His greatest pleasure was fixing things – a close second was teaching others how to fix them.

Who knows? In another life, I could have been a teacher. Even a headteacher, perhaps.

Reece leaned in closer to watch, his teenage indifference fading into genuine interest. 'So now we just clean them?'

'You do! Get that sandpaper I gave you.'

Peter supervised as Reece carefully cleaned each contact point. 'Steady now. You're not sanding a bloody fence, lad. You'll wear them down to nothing.'

To be fair, Reece was trying, and for someone who'd clearly never got his hands dirty, he was a reasonably quick learner.

Tongue caught between his teeth, Reece worked.

Maybe the cocky little sod had some hope after all.

Just before the last contact, Peter put his hand on Reece's arm. 'Listen, lad. Before we finish this... I need you to renew your vows.'

'Eh?'

'Don't worry, lad, we're not talking about marriage... I'm talking about your promise last night.'

'Ah...' He nodded.

Peter shook his head. 'Word for word, laddie.'

Reece looked over both shoulders, checking there were no witnesses to his moment of humility. 'I promise not to drive like a dickhead again.'

Peter nodded. 'Good... now you're promoted to "civilised youth in training".'

Reece smiled. 'Thank you.'

The gratitude caught Peter off guard. 'Good lad.'

They finished the job together, and Peter showed him how to reseat the cap properly. 'Try it now.'

The engine turned over immediately, far more smoothly than it had done prior. Reece's face lit up.

After Reece killed the engine and stepped back out, Peter clapped him on the shoulder. 'My father always said to me, Reece, we can all make good choices. That's what gives us all a chance.'

The words felt hollow in his mouth, given his mountain of pills and destined outcome... still... it'd served him for most of his life, and maybe there wasn't anything wrong with being hypocritical if it helped set this young man straight.

He clocked a Range Rover Sport pulled into his driveway – a far cry from the beaten-up Corsa he'd just been servicing. It was certainly out of place on this estate. A peacock among sparrows.

Two people emerged: a woman with striking red hair pulled back so severely it looked painful, wearing a suit that screamed authority, and a man whose attempt at professionalism was completely undermined by what had to be the most ridiculous moustache Peter had ever seen.

'Police,' Reece said.

'And how do you know that, lad?'

Reece lowered his eyes. 'Grew up with cars like that pulling up on our driveway.'

The ghost of Reece's father – another life cut short by poor choices – hovered between them.

Peter clapped him on the back again. 'Thanks for the heads up, son.'

He watched the officers approach his door with that stride he'd seen countless times during his security days – purposeful, measured, the walk of people who carried serious news.

As he walked back to his home to meet them, he felt the weight of watching eyes – Reece behind him, Lucy and Mia in their doorway, even that waste of space next door, Jake, peering out like a nosy schoolboy. The street had always been full of curtain-twitchers, but this was different. They knew something was coming.

He glared at the neighbour. *Away with you! You may be a bastard, but I won't point out your drug den. Not as miserable as your girlfriend seemed to think, eh?*

They were knocking on his door.

'Can I help?' he said from the top of his driveway.

The man with the ridiculous moustache turned and held out a warrant card. 'Mr Watson?'

'Yes?'

'DS Moyes, and this is DC Miller. Have you got a minute?'

I reckon you want more than a minute, he thought, regarding their serious eyes.

Chapter Forty-Nine

THE LOUNGE WAS IMPRESSIVE, with mahogany bookshelves lined with leather-bound classics, oil paintings of pastoral scenes in gilt frames, and a baby grand piano commanding one corner.

A towering real Christmas tree dominated one window, its branches adorned with hand-blown glass ornaments and twinkling white lights that must have cost a small fortune. Artfully arranged garlands of fresh pine and burgundy silk ribbons draped the mantelpiece, while crystal bowls filled with gold-dusted pinecones and cinnamon sticks perfumed the air.

Stephen wasn't just cultivating cultured affluence through his polished pronunciation; he had woven it into every aspect of his life.

After Frank and Gerry sat on the sofa, Stephen stayed standing.

Was he maintaining the higher ground? He'd spent a large part of his life as a headteacher, after all. Such habits would die hard.

It was troublesome, though.

'Please sit, Mr Walker,' Frank said.

'Just call me Stephen... and tell me, please,' he said as he sat. 'Was she murdered?'

'We suspect so,' Frank said, watching Stephen's face carefully. 'You seemed very shocked, Stephen... but she's been missing since 1989?'

A flicker of something – *shock? Guilt?* – crossed Stephen's face before he regained control. 'Yes, well, of course I'm shocked. Many people just assumed she'd left. I went with that view. After all, she must have been what? Twenty-one, twenty-two, when she left Ruswarp? I remained optimistic. Oh, this is dreadful. Awful. I have a daughter, you know. Imagine that poor mother. Is the mother still alive?'

Frank nodded.

'I can't believe it.' He rubbed his temples. 'Where was she found?'

'In the old silo close to here,' Gerry said.

'What?' Stephen's eyes widened. 'The one that came down the other day?'

'Aye.' Frank opened his notebook to a fresh page. 'We've kept the body, Sarah's body, out of the press – for now. Won't be long, but we'd appreciate your discretion for now.'

'Of course... of course...'

'Did you never wonder, in all these years, where she might have gone?' Gerry asked.

Stephen narrowed his eyes, thrusting out his palm with the practiced authority of someone used to silencing rooms. 'Hang on... what's being implied here? She was my student until she was eighteen. What makes you think she was so firmly on my mind? It was almost four years after she left Riverside. I had many students. Many, many students in my career. Some, alas, passed young, whereas many left here in search of careers. With that in mind, I find that question, a little, I don't know, antagonistic.'

'We apologise,' Frank said, though he didn't mean it. Something about these wealthy folk with their accolades and sense of importance always did set his teeth on edge.

Frank reached into his pocket and withdrew a photograph of Sarah Matthews in her nursing uniform. He placed it carefully on the coffee table's polished surface. 'Can we just confirm that we're talking about the same girl, please?'

Stephen reached forward, picked it up and squinted at it through his spectacles.

Frank caught the sharp intake of breath– and the slight tremor in the former headteacher's fingers.

He glanced at Gerry's notebook, catching her precise notation: *emotionally invested.*

Agreed, Frank thought.

'Yes, that's her,' Stephen said.

'Thank you,' Frank said, making a note too. 'Can you recall what kind of student she was?'

'No bother, as far as I recall.' Stephen looked up at Frank.

'You know about her background. She'd been troubled?' Frank asked.

'Yes, everyone knew. I was aware of the problems she'd had. Her father... he died, you know, in prison... And shoplifting... I'm glad she found her way to us. She could have ended up in juvenile detention. She became an excellent student.'

And do you credit yourself with helping her, Stephen? Frank thought, his mind darting to those lines of poetry again. *Some gifts come with strings attached, pulling tighter, day by day, until you can barely breathe.*

And did you take something in return?

'She was with you between 1983 and 1985 before leaving for university in Middlesbrough,' Gerry said. 'Is that correct?'

'It sounds about right – I'd have to check,' Stephen said.

'How close were you to Sarah?' Gerry asked.

He widened his eyes. 'Again – is that an appropriate question?'

'It's a murder investigation, Stephen,' Frank said.

He shook his head. 'Close to? What does that even mean?'

'We've spoken to Margaret Matthews, her mother. She seems to recall a special relationship – between you and her daughter,' Frank said, leaning forward.

Stephen creased his brow. 'A special relationship?' He looked off in the distance as if trying to remember. 'I helped her with some writing, if I recall. Is that what she was referring to?'

Some writing!

'Her mother recovered a lot of poetry. She credits you with assisting her daughter with it for a considerable length of time.'

He looked very uneasy again – in the same way he had when he'd answered the door. 'She was talented, and needed little help – although, yes, okay, I helped her.'

'Could you help us understand this talent?' Frank asked, still leaning forward.

'Well, I'm assuming at this stage you've read her poems. Sarah could write. It was raw, yes... but genuine... very genuine.'

'You sound enamoured by her?' Frank asked.

'Again, that question unnerves me. Look, I appreciate poetry. I also appreciated students from more challenging backgrounds who needed encouragement... enrichment. I offered her a place in a poetry writing group I ran while she was at Riverside. She rose to the challenge. I was fond of her writing. Does that make me a suspect?'

'We're just trying to establish the context and the relationship at this stage,' Frank said.

That didn't put Stephen at ease, which had been Frank's intention.

'Did you stay in touch with her after she left college?'

'Not purposely, no. She popped by every now and again, to the school, while she was on her university breaks, but they petered out. I don't think she visited for more than a year.'

'How did this poetry group work?' Gerry asked.

'At the back end of 1983, I set up the group. I wanted to keep the group tiny and exclusive... you know! After all, I had a very trying job with lots of expectations to manage as it was. I allowed many students to submit, but I clarified that I was only going to select four.'

'And who were the four?' Frank asked.

'Cassie Sinclair, Sandy Greene, Kayleigh Cotton, and Sarah, of course.'

'All female?' Frank asked, scribbling down the names.

Stephen took a sharp breath. 'Yes... Very few young men applied. I chose the four best on merit, not gender.'

'And how did this poetry group work?' Frank said.

'I met with them once weekly and read their work with them. I offered them critique. Just critique. It was up to them if they changed them. I didn't want to dampen their individual talent. I enjoyed the process, and they did too. In fact, I remember it as one of the highlights of my career.'

Frank nodded. 'Have you stayed in touch with any of them?'

'Only Sandy... the rest, sadly, no. Sandy, actually, has been published in quite a few notable anthologies. Feel free to speak to her. She'll vouch for my character.'

'I'm not calling your character into doubt, Stephen... we're just trying to build a picture. But, on that note, did anybody have any issues with this group you were running?'

'No! Why would they?'

Frank shrugged.

Gerry opened her bag and took out the two poems that had 'submission' written across the top. She started with the one that didn't have a line through the word: 'The Beginning'. She slid it over the table. 'Do you recognise this?'

Stephen's hands trembled again as he picked it up.

His eyes grew misty as he read. 'Yes... I remember. It was Sarah's submission.'

'It is very polished and structured,' Gerry said.

'Yes, it is. It was impressive.'

'But, nearly all of her other poems are in a completely unique style. You referred to it as raw and genuine, before. I'd agree.'

Stephen nodded. 'What's your point?'

'I suspect different people wrote them.'

Stephen creased his brow and sneered. 'Why?'

'The voice is completely different.'

'That makes no sense. People can change their voices. Adapt, evolve?'

'But to that extent?'

'Why not? She was young!' He pushed it back. 'No, sorry, I don't agree. She wrote that submission.'

Frank noted that Stephen really didn't like Gerry's line of questioning. Why? Was it because he was having his expertise questioned? Or maybe he was hiding something?

'How many years did you run your poetry group, Stephen?' Frank asked.

'Ah, well, see... this was the only one. It was a lot of pressure... a lot of work... the governors weren't happy with me dividing my time. So, I called it a day when these four girls left.'

Unhappy about dividing your time? Frank wondered. *Or is something else going on?*

'Could you not have asked another member of staff to run the group instead?' Gerry asked.

'I put it out there, but, alas, no one seemed interested,' Stephen said.

'Where did you meet the girls for the sessions?' Frank asked.

'My office,' Stephen said. 'There were only four.'

'That was my next question – so always as a group?'

There was a slight pause, before he said, 'Yes.'

'You sure?'

Stephen's expression suggested he didn't know how to answer that. 'Usually.'

'Usually?'

'Yes, I occasionally met them alone... if they came with additional poems during that week. They might visit during the school day or straight after school, nothing suspicious. You can ask Sandy if you don't believe me.'

'We will,' Frank said. He fixed him with a stare. 'Problem is we can't ask Sarah.'

Stephen took a deep breath and glared. 'There was nothing inappropriate about my sessions.'

'I'm not saying there was,' Frank said. 'I'm just pointing out that I can't verify it.'

He nodded. 'Yes... times were different, then... less

suspicious. I should have been more sensible, but I assure you nothing untoward ever happened.'

Frank nodded, jotting something down in his notebook.

'Do you know anything about Tommy Reid?' Frank asked. 'Sarah's boyfriend at the time of her disappearance.'

'Just the same as everyone else. That it was the same boyfriend she had when she was younger.'

'When she was thirteen,' Frank added.

Stephen gave a sad nod. 'Unforgivable.'

'Well, she forgave him,' Frank said.

'Clearly, a mistake.'

'What makes you say that?' Gerry asked.

'Oh, I don't know. It sounded like he was no good, but, like I said, I didn't know him.'

'How about Dr Hannah Wright, the child psychiatrist, she was being treated by?'

'I knew Hannah. She was a good person, and her loss was tragic. I know Hannah helped Sarah a lot when she was younger, and Sarah was very grateful – you could see that in some of her poetry.'

Frank took out the photograph of the man pictured with Dr Hannah Wright at Sarah's riding events. 'Do you recognise this man?'

He shook his head. 'No... sorry...'

'Also, can you tell us anything about Clive Morton?'

He looked rather taken aback. 'Clive Morton... the one who died in the gas explosion along with Hannah Wright?'

Frank nodded.

'Just that he was an odd piece of work. He worked at Riverside for a time.'

Frank nodded again. 'I was going to ask you about that.'

'Not much to ask, really. He worked there for a short time. Personally, I never had much to do with him, until the complaints came in. Turns out he was unnerving some students by watching them and passing comment on their conduct... that kind of thing. Hannah did actually speak to me about him at one point. She knew him and stated that, in her opinion, he was misunderstood; she believed he was only trying to be helpful and caring. But he was socially awkward. Very awkward. He'd have had a diagnosis for it these days, no doubt. She obviously believed in the courage of her convictions because she gave him a job. He never actually did anything, but they didn't feel safe. When he told a girl that her skirt was too short, and that he was concerned about her, it was the final straw. He couldn't be around young people. The governors asked him to go.'

A sound from the doorway drew their attention – the whisper of silk against wood.

'Caroline?' Stephen said, rising.

Caroline Walker stood there like an apparition – silver hair dishevelled against her silk dressing gown, her eyes carrying that peculiar mix of confusion and clarity that often came with dementia. Her eyes moved between the face of every occupant in the room. Gerry straightened in her seat, eyes sharpening, no doubt cataloguing every detail of this unexpected development.

'Caroline,' Stephen said. 'You should be resting. Please, dear, go back to bed.'

She moved into the room with an almost ghostly grace, clutching a leather-bound album to her chest like a shield. 'Caroline... no... how did you?'

She placed the album on the coffee table. 'I heard his secrets whispering to me.'

'Caroline.' Stephen darted for it. 'Don't be ridiculous – put it back!'

Frank was there first. 'Where's this from?'

'His safe,' Caroline said.

Safe?

He opened the album to a handwritten poem taped in. Alongside it was a picture of a young woman sitting on the sofa, looking up at it.

Sarah Matthews.

'Why was this in your safe?' Frank asked.

'Memories. That's all they are. It's not how it seems, how you will interpret it! They're just poems and the poet's picture.'

Frank flicked through page after page of poems and pictures of the four young girls. Frank frowned. 'Again and again...'

'So?'

Frank wasn't sure. Aye, it could all have been perfectly innocent... until...

He stopped at the last picture.

Sarah Matthews blowing a kiss to the camera.

Chapter Fifty

Sharon noticed the child's pink jacket hanging by a larger one in the hallway as she removed her shoes.

She took a deep breath, pushed aside the sadness threatening to cloud her judgement, and followed Peter Watson into his home alongside Reggie.

Peter sat in the only chair in the lounge. 'Sorry, no sofa,' he said, raising one of his eyebrows and crossing his arms. 'But I guess it doesn't matter as this will only take a minute?'

'We can stand,' Reggie said, a smug edge to his voice that made Sharon want to kick his ankle. Had he forgotten what this man had been through?

On the mantelpiece, a bowl filled with paracetamol sat next to a framed photograph of a woman – presumably Donna, Peter's late wife. Strange. Why was he keeping so many pills there? When he caught her looking, his chin jutted out defensively. He held up his hand. 'Arthritis. It hurts to push the painkillers from their blister packet. So, I do them all when I'm not feeling so bad.'

'Good thinking, Mr Watson... What happened to your head?'

'Another hazard of being old. I caught it on the mantelpiece...' He made a show of checking his watch. 'You promised a brief visit ... this doesn't feel brief. And, well, with the world in flames, and it is – wouldn't you agree? – surely a seventy-four-year-old man's aches and pains aren't the police's priority?'

Reggie reached into his jacket, pulled out the photograph of Sarah Matthews, and held it out – without a word. Sharon winced internally. It felt too aggressive to her. Reggie was usually better at controlling his frustration. It seemed his psychosomatic cough seemed to be affecting his mood.

Peter took the photo. His eyes widened. 'What? What's this?'

'You know her...'

'Aye.' He stuttered as he spoke. 'I-It's Sarah.' His eyes lifted to meet theirs, carrying a look of such raw desperation that Sharon felt her chest tighten. 'Is she okay? Tell me she's okay?'

Reggie leaned in. 'She's—'

Sharon grabbed his arm, stopping him before he could go in for the kill. 'We've some unfortunate news, Mr Watson.'

She explained, and the colour drained from Peter's face so rapidly that Sharon thought he might faint.

The silence that followed felt as thick in the air as it'd done in the Reid household.

Peter's earlier defensiveness crumbled, leaving behind a man who looked vulnerable. Fragile. Even Reggie, who'd been so bombastic moments before, seemed to deflate.

'Can I grab some chairs from the kitchen?' Sharon asked, uncomfortable with how they both now loomed over this diminished elderly man.

'Let me,' Reggie offered.

While Reggie was gone, Sharon watched Peter trace Sarah's features with weathered fingers that trembled slightly.

'No... that's not right...' Peter said.

'Sorry?'

'She was supposed to be in Australia.' He shook his head, his face greying. 'She went to Australia.'

'When?'

'In 1989 of course.'

This couldn't be true. Her passport would have been flagged during the missing person's investigation if she'd left the country.

Reggie set up two kitchen chairs opposite Peter and they all sat.

'Did she tell you that's where she was going?' Sharon asked.

He looked at both of them. 'What aren't you getting? She went... she must have come back... that must be it. She must have come back and—' He put his hand to his mouth. 'Oh God, really?' He stared at Sharon. 'Sarah, really?'

Sharon nodded. 'I'm sorry.'

Peter wept.

Sharon and Reggie exchanged a glance. She saw the guilt on Reggie's face now. The man sitting before them looked absolutely broken.

After a couple of minutes, he looked up at them, red-eyed. 'She was like a daughter to us...' He looked up at a picture of a woman on the mantelpiece next to the pills, presumably his late wife. Peter then looked at their faces again. 'How did you two end up here?'

They explained about Roger Grip and the shoplifting.

'Aye, Roger...' His top lip curled up. 'He was a dickhead

if there ever was one. Though I suppose he wanted to keep his job. I was happy to chuck it.' He gulped and fell silent for another moment.

He stared at the photograph of her in her nurse's uniform. 'Ha! Look at her on this – butter wouldn't melt... but I'm telling you this girl had fire in her belly. Our girl...' He glanced at his late wife again. 'The day I caught her, she was this little thing, all fire... clutching a book on bloody horse, if you can believe it.'

Sharon nodded.

'Outside, when I caught her, I couldn't help it. I had to know. Horse riding! She looked at me with those eyes of hers, full of fire, and snapped, "Because I hate everything ... everything... apart from horses! I don't know why, but I like horses!" Poor little lass! She told me she already had two charges, and a third would mean her being banged up in a juvenile centre. That wasn't happening on my watch. I let her go but told her to meet me for a coffee later. I didn't expect her to. But she met me, and that was it really. We hit it off.' He rubbed at his eyes and then pointed at Reggie, and then Sharon. 'Not in that way, mind, so knock whatever you've come here with out of your heads. Friends. She was a child, and I'm not like that.' He looked at the picture of his late wife again. 'Neither of us were.'

'So, you stayed in touch?' Sharon asked.

'Aye... you could say that! She was always coming round to visit me and Donna. Mainly weekends like, when she could catch some free time between her horse riding, but sometimes, she turned up during the week for some tea, around five, to watch the soap operas. She bloody loved those Australian soap operas! Always on about Australia she was. Obsessed with the bloody place. *Neighbours, Home and Away*... I tried to explain that life probably wasn't that dandy. It wouldn't all be sunshine, beaches, handsome boyfriends, and friendly neighbours.' He pointed at his wall. 'You want to see my neighbours these days – anything but fucking friendly. Excuse my language.'

'So, both you and your wife were close to her?' Reggie said.

'Aye... like I said... she came to see us a lot. My wife was a paediatric nurse. She's a way with kids, you know. Ha! Meanwhile, Sarah, just took the piss out of me.' He smiled, tears dripping in at the corners of his mouth. 'I used to play the fool – flick her ears and run off that kind of thing... to be honest, it was nice to have a youngster about the place...' He looked off into the distance.

Sharon thought of the small pink jacket and her heart sank.

'How long did this go on for?' Sharon asked.

'Oh... bloody years...' Peter said. 'At first, we just wanted to really encourage her to make good of her life. She had another positive influence too – a doctor, Hannah Wright. Sarah made us promise never to talk to her. She was always so desperate to keep parts of her life separate. Before we knew it, she was part of our lives, dropping in and out at whim. Sixteen... seventeen... I always thought she'd be a writer. She started writing poetry at sixteen – bloody good stuff, too. You should see them. Proper emotional. I'd like to think that the time we had with her, those moments she snatched between her normal life, was enough to put her on the straight and narrow.' His gaze turned distant, seeing something far beyond the room's walls. 'I remember one time, she insisted on taking me riding. Said I needed to understand why she loved it so much. I wasn't a natural like her, but I saw why she did it – why she needed that freedom. Some things that had happened to her in her life... her father...' He shook his head. 'She had spirit. But she'd a lot of baggage too. Needed to burn it off.'

He stood up, groaning over his arthritic stiffness. 'Wait a moment.'

Sharon watched him shuffle into another room, returning with what looked like a greeting card. An eagle soared across its front, wings spread against a blue sky. 'She gave me this,' he said, opening it carefully. 'She stuck a typed poem inside, too. Listen to this.'

His voice trembled as he read, '"Peter... Through darkness you showed me light, when chains bound me, you gave me flight. Always your special friend, Sarah".' He swallowed hard. 'Nice, huh? No one's ever given me something like that.' He whispered the last part, closing the card as if it were made of glass.

He cried again as he sat. Again, Sharon and Reggie were patient.

Eventually, he looked up, rubbing at his eyes. 'I was so happy when she made it to Australia. She'd vowed to for so many years, and I believed her. And then she did it! She'd such strength, that girl. She stuck her fingers up and told this place to get stuffed. Why the bloody hell did she come back to this dump? And then what happened?'

'What makes you think she made it to Australia?' Reggie asked.

Peter grimaced. 'What's this? I don't think, I know!'

'I'm sorry, Peter,' Sharon said. 'But I think someone misled you somehow—'

'Ha! No dear, wait there...' He went back to the drawer and came back with a postcard. He passed it to Sharon. She regarded the Sydney Harbour Bridge. 'Read this... and I think you'll see that you're the ones who've been misled.'

Chapter Fifty-One

'She had that type of humour. What can I say? Playful. Silly sometimes...' Stephen said, referring to Sarah blowing him a kiss. 'God knows she'd had a tough enough life... she often could be silly and immature, probably to shake off all the gloom. I remember that photo well, and it isn't what you think. She asked me why I always wanted a fresh photo every time she produced a wonderful poem. Her, and the other girls. And I said... to capture the moment... the moment the poet releases their magic to be seen in the world. It was just a silly tradition I enjoyed. I told them that if any were ever published, then that would be the image that could go alongside it. Kind of captured in the moment, you know? Then, on that last time, she thought it was funny to blow me a kiss... she was just cheeky like that... there was nothing in it!'

'Then why keep it?' Frank asked.

'I kept them all!' Stephen grew red faced now. 'I hate having to justify this special time. I helped them. And they got so much from it!'

He'd looked the picture of health before, but was now

wobbling, and Frank didn't want him blowing an artery on him. 'Please... sit down, Stephen... and take some deep breaths.'

As Stephen did that, Frank considered. Truth be, he didn't know what to make of this. It was odd, sure, but it wasn't the first time he'd come across behaviour he considered odd but was a perfectly harmless tradition in the eyes of someone else.

Someone blowing a kiss at a camera was hardly enough to prove Stephen had abused this girl or groomed her.

Still, it didn't look good... and just further cemented Stephen's position as a major suspect in Frank's mind.

'Why keep them in your safe though, Mr Walker? It seems strange.'

'Are you not listening? These are some of my happiest memories, of course. They mean a lot to me. It was a highlight of my career helping those girls realise their talents! Why wouldn't I want to keep them stored carefully?' He looked at his wife, Caroline, who was now looking off into space, as if she'd completely forgotten what she'd just done. 'I mean if I'd something to hide, would I really let my wife have the code for it?'

'Is this true, Mrs Walker, do you know about this?'

Caroline was pale. She looked around. 'He's a good man... Stephen... he should show you around Riverside this afternoon when he goes back to work... the place is unrecognisable since he started there.'

'I need to take my wife back to bed,' Stephen said, glaring at Frank. 'Unless you plan to arrest me over some old poems and photographs I hold dear?' He stood and went over to his wife.

Of course, Frank had more questions, but he looked at Gerry and made a decision.

He'd give Stephen a breather, at least until they'd spoken to the surviving members of the poetry group.

Caroline stopped at the doorway, her eyes suddenly sharp with clarity. 'Whispers,' she breathed, the word hanging in the air. 'Always whispering.'

Stephen touched her arm. 'Dear, please—'

She pulled away from him, her voice rising. 'No one will ever destroy my husband, you know?' Her gaze locked onto Frank with an unsettling intensity. 'You can try, but you'll never win.'

Frank felt the hairs rise on the back of his neck. He caught Gerry's eye. Her usual analytical calm had slipped for a moment, replaced by an expression he rarely saw – genuine unease.

Frank stood. 'Stephen, we'll show ourselves out, but we'll be back in touch... probably later today.'

'I'm sure you will,' he muttered.

'He helped them reach for the stars.' Caroline's voice dropped in volume as she headed up the stairs. 'Reach for the stars, and all you do is whisper... whisper...'

The words seemed to follow them down the hallway, making Frank's skin crawl.

After they left the Victorian townhouse, he stood and regarded it. 'Reach for the stars, eh? Well, Sarah reached them, and not, I suspect, in the way you meant, Mrs Walker.' He sighed and looked at Gerry. 'What did I say when I walked in Gerry?'

'You said: "Ready to see what's beneath that polish?"'

'Aye, and do you know what... I feel there's a lot more polish to come off before we're through.'

Chapter Fifty-Two

Peter and Donna. I flew! And the beaches are beautiful, and the boys are handsome. Although, I've yet to meet the neighbours. Let me be – keep it quiet. Love your eagle, Sarah x

THE STAMP SUGGESTED it'd come from Sydney via international airmail.

15 December 1989.

This was intriguing. But it also felt completely impossible.

When investigating where Sarah Matthews had disappeared to, flight rosters would have been a must.

Sharon made a note to double check, but she'd be very surprised, extremely surprised, if her predecessors would have been that incompetent.

'We have to take this in,' Sharon said. She was already thinking about handwriting analysis – they'd a pile of handwritten poems to compare it to...

He nodded. She'd expected him to put up a fuss, but he didn't. 'Do you believe me now?'

'I believe you received this card... but I don't believe she left the country,' Sharon said. 'I'm sorry.'

'But that makes no sense.'

'No, it doesn't,' Reggie said. 'But we'll do our best to get to the bottom of it.'

Reggie shifted in his chair, wincing as his back cracked against the hard plastic. 'While we're on the subject of your relationship with Sarah, what happened when she went away to university?'

'Aye...' He lowered his eyes. 'That was when the distance between us started to build. I mean, it wasn't too far, it was only Middlesbrough, but her time became limited, and she insisted we didn't make contact – she didn't want her mother finding out and becoming upset at what she called her "double life". I remember the day before she left... it was the beginning of September, 1985, she came and had dinner. She said we'd been like second parents to her. It was sweet... wonderful even...'

He rubbed his eyes. 'We were all in floods of tears. This eighteen-year-old in awe of us for how we'd helped her... but then, it faded... I guess that happens to us all when the children leave home, and who were we kidding – I'd only really known her for four years. It was all very inevitable. In the first year, she visited on her holidays. About three times in total. That was okay. We were proud and let her know we were.'

He looked up at Donna. 'And imagine if I'd have had her arrested that day? That third offence. What a waste. Look what we were part of. She was going to be a paediatric nurse – like Donna!'

'Still, visits became less and less; then, after she finished university, she came a few times, but she'd grown into a woman now. She had her own plans and dreams. She was doing well in her job. I think we saw her a few times in that final year, but the reality was she'd completely changed – as people do. We were content that she was happy. Until... well, until we just stopped hearing from her.' He took a deep breath, forcing back more tears.

'When we hadn't heard from her in a good while, I went to see Dr Hannah Wright, hoping to catch Sarah at work. But she wasn't there any more. Hannah had asked her to leave because she'd got back with that absolute knacker, Tommy Reid. Tommy Reid! Of course, we knew the story from when she was thirteen. She'd told us all about that; how could she have done something that stupid? He sounded like a complete idiot... and his mother... well, she sounded bloody loopy, too.'

Sharon exchanged a glance with Reggie. His eyes echoed her thoughts. *You can say that again!*

'I was devastated! Can you imagine? Throwing away everything she'd worked for! But Hannah insisted this was the right move. Let her realise and she'll come back. She asked me to stay out of it, and I did. I knew she'd feel ashamed of what she'd done, and that's why she couldn't face me, so it was a struggle not to see her.' He nodded at Donna's photograph. 'She agreed with Hannah though... so, I let it ride, we let it ride, hoping that she'd see sense.' His sigh seemed to carry decades of regret. 'And then she was gone... just like that. Awful, awful time.' He stroked the eagle on the card. 'I know she gave me this long before, but I believed there was a message in this image. She'd always wanted to fly away – to Australia. So when they never found her, I assumed – *hoped* – she'd finally spread her wings and gone on an adventure. Then, that postcard showed up, and I thought my prayers had been answered.'

'You didn't think of bringing this to us?' Reggie asked.

'Of course not, man. What are you? Soft in the head? Ha. Lock me up now, but she wanted away, and she got away – I wasn't about to be the one responsible for dragging her back to where she didn't want to be!'

His eyes brimmed with fresh tears. He stood, groaning. 'You'll have to excuse me.' Peter pushed himself up with painful slowness. 'Need to use the facilities.'

After Peter's shuffling footsteps faded, Sharon caught Reggie staring at her. 'I can see your heart bleeding,' he said.

'Jesus, really, sir... and yours isn't?'

'When you get to my age, Sharon, you lose count of how many times you've been lied to – as effectively as that, by the way.'

'But that postcard?'

'He may have done it himself,' Reggie said. 'I've seen it before. A woman was in denial over killing her husband, so she wrote herself a valentine's card from him. Tricked herself. Denial and grief can do funny things. Well, I mean, she obviously didn't write it, did she?'

Sharon shook her head. Surely, that level of anguish couldn't be faked. His phone beeped. 'Look at that.'

He turned his phone. It was a message from Sean.

> Records show Peter Watson owned a red
> Ford Fiesta between 1985 and 1990.

Her eyes widened. She gripped the edges of the plastic chair. *Surely not?*

She expected him to say something smug, but his face remained blank. Perhaps he'd been hoping as much as she had that Peter's grief was genuine.

Chapter Fifty-Three

Lewis's fingers ached. He'd spent the night clutching both his mobile and the mysterious photograph, unable to let either go. He must have tried the number dozens of times overnight, but every time, he'd received the same engaged tone.

He wasn't sure if he'd slept – maybe he had dozed off intermittently.

He needed some fresh air.

Before he left the house, he stared down at his frail father. 'One last sick joke, eh? Got your pathetic son chasing shadows?'

Without really thinking about it, he walked to White Hart, not for a drink – though God knew he needed one – but because this was the place that had destroyed his life. His mind was already tortured, why not torture it some more?

Lewis first recalled Gregg Ince's bones cracking against porcelain, and then the police rightfully dragging him out of society.

Three years ago.

Why had he done it?

Good question.

The memories of that evening were fragmented, distorted by alcohol and fury. Isobelle had demanded he leave, declaring the end of their marriage. In the pub, his anger and frustration were too volatile to contain. In the toilets, a pissed Gregg Ince had eyed him up and down, asking him what the fuck he was looking at.

Gregg became a convenient way to vent.

Then it was a blur, and all he could hear now, in his memory, was the sickening crack of a skull against the urinal.

Next, he wandered across town until he was opposite the home he'd shared with Isobelle. Morning sunlight caught the kitchen window like a spotlight on a stage he'd abandoned years ago.

His son sat at the breakfast table, spoon halfway to his mouth.

Ten years old now, though Lewis hadn't seen him since he was seven. His feet carried him forward before his brain could object, hand twitching at his side. The urge to tap on the glass, to call out to his son, was overwhelming.

He stopped at the gate, reality crashing back. What would his son see if he knocked?

A stranger? Or worse...

Would he look at me the way I look at John?

But didn't he have to try?

The opportunity might never come again.

Heart hammering, he opened the gate.

Through the window, Lewis saw a tall man appear behind his son, ruffling the boy's hair with casual affection. His son looked up with a smile that pierced Lewis's heart – pure, unguarded love for the man who'd replaced him.

Lewis stumbled backward, the gate clanging shut. Father and son looked toward the sound, but Lewis was already turning away, bile rising in his throat as he ran.

What right did he have to shatter their world? To drag his boy into the same cycle of abandonment and return that had poisoned his own life?

Lewis ran all the way back to his father's home, each footfall echoing with shame. Out of breath, he looked up at the bedroom window, wondering if his father was still alive.

Are we really so different, John? The thought followed him up the driveway like an accusing shadow.

Maybe that's why you kept that mysterious woman's picture hidden – another reminder of choices made, lives abandoned. We both escaped from responsibility. You watched us grow from a distance, and now I'm doing the same.

After all my condemnation, I've become you. Like father, like son.

The house felt emptier than ever as he let himself in, Jamie's smile searing in his memory alongside the face of the man who'd taken his place – all those moments he'd never share with his son burning holes in his heart.

Mark nodded as Lewis passed. His father was still alive then.

He wiped sweat from his brow as he headed up to see the old bastard.

Is this my destiny, too? To die alone, surrounded by photographs of moments I missed, until the grim reaper comes?

Chapter Fifty-Four

'MR WATSON.' Sharon chose her words carefully. 'On the night that Sarah disappeared, she was seen outside Bridge Inn climbing into the passenger seat of a red Fiesta. This was the last time she was seen.'

Peter nodded absently, his face blank – he clearly hadn't grasped the significance.

'You were the owner of a red Fiesta between 1985 and 1990,' Reggie added.

He nodded. 'Yes.' His brow furrowed as understanding dawned. 'But... so? What are you saying?'

'We're just establishing facts,' Reggie said. 'An eyewitness said—'

Peter's voice sharpened. 'Yes, I heard you the first time. But there were a lot of red Fiestas in 1989. It's nothing more than a coincidence.'

Sharon glanced at Reggie. Without registration numbers, CCTV footage, or a living witness, the red Fiesta connection felt paper thin 'Where were you on October 12, 1989?' Reggie asked.

'Are you serious?' Peter snapped.

Reggie nodded.

Peter ran a hand over his face. 'Bloody hell. How do you expect me to remember? All I can tell you is that when I heard about Sarah going missing, I was usually working evening shifts at the Royal Oak in Whitby.' He squeezed his eyes. 'Monday through Wednesday, Saturday and Sunday. Would that cover the date?'

Reggie nodded. 'Yes, but I thought you ran a security business?'

'Aye, but they were some tough years. Mortgage payments eating us alive. You could maybe confirm that with whoever runs it now... they might have kept a record of staff.'

Unlikely, Sharon thought, *but we'll check it out, anyway.*

'Did Donna drive the car too?' Sharon asked.

'Aye... but I'm telling you, that wasn't our red Fiesta. Like I said, how many red Fiestas do you think were around then!'

'Can you remember where Donna was that night?'

'Ha! Are you serious? Here, resting probably! She was a bloody nurse for God's sake!'

His voice cracked with sudden emotion. 'I mean, what are you even suggesting?' He pressed a hand to his chest. 'My Donna! Bloody hell! She wouldn't harm a hair on anyone's head. She was a kids' nurse. Desperate for Sarah to continue being a nurse. And that becomes grounds for what? Putting her in a fucking silo and...' He choked on the words, unable to finish.

'It's okay,' Sharon said. 'We just have to cover everything. I'd struggle to believe that too.'

'Good!' Peter's hand shook as he gestured at Donna's photograph. 'All we ever wanted to do was help her. Our mistake was not going to see her after she went back to that dickhead, and Hannah warned us off! Sarah had spent her whole life being written off! I should have been first to that sodding door at the Reids', pulling her out!'

They tried asking more questions, but the suggestion about Donna had broken something in him. His responses dulled to single words, his eyes fixed on Donna's photograph as if he'd forgotten they were there.

Finally, they thanked him for his time.

At the door, Peter's fingers closed gently around Sharon's arm. His eyes met hers, deliberately excluding Reggie. 'I loved Sarah like she was my own.' The words carried the weight of a confession.

Sharon nodded, letting her expression convey her belief in his sincerity.

They were halfway down the path when Reggie cursed under his breath. 'Shit... the man with Hannah! The boss will have me...' He jogged back as Peter was closing the door. 'Sorry, sir, one more thing – do you recognise this man?' He thrust forward the photograph of the unknown figure at the horse riding competition with Hannah Wright.

Peter took the photograph and studied it carefully, his eyes moving methodically across the image.

For a moment, Reggie thought he might just recognise him.

But he shook his head and handed it back.

Then, with one last sad look at Sharon, Peter closed the door with a quiet finality.

Chapter Fifty-Five

It was afternoon, and Christie's head throbbed from last night's overindulgence. No doubt, her bruised temple, caused by her mother, was also playing its large part. She'd called in sick, on this, only her second day!

She'd taken the job after the last English teacher had unexpectedly quit because of ill health, hence the strange start date. It had felt like an opportunity for Christie to impress them. To ride to the rescue, like a real Walker would! Show them she was just like her father – an excellent teacher and leader. Yet, here she was, off sick already; ironically, because of the bloody man that had inspired her. Plus, it was only two days until they broke for Christmas – this wouldn't be what the current head and the governors had been hoping for. Not at all.

Her life felt in fucking tatters.

But she hadn't got time to dwell on this now. What she needed was answers, and fast, in order to make sense of everything. So, if Georgina Prince wouldn't give them willingly, Christie knew someone who would.

Nancy Keegan was one of three governors from her

interview panel, and the only one remaining from her father's era as headteacher. At seventy-eight, she should have retired years ago, but widowhood, and having no children, had left her clinging to the role like a lifeline. Nancy had always adored Christie's father, constantly praising his service to the children of Whitby and Ruswarp.

Looking back, Christie realised her own appointment had been inevitable with Nancy on the panel.

If anyone knew anything, then Nancy would.

Christie freshened up as much as was possible and headed to Nancy's home.

Nancy still possessed a youthful energy, which made her seem decades younger than she was. 'Christie? Shouldn't you be at work?' She pointed at her bruised and grazed temple. 'What happened, dear? Are you okay?'

'My mother... she pushed me.' Christie had intended to make up some lie, but it just slipped out. 'She didn't even recognise me.' Her voice cracked.

Nancy shook her head. 'Oh, you poor thing. Come in.'

The kitchen was warm and inviting. Nancy busied herself with making tea. When they were both settled with steaming cups, she reached across and patted Christie's hand. 'I'm so sorry about your mother. Caroline is an admirable woman. What a wonderful teacher she was, and what a great service she did to Ruswarp. It is such an awful disease.'

Christie smiled with gratitude. She nudged a tear away, took a sip, steeled herself, and then regarded Nancy with a more serious expression. 'Do you know what happened yesterday at Riverside?'

'Sorry... no. They treat me with bloody kid gloves these days. What happened? Nothing serious, I hope.'

'I don't know, Nancy. It felt serious. It felt fucking horrible.' She broke off. 'Sorry for my language.'

She winked. 'I may look like a sweet old lady, but I've been around a fair old while, dear. Lay it out. Fucking warts and all.'

Christie smiled, but as she spoke, her face dropped again. 'A woman called Georgina Prince came to see me.'

Nancy's face also dropped.

It was sudden, too, and the colour left her face immediately. Her teacup clattered against its saucer.

Christie reached for her hand. 'Nancy, are you okay?'

'Georgina? Really? And they didn't let me know? Imbeciles.'

'So, you know her?'

She nodded, slipped her hand free of Christie's, and turned to one side. Christie detected shame. 'Of course. I knew her son was at the college... but I never expected her to approach you. Now why would she do a bloody thing like that?'

Good question. I was hoping you could tell me!

Nancy was wringing her hands together now, and Christie really hoped she didn't clam up and start keeping secrets from her – rather like her father had done. 'She was furious, Nancy. Saying all sorts of strange things. She suggested my father had been up to no good in some way, and that made me, in some way, a risk for her son—'

Nancy cut her off sharply by suddenly turning and glaring. 'Listen to me, Christie – that girl has never been well.' She tapped her temple. 'Not one bit. You need to understand that. Jesus... that puddled little bitch!' She stood abruptly, turning away.

Hearing a woman in her mid-fifties being referred to as

a 'girl' and 'a little bitch' was peculiar, but seeing Nancy losing control was far more disconcerting.

'We tried to do right by her, you know... and now...' She spun back to face Christie. 'What did she say exactly?'

Christie recounted everything – the classroom confrontation, the 'reach for the stars' bracelet, the reference to 'poison apples.' Then, she described her mother's words: 'vicious, vicious girl'.

With each detail, Nancy's expression grew more strained. 'Well, Georgina was the vicious girl all right! She almost ruined everything! Caroline, in her confusion, must have seen her in your place – I'm so sorry, Christie... so sorry your mother did that to you... but it wasn't aimed at you, you must understand that.'

Christie nodded. It made her feel slightly better. Why couldn't her father have said that to her though? Settled her anxiety with the truth?

'Excuse me a moment – I need a drink.' Nancy left the room. A moment later, she returned with two glasses of amber liquid over ice. 'Southern Comfort. I apologise, but I need this. Would you like...'

Christie's stomach lurched at the thought, memories of last night's wine still too fresh. She shook her head.

Nancy sat back down, taking a long pull from her glass like a woman seeking courage.

'Firstly, both you and your father are wonderful. "Poison apples"? Jesus wept!' She screwed up her face in disgust. 'Absolute balderdash.' Nancy sighed deeply, the sound carrying the weight of buried secrets. 'I'll tell you dear because it won't do for you to continue poking around in this. But after, you must let it go, okay? She almost destroyed your father's career once – if we breathe life into this drivel again, then, well, I dread to think what she'll destroy. His legacy, even! It was the poetry club. Your father mentioned it at some point to you, I'm sure?'

Christie nodded vaguely, remembering fragments of conversation from a long time ago. She said what she knew of it, and Nancy filled in the gaps. 'Teaching them as a group was never the issue... it was the fact that he spent some time alone with them, individually, helping them. It opened the door to accusations, I guess. The world is more cautious now. I don't suspect he'd have got himself into this position had this been recently.'

Christie nodded. Very few members of staff would put themselves into this position these days. She'd been advised to leave the classroom door open when speaking to a child alone, and she saw very few teachers not following the same advice.

'He made a mistake, it's clear,' Nancy said. 'A headmaster spending time alone with female students... he really should have been more mindful... but, like I said, policies and procedures just weren't what they are now.'

'What were the accusations?' Christie asked.

'I'll get to that, dear!' Nancy's voice suddenly carried a defensive edge.

Christie knew how much Nancy admired her father, but she was still surprised by the elevated tone. 'Okay.'

'He was a good man, Christie, your father. Still is! He did all this from his heart – looking for talented children with little prospect and elevating them. That was how he spent most of his career. Your father wasn't a rich man then, but don't you think your father could have made his money at that age? Of course he could have done! He was a true leader, inspirational and full of ideas. He could have made a fortune, but he chose to improve lives.' Her lip curled with decades-old contempt. 'And then Georgina Prince, the jealous, spoilt little brat, turned up like some kind of bloody wrecking ball!'

She took another fortifying sip. Then, she looked down into the liquid, and swirled it around, ice clinking against the glass.

'Georgina applied for the poetry workshop. Stephen made it clear he could only mentor four. He was a busy man. Georgina wasn't the only one rejected – most took it in their stride. But not her. No, Georgina had always been entitled, always prone to destruction. Turned on her best friend... accused her of stealing one of her poems for submission! I mean, how ludicrous! Did she really believe that Stephen wouldn't be able to tell the difference between the way they wrote poems?'

'Who was the best friend?'

'Sarah Matthews. Yes... a rather interesting story with her... disappeared when she was in her early twenties, but anyway, I digress... The reality was that Sarah was very talented, and this made Georgina bitter and jealous. Not only did she end their friendship, but she then turned her spite onto your father. The accusation was... I don't know... so outrageous, so exaggerated, how could anyone believe it? She claimed she burst into Stephen's office one day and found them half-clothed and kissing. I mean you can credit the gumption on the girl.'

Christie's blood ran cold. 'And you investigated?'

'Of course! We're duty-bound, Christie. Things were laxer then, but they weren't ridiculous. We were diligent, don't you worry about that. More diligent than most would have been. Your father! I mean, how absurd! But we gave it credence, for a time, asked your father to take a week off while we looked into it. We spoke to Sarah, spoke to all the girls, all of them, a complete pack of lies. Your father wasn't that kind of man as well you know. He never touched any of them, and all four were happy to say that. Yes, they loved the man, who couldn't? But not in that way, good lord, no.'

The vehemence in her voice made Christie flinch.

'But the insolent girl wouldn't let it go. Said that she went to confront him about her, and he cornered her in his office, put his hand around her throat, accused her of being jealous, and kissed her forcefully. Apparently, he said, "Is this what you're jealous of? You feel underappreciated?" She said she'd to force him off and make a run for it. Ha! Can you believe it, Christie? From one extreme lie to another.'

Christie nodded. She wanted, so badly, to be as adamant as Nancy.

No part of her could ever live with the consequences of this – if it contained even the slightest grain of truth.

'What happened?'

'Listen, and this is where you truly know it's a lie. Her parents threatened to go to the police unless we paid some kind of compensation. I mean, what manner of parent would do that? Yes, the police would dismiss it as nonsense, we knew that, and Georgina would make herself into a laughingstock, but still... what parent would just give up and ask for money unless they knew it was a lie, too? So, that's what happened. It seemed the best option—'

'Sorry...' Christie shook her head, confused. 'What happened exactly?'

'We paid the compensation.' Nancy looked away and took a drink. 'Well, we thought it better to do it. I mean, as much as it was complete balderdash, who wanted the press involved? Better just to pay the money, move her on. Your father was doing such a great job with the school – we didn't want to slow it, jeopardise it, you know?'

'So you paid her and her parents off?' Christie's voice trembled with disbelief.

'Don't worry! Not at the amount they wanted, we got it down to a more reasonable number.'

'No, I'm not worried about that. You can't pay someone off... that's just unacceptable. Completely unacceptable.' She tasted bile.

'I know how it sounds, but look, it was a different time and—' Nancy grabbed Christie's hands with desperate intensity. 'Think of the alternatives – your father's reputation dragged through the mud, his career destroyed. Besides, the added bonus was that Georgina's father was also a police officer. It meant that it'd be well and truly over. No further issues down the line. Public knowledge of this agreement would ruin him!'

'I'm sorry, Nancy, but this isn't making it sound any better!'

'It was so long ago... and think about it! Think of what we preserved. Think of all the lives he's touched. You think he would've been given that OBE with that vile lie out there in the public sphere – in this day and age? Which is precisely why this needs to be quietened down now, Christie. Because this was a different time, and you know what would happen if this story got out.'

Christie pulled her hands away. 'But... I can't... that's just awful.'

'So you believe those vile lies about your father?'

Christie didn't think she'd ever seen anyone look as indignant as Nancy did now.

'It's not that! It's the cover-up. The lack of transparency. It goes against everything I believe in.'

'Funnily enough we all believe in it until it involves us. I think when you've had a good think on it, dear, you—'

'No! I could never make peace with this.'

'You'd have done the same.'

'No, I wouldn't have, I would've—'

'Ruined a wonderful school? Those young adults were getting an education they'd never have had otherwise. And you'd have set fire to it over some spoilt princess's lies.' She squeezed Christie's fingers. 'We'd an opportunity to stop it happening. So yes, we paid her family. And I'd do it again. In a heartbeat.'

'But what if it is true... what if it wasn't a lie?'

'Are you seriously asking me that question?'

'Why would she come to the school now? Why drag her son out of my lesson? Why cause a scene?'

'For the same reason she did back then!' Nancy's smile was pitying. 'Bitterness, jealousy... and a dash of madness, too, perhaps... Besides, having her son taught by you reminds her of her shame, her poor behaviour. Better for her she just moves him. Makes a snide little point on the way. I don't think we'll hear from her again. She won't want to expose her shame any more—'

'I don't know... I looked into her eyes, Nancy... she didn't look like she thought she was a liar.'

'Well then she's still delusional! And, to be honest, I doubt she'll want to ruin her father's name either. No... I think it could be done, but you dear, need to get perspective, and sorry to say it, as I'm not your mother, but get a grip because—'

Christie yanked her hands back and stood on shaky legs. 'This is wrong. All wrong.'

'Listen to me, dear.' Nancy stood; her voice carried the weight of authority. 'Your mother is sick. You don't want to do anything silly. Your father is a wonderful man, take it from me. No good can come from any discontent. I advise you to ignore what happened and get back to work. Those kids need you. A Walker in the building is always in everyone's best interests. I say that from my heart.'

'I have to go...' She marched for the exit, ignoring Nancy's calls to stay a while longer.

Her journey home passed in a blur of confusion and doubt, her mind spinning like a broken compass.

Chapter Fifty-Six

Rylan was inspecting the new Christmas tree in the incident room corner.

Frank was curious too – where had it come from?

Chief Constable Donald Oxley, trying to bring festive cheer to HQ?

Nah, he thought. *Too surreal.*

Someone in this room had put it up. He narrowed his eyes - did someone on his team have too much time on their hands?

He looked between their faces, deciding it was best not to know.

If he challenged it, he'd earn himself another unflattering nickname to add to the list. Probably *Scrooge* or something like that.

'So... Stephen Walker OBE.' He infused each letter with carefully measured derision. 'He's well regarded. Seems that every corner we turn, someone's singing his praises. Sean, you spoke to the governors?'

'Two of them. And both practically wrote his eulogy.'

Frank snorted, while Sharon and Reggie also grinned over his sarcasm.

Sean straightened up in his chair, a proud look on his face. 'Some quotes...' He looked down at his notes. '"Transformative leadership", "visionary educator", "champion of the disadvantaged". They're even planning to name a building after him.'

'Tell them to hold off on the sign,' Frank muttered. He gestured at Clara, who'd been analysing Stephen's finances. 'It seems his golden reputation led to bars of solid gold, too.'

Clara's fingers never left her keyboard as she spoke. 'He rubbed shoulders with the right people during his career – MPs, business leaders, philanthropists. The connections that open doors. After retirement, he built a significant investment portfolio, had political influence, and earned an OBE. He had become very wealthy.'

'Aye, I'd say his prestige afforded him great opportunities after...' Frank said. 'But I'm thinking about now, or the present. Four girls, alone with him, and those photographs locked away in his safe like some kind of... trophy. Doesn't conform to many safeguarding policies I know of. I don't like it.'

Reggie said, 'It was the mid-eighties, boss.'

Frank's patience frayed slightly. 'I know, Reggie. I was making a point, not showing ignorance. Just because policies didn't include "safeguarding" in their titles doesn't mean they shouldn't exist. Common sense existed back then.' Frank's voice hardened. 'And how many people have we found guilty following folk looking the other way? This should heighten our suspicions, not dampen them.'

'Don't worry, boss,' Reggie said, stroking his moustache. 'Mine are heightened.'

He stopped himself short of telling Reggie not to do that with his moustache.

'And,' Sharon said, 'he knew Sarah Matthews, in particular, was vulnerable. He knew of her turbulent history.'

Frank nodded. 'If not for his wife exposing his photo albums, he may never have admitted being alone with them.' He turned back to Clara. 'Any luck tracking down the other three girls from the group?'

'Cassie Sinclair died five years ago – suicide after battling bipolar. I've requested files to find out what drove that. Sandy Greene, the published poet, is in Canada – planning to speak with her later. Kayleigh Cotton is in York – she spoke positively about Stephen. She said that he was never anything but respectful towards her... but she mentioned something interesting. A few months into their poetry group, he gave her a rather snazzy little bracelet. Gold plated and engraved. It said, "Reach for the Stars". She admits it made her feel rather special, at least until she realised he'd gifted the same bracelets to the other three girls in the group!'

'Probably got a bulk deal at a discount. Sleezy prick...' Reggie said.

'Eh, Reggie, tone it down, fella... We don't know enough yet for that kind of chat. But, aye, I admit, it does sound rather creepy... like keeping pictures in a locked safe! Reach for the stars... telling them to be ambitious.'

Gerry's hand shot up.

'Aye, Gerry?'

'There's a relevant quote from one of her poems: "A chain of gold. A beautiful bond. Wrapped around us." It comes from the poems that I suspect were written around the time she was part of that poetry group. It could be a reference to that gift? It could also be a reference to how close they became?'

'Inappropriately close?' Reggie suggested.

Gerry still had her hand up. She wasn't done yet. 'There's another one I've highlighted from the same period, I believe. It speaks of her feeling indebted: "There are no payments high enough for such gifts. How can a price be placed on light when it comes into the darkness?"'

A heavy silence descended over the room, broken only by Rylan's soft padding as he returned to Gerry's side.

'I'm sorry, boss,' Reggie breathed. 'But that's sleezy.'

'Chuffin' dark is what it is,' Frank said, pacing, his footsteps echoing his racing thoughts, 'but even if there's something in these words, we can't say for certain she's referring to Stephen's "gifts" of "light". It could refer to Hannah Wright, who took her under wing, paid for everything. Or Peter Watson, who spared her juvenile detention... Sharon and Reggie?'

Sharon leaned forward, choosing her words carefully. 'Peter's grief felt genuine, sir... to me.'

Reggie nodded. 'Me too, but I'm still open-minded. That he drove a red Fiesta can't be dismissed easily... but you know, it was raw, his anguish...'

'We've talked before about outstanding actors,' Frank said, raising an eyebrow.

'The man has been through a lot,' Sharon said. 'In his life. He was rather hollow.'

'That could make him more of a concern?' Frank played devil's advocate.

Sharon shook her head. 'I don't know. He was despondent. Too despondent to link to that silo and whatever went on in there... at least for me. When we told him, and showed that picture of her...' She looked down sadly. 'Well, it'd be so hard to fake... and I really think he believed she was in Australia. He wouldn't let it go. I also think he still believed it by the end.'

'Yeah, what of that? Who could have sent him that? And why?' Frank asked.

'The most obvious answer would be the killer,' Gerry said. 'Perhaps wanting him to take it to the police to cast doubt on their investigation and make them give up on it? I mean, it seems obvious to us it wouldn't work – that a passport check would be issued – but to the killer? Maybe not.'

'So could the killer be in Australia?' Reggie asked.

'Anything's possible... they could have gone on holiday, sent it, or even asked someone to send it from overseas? A relative, perhaps?' Frank asked. 'Okay, Clara, if you could look around the time that the postcard arrived – December, wasn't it? Anybody from Ruswarp or nearby emigrate around that time? Or at least head there on holiday? Let's focus in on all our suspects – any relatives, friends in Australia or nearby that could have arranged the card. But then, they'd have to be complicit, which is another gigantic leap.'

Clara nodded.

'And what of this red Fiesta?' Sean asked.

'There were over 15,000 red Fiestas registered in North Yorkshire in 1989,' Gerry said.

'Why couldn't Malcolm have got that bloody registration plate, eh?' Reggie asked.

'The red Fiesta evidence, from an unreliable witness, is the most frustrating part of this whole bloody case – but let's not make the mistake our predecessors made. Something will still come from it I feel. A drunk witness is better than no witness,' Frank said.

'Except in court,' Reggie said.

'We'll worry about court when we get there.'

'If,' Reggie said.

'*When*,' Frank said with a raised eyebrow.

'Also, let's not neglect to contact this Royal Oak – see if they've kept employment records of Peter's time there. If we can see if his alibi stands up, it may save us some legwork further down the line.'

Frank strode to the window. 'Christ on a bike... the white stuff is back!' Snow swirled against the backdrop of a setting sun. 'I hope it doesn't maroon us again. Oh, before I forget, has anybody had a sniff on that man with Hannah Wright on the photographs?'

Silence and a lot of shaking heads.

'Don't all shout at once—'

'Oh, I meant to say,' Sean said. 'It's no biggie, yet, but we know that Hannah's patient records were destroyed in the explosion, but I've struck gold with the NHS referral records. They'll be over tomorrow. Might give us a lead on our mystery man. Might be a parent of a patient, perhaps?'

'Good thinking, Sean. It's definitely something worth looking at.'

Colour rose in Sean's cheeks as he ducked his head, fighting back a grin.

'Ah shit,' Frank said, tapping his forehead. 'Almost forgot. Clive Morton? Stephen mentioned him intimidating students...' He went through what Stephen had said about him being overly friendly.

'Got the same story from one governor,' Sean said. 'Complaints about lingering stares at female students, comments about their uniforms. Advice on how to dress in a less provocative way.'

'Bloody hell,' Reggie said. 'And yet Hannah Wright gave him a job?'

'They let him go quietly. There were no formal complaints,' Sean explained. 'Maybe Hannah didn't know when she hired him as a gardener?'

'No,' Frank said. 'Stephen told me that she thought people misunderstood him. That he was a kind soul, who just came across as inappropriate.'

'Seems she went about trying to prove her point,' Reggie said.

Sean shifted in his chair. 'I tried following up with that call to Clive's widow, Becky Morton, but the phone was disconnected. I managed to speak to her nurse in the NHS, who visits daily. He claims Becky's decline has been rapid this year. Memory's going, communication's breaking down. She's still mobile but housebound, and he thinks a care home placement isn't far off.'

Frank absorbed this information, feeling the weight of time pressing down. With historical cases like this, he knew how quickly connections could disappear – each death taking potential answers to the grave. The smallest detail could crack everything open, but their window was closing fast. 'Sean, it might not seem like much now, but keep it in mind. In fact...' He ran a hand across his face, weighing options. 'Sharon and Reggie – would you visit Becky tomorrow? Yes, I know it might seem like a long shot, but we're too vague on Hannah and Clive, and what if she knows this mystery man? She might be one of our last links to the whole bloody thing. I don't want to wake up next week and find out we need to talk to her, and she's already passed.'

'No problems, boss. As long as she doesn't smoke, I'll be fine with that,' Reggie said.

'Yes, Reg, I noticed your cough had improved.'

'Some brisk walking earlier helped,' he said.

'Aye,' Frank said. 'Bet it did... maybe you could take a brisk walk to the barbers for this?' He pointed at his lip.

'Hilarious, boss.'

'To a more sombre note. Tomorrow, I'm meeting Margaret Matthews at the morgue. She wants to see her daughter.'

Sean said, 'Is that wise? She should just remember her how she was.'

'She'll be gone herself within a couple of months,' Frank said. 'I think memories are the last of her concern... I think she just wants to be close to her child one last time.' Frank straightened. 'While I'm with her, I'll press her more about Stephen Walker – see if there're any more poems, or anecdotes, squirrelled away.' He looked at his watch. 'Right then, let's wrap this up. I'll make a note of everyone's assignments for tomorrow and pin them on the board.'

As Frank wrote up the assignments, movement caught his eye. Reggie was at the Christmas tree, clearly retrieving the bag he'd brought it in! The madman then placed one final bauble with theatrical care.

You've got to be kidding me. Christ alive.

Reggie wasn't satisfied with just being the fittest old man in Yorkshire – he now wanted to be Mr Christmas, spreading cheer like a silver-haired Santa!

The only thing that saved Frank's inferiority complex from worsening was Reggie's bloody awful attempt at facial hair. No amount of festive spirit could compensate for that monstrosity.

Chapter Fifty-Seven

Through darkness you showed me light. When chains bound me, you gave me flight.

For most of the day since the detectives had visited, Peter had sat in stunned silence, holding the eagle greeting card from Sarah with a trembling hand.

He said they could take the postcard, but not this.

No.

This was one of three possessions he wanted with him when he died.

The postcard, however, it seemed, had been some kind of lie. It'd never been *his eagle,* after all.

How many times today had he reminisced over his times on the sofa, Sarah on one side, Donna on the other?

He'd lost count.

Sarah had always dreamed of sunshine and distant shores, longing to trade Whitby's cold beaches for Australian warmth.

And, for so long, for decades, in fact, he'd believed that she'd reached that promised land.

He sat and cried.

'But you didn't, did you, Sarah? You never flew.'

He sank into his chair, pressing trembling hands against his eyes, as if he could hold back the grief. If he concentrated hard enough, maybe he could reach back through time, grab hold of himself and tell him to get round to Tommy Reid's. Beg her to come home with him.

He never should have listened to Hannah Wright and stayed away.

He dropped his hands.

Outside, it was growing dark.

Suddenly, like a tomb closing in, he felt the walls pressing down on him.

I don't have long left now, he thought. *There's only so much more I can take.*

His breath came in short, desperate gasps. He needed something – connection, warmth – anything to anchor him.

Lucy.

Before he could think better of it, his feet carried him across the street to number 5, a fresh bout of snow whirling and peppering his face.

He knocked too hard, too urgently.

But this was it now.

Lucy was the last connection to humanity he had left, and he still owed her daughter, Mia, that apology.

Lucy opened the door. Her face was tight with concern. 'Peter... are you okay? What happened?'

'I need to...' The last words stuck in his throat like thorns. *See you.*

'Peter?'

He closed his eyes and shook his head. 'Sorry...'

'Don't be... come in.' He felt her hand on his arm, pulling him inside. He allowed her to do this.

After she closed the door, he looked at her. 'I don't know how much longer I can do this.'

'Do what?'

Live.

The truth hovered on his lips before retreating, unspoken. 'Is this about earlier?' she asked. 'Those police officers Reece saw...'

He nodded, tears tracking down his weathered cheeks. 'Partly that... and partly everything else...' Shame crept into his expression. 'I found out I lost someone else today... someone else that was so important to me. I've *lost* everyone that I ever loved.'

'Who? When?'

'Sarah. It was so long ago. But it doesn't make it any less painful.'

She ushered him inside before his dignity could fail him completely, leading him to the lounge where Mia sat cradling Sophie. The baby's eyes found his immediately, as if she'd been waiting for him.

Her face split into a sunrise smile, and for one blessed moment, he felt some of those shadows recede.

He moved towards the child as if drawn by an invisible thread.

Sophie giggled, and more of those shadows retreated.

'Look how happy she is to see you,' Mia said.

'Aye,' Peter whispered, reaching out with trembling fingers.

Sophie's tiny hand found his finger, gripping it with surprising strength.

For a moment, he felt distraction, warmth... respite from the darkness. 'I'm sorry for yesterday, Mia...'

'It's okay,' Mia said. 'You were tired... I was forceful.'

'No, don't make excuses for me.' He shook his head. 'Really, I'm done with that. I was wrong, and I'm sorry.'

'It's forgotten,' she said.

He stared at Sophie, who was still clutching his finger, and rocking, so happily, in her mother's arms.

'Can I hold her now?' He met Mia's eyes. 'Please?'

Mia smiled. 'I don't think you've a choice. She's desperate for you to do that.'

He smiled through fresh tears. 'Oh God, I'd like that. I'd like that very much.'

He settled into the chair. Mia placed Sophie in his arms with careful precision. The baby nestled against his chest, her warmth achingly familiar. She giggled and kicked her legs gently, looking up at him with complete trust. He leaned down, breathing in her sweet, powder-fresh scent, feeling the silk of her hair against his chin.

Behind his closed eyes, he saw Donna sitting opposite, her smile radiant with approval.

For the first time in years, he let himself feel whole.

'Are you okay?' Lucy asked.

'Yes...' He opened his eyes, not bothering to hide his tears. 'Never better.'

He returned Sophie after she grew drowsy, and Mia placed her on the mat.

Still, like sunshine after a storm, the feeling of bliss lingered.

He watched as she drifted off to sleep on her mat, her face peaceful, tiny fingers still curled as if holding onto something precious. Then Peter said, 'I want to tell you both about someone now... is that okay?'

'The person you mentioned at the door?' Lucy asked.

'No, although she's special and I'll tell you about her too, sometime. No, now I want to talk about Penny.'

'Of course,' Lucy said.

He took a deep breath. He exhaled. 'Just a moment… it's been so long. So long since I spoke.'

'Take your time,' Lucy said.

He closed his eyes and smiled.

And there she was – his beautiful six-year-old daughter, smiling back.

Chapter Fifty-Eight

NO MATTER *how many weather warnings were issued, snow always felt like a surprise visitor.*

Especially, Peter imagined, for a six-year-old.

Peter felt the warmth of Penny's hand in his.

She was as light as a bird, but he could feel every one of her skips and bounces.

He smiled down at her as she glided her yellow paper crane through the air.

'Clara was poorly today. I shared my orange with her.'

'That's kind of you,' Peter said.

Penny beamed up at him, and there she was – Donna – glowing behind those eyes.

'I share because Mummy shares.'

'Aye, I know,' Peter said. 'You and she are two peas in a pod.'

They both had that endless desire to help others, to make the world a little better.

'But she's curious,' Donna would say. 'Curious and enthusiastic. That's on you, Pete. Our girl's got the best of both of us... and none of our nonsense.'

The road was busy. Bustling. Cars rushing to outrun the weather. Risking their safety to reach safety.

At the bus shelter, they huddled together on the cold metal bench, Penny's legs swinging in empty air as she continued flying her increasingly damp paper crane.

Thursday was the day they caught public transport.

Penny loved buses and trains – they alternated weekly.

'You want to keep that crane out of the snow,' Peter said.

'Kylie!'

'Who?'

She giggled. 'Kylie the crane.'

'Ah, of course.' He laughed.

'Miss Wilson says that in Japan, if you make a thousand, you get a wish!'

'What would you wish for?'

'A puppy.'

'How many cranes did you make?'

'Two.'

The puppy, then, was a long way off.

Not that Peter was averse to a puppy. After all, they'd discussed it. Donna liked the idea. He'd hated it at first, but he always came round to what his two girls wanted.

'Is that your second?'

'No, my first. My second is in my tray at school.'

'Well, keep Kylie safe, then,' he said. 'It's your first and it's special... and very perfect.'

A gust of wind caught them by surprise. Penny squealed.

He watched the paper crane swooping off.

'Daddy!' *Her face crumpled as it danced away, up and down, flashing yellow against the snow and gloom. A series of gusts prevented it from settling. Up and down. Dancing backward through the gloom.*

He caught Penny's shoulder, stopping her before she

could move to chase it. He didn't want her running close to traffic. 'Stay here, dear.'

He sprinted after Kylie, shielding his eyes against the oncoming headlights. The yellow paper crane stayed just beyond reach. Each time his fingers brushed it, another gust would steal it away.

If the crane reached the road, it'd be crushed. Lost forever.

Traffic rushed past like an angry river, horns blaring.

Penny's voice carried to him, thin with desperation: 'Please, Daddy, catch Kylie!'

'I'm trying!' he called back, not wanting to let her down.

Penny believed in him so completely.

These were the years when Daddy could do anything. And he relished them.

Here it was! His fingers closed around the crane. He stopped against a lamppost and turned, holding it aloft. 'Got it!'

There was a screech of tyres. Followed by the sound of metal scraping against metal. The surrounding darkness vibrated.

Glass showered the night. Glinting like snow in the streetlights.

Shards swirled and circled one another.

He gazed into them, and thought of stars exploding, wondering for a moment if a car bonnet folding into a bus shelter was the signal that his world was next.

Stars... worlds folding like paper. Origami.

If not for the hellish sound of twisting metal, and the devilish smoke in his nostrils, he may have lost himself at that moment. Caught between collapsing galaxies and terrifying tragedy, but he didn't.

Instead, he screamed his daughter's name as she disappeared inside the implosion.

'Penny!'

And then he ran, keeping the paper crane safe, unbroken, uncreased, against him, like all their lives depended on it.

Chapter Fifty-Nine

From the dead world, had risen another.

For so long, he'd lived inside it.

On a star he didn't understand. Nor care to understand.

If not for Sarah, Donna and then Bryan, he'd have left it long ago.

But something was shifting inside this world that he'd ambled through, ghost-like, and functional. Something was stirring.

He hadn't spoken of this in so very long. And now he'd just silenced a room with his tale.

For a long while, he stared at the floor and let the silence linger.

He'd known this story would steal their words – he'd been ready for that.

Eventually, he looked up, but still nobody spoke.

Mia's cheeks were wet, while Lucy stared at him, face gaunt, expressionless.

Mia's steps were unsteady as she left the room in tears.

Guilt twisted in Peter's gut.

This tragedy was so heavy for someone so young.

He took a deep breath.

For everyone.

'I'm sorry,' he whispered. 'She's *so* young. I really should have known better.'

Lucy crossed the room to him and sat beside him. She took one of his hands in both of hers. Her grip was almost painful. She still couldn't speak.

Now her eyes were full of tears.

After finding out about Sarah, he'd cried for most of the day. He really believed that there were none left. Still, he was unsurprised when more came.

But the tears felt different from usual.

They came more as a relief. A purging, perhaps.

'I'm sorry. Don't pity me. I'm too long into this whole game for that. Please don't tell me it wasn't my fault. I've lost count of the number of times I heard that in the weeks and months after. I stopped talking about it. For so very long. But while Donna was here, I still had someone to share it with. Now, I've no one... so I'm sorry...'

'Who are you apologising to, Peter?'

He creased his brow. 'I don't understand.'

'Why apologise to me, or Mia? Why? You've done nothing but share with us. Open up to us. Be *here* with us.'

'I know...'

'So, who are you apologising to, Peter? *Who?*'

His eyes filled again, and tears ran down his face. 'Myself. I'm apologising to myself... I don't know why...'

'I think you do.'

'I miss her so much... I miss them all so much...'

She leaned forward and embraced him.

He held her back and cried for an immeasurable length of time.

Afterwards, they sat together, hands joined, until Sophie stirred and brought her giggles back to the room.

'Do you want a drink, Peter?' Lucy asked.

Peter shook his head. 'No, thank you, but there is something I'd really like...' He smiled down at Sophie.

Lucy understood. She lifted Sophie carefully.

'Can I?'

She placed Sophie in his arms. He pressed his nose against her downy head, breathing in that perfect baby smell.

∼

Penny was impossibly small on that, her first day.

So fragile.

Yet he held her.

'Loosen your arm... you won't break her.'

'Unbreakable, she is.'

'Like me.'

'No argument.'

'And you too, Peter. You too.'

He'd pressed his nose to Penny's head, breathing in that new-life scent. He felt his heart expand beyond what he thought was ever possible.

When she stirred, his arms adjusted instinctively, as if they'd always known how to do this.

Had he really been waiting all his life for just this moment?

His daughter's eyelids lifted.

'Hey there,' he whispered.

Penny's eyes found his.

'I'm the luckiest person alive.'

A tear ran down his face.

'I know she feels the same way.'

'This is the world I was born for, Donna. This is the star that I want to live on.'

Chapter Sixty

Frank sat by the lounge window, eyes tracking the barely lit street outside.

The forecast had suggested it'd fall lightly for now, but more heavy snow would come in the early hours.

With Christmas Eve this coming weekend, many would rejoice over a white Christmas.

But not Frank.

And not just because of work implications, either, but because bad weather made the return of the hooded mysterious figure less likely.

What had he wanted?

The question had lurked all day, plucking at his mind as he'd tried so desperately to do right by Sarah Matthews.

But the mystery fed on him like vultures over a carcass.

His phone buzzed with a fifth message from Evelyn. They were both the slowest texters in the world, so the conversation had lasted almost an hour. In a way, the gentle flow of their back and forth was a comfort, something unusual in this day and age.

Evelyn had escaped the hospital today, and she was

currently talking about how her daughter was readying the chains and padlocks again to keep her away from civilisation.

A genuine laugh escaped him – when was the last time that had happened?

He looked forward to their meeting at the park on Christmas Eve with an anticipation that felt almost foreign.

Her recovery had certainly given him a lift.

He looked up.

Movement caught his eye. Gerry, with Rylan padding faithfully beside her, made her way up his path.

Frank checked his watch, frowning. This was more than unusual – it was unprecedented. Gerry had a carefully maintained schedule. It must be serious for her to deviate.

He opened the door before she could knock. The sight of her face stopped him cold. Her eyes were red-rimmed. In all their time together, he'd never seen her composure crack like this.

'How do, Gerry?'

She shifted uncomfortably. 'I know coming late is irregular, sir... so... I apologise.'

'Don't apologise. Me and irregularity are close friends,' Frank said. And Christ, wasn't that the truth – it'd been years since he'd known his arse from his elbow. Only recently, with Gerry's methodical influence, had any semblance of order returned to his life.

She was welling up.

Christ!

This really was unprecedented.

He didn't know whether to embrace her. She was autistic and rarely liked to be touched – he'd hate to make this situation worse. He refrained.

'I'm sorry *again*.'

'Enough of the apologies, Gerry!'

She looked confused. *Again, unusual.*

'I really don't have anyone else to talk to...'

Frank tried not to feel wounded by that. At least he was a resort. Two years ago, he wouldn't have been anyone's. 'I'll put the kettle on then.'

She shook her head.

Of course, he thought, remembering she wouldn't drink it if someone else made it.

'I've got water... so come and sit down. Let's get to the root of the issue.'

Chapter Sixty-One

THEY SAT in silence for a time.

Gerry stroked Rylan while she drank from a fresh bottle of Perrier water.

Eventually, she said, 'It was you, Frank, or Dr Samuels. However, talking to Dr Samuels wouldn't have helped this time. His priority is me... *only* me... and he'd advise me that Tom should be accepting of exactly who I am.'

Frank nodded. 'He's got a point, I guess. Sometimes your way or the highway is a good call.'

'I was hoping you could be a little more open-minded – maybe, consider Tom's feelings, too?'

But you're still my priority too, lass, Frank thought. 'I'll try,' he said.

'Tom called two hours ago...' Her voice carried a fragility he'd never heard in Gerry before. 'To tell me we're finished... it's over.' She took a deep breath. Frank could tell she was trying to stop herself from welling up again.

'I'm sorry to hear that.'

She nodded. 'He says we're too different. That it won't work out.' Her hands stilled in Rylan's fur. 'At first, I took it as it was. If he isn't happy, then he isn't happy. That's the logic, rational approach. But then, within an hour, I experienced a sudden sense of loss. And it seemed to increase. It's disconcerting. I know I can differ from others, and I accept that, but what does that actually mean? In practice? That I'm not able to pursue a relationship with someone I like – especially, if they're neurotypical?'

'Did he elaborate on the call?'

'He said he felt controlled. That there's no room to breathe. He said spontaneity is important in relationships. He said you can't schedule and document everything. That love isn't a spreadsheet.'

Frank shifted uncomfortably. His heart ached to defend Gerry, but there was truth in Tom's words, he guessed. He felt some sympathy for the lad.

'The last thing he said was that he felt like he was living in a laboratory experiment sometimes.' Her voice broke on that last word.

Slow down, fella! That's a bit bloody harsh, Tom lad, he thought, his sympathy suddenly diminishing.

'Is that what I'm really like? Controlling?'

Christ! Not a question he wanted to tackle, but she'd come to him for honesty. Still, some swerving felt appropriate. 'We *all* have our moments. It's the intentions that matter and your intentions, Gerry, are good. Look at me!' He patted his shrinking stomach. 'You've probably added years to my life with your...' He stopped himself short of saying 'orders'. 'Good intentions.'

She met his eyes for the first time in their conversation. 'You mean that?'

'Of course!' He paused. Now this was the hard part, but she'd come to him for help – not to bash Tom. 'Dr Samuels is right. You don't have to conform to anyone else's expectations. But I guess any relationship needs a halfway point, you know? Compromise.' He took a deep breath, feeling like he was walking through a minefield. 'What caused this? Not those marriage considerations?'

She nodded.

'Which ones in particular?'

'We didn't get around to reading them together.'

'So, what was bothering him, exactly?'

'The number of points – he saw the document on my computer...'

'How many points were there?'

When she told him, he had to force back an exclamation.

Christ almighty!

Chapter Sixty-Two

GERRY PLODDED through her extensive list, which she had access to on her mobile.

Frank recognised the comfort she found in organisation and so was as supportive as he could be.

'Having Rylan sleep on the left side of the bed *has* to be non-negotiable,' Gerry stated, as if reciting a fact from a textbook.

'I see that,' Frank said, knowing firsthand how Rylan's consistent presence helped ground her, especially during difficult cases. 'That's reasonable.'

But some points made Frank wince. When she reached the scheduling of intimacy, in particular.

'Tom says spontaneity matters, but I don't understand why unplanned encounters would be superior,' she said.

Frank coughed. 'Aye, well, maybe ask someone like Helen about that one... shall we move on...It's quite a list.'

When she reached the point about keeping emotional discussions away from mealtimes, he found himself nodding in recognition. How many dinners had ended with Mary or Maddie in tears, while he'd sat there silent, too exhausted from police work to offer anything but stony silence? The memory stung - their frustration at his emotional unavailability, his own guilt at being unable to bridge that gap. After twenty minutes, Frank asked how much was left in the list.

'We're about halfway.'

Jesus, he thought. *My head is spinning, and I'm a passive observer. Imagine marrying into it?*

It was time to offer some words of wisdom.

And hope he didn't lose one of his few friends left in the world. 'Okay, first, Gerry, you know if you've children, nearly all of those plans go out of the window?'

Her face drained of colour so quickly it took his breath away. He hadn't meant to go in so hard. 'But... there're lots of positives to having children, too,' Frank insisted. 'They're cute... to begin with, at least. Some people like feeling depended on...'

Her expression suggested he was digging himself into a deeper hole.

'I've included a section on children,' Gerry said. 'Do you want to hear it?'

He sighed, leaning forward in his chair. 'Gerry, I mentioned children to point out that life can get a little unpredictable.'

'I understand, sir. That's why I made the list.'

'Aye, so you did. Can I be blunt?'

'Yes. That's why I'm here. Because I knew you'd be.'

'Forget Tom for a second. I think you first need to ask yourself what you want out of a relationship?'

'I did that before all this. I wanted compatibility, so I assessed it. Ninety per cent was our alignment!'

'I remember, but maybe you aren't compatible if you want that level of control and he doesn't?'

'So, you're saying the level of control is fine – I've just opted for the wrong partner?'

He took a deep breath, thinking, *No, I imagine 99 per cent of potential partners will find that list as appealing as gum surgery...* 'It's possible, but if you want my honest opinion, I think this list is too rigid. And I think you'll struggle to find anyone compatible while it continues to exist.'

'So, I should get rid of the list?'

'I don't think the list is the issue, per se. I think it's... Gerry, do you love him?'

'Love him?'

'Aye.'

Expecting a convoluted answer, he was surprised when she said, 'Yes.'

'Okay.' He nodded. *That's a start*, he thought.

'I feel the loss, I told you.'

'I can see that... so... you know love differs from absolutely everything else, right? *Everything*. And it's especially different to work. We can't analyse it like a crime scene, compartmentalising it into different leads. It's very different.'

'Messy?'

'Aye, messy.'

'I never really liked messy.'

'Aye, but you like Tom, don't you? If you love him, then maybe it's time to accept some mess.'

She looked down at Rylan and stroked his head.

He felt a warming sensation inside his chest. She'd been there for him, in so many ways, since they'd first met. Or, rather, in his face... but she'd helped him. She really had. He wanted to help her now. 'Tell me about the times when you weren't thinking about rules or assessments when you were with Tom. Just... moments.'

Her brow furrowed. 'I don't understand.'

'You know, times when you felt close to Tom.'

'I thought you didn't like to talk about those moments?'

'Outside of the bloody bedroom!'

She was quiet for so long, he wondered if she'd understood, but of course she had, and the answer was gentler and more heartfelt than he'd expected. 'We watch nature documentaries together. Even though I already know most of the information, I enjoy his explanations. His enthusiasm. The way he gets excited about things I find obvious. It makes me feel lighter. Not so much amused, just... I don't know.'

He smiled. 'Endearing?'

She nodded. 'Is that relevant?'

'Aye, Gerry, lass. Aye.' *And it's probably the most relevant thing you've ever said about this relationship.* 'Continue...'

'He's always trying to help. Brings me bottled, unopened water without being asked. Organises the living room exactly how I like it if something goes out of place. He learned all Rylan's routines...' Her voice cracked, but this time, the emotion wasn't from loss.

Frank felt her realising.

'He cares about the little things that matter to me... more than I realised.'

'Gerry, ask yourself, does he need a list of rules to make you happy?'

She stared off into space. A tear tracked down her face. 'No...'

'Well, there you go.'

'But what if I need them, sir... to be happy? What'll happen to me without a safety net?'

Frank sighed, feeling the weight of her trust pressing down on him. 'I don't know.' And he really didn't. 'You can only have my opinion, for what it's worth. Love isn't about controlling everything, Gerry. Maybe it's just the opposite.'

'Do you think I'm loveable, Frank?' The directness of her question caught him off guard.

Bloody hell – how do I answer that?

Truthfully?

He gave it a go. 'You're one of the most loveable people I've ever met, Gerry...'

She stared straight at him and held his gaze. It was unusual and testament to the surprise his comment had caused.

His cheeks inflamed. 'But not in that way, of course.'

'In what way?'

'The Tom and Gerry way – good lord! Sorry, not the cartoon way, obviously... your way with Tom. I see you as loveable... like a daughter...'

She looked confused. 'I am very different from Maddie.'

'Aye... I know... but that's not really what I meant.'

She lowered her eyes and thought.

A tear welled in his eye, but he quickly blinked it away.

They returned to silence for a time.

Eventually, she sighed and looked up. 'I ruined *everything*. Tom's given up.'

He shook his head. 'No, Gerry. He proposed to you. That's not the action of someone who's willing to give up easily. There could be life in this yet.'

Chapter Sixty-Three

Frank was just getting ready for bed when he received a message from Gerry.

> Thank you, sir. Just got home. I tried calling Tom. He still isn't answering. But I feel more positive now. Thank you again.

'Come on lad,' he said out loud. 'Answer your bloody phone. You might just like hearing what she has to say...'

An idea occurred to him. He went to his contacts and scrolled through to a number on his phone Gerry had once given him as an emergency number.

Tom.

Was it a good idea? Frank Black, relationship counsellor?

He wasn't sure it had a ring to it.

Closing his eyes, he thought about her on his doorstep, coming to him for help.

She'd no parents.

At the moment, he'd no daughter – at least, not in his life.

It felt right to help. He'd do it for Maddie, and her father would have done it for Gerry.

'Hello?' Tom's voice was wary. 'Frank? Is everything all right? Gerry?'

'Aye. Don't worry. Everything's fine, son. I guess Gerry gave you my number, too, then?'

'Well, she said I was an emergency contact – guess she didn't want me ignoring an unknown number?'

'Makes sense. Thorough.' *Definitely her way,* he thought.

'Yes – how can I help?'

'Can I have a minute? It's about Gerry...'

'You said she was fine?'

'Aye, she is. Well, she's okay-ish, I guess. Could be better.' *Shit, get to the point, Frank Black.* 'Not good at all, actually.'

'Go on.'

'Okay... tell me if I'm out of order.'

'I will.'

He took a deep breath. 'She loves you, fella.'

He waited. The silence stretched between them like a rubber band about to snap.

Bloody hell, this really is none of my business. 'Tom?'

'Frank, I need to tell you something.'

'Go on...'

'You *are* out of order.'

Cocky little scrote, Frank thought. 'Hear me out.' He took another deep breath and said, 'You know when I first met Gerry, she drove me bloody mad? Everything had to be just so. Wouldn't let up about my diet, my smoking, my car... anyway... but now I know the truth. She cares about me, she really does. And the thing is, she cares about you,

Tom, too. A lot. A chuffin' lot. Like, the love version of a lot!' He broke off, knowing he was rambling.

'You know about the proposal, then?'

'Aye...'

'That was private! I can't believe she's telling everyone!'

Hearing the outrage in Tom's voice caused a rise of irritation in Frank. He pushed it back down. *He's just sore*, he thought, *probably a pleasant lad when you get to know him.*

'It went down like a lead balloon...' Tom continued.

'Ah, you see, that's why I'm phoning. It didn't.'

'Ha! I was there.'

'I know, but—'

'But what? It was a disaster!'

Well, if you let me finish, lad... 'Think about it, who'd write a document that long for a marriage they weren't into?'

'Someone who's only worried about herself?' Tom said.

That wasn't really the answer he was looking for. He'd had to push back another wave of irritation. 'Now, we both know that isn't true.'

'Do we?'

'Okay, Tom, listen, I'm only going to ask one thing of you. One thing. Then, I'm gone...' *So I can take some deep breaths,* he thought.

'Yes.'

'Please phone Gerry. Just the once. See what she has to say. I think she finally understands something.'

'Oh, like what?'

Frank gritted his teeth. *You're really grating on me now, fella... still, I'll keep buttering you up, for her.* 'That you're endearing, and she wants to be with you. List or no list.'

'Really?' Tom's voice held a note of excitement.

Frank felt a small sense of victory – he'd done his job.

'Bye, Tom.' He hung up. Better that way. The kid was pushing him too far – Frank might snap and then Tom may just be fleeing the country with a boot up his arse. That might feel good, but it wouldn't do anyone any good.

Well, Gerry lass, he thought, *not sure if I'm keen personally, but I'm not the one who has to marry him. He's a lucky fella; he better get on and realise that, or I'll have to put my list together for him.*

Chapter Sixty-Four

STEPHEN WATCHED Caroline as she slept.

He reached out, his fingers hovering close to her elegant cheekbones, but he didn't touch, not wanting to disturb her.

'My darling,' he said, a tear running down his face. 'How you glow... even now. How you still glow.'

But he'd be lying if he didn't admit that the glow was diminishing. Bit by bit. A little more every day.

Every night, he'd lie in the darkness, terrified that when he woke the next day, her glow would have gone completely.

And yet, as his entire world collapsed – his life with Caroline, his relationship with his daughter, his legacy – his health remained.

I'm going to outlive all of this chaos and destruction.

He closed his eyes and rubbed his forehead.

What a horrible thought... and one which made him wonder if he'd be better off like Caroline. A mind fragmenting. Consciousness fading like watercolours in sunlight.

It sounded perverse, but preferable to watching everything become dust.

The knock at the door startled him.

He opened his eyes. Caroline was undisturbed. Her chest continued to rise and fall.

Christie, I expect, he thought. *Demanding more answers.*

He left Caroline in bed and headed downstairs, fastening his dressing gown.

He opened the door to Georgina Prince.

Sharp adrenaline ran through him like jagged glass. 'You shouldn't be at my house.'

She narrowed her eyes. 'I know.'

'You just couldn't leave it, could you?'

She took a deep breath and shook her head. 'No, I couldn't. Seeing you brought everything back.'

'Your lies? What do you want, Georgina? Another payday?' He tried to add authority to his voice as he'd done in his career so many times.

Her sneer stripped away that authority like paint under acid.

'You think I saw any of that money? Any of it?'

'I'm sure it improved your family's life—'

'It never improved mine.'

'So, that's what you're here for, more money?'

She shook her head.

'What then? Christie confronting you like that at Riverside was unacceptable—'

'I tried to stay quiet. For so long, I did. But there was a line. Your daughter teaching my son? How could you expect me to allow that? You tarnished lives – I couldn't allow it to happen to Jamie. And now, well, now, you've woken me up. I can't ignore who you really are. What you did! I just can't!'

He snorted, though his hands were trembling. Her

words were like hammer blows. But he needed to maintain an air of control. 'What is it you want?'

Her voice dropped to a whisper as sharp as steel. 'I want you to admit you're a liar.'

'I'm not.'

'Yes, you are. A fucking good one at that! A seasoned one! Poor Sarah.'

He wondered if she knew about Sarah's remains. Possibly not. He didn't wish to antagonise the situation further on his doorstep. Let someone else tell her. 'You're delusional... always were.'

'Nancy Keegan called me,' Georgina said. 'After your daughter went to see her. She said the same thing to me. Delusional. Strange, isn't it, that everyone always believed you, and not me?'

'Because I'm not a liar!'

'I see you'll never admit it, so I've changed my mind. I'm here to see Caroline, your wife.'

'She's ill and you're not welcome.' Stephen stepped forward, ready to shut the door. 'Now go away before I call the police.'

Georgina's foot blocked it. The force of her sudden push then sent him staggering backward. He hit the wall, and the impact knocked the wind out of him.

Georgina stepped into the house and closed the door behind her. 'Don't get in my way, old man. You aren't what you were.'

Gasping, he reached into his pocket for his mobile phone and held it up. 'I've enough left in me to call the police.' He opened the keypad.

'Do it. The first thing we'll discuss is that meeting with the governors.'

His fingers froze.

'Where is she? Upstairs?'

'Get out of my fucking house!'

'I'm not leaving until I've told her everything, and until she's got you to admit you're a liar.'

'Your version of the truth isn't the truth!'

'Yes, it is.' Georgina was now standing at the bottom of the stairs, looking up.

The sight that greeted Stephen froze his blood: Caroline stood on the stairs, wearing her nightie, her face carrying that emptiness that had become increasingly familiar.

'Ah, we have guests,' Caroline said.

'I'm here to see you, Mrs Walker.'

'She's just leaving.' Stephen's voice cracked like thin ice. 'And you need to go back to bed, Caroline, and rest.'

'Don't be silly, Stephen, I'm fine,' Caroline said. 'Are you here to see me, dear?'

'Yes,' Georgina said.

'Then come up. Please.'

Stephen watched, helpless as a child, as Georgina started up the stairs. Halfway up, she looked back at Stephen and smiled. It was like a dagger, going deep into him, forcing him against the wall, gasping for more air. 'No.'

The woman was driving nails into the coffin of everything he'd built!

Chapter Sixty-Five

Mark leaned in close behind Lewis. 'It won't be long now.'

His words were so soft, they seemed breathed rather than whispered.

The truth about John's other life would soon be gone forever.

He looked down at his father's hand. Should he take hold of it? Be with him at the end as he embarked on that final journey?

Do you deserve that?

But then, would I deserve it?

Lewis thought about what he did to Gregg Ince, and then about abandoning his son.

Maybe I don't, John. Maybe I don't deserve anyone with me at the end any more than you do.

The thought made him panic. His heartbeat thundered in his ears, and the walls suddenly seemed to close in. He pressed his fingertips against his sternum, closed his eyes, and used the grounding technique he'd learned in prison. Five points of contact: fingertips on chest, feet flat on floor, back against chair. Focus on the weight of each point. Breathe into the pressure.

For a moment, he felt anchored in the present.

But, then, following one exhalation, he felt himself in the past's undertow, and a memory dragged him under.

A football pitch. Mud-speckled boots.

Three misses. Each attempt worse than the last.

The jeers of his teammates. And the intensity of failure.

'Wide open goal, mate! Even my gran could've scored that!'

At home, shame burned inside, Felix – always the stable one – said, 'Get your boots.'

Three hours under a bruised sky. The thud of leather against leather. Felix's voice carried endless patience as he showed positioning, timing, follow-through.

'You've got this, little brother. One more time.'

The sun sank behind the goalposts like a deflated ball.

'One more time.'

The following week, everything clicked. A ball arched. Into the top corner. Perfect.

But that night his house had been empty.

Silent.

The note on the kitchen table.

That was the loudest thing he'd ever read.

Felix was in the hospital. Sick.

In the present, he tried grounding himself once more, but went under again, into another memory.

His mother's hand was in his. Tears in her eyes. 'I lost everyone. But not you.' Her other hand pressed into his cheek. It was cold. 'My sweet boy. You'll make such a good husband, such a good father.'

He wanted to tell her it wasn't true. Ask for her help. But how could he? That would mean burdening her with the knowledge that his experiences had left him hollow inside. That he would never be good for anyone.

How could he break her like that?

The next day, her face was slack. The morning paper was unopened in her lap.

He held her hand while she sat in the armchair and waited for her to be taken away.

She would've known little pain.

Was this a mercy?

Or just another wave which would eventually drag him deeper into the darkness?

When he returned to the present, he was holding his father's hand.

His skin, like his mother's that morning, was papery and cold.

Instinctively, he went to pull his hand away, but subjected to another memory, he froze.

He was burning up with fever.

His father's hand was in his. He was sitting alongside him. He sat for hours and hours. Day upon day. Reading him stories. 'Oh, the places you'll go,' his father read.

And Dr Seuss wasn't wrong.

Not one bit.

With his father beside him, he soared.

And afterwards, he slept, exhausted in his father's arms.

Back in the present, he thought, *Why had I forgotten that?*

John's eyes fluttered beneath paper-thin lids, lips moving in silent speech. Still clutching his hand, Lewis leaned closer towards his dying father.

'Dad.' His breath caught in his throat. He couldn't remember the last time he'd called him that. He took a deep breath. 'Before you go... please know that you're not alone.' He blinked away tears.

John's breathing was now little more than a shallow hiss.

Sudden movement in the doorway drew his attention.

He expected to see Mark, but through tears, he saw two women – one elegant older woman who must have been in her seventies, with swept-back silver hair, the other perhaps in her mid-thirties, carrying herself with the same precise grace.

'Who...?' Lewis began, but he didn't need to finish the question, because he already knew.

He felt it in every part of his body.

'Quickly,' he said.

The elderly woman moved to John's other side. The way she took his hand and looked down at him showed the familiarity of long intimacy. She didn't cry, just nodded, thoughtfully, a gentle smile playing on her lips. Her presence seemed to fill some space in the room that Lewis hadn't realised existed.

The younger woman placed her hand on her mother's shoulder, tears gleaming in her eyes.

Lewis turned back to his father and wiped the tears from his eyes.

'Don't be afraid, Dad.' He squeezed his father's hand gently. 'Oh, the places you'll go...'

And so, John White died as he'd lived – trapped between worlds, torn between families, lost between truths. But this time, at least, those worlds had finally collided, united in witnessing his final breath.

Chapter Sixty-Six

His afternoon with Lucy, Mia and Sophie had altered something in Peter.

Although, sitting here now, in his armchair, he conceded that the specifics of that alteration were a difficult thing to determine. Changes, he knew from experience, were hard to measure. And he'd been fooled before.

Grief could be a nasty animal. It'd retreat like the tide, only to surge back later, with more intensity. Sometimes, like a tsunami.

He knew the loss of Penny and Donna would always be a storm within him – to varying degrees. To hope otherwise would be false. There'd be calmer weathers, sure, but he didn't believe for a second that the thunder and lightning wouldn't return.

And now, of course, he'd another loss to contend with.

Sarah.

For hours he sat in his chair, Sarah's unfulfilled dreams of Australian beaches and neighbours worth a shit nagging at him. While, at the back of his mind, something else tugged at him.

It took him over an hour to admit to himself what that was.

It was their red Fiesta.

Until this moment, he'd genuinely believed his argument to those officers: 'There were a lot of red Fiestas in 1989... it's nothing more than a coincidence.'

But doubt has a nasty way of building, doesn't it?

In terms of investigating it, he had something in mind, but he really didn't want to go there.

Thirty minutes later, he had to concede that he had no other option, really.

He reached for the house phone and dialled a number he knew off by heart, but hadn't used in over a year.

Denise, Donna's younger sister, answered the phone. 'Hello?'

Frank and Denise hadn't spoken since Donna's funeral. She'd wanted to play 'You Are My Sunshine' – Donna's favourite song. He'd refused, saying it was too cheerful for a funeral. He'd been more than just resistant – he'd been cruel, lashing out like a wounded animal. The situation would have outraged Donna.

Over a year later, the shame still burned, but he'd been too pathetic and miserable to apologise.

'Denise...'

'Peter?'

'Aye.'

He heard her deep breaths.

Eventually, she said, 'You caught me by surprise.'

'I'm sorry for what happened. You know? Between us at Don's funeral... Well, you were right, and I was wrong. A right dickhead, aye. Donna would have been horrified and, well—'

'Peter?'

'Aye?'

'Stop. Apology accepted.'

'So, you no longer hate me?'

'I never did. The hate was only ever coming from one place.'

He gulped. 'Aye... it was her favourite song. I wish I could go back. She used to sing it everywhere, like. While cooking... in the garden. And in the bloody sunshine! If I could go back, I would.'

'Thank you, Peter, for apologising... now, how are you?'

He gave her a very brief update on his life, trying to be positive. He talked about the new neighbours at number 5, and how nice they were. She, too, talked about the last year. It'd been difficult, but she was moving on.

Then he explained about Sarah Matthews. A few times, he felt himself welling up and paused.

She was quiet for a while. 'I'm so sorry. I know how close you and Donna were to Sarah.'

'Aye...' He took a deep breath. 'Did she ever talk to you about seeing Sarah again before she disappeared?'

Denise was silent. He didn't like that.

'Look, Denise, the police mentioned a red Fiesta... The night she disappeared, a witness saw Sarah being picked up...'

The silence continued.

'Denise?'

He heard a sudden sharp intake of breath. In that moment, it became clear. Denise knew something. His heart sank. 'Denise, I need to know.'

'Peter...' Her voice cracked. 'Donna made me promise...'

Peter shook his head. *Donna, what did you do?* 'No, Denise... Don has gone. We're still here. That isn't fair. You need to talk to me.'

'She did it for you; she didn't want you to carry any more than you were already carrying...'

He gritted his teeth and squeezed his eyes shut. He wanted, now, to shout from the top of his lungs, get to his feet, potentially unburden himself by tearing this room apart – but he needed to keep it in – at least a moment longer. 'Tell me.'

So, she told him, and each word was like a stone. Donna must have carried some weight over all those years, keeping it from him. When she finished, he sat in silence, struggling to process it.

'You need to call this number,' he said finally. His hands shook as he recited the number the police had given him earlier from a piece of notepaper. 'Tomorrow morning. First thing. Please. Early as you can.'

'Wouldn't it be best if you just told them?'

'No, she confided in you. They'll prefer it from a witness. Not second hand from me. Besides...' He looked at the bowl of paracetamol waiting on the table – *after this, I really have had enough*. 'I'm otherwise engaged.'

'Peter... I'm sorry... she wanted you to be happy.'

'It's okay, Denise. I kind of get that. And to be honest, deep down, I probably never really believed she made it to Australia. In a way, it was convenient.'

'She worried you couldn't cope with it again... not after...'

'Penny, aye. At least I know Don loved me, eh?'

'With all her heart, Peter.'

'Aye... oh, and before I go, Denise, don't forget what I said. I was a dickhead and a fool.'

'Peter!'

'No, listen. Don used to sing that all the time. All the

time. To Penny. To herself. To me. It would've been just perfect... thank you.'

He hung up before she could respond and then left the phone off the hook.

He immediately went to the kitchen and ran his fingers over Donna's apron, faded but still holding the ghost of her shape. 'You should have told me, Don, love. You should have told me.' He rubbed tears away. 'But I understand why you didn't.'

With steady hands – steadier than they'd been in days – he poured a glass of water to take his tablets.

The stairs creaked under his feet as he carried the glass, the bowl of tablets and the eagle card upward on a tray. At the top of the stairs, he glanced at the wall alongside Penny's old room. He smiled at the lines in permanent marker, which had recorded Penny's growth until the age of six. He regarded Donna's favourite painting of the Abbey...

Before he went into the room, he looked at the eagle on the card again.

'Ah, Sarah... you're flying now, ain't you? Free as that eagle you always wanted to be. Nobody could ever keep you in chains.'

In the bedroom, moonlight painted silver paths across the floor as he set down his tray on the bed.

He sprayed Donna's perfume – that light floral scent she'd worn every day of their marriage.

Then he reached into his bedside drawer and withdrew a small box, smooth by years of handling. Inside was the paper crane. The yellow had faded slightly, but its creases were softened by time.

He placed it on the tray.

He heard Penny's voice in his head. 'Look, Daddy! It still flies!'

'That it does, love. Like the eagle... like you Don...'
Like I want to.
The pills felt impossibly light in his palm.
That was good.
In order to truly fly, it was better to shed the weight.

Chapter Sixty-Seven

THE SNOW HAD COME DOWN HEAVILY overnight.

Christie heard that the school was closed and sighed. It saved her from having to decide whether to phone in sick again.

She'd laid off the wine last night and had got a reasonably good night's sleep. She felt ready to speak to her father about what Nancy Keegan had told her yesterday.

Speak to him? Who was she kidding?

She was ready to confront him.

She opted to walk the fifteen minutes to their home. It really wouldn't be worth taking on the weather in her car.

En route, she tried to make sense of what the governors and her father had done back then. In Christie's opinion, paying off Georgina Prince was unforgivable.

It was also a gross miscalculation on their part. Buying silence? If it ever came to light, how would it look like anything other than guilt?

Her father had often told her that no good ever came from deceit.

The irony of his words was now twisting like a knife in her guts.

She walked through town, snow crunching underfoot.

Ruswarp unfolded before her like pages from a family album. She passed the butcher's shop where she'd done her work experience. The memory of fresh bacon every morning for two weeks made her smile. Mr Thompson still stood in the window, arranging his display with the same careful precision he'd shown twenty years ago, albeit more slowly.

The Bridge Inn came next. Steamed-up windows prevented her from seeing inside. She recalled a family meal there many years ago, when they'd celebrated her A-level results. She could still see the pride on her parents' faces. Her father had ordered champagne. She'd never been a fan, but that day it'd tasted of victory and possibilities – like sunshine and fresh air.

Beyond, a snow-tipped spire rose. How many times had her father's voice filled that church during prize-givings and grateful sermons delivered to his community? His voice, carrying that perfect mix of authority and compassion, had always inspired her.

The cricket ground, blanketed in snow, came into view. She remembered summer evenings watching matches with her father, his voice patient as he decoded the game's arcane rules. She could still picture his hands moving as he mapped out strategies, teaching her to see beyond the obvious – just as he had with generations of students.

She'd always assumed that he'd touched so many lives positively.

The prospect of him actually ruining them made her want to collapse to the ground in despair. Christie's memories were of a man who'd dedicated his life to others. She couldn't align them with this depiction of a monster.

She so hoped, and prayed, that Georgina was a bitter liar.

And if she was, then, over time, she might be able to make peace with what the governors and her father had done.

Maybe even feel grateful?

After all, it'd worked until now, and she'd had her family for over three decades, a loving family, at home for her.

As she turned onto their street, Christie felt resolve hardening in her chest. Tomorrow, weather permitting, she'd return to school, head held high. Let the whispers, the lies, curl like smoke – they'd most certainly burn out.

And then the truth would remain.

Her father would continue to be the man she'd always believed him to be.

The first flash of blue lights against the house windows stilled her enthusiasm.

Then her heart stuttered as she rounded the last bend and confirmed her fears. Police cars painting the snow in cobalt pulses outside her parents' house.

Was this it? The end of the line for her father?

She also saw an ambulance wedged at an angle across the drive – its back doors wide.

Christie quickened her pace, careful not to slip on the snow. She noticed her parents' neighbours, standing in their doorways like silent sentries.

She reached her garden gate just in time to see two paramedics wheeling out a gurney, a white sheet draped over a body.

Mum?

It was an obvious leap. Her mother was the one who'd been deteriorating.

'No... please, God, no.'

Christie's knees buckled, her hands finding the rough stone of the garden wall as her eyes tracked the gurney, her world completely reduced now, to a white sheet and its terrible outline.

The gurney's wheels crunched a path through fresh snow as it slid past her.

She looked up at the doorway and saw her father's face, bloodless and ancient in the morning light.

Oh, God... Mum...

She put her hands to her face.

Chapter Sixty-Eight

LUCY HAD BARELY SLEPT.

At least she had been able to tend to Sophie whenever she cried, giving Mia some much-needed rest.

Peter's tale had been a tough one.

The one time she'd dropped off, she'd dreamt of that moment when Peter's trembling fingers had moved through Sophie's hair. It was at that point she'd seen the true extent of his grief and longing.

She recognised it, because she felt it too, over the loss of her husband.

Losing what was precious had chewed both of them up, and they were always drowning, catching glimpses of a surface they couldn't break through.

Every day, Lucy masked her pain, fought on, for her children, for her grandchild...

But now that Donna was gone, and his dog was gone too, who'd anchor Peter to this world?

Since their first encounter at the door two days back, she had understood Peter. To others, he may seem a bubbling mass of anger, frustration and aggression, but not to her. He still had a high degree of fundamental decency. His lot in life had tried to extinguish that. However, if you were genuinely kind, your decency would never disappear. It would always be there. Buried. But there.

He'd fixed her kitchen, her son's car, and had wanted nothing for it. Later, he'd held Sophie like she was the most precious thing in the world.

Here was a man who'd chased a paper crane through winter streets for his daughter and experienced the unthinkable; who'd nursed his wife through illness and spiralled away into loneliness.

This weekend was Christmas. The thought struck her with sudden clarity – *on such a day, no one should be alone with their ghosts.*

Without another thought, she was out the door, unsurprised by the snow, having watched it fall for most of the night through her bedroom window. She crunched through it to his home. The lounge curtains were drawn. The morning light caught the condensation on his windows, making them gleam.

She went down the path to his door.

Taking a deep breath, she took a moment to orientate herself, prepare her invitation. The surrounding air was biting, but the skies were clear, and everything was quiet and still.

She knocked, the sound splitting the morning stillness like breaking glass. A few snowflakes, disturbed by her movement, drifted down from the porch roof.

She pulled her coat tighter against the cold and waited. He might need time to rise, put on a dressing gown.

But the silence stretched on.

So, she tried again, monitoring the curtains, watching for any flutter of movement, any sign of life within. After the third knock, she felt a sense of dread, but waited a whole two minutes before it crystallised into a sense of urgency.

She looked down at her feet and then around at the snow. The pristine white surface told its own story – there were no tracks leading the other way. That ruled out the possibility of him going for a walk early this morning, unless he'd left before the snow stopped? But she remembered watching it, stopping around 4 a.m. Had that been too early for a walk?

She peered through the window, homing in on a sliver between the curtains, but the living room was dark and empty. His chair sat vacant.

She tried calling out to him through the letterbox. Then, the handle, but the door was locked.

Her heart was now hammering against her ribs.

She circled to the back of the house. The garden lay under an unbroken blanket of white. No footprints marred its surface – again, that didn't rule out a night walk, but it'd been heavy snow... A few hours, wandering aimlessly, out in that temperature could be serious for a man of his years, and no footprints suggested a return either.

The more she considered it, the more desperate she felt.

She knocked on the back door a few times. The sound echoed hollowly. She tried the handle. Again, locked.

Back at the front, she knocked again, longer this time, more insistent. Neighbours emerged from their homes like curious birds, drawn by the commotion. She asked if anyone had seen him leave. Their head shakes only deepened her certainty that something was wrong.

Five minutes passed. Then ten. Her knuckles were raw from knocking, her throat tight from calling his name. The dread that had been building in her stomach wasn't just certainty any more – it was terror.

She could already imagine the emergency services dismissing her concerns – just an old man having a lie in or out visiting someone. 'Give it a few hours,' they would say. She pulled out her phone, fingers trembling as she dialled, vowing to kick the door down herself if they suggested waiting.

The operator was just asking what service she required when a police car slid down Peter's drive.

Chapter Sixty-Nine

THE SILENCE in his father's room felt thick enough to touch. Lewis stood in the doorway, watching as morning light crept through the windows, casting John White's lifeless face in shades that made him look carved from stone. The mortuary transport had been delayed by the weather – though the snow had stopped falling, the roads still needed gritting before they could safely navigate them.

Lewis had spent the night on the sofa downstairs, leaving the spare rooms for John's unexpected visitors.

His half-sister's name was Rosie Cross. She was thirty-four years old. That means he would've been twelve when she was born.

Her mother, Anais Cross, was in her late sixties, and so would have been a similar age to his mother while they were conducting their affair.

During the night, Lewis had peered into his father's room on several occasions, to see Anais holding his father's hand.

He wondered if she'd spent the entire evening here.

Now it was morning, he craved answers. He coughed gently to indicate his presence.

Anais didn't turn, but her fingers continued their gentle dance across his father's hand with a tenderness that made Lewis's chest tight.

'I never expected to be here when it happened,' Anais said. 'If not for your call...'

'How did you know the address?'

'Oh,' she sighed. 'I've always known this address. I haven't seen your father for almost three and a half decades. Since the day he moved here and told me it was best that he never saw me again.'

Lewis let out a dry laugh. 'Yeah, that doesn't surprise me. I barely saw him after I turned ten. Guess we've a lot in common. This man spent his life turning his back on people he was supposed to love.'

'Quite the opposite, actually,' Anais said. 'He thought he was doing us all a favour by locking himself away from us all. He considered himself some kind of curse. Your father, in his own way, loved too much and too hard. That was what destroyed him... and his relationships. He believed his behaviour, and personality, led to all this tragedy. Poor karma.'

Lewis snorted again. 'My father didn't believe in karma. That merely sounds like self-pity to me. He led his life, did what he wanted and then the guilt kicked in...'

Anais lifted her gaze to his. 'He adored you, you know. You and Felix. He used to talk about you often...'

Hearing Felix's name made him flinch. He felt a surge of irritation. 'What about my mother?'

'In his way, he loved her too.'

'In his way?'

'Yes, he learned he couldn't be with Elizabeth...'

'Because of you?' Lewis's words carried the sharp edge of decades of abandonment.

She shook her head. 'It's not that straightforward. Remember, it ended the same way between us, as it ended up between him and your mother. John was never meant to be with one person. It wasn't his nature. He felt it in himself. He did fight it. But it just tore him up, over and over; eventually, he thought it best if he just went away. He was convinced that distancing himself was the best thing he could give any of us... the only thing he could give us—'

'He wasn't even there when his own son died!'

'I know.'

'It's a disgrace.'

'I agree.'

'So, how do you expect me to feel pity?'

'There can be no excuse. Not really. I understand that. All I'll say is this. When he was told about your brother's impending passing, he was overseas. He'd never have made it home, and he knew that. Still, he booked his flight, but such was his guilt and trauma that he drank himself half to death in the airport and they wouldn't let him on the plane. By the time he sobered and the next flight came along, your brother had passed. His pain was unbearable.'

Lewis gulped and looked away. He felt a tear in his eye. 'I know the pain was unbearable. I felt it too. He should have tried harder.'

'Maybe so... But—'

'What was his excuse for not being at the funeral?' Lewis's voice cracked with old rage. 'Guess he couldn't face the pain, then, eh? We all had to face it without him.'

'I know.' She shook her head, as if trying to dislodge painful memories. 'He couldn't ... because...'

'Because?'

'He wasn't allowed.'

'Come again?'

She fixed him with a stare. 'He was committed.'

'What?'

She nodded. 'Yes, he came back to me. A mess. The day before the funeral, he got up early and threw himself off a bridge, Lewis... they pulled him from the water half-dead and completely broken. When they dragged him out, he was incoherent, and they locked him away so he couldn't harm himself. He begged me not to tell anyone. He didn't want Elizabeth and you feeling that pain on this particular day.'

Lewis looked away, a tear running down his face. He could feel his resistance cracking. And he didn't like it. 'He should have told us, damn it!'

'I agree, but he didn't... and here we are... He loved you. Felix's death broke him.'

He shook his head, desperate to keep resisting. 'You're a lot more forgiving of my father than my mother was.'

'I can't speak for your mother, Lewis – that wouldn't be fair.'

'Did she know all this?'

'I don't know. That's the truth. But even if she did, it might not have made any difference. After all, she couldn't accept who your father was...'

'Work obsessed? An alcoholic? A womaniser?'

'These are some of the terms used for his problems. I'll not defend him from that, but I do think your father was more complex. He fought hard in himself. Very, very hard. He led a painful life. And your mother couldn't forgive him, couldn't accept him, and I think that's fair. Really fair. She'd a right to make that choice.'

'Yet, you accepted him?'

She furrowed her brow. 'To an extent. Although, I never believed we had a future.'

'So, my mother was stupid for believing that.'

'Your mother wouldn't have truly believed it either. She'd have tried. Convinced herself she could change it.'

'So you forgive him?'

She traced her thumb across John's knuckles. 'Yes. And I pity him. And you know love is intensified by pity, I guess. So, I forgave him, I pitied him and I loved him. Your father battled countless addictions. And he believed that what happened to Felix, and then to...' Her words stumbled to a halt. 'Well, he thought that was his fault and he didn't want to pass any more pain to you... to me... to any of us.'

Lewis leaned forward. 'How did you meet? I want to know everything.'

She swallowed hard, her eyes fixed on John as if seeking permission. 'I'm not sure you'll be happy hearing everything, Lewis.'

'Oh I will!' Lewis narrowed his eyes. 'And let's start with this: why the fuck did you even come here if you've not seen him for three and a half decades?'

She squeezed her eyes shut, tears gathering at the corners. 'Because you phoned... because he mentioned Rosie... I sensed he didn't want to be alone at the end... that despite everything, he wanted his family.'

Lewis shot to his feet, energy surging through him. This was unbelievable. Not just another family – but a whole web of secrets that somehow connected to his own. He turned and pointed. 'To find out he'd a daughter like this, that I've a sister... do you have any idea what this is doing to me' – he pointed to his head – 'in here?'

'I can imagine, but there's more, and it'll make the storm worse before it gets any better.'

'I think I'm beyond shocking, don't you? There's no need to hold back.'

She sighed and lowered her head. 'He had another daughter.'

'Another?' The word exploded from him as his eyes locked onto his father's still face.

Maybe I'm not as unshockable as I thought.

'Jesus – who the hell are you?' Lewis asked his dead father.

'She came first. Before Felix and you. Not with me. Not with your mother. But that didn't make her any less special to him.'

'Who is she and where is she? Can we not invite her around too?'

She clutched John's hand as if it might anchor her to the present. 'I'm sorry, John...' She shook her head. 'This is for the best. The truth out now. Everything. It'll cost me. Cost me dearly. But then, the peace that comes from it... for all those remaining... it is a price worth paying.'

Lewis shook his head in disbelief as he watched this stranger justify the truth to John.

Anais turned and met Lewis's gaze, her eyes suddenly ancient with grief. 'Your older sister is gone, Lewis.'

'Gone? Where?'

A pause.

'You mean she's dead?'

Her fingers clenched John's lifeless hand, her knuckles whitening. 'Yes... a long, long time ago. And no one blames themselves more for this than John.' She rose slowly, age and exhaustion evident in every movement. 'I think it's best we go downstairs, so that you both hear this. Rosie, too. That's fair—'

'Rosie doesn't know?'

Anais shook her head, something like fear flickering across her features.

'No. And it'll be hard. Because it involves me.' She looked down. 'It's always involved me. I'm not who she believes me to be. Her own mother, can you believe it? Poor child. I'll have to stand in judgement of that.' She looked up. 'Come down and I'll tell you both a story... one I've never told. I always feared it'd be the death of me! You'll need to listen carefully when I tell it, because I don't think I'll be well enough to tell it a second time.'

Chapter Seventy

The winter morning air bit at DC Sharon Miller's fingers as she brushed the snow from the roof and the windscreen.

Once she finally had visibility, she attempted to manoeuvre the car off her drive. Predictably, the wheels protested, but she made it some way, before they began spinning in a patch of snow. She put the car in neutral. This wasn't looking good. She sighed.

Okay, one last go.

She took a steadying breath, gritted her teeth, checked her mirrors, and slipped the car back into reverse. Bracing for the wheels to spin, she almost cheered when the tyres caught, and the car moved backwards.

The roads here had been gritted, but she still went slow and crept along. Up ahead, three other drivers shared her caution, creating a delay at the roundabout.

A glance at her watch confirmed her fears – she would never get to Reggie in Ruswarp in time to interview Becky Morton. She called him hands-free but got only his voicemail. She left a brief message.

The early morning roads were eerily quiet. Most sensible people were not willing to tackle the snow, but increasing her speed too much was a definite no-go.

The hands-free startled her.

She cursed when she saw Sean's name on the display rather than Reggie's.

'Morning, Sean. Make it quick – I need to focus on the—'

'Sharon... thank God.' His voice was edged with tension.

'What's wrong?'

'No one is picking up! Gerry and Frank are at the mortuary, I guess.' Sharon couldn't remember last hearing Sean so flustered. Sean was usually too laid back for such behaviour. 'Reggie is off grid...'

'I know, just tried. You're through to your last resort, then!'

'We've just had a call from Denise Outhwaite – Donna Watson's sister. She confirmed it was Donna driving the red Fiesta that night in '89.'

'Jesus.'

'She picked up Sarah. Malcolm's witness statement was accurate, after all!'

'Except it was an older woman, not a man?'

'Well, yeah, apart from that. Guess it was dark, though.'

A surge of irritation went through her. She'd trusted Peter. 'He lied to us!'

'No. Denise said Donna had never told him.'

'Eh?'

'Because she couldn't bear to, apparently. He was so close to Sarah, and didn't want him to know that she'd tried to talk sense into Sarah and failed.'

'I can't buy that...'

'Sarah had admitted to Donna that she was pregnant.'

Sharon's eyes widened.

'Donna thought that if she told Peter, he'd go around there, all guns blazing, and she didn't want it ending in disaster. Also, Sarah made her promise not to say anything.'

'Okay, okay,' Sharon said, indicating right and carefully turning onto another main road, which, fortunately, was well gritted. She cautiously increased her speed.

'Anyway, Sarah demanded that Donna pull over and let her out. She was hysterical. Told Donna that she didn't want her driving her back – that if Tommy saw her... he'd ask too many questions... and she couldn't cope with that now. She didn't want him to know she was pregnant yet. Donna pulled over, apparently, not intending to let her out, because they were in the middle of nowhere, but to calm her down... talk sense into her.'

His voice cut out. Sharon took a deep breath. 'Shit... shit... Sean?'

Nothing.

Crap! She was about to redial when his voice came back. 'Hello, Sharon?'

'Yes, you're back. It was the reception.' She sighed with relief. 'What were you saying?'

'After Donna stopped the car, Sarah wouldn't calm down. She hugged Donna, kissed her, told her she loved her and just got out...'

'Where?'

'I'll get to that.'

'You said it was in the middle of nowhere...'

'It was... kind of... *just* let me finish!'

'Okay! Keep calm!' She realised how hypocritical that sounded.

'She told Donna she shouldn't come after her,' Sean

said. 'That she knew her way around the woods and the way back... and that Donna didn't. If Donna didn't chase after her, Sarah promised that she would visit her and Peter before the end of the week.'

'So?'

'Well Sarah got out, and Donna did what she was asked. Lingered around in the car until it was clear she wasn't coming back and then headed home. She told Denise that the promise of a visit was too good an offer to pass up.'

'All that, and then she didn't show up within the week? What must have been going through her head?'

'Christ knows... and that was when she probably should have told Peter, but didn't.'

She sighed. 'Because of the pregnancy... She was also probably worried he'd fly off the handle, march round to Tommy's.'

'Maybe. And then they both found out she was missing.'

'She *definitely* should have said something then!' She stopped herself saying *stupid woman*. She'd known desperate and sad people do worse when faced with tragedy, and they weren't always stupid.

'I know... it's mad, huh?' Sean said. 'But Denise insisted Donna was a good person, and she definitely made the wrong decisions here. When it was clear that Sarah was gone, possibly dead, she went into protection mode. Remember what had happened to his daughter? Penny? He'd a history of depression and two suicide attempts following that... she didn't think he could cope with another tragedy. I guess he saw Sarah as some kind of surrogate daughter?'

'Yes... oh my God, Sean!' Sharon said.

'What's wrong?'

'She arranged that Australian postcard, didn't she?'

'Yes.'

'Fucking hell! That's ridiculous. What if her body had shown up? How would that have bloody looked to Peter?'

'She waited a few months before arranging it. She must have assumed that Sarah would never show, and then she asked a friend to send the postcard – someone who'd emigrated to Australia. Denise says she doesn't know the name of this friend. Nonsense, of course. She just doesn't want to get her in trouble.'

'This is beyond irresponsible. Especially since Donna was the last person to see her alive. Ludicrous.'

'Seems that way to us, I guess. Denise said that Peter would have blamed himself. That he was this kind of person. Donna wouldn't accept that,' Sean said.

'Okay, we need to get back to Peter's house...'

'I've already arranged for officers to pick him up.'

'Good... and keep trying Frank. I might lose the signal when I reach Reggie. Ah shit, almost forgot. Where was Sarah when she got out of the car that night? You said middle of nowhere?'

'Wasn't exactly the middle of nowhere. It was just outside Ruswarp. It was by a small patch of trees. It's crazy, but when we circled it on the map... well, you won't believe where it was close to. Coincidence, I'm sure, but—'

'Just bloody get to it, Sean!'

Sharon's eyes widened when he did. The adrenaline caused her to speed up. Fortunately, she was still on a gritted road. 'Sean, keep trying everyone. Get this information out there.'

After ending the call, she tried Reggie again. Still nothing but voicemail. She left him a message detailing

Sean's revelation, then slammed her palm against the steering wheel and swore.

She needed to hurry.

Instinctively, she veered onto a side street that would cut through and save her time.

Bad move, Sharon.

The mistake hit her instantly.

She found herself on a road that hadn't been treated, working her way past cars, half-buried in snow.

Bad fucking move.

The car's handling deteriorated.

She eased onto the brake pedal but clocked that the wheels were already losing their battle with the ice. The steepening gradient ahead promised nothing but trouble, and unless her tyres found grip soon, a skid was inevitable. What an idiot!

The intersection with the main road loomed closer.

A few cars crawled past on that main road, moving cautiously. If she didn't stop soon, she'd be crossing the path of a vehicle!

'Fuck...' She pumped the brakes gently, but it was completely useless. 'Fuck...'

A full lock would surely send her into a spin.

Several heart-stopping metres from the intersection, she realised she'd no choice. She hit the brakes. The steering wheel became frighteningly light in her hands. All traction vanished.

Time seemed to stretch as her car slid sideways across the ice. Raw fear whiplashed through her as the vehicle rotated a full 180 degrees, leaving her staring back the other way, the summit of the hill growing smaller. She glimpsed in the rear-view mirror and gagged. She was a metre or so from the main road. Instinctively, she reached for the door handle to jump, but it was useless. She was already in the centre of the main road, watching the inevitable impact approaching. She squeezed her eyes shut. Glass peppered her face and cold air rushed in.

Chapter Seventy-One

Fingers trembling, Margaret Matthews smoothed imaginary wrinkles from her blouse. Then she looked up and smiled at Gerry. 'Where's Rylan?'

'With my neighbour,' Gerry said.

'How is he?'

'He'll be happy because my neighbour can spare him over an hour to run in the park.'

'Ah... he's such a beautiful dog.'

'So is Jasper,' Gerry said.

Margaret's eyes drifted over to the glass window that looked in on the mortuary.

'Dogs know and understand far more than we give them credit for,' Margaret said.

'Couldn't agree more,' Frank said, moving to stand alongside her. The last few months with Rylan had really opened his eyes.

'Don't you think that shows that we understand far less than we give ourselves credit for?' Margaret added, still looking through the window.

Aye, now ain't that the goddamned truth, Frank thought, eyes joining Margaret's in that sad journey through the glass. 'Are you ready?'

'I'm not sure.' She sighed.

'There's no shame in not going in,' Frank said. 'No shame whatsoever.'

Margaret met his gaze. 'I know that... but let's go.' Her voice now carried the quiet certainty of someone who'd made peace with impossible choices. 'I want to be with Sarah one last time.'

Frank nodded.

Understandable.

He thought of all the times he'd sat in Maddie's empty room, trying to feel her presence in the hollow spaces she'd left behind. How many nights had he spent wondering if he'd one day be in Margaret's position, walking through a door like this one?

He stepped to one side and opened the door for her. She paused alongside him, her eyes finding his. 'I dreamt about finding her one day...' Her gaze drifted forward before returning, weighted with meaning. 'In different circumstances, yes, but still. I'm grateful for this last opportunity.'

As she entered, Frank felt something crack inside his chest. He, too, dreamt all the time about finding Maddie, creating hopeful scenarios time and time again. Were they also just lies? Was the outcome as inevitable as Sarah's? And if so, would he ever be able to face an outcome with the same grace as Margaret? With such dignity?

Margaret's slow steps weren't because of her age. Frank could tell they were deliberate. He used the opportunity to close the door behind himself and nod at Gerry looking in through the viewing window.

When he turned back, Margaret was lowering herself into a chair alongside Sarah. A mortuary technician in green scrubs approached, offering quiet condolences.

Frank clasped his hands together as if he was a mourner at a funeral and bowed his head slightly.

'I'm ready,' Margaret said.

The mortuary technician's voice was gentle but firm as he asked that Margaret didn't touch the body. Then he drew back the shroud.

The sigh that escaped Margaret was so quiet that Frank almost missed it. But he caught it. Just. Such a gentle sound yet carrying such agony that it shook Frank deeply.

He left the room and stood alongside Gerry.

They both stood there for a minute before Gerry looked at him. She clearly wanted to say something.

'Go on.'

She nodded. 'Tom wants to meet tonight. It sounds... positive.'

She turned her attention back to the mortuary.

Frank felt warmth spreading through his chest. 'Bloody fantastic, Gerry. I needed news like that.'

She looked back at him. 'I wasn't expecting it.' Then, back to the mortuary.

'I was,' Frank said, still not taking his eyes from Margaret. 'Tom strikes me as a man with a good head on his shoulders. Was only a matter of time before he saw sense.'

'He said you spoke to him.'

'Ah... did he now.'

'Thanks Frank.'

'Wasn't sure how you'd respond to be honest.'

'I like that you care.'

Aye, lass, I like that I care too, he thought.

'What did you say?'

'The truth... your precise nature isn't to control, but rather your way of creating order from chaos... of building frameworks to support the things that matter most.'

'You once said that sometimes love is learning to dance without knowing the steps.'

'I did. You understand that now?'

'I think so.'

Through the window, Frank watched as Margaret maintained her vigil. She respected the mortuary technician's request and made no movement to touch her daughter's remains. She simply sat there, drinking in these last moments. After ten minutes, she turned in her chair and gestured for them to come in.

Their footsteps echoed in the sterile space as they approached.

They stood alongside Margaret and looked down at Sarah. Her body curved inward – like a child seeking comfort in sleep, or someone trying to disappear. Frank preferred the former interpretation.

'Would you read this?' Margaret's hand trembled as she held out a creased sheet of paper. 'I can't. My eyes are so tired.'

Frank recognised Sarah's handwriting immediately: the same careful loops and whorls they'd seen in her other poems, though these looked shakier, as if written in haste or distress. This one hadn't been in the pile Margaret had given them earlier, but now wasn't the time to question why. He cleared his throat.

'There's emptiness between memories. Spaces between heartbeats.
Everything else is noise, chaos, endless and pressing.

Something missing. Taken. A presence known by an absence?
Who should be there amongst the endless, quiet?
Who are you? Are you real?'

Margaret's fingers shook as she reached up to retrieve the paper.

Frank handed it to her, but made a mental note to ask for it later.

He looked at Gerry, wondering if she knew who the poem could refer to.

Margaret wiped at her tears with trembling fingers. 'He's real.'

'Sorry?' Adrenaline made him lean in. 'Margaret?'

When she didn't immediately respond, Frank took a deep breath, wondering if grief had confused her words.

Margaret bent toward her daughter's remains, her voice dropping to something between a whisper and prayer. 'Deep down, you knew, Sarah, you always knew.'

Frank exchanged a questioning glance with Gerry. He stopped himself from probing her again, because he sensed she wanted to tell Sarah something first. Something, he realised, that would be very significant.

'I'm sorry for keeping it from you.' Her words carried the weight of decades. 'I always planned to tell you. But the time was never right.' She lifted her eyes to Frank's, guilt and apology warring in her expression. 'Frank, I'm sorry. But I just couldn't tell you before I told her first. That's why I needed to see her. It wouldn't be right.' Her attention returned to the remains of her daughter, her voice carrying the tremor of someone about to unleash a long-held truth. 'Sarah...'

Frank felt the adrenaline tearing through him now, and

he had to keep his hands clasped behind his back to keep himself still.

The silence felt tangible, as though the very air was holding its breath, waiting for Margaret to speak.

He glanced at Gerry. She looked calm, but surely she must be feeling the same thing.

Chapter Seventy-Two

Christie sat alongside her father in the police waiting room.

Despair raged inside her, but she forced herself to stay composed.

Her father was crying, but he was fighting it. He muffled his sobs against his sleeve, struggling to maintain the dignity that had always defined him.

If she lost it, she feared he'd dissolve – and despite everything, here was a man who she'd always admired and adored more than anyone.

No. She'd remain strong. Just like he'd always taught her to. 'Be there to guide others through a crisis if you can. That's the mark of a leader.'

She'd not contacted her brother yet, because he was overseas and there was a significant time difference. She'd do that later, when she'd fully processed what had happened.

Christie slipped her arm around him, feeling the tremors running through his body. Her mind drifted back to earlier that morning, when she'd watched the gurney being wheeled past her in the garden.

She'd believed that the person on the gurney had been her mother.

It hadn't. Although the truth was still devastating.

She recalled the moment she'd seen her mother standing at the door in her nightgown, and the relief she'd felt...

'Mum!' Christie lurched forward.

A police officer held her back while another stepped between her and her parents. 'Ma'am, please stop.'

Christie watched over the shoulder of the officer as her father draped a coat over her mother's shoulders and another officer came to her side to take her arm.

'Let go of my mother,' Christie said. 'She's sick.'

'Christie, please...' It was her father.

They led her mother past. She was trembling. At least they weren't using handcuffs.

She turned and watched her being escorted to the police car.

'Mum!' Christie called.

When Caroline turned at Christie's call, her gaze seemed to pass through her daughter like light through glass, focused on some point far beyond the present moment. The hollow cheeks and fragile frame spoke of a woman already half-gone from this world.

'We need you to be calm, miss,' one officer said.

She glared at him.

His face carried the particular strain of someone forced to witness family tragedy – sympathetic but resolute.

'Christie...'

Her father touched her shoulder.

He was now beside her. She looked at him. The sight crushed something inside her. His face was blotchy from crying, his shoulders slumped. In all her years of watching him command rooms, she'd never seen him so utterly diminished.

'This is my fault,' he said.

'What happened, Dad?'

His face crumpled like burning paper.

She embraced him, feeling his body tremble.

'I'm sorry,' he whispered. 'I'm so sorry, but I must go.' Every word caught in his throat. 'They said I could go with her.'

Christie pulled back, her hands trembling as they cupped the face she'd looked up to all her life – carved into pieces by guilt, confusion and grief.

'What happened, Dad? You must tell me!'

His eyes were red-rimmed, haunted by a darkness deeper than grief. 'She came back. Not for you this time... but for me. For us. I should have known this would happen. She hadn't changed. She was like a force of nature. I should've known that she'd never stop.'

Christie felt her blood run cold. 'Georgina came here.'

Here it was – everything she'd feared from the moment Nancy had told her.

Lies and secrecy could never work.

They always caught up in the end.

'She's dead.' He flinched as he said it.

Her breath caught in her throat. She stared off at her mother. God... no... please don't let it be so...

She looked back at her father.

He'd already turned away – he looked like a man suddenly cowering from his own shadow. 'It wasn't her fault. It wasn't your mother's fault. Okay?' His voice was desperate. 'She's sick. She didn't understand.'

Christie gently turned him back toward her, feeling the tremors running through him. 'How?' Her own voice sounded even more desperate than his.

Tears carved paths down his face as the story spilled out in broken fragments. 'She came into our house with her lies... shouting and attacking me with those lies... How could Caroline cope with that? You know how she is. Your mother invited her up... she was so confused. Except... at the top of the stairs... God, I can't even say it!' He took a deep breath. 'Your mother had a hammer, from the spare room...' He pulled away as if physical distance might somehow lessen the horror of what he had to say. 'I couldn't stop her. It was too late. Before I realised, she'd swung and... God... Georgina was falling...'

As if summoned by the word, a white-suited officer emerged from the house, carrying a clear evidence bag. Inside, a hammer was visible, its head dark with dried blood. Christie recognised it and felt her stomach turn. She swallowed, fearful she might vomit.

How many times had she watched her mother and father use it to hang pictures, to build the framework of their perfect life?

An officer beckoned to her father. 'Sir, we're leaving.'

'I must go with her,' Stephen said, moving towards the officer.

Christie felt bile rise in her throat as she started forward, but the other officer blocked her off. 'We'll take good care of them.' The officer's voice carried practiced gentleness.

Christie watched, helpless, as they helped her mother into the police car, Caroline's movements as uncertain as a sleepwalker's. Her nightgown caught on the car door and an officer had to free it, the gesture absurdly tender in its horror.

In the harsh fluorescent light of the waiting room, her

distressed father's words became a desperate litany. 'It's my fault.' Each repetition seemed to age him further, stripping away layers of carefully maintained dignity.

Christie pulled him tighter against her.

'Georgina said you'd spoken to Nancy.'

Christie took a deep breath. 'Yes. I know about the cover-up... about paying her off.'

'I'm sorry... I felt like I'd no choice, at the time. At first, I wanted to just go to the police, but the governors talked me out of it. Nancy can be so convincing.'

Christie nodded. *I'd noticed*, she thought. 'But those things you were accused of, are—'

He pulled back from her, his eyes widening. 'God, you don't think? Flower? You can't—'

Christie studied her father's face - the deep lines of exhaustion, the trembling lips, the haunted look in his eyes. He seemed to have aged a decade in a single night. The proud man seemed to be gone, replaced by someone fragile and desperate. The desire to ask more questions, to probe deeper into Georgina's accusations, was overwhelming, but seeing him like this - so broken, so vulnerable - made her throat tight. How could she add to his suffering now?

'It's not true. None of it.' He continued, his voice cracking.

'I believe you.' The words felt hollow in her mouth, but they were what he needed to hear in this moment. She followed the instinct to protect him, even if the doubts still churned in her stomach. The accusations would have to wait.

'Thank you, flower... but... I've made a dreadful mistake. I've made a mistake. The governors bribing Georgina's family. The truth of what happened will surely come out now.' His emphasis on the word, *truth*, fell between them like a confession, making her skin prickle.

'Does Mum know about Georgina?' Christie asked.

'Some of it... but she'll struggle to recount the details. She lashed out because she felt we were under attack – I'm not sure she understands, fully, who Georgina is any more. It's me who should be held accountable for it. Not your mother.' Stephen pressed his fingers to his temples as if trying to physically hold his thoughts together, his skin grey with exhaustion. 'But they're not listening. They're only interested in what happened. I'm so tired... confused... I don't know what to say or do.'

'We let the solicitor handle it. As he said, Dad, it's diminished responsibility.' Christie's voice carried a certainty she didn't feel.

'She can't stand trial!' His shout echoed off the institutional walls, making several heads turn.

'We're getting ahead of ourselves,' Christie said, though the same fear coiled in her stomach.

'I sat with that body all night, Christie.' His voice dropped to a whisper, horror threading through each word. 'I didn't know what to do. I couldn't think straight. I still can't. I wouldn't call them. Can you believe it? I thought about burying her – how ridiculous. Should I have done?'

'No. Of course not.'

'What choice did I have but to tell the truth?'

'None.'

'So... should I tell them the truth about Georgina? About my lies?'

Panic hit her full force.

If he did that, then what? Would she lose both parents to the justice system in a single night?

The two people she'd adored the most in the world?

Such a prospect was unthinkable.

'No.' Christie turned into her father's embrace, her own carefully maintained composure finally crumbling. Her tears soaked into his shirt. 'Say nothing... not yet... let's wait for the solicitor.'

She buried her head into his chest, wondering if she was now making herself complicit in a deceit that raged against every value she'd believed herself to hold dear.

Maybe.

But then an image rose in her mind. A police car pulling away from their home, her mother's face pressed against the window, pale, lips moving in silent conversation with ghosts.

And her own values fizzled away.

Chapter Seventy-Three

Lucy stood beside the police car, while two plain-clothed officers explored the house.

Their arrival had frozen time.

Mia was alongside her, gripping her arm.

Peter's front door hung askew after the forced entry. The sound had brought many neighbours to their doors, but they didn't speak. Sycamore Close was gripped by silence.

Lucy didn't want everything to spring back into action, because when it did – there'd be a new reality. A truth she'd have to face.

Peter was gone.

She'd known it, felt it, from the moment she'd seen the shadows and grief behind those eyes as he'd told them about Penny and had embraced Sophie like it may just be his last act on earth.

The officers had tried to dismiss her concerns initially, but their reluctance evaporated when control confirmed Peter's two previous suicide attempts.

She took a deep breath, realising that it was time... she

needed to come out of the frozen silence. She started forward.

'Where are you going, Mum?' Mia asked.

'I need to know,' Lucy said and stepped into the home, past the broken door.

She regarded the two pink coats. Donna's and Penny's.

Then, with a tightness in her chest, she approached the bottom of the stairs.

The sound of creaking floorboards filtered down from above, punctuated by the indistinct murmur of voices.

Lucy strained to make the voices distinct – to catch even a hint of what was happening, but she couldn't.

Fuck this...

She stopped about two-thirds of the way up, so she could see onto the landing. The low, urgent voices were coming from the room at the centre.

'Is everything okay?' she asked, the words escaping before she could stop them.

One officer appeared in the doorway. Lucy's eyes fixed immediately on the object in her hands – the same bowl she'd noticed two days back, sitting on Peter's side table. The same bowl that had been full of paracetamol.

The bowl was empty.

She placed her hand to her mouth.

'Mrs Coombes, you shouldn't be in here,' the officer said.

She dropped her hand, tears already filling her eyes. 'Just tell me, please. Is he...?' She put her hand back to her mouth to hold in the reaction that was sure to come.

'There's no one here,' the officer said.

Lucy gripped the banister tighter, her legs weak beneath her.

'The house is empty,' the other officer said, coming into

view. 'We could do with taking a statement from you, concerning his state of mind. Maybe try to work out where he is.'

'Why are you even here?' Lucy asked.

The officers looked at one another. The woman said, 'We're not really permitted to say.' She regarded her partner. 'Why don't you handle interviewing Mrs Coombes? I'll go door to door to see if anyone saw him leave. We also need to get ANPR out on his car...'

'His car has been stolen – he didn't drive.' Lucy's own voice sounded distant to her, as if spoken by someone else.

'There's been no reports of a stolen vehicle,' the male officer said.

The disorientation intensified and she turned away and faced down the steps. 'I know nothing about that...' She wondered if he'd not bothered to report it simply because he hadn't envisaged ever driving again. 'He also had a head injury...' She looked back up. 'Said he caught it on the mantelpiece. I bandaged it for him. It looked bad.'

'Did he go to the hospital?'

'He said so.'

The female officer looked at the male officer. 'Check that too.'

'He must have left before the snow stopped,' Lucy said. 'There were no tracks in the snow.'

'Good thinking.' The male officer got out his phone, presumably to check weather records.

'Four in the morning,' Lucy said, remembering how she'd watched the snow fall while wrestling with her concerns about Peter.

The officer looked at her, raising an eyebrow.

'I told you, before, outside. I couldn't sleep. After what he told us about his daughter.'

'Okay,' the male officer said. 'Let's get a proper statement. Downstairs? Or at yours?'

'Mine. I can't think straight here. Number 5.' She was desperate now to escape from this hollow space that still held echoes of Peter's presence.

Outside, Mia came running towards her.

'He's not there,' Lucy said, pulling her daughter close, feeling the tremors running through both their bodies.

Chapter Seventy-Four

FRANK RANG THE DOORBELL, Margaret's words from the mortuary echoing in his mind...

'Sarah... I never told you about Rory's older brother. He was your real father, Sarah, following a brief affair I had with him in 1966, and I'm so sorry, my sweet, for keeping this from you... but it was never the right time.' She lowered her head. *'When you were troubled, I didn't want to make things worse... and when you were happy, well, I didn't want to bring your mood down. I like to think I would've told you one day, but I just don't know. Maybe I was a coward? Maybe the time would never have been right.'*

Afterwards, alone with Frank and Gerry, Margaret had elaborated.

'You remember me telling you about his brother?'

'Aye. We looked, but we found no record. I would've followed it up at some point.'

'Because he was Rory's half-brother, you see. Their relationship isn't on record. Rory, himself, didn't even know about John until he appeared, seemingly out of nowhere, in 1965. He was the product of one of his father's earlier

dalliances. Of course, nobody was doing DNA tests back then, so I guess it's not 100 per cent – but I'll tell you now that they'd a similar look, you know, him and Rory. In their eyes.'

'So, Sarah's father's real name was John?'

'John White. And he was a handsome devil, Frank. A real charmer. I fell for him, but I was stupid, because I knew I wasn't the first person who fell for him, and I wouldn't be the last! But he just had this way, you know?'

'Did Rory ever find out?'

Margaret nodded. *'And they didn't talk again. So, John, despite being Sarah's father, was in her life for barely two minutes. He crawled back into the woodwork. I never knew the truth about him – did he have another family? For all I know, he could have died before Sarah was even born... Who knows? Rory forgave my mistake, but it ate away at him – ground him down over the years. Like I said the other day, there had been goodness in Rory before... I guess it was my actions that destroyed that. He became bitter and aggressive. Maybe he took it out on Sarah because he knew she wasn't his? I'm sorry for not telling you two days ago, but I could never give you the truth before Sarah...'*

'I'm going to show you a picture of Dr Hannah Wright at one of your daughter's horse riding events. Can you tell me if you recognise the man with her?'

'Good lord, Frank... how could it be? That's him! That's her father. John White.'

The door before them opened. A tall, broad-shouldered man stood there, his eyes carrying dark shadows. The mark of exhaustion. Frank's attention caught on the dark ink adorning his wrists – he could make out the shape of letters. He reached up for his spectacles so he could read them, but they weren't on his head. He recalled pulling them off in the car and rubbing his temples when Sean had been filling them in on Donna Watson and the red Fiesta... he must have thrown them in the door pocket.

Well, he'd have to do without now.

Frank showed his warrant card. 'DCI Frank Black. This is DI Carver. We're looking for John White. Who am I talking to?'

'His son, Lewis White.'

'Okay, Mr White.' Frank nodded. 'Is your father home?'

Lewis's eyes darted between them before gesturing upwards at the ceiling. 'Upstairs...'

'Good... good. Could you ask him to come down, please?'

He shook his head.

Frank didn't detect aggression, but the reaction was odd. 'Sorry?'

'He can't.'

There was something else in the man's eyes – that distant look that came with fresh grief. 'He's sick?'

'Dead,' Lewis said with a weary nod. He rubbed his eyes. 'Last night... cancer.'

Frank and Gerry exchanged glances, both recognising time fraying another thread of their investigation right before their eyes. 'I'm sorry for your loss.'

Lewis nodded again. 'I actually thought you were here to collect him. What with your suits and everything. The weather's delayed collection.'

Frank reached into his inside pocket and pulled out one photograph from one of the riding competitions. He held it in front of Lewis, his thumb just above the man's head. 'That's your father?'

Lewis leaned towards it. 'Yes, a lot younger.'

'From the early eighties,' Frank said.

'Not long after I was born then.'

'Do you know who this is alongside him?' He moved his thumb across to Hannah.

Lewis stared. 'She looks a little familiar, but... no. You know, my father was a rogue. The man has more conquests than I dare to count. No idea, sorry. The story of his bloody life!'

'We could do with hearing as much of this story as you know,' Gerry said. It was the first time she'd spoken, and Frank wasn't sure if she was being sarcastic, or had taken those words literally.

'The truth is I know little.'

'It's important, Mr White,' Frank said. 'We're investigating a murder, you see. Of a young woman. Sarah Matthews. Does that mean anything to you?'

Lewis shook his head. 'No... sorry...'

'She went missing in 1989.'

'I would've been eleven years old,' Lewis said. 'At that point, I hardly saw my father. Look... I've company right now.'

'Who?'

He sighed. 'One of his old flames. But don't get excited, there were many. Still, I'm waiting to be enlightened. I've just found out I have a younger half-sister. As you can imagine, to say this is emotional would be an understatement. I won't mind coming down to the station and—'

'Lewis?' It was a woman's voice.

Lewis turned. 'It's not the undertakers.'

'Oh. Who is it?'

'It's the police. They wanted to speak to Dad.'

She stepped closer, smiling. Frank returned her smile and then his breath caught.

He looked at the photograph.

This woman was almost the spitting image of Dr Hannah Wright.

Impossible! She'd be in her seventies by now if she'd survived the explosion. He took a deep breath to steady himself, reminding himself that he'd no spectacles on and so could be mistaken.

An elderly woman stepped from the lounge and joined them, her gait matching the younger woman's exactly. Mother and daughter.

It was undeniable.

'Dr Hannah Wright?' Frank asked.

The reaction was subtle but unmistakable – a slight stiffening of her spine, a flash of something like fear crossing her weathered features. She looked down at the floor for a moment, then met Frank's gaze. 'Forgive my reaction, it's been a long time since I heard that name.'

'Yes,' Frank agreed. 'Not since 1991, I expect.'

Lewis and the young woman turned to Hannah, their faces masks of shock.

Hannah's shoulders squared, as if preparing for battle. 'You're just in time. I was just about to begin.'

Chapter Seventy-Five

Despite Becky Morton's farmhouse being off the beaten track, Reggie's Range Rover Sport navigated the accumulating snow with ease. He did, however, worry about Sharon's journey.

As he negotiated a narrow snow-covered road slicing through a patch of trees, he concluded that there was no hope of her getting anything other than a 4x4 down here.

He should've just picked her up – they only lived twenty minutes apart!

He parked up, killed his engine, and reached into his jacket pocket for his phone. It'd be best to call her and tell her to hang back. After all, how long would this meeting realistically take? An elderly woman in poor health? He imagined it'd be done and dusted in a few minutes.

He groaned when he saw there was no reception.

After looking in the rear-view mirror at the narrow dirt road he'd just navigated, he decided that the safest option was to head back and meet Sharon en route, or at least find a spot of reception to call her, and prevent her from slipping up and getting herself snowed in.

He started the engine, but movement caught his eye – the farmhouse door had opened.

He squinted.

Becky Morton sat in her wheelchair watching him.

He rubbed his moustache. The last thing he wanted was to unnerve the poor woman by parking up and then immediately driving away. She might think she was being scoped for a burglary! No, best to go in. Surely she'd have a landline with which he could warn Sharon.

Snow crunched beneath his feet as he left the car. This pristine white blanket was much deeper here than back in Whitby. The snow reached his shins. The overhanging trees had obviously protected a week's worth of build-up from the rain and sun alike.

Her nurse was supposed to be visiting daily. They would surely struggle today, unless they had transport like his.

He raised his hand in greeting as he approached.

She remained motionless, almost spectral in her chair.

Flanking his path were two life-sized ceramic angels. Snow-draped wings spread wide against the grey sky. Their blind eyes and frozen expressions sent a chill through him.

Closer to the doorstep, a weathered stone crucifix rose from the snow. Above the door, a ceramic dove perched, its wings spread in eternal flight.

He mounted the steps, drawing out his ID with a gloved hand. Becky seemed constructed entirely from angles and edges, her silver hair pulled back severely from a face mapped with deep lines. 'Good morning, Mrs Morton. Detective Sergeant Moyes. I was hoping to ask you a few questions.'

'Like the Magi following the star.' She spoke with a

blend of suspicion and intrigue. 'You come seeking truth on a cold morning.'

With absolutely no idea of how to respond to that, he simply nodded and said, 'I won't take up too much of your time.'

Her eyes narrowed and she studied him with a growing intensity. 'Is it about Clive?'

Feeling the cold chill in his veins deepening, he nodded. 'Partly... yes...'

'Would you like to come in and see him, then?'

He took an involuntary step back, the chill now ice cold. 'But Clive passed in 1991?'

'Yes. Of course. He may not be here physically, but that doesn't mean he isn't here. He'll know you when you come inside, but that's good. Because if he trusts you, then I'll trust you.'

Reggie nodded. Was this peculiar show a shot at humour – a lonely woman's whimsical attempt to amuse herself? Or was she losing her marbles?

He plumped for the latter.

This made him feel some sympathy as she turned and wheeled herself in.

There was nothing to worry about here, he reassured himself, and felt lighter as he crossed the threshold, but then she stopped so abruptly he nearly collided with her. 'Sorry, Mrs Morton.'

She spun her chair. 'Please call me Becky. We never did well with formality here. Clive says it creates unnecessary barriers between souls.' She smiled. 'Now, close the door, there's a good boy.'

Reggie raised his eyebrows but did as she asked, closing the door behind him.

Chapter Seventy-Six

Dr Hannah Wright sat with impeccable posture in a high-backed armchair.

At first, she'd insisted on John's son, Lewis, and her daughter, Rosie, being present for the story, but Frank had been firm in his refusal. He clarified that this was a police interview, and cautioned her. She had faked her own death, and now it was time to face the consequences.

'For almost three and a half decades, I've been Anais Cross. Please excuse me if I seem a little unfocused and disorientated at times.'

You seem quite the opposite, Frank thought, studying the renowned child psychiatrist from his position on the sofa alongside Gerry. She carried the same air of authority he'd seen in the photographs. Everything about her radiated control – her perfectly manicured nails, stylish white hair, and her eloquent choice of words.

'I thought she'd never be found.' Something flickered in her eyes – *grief, guilt?* Frank couldn't quite tell.

'An old silo...' Her composure cracked slightly. 'What a

horrible, horrible thing. Maybe it's best that John never knew that. The pain and guilt he felt were bad enough.'

Frank was still reeling from the revelation that John White was Sarah's father – yet he knew so little about him. 'So, from the get-go, you knew John was Sarah's father?'

'Yes, because he approached me after Rory Matthews was imprisoned.'

'Did Sarah ever know?'

'No. They met, of course, but we simply told her he was my partner. He didn't want her to know. He liked that they talked and had some contact – he was concerned that if she knew she'd resulted from an affair with Margaret, it'd fracture what little of a relationship they had.'

That aligned with what Margaret had told them. John had been happy to let Sarah believe she belonged to his half-brother, Rory.

'Over the coming months you may hear a lot about John. Mostly negative, but he'd a side to him, a quality that few saw. The drinking, the women, the self-destruction – they were there. I can't deny it.' She drew a breath and shook her head. 'A combination of my training as a therapist, I guess, garnished with a slightly reckless nature myself, allowed me to see something in him that really appealed. His true qualities. Though if you asked poor Lewis in there, he'd likely disagree. But there was always something about him... he was a passionate man, who never truly let go of anyone. He was always there, watchful. Just keeping enough distance so as not to cause any destruction. Ever vigilant.'

'So, you're saying he monitored Sarah's childhood?' Gerry asked.

Hannah nodded. 'As well as the childhood of his other two other children. He had Felix White in '75. Lewis, in the room next to us, '78, if I remember right. Then, Rosie, our daughter, in '91.'

'Where's Felix?' Frank asked.

'Unfortunately, he died in '88. Meningitis. It was awful... just awful. John was overseas and didn't make it back. Following a suicide attempt, he was committed for a few months. He never recovered from that. He thought himself some kind of curse. Paying the price for his hedonistic lifestyle. By that point, his marriage with Caroline was in tatters. She'd endured his behaviours for over ten years. After Felix died, they divorced. Again, he watched and supported Lewis from afar, but never really saw him or spoke to him.'

Admittedly, Frank was struggling to see these 'qualities' she'd referred to moments before. A man estranged from all of his children, apart from maybe Sarah for a time – but she'd never even known the truth. Solving his problems with money. Frank had had a gutful of people like that in his career.

That he was blaming himself, living a self-imposed exile, just felt like self-pity and excuses to Frank. In his honest opinion, this hedonistic money man should have faced up to his responsibilities properly.

So, Hannah, he thought, *how did you end up tangled in this web?*

He rephrased it for the actual question, though. 'So you and John met just after Rory went to prison. When was that? 1981?'

She nodded. 'He'd heard about my reputation for privately counselling children. He offered a substantial sum for me to counsel Sarah. I accepted.'

'And you called it research?' Gerry pressed.

'Yes, but it had to be that way. He didn't want his name

against the funding. So, I claimed it was pro-bono, and for research...'

'And her mother, Margaret, knew nothing about this arrangement?' Frank asked.

She shook her head. 'I simply visited Sarah at school and then offered my services to Margaret pro-bono. Sarah's story was a tragic one. Nobody questioned my motives. John funded the costs of everything, including the horse-riding lessons.' Her voice softened. 'It was his way of trying to be her father from a safe distance. He knew her emotional wellbeing was poor, and he believed he could help her through me.'

'And when did you fall in love with him?' Gerry asked.

The bluntness made Hannah flinch. 'Not immediately. But we got closer and closer as I reported back to him. He came to some horse shows with me. We got on well... I saw the goodness in him...'

'Did John have Rory Matthews killed in prison?' Gerry asked bluntly.

Frank looked at his colleague – it was an even bigger thunderbolt of a question.

'I don't know,' Hannah said softly.

'But you're not denying it?' Frank asked.

'I'm simply saying, I don't know. And I won't speak on his behalf. It wouldn't be right.'

'So you've suspicions, then?' Frank asked.

'Please, DCI Black, I'm not comfortable speculating.'

He suspected it to be the case, though. Rory had been a dangerous man. John was a wealthy man who'd a daughter who'd suffered abuse. He'd have had powerful connections. The pieces aligned with uncomfortable precision.

Still, he left it for now – this wasn't his priority.

'You said before that John would always act in Sarah's best interests?' Gerry said.

'Yes.'

'So why did he stand by while you asked her to leave her job with you in 1989?'

Hannah's sharp intake of breath echoed in the quiet room. 'Let's be clear – I loved Sarah. She was like a daughter to me. And not just because her father was my partner, but because of the time I'd spent with her. Years and years in her recovery. I was never closer to a patient. And, also, you should know that she was compassionate, loving, and nothing like the wild creature some others painted her as!'

Frank nodded. Unlike with John, she'd his complete agreement on that – Sarah had been compassionate, and she'd suffered, in so many ways.

Tears gathered in Hannah's eyes, her composure cracking further. 'Tommy Reid. He was like poison to her. After the first time, who'd have thought she'd make the same mistake? But people do, don't they? Repeat their mistakes. The second time around, though, she wouldn't listen to me any more. Not at all. John and I discussed it. Together, we thought if we shocked her by pushing her away, she'd soon see sense. Come back to us...' Her voice cracked. 'We never imagined...'

'Did you know who Peter and Donna Watson were?' Frank asked.

She shook her head once more.

'So,' Frank pressed. 'She never told you about the security guard who helped her. Her friendship with the couple, who she came to see, well, in a parental role?'

Still shaking her head, she looked down.

Frank explained the background behind Peter and Donna.

She took a moment to process it and then looked up. 'I'm happy that they made her happy for a time, and vice versa, but I knew nothing about it. But this isn't surprising. Not one bit.'

'What do you mean by that?' Frank asked.

'She was so complex. In fact, she was the most complex child I ever treated. The way she could compartmentalise was almost unprecedented – at least, in my experience. She was able to keep so many facets of her life separate – stop them intertwining. Earlier, in her therapy, I toyed with the possibility that she had dissociative identity disorder – you know, different identities and lives. I mean, how else could she do it so effectively? She'd grown up under an abusive father. Trauma had fractured her. Led to her leading secretive lives.

'Obviously, that didn't turn out to be the case, but I'm not shocked about learning things I didn't know. She wouldn't tell me about her experiences with Tommy Reid. I certainly didn't know about Peter and Donna. She never even told me about her poetry – I only found that out from her mother.'

'Did she ever discuss Stephen Walker?'

'Her head teacher? No. But many of the younger adults I've treated spoke about him. By all accounts, a wonderful man. Supportive and kind. Like I said, I never even read a single poem she wrote – despite her being part of some poetry club with him. I so wanted to read those poems. From the first day, I told her I wanted her to treat me like a diary. Pour everything into me. She made me think she was doing that, but like I said, it soon became obvious she wasn't giving me much.'

Frank thought of Sarah's poems, each one a different facet of a fractured life – the secret relationships with Peter and Donna Watson, the hidden pregnancy, the desperate search for connection. How many versions of herself had she created to survive? How many masks had she worn before her final, terrible end?

'I'm assuming the poems are with her mother?' Hannah asked.

It was presented like a question, but Frank decided not to answer it. He was still uncertain where he stood with Hannah. Why had she faked her own death?

Realising that she wasn't going to have her question answered, she went straight into another. 'You say it was Donna Watson who drove that red Fiesta?'

Frank nodded.

'You know, John spent a fortune in those years when she disappeared. Following every lead, every whisper regarding that red Fiesta. He vowed never to stop. To never write it off as a false, drunken witness statement.'

If only we'd taken that stance back then, Frank thought.

'Obviously, he did stop once we knew for sure that Sarah was dead. I mean there was no point, then, was there?'

Frank narrowed his eyes. 'Wait... did I miss something? How did you know? Hang on, do you know who did it?'

'Why, yes, of course, don't you?'

Frank shook his head.

'Sorry, DCI – I assumed you already knew. I mean, how would you have found poor Sarah otherwise?'

'The silo was brought down by a joyrider,' Frank said. 'We only recently found out about the red Fiesta.'

'Oh, I see, I'm not from around here. I assumed when you told me that Sarah was last seen near the Morton property, running from Donna's car, that you'd most certainly have spoken to Becky Morton. And she must have told you he'd put her body in the old silo. Hence, how you found her—'

'Sorry, rewind...He? Clive Morton?'

She nodded. 'One hundred per cent.'

Frank and Gerry exchanged a glance, before he looked back at Hannah. 'How do you know it was him?' Frank asked.

'*He told me.*'

Chapter Seventy-Seven

Becky Morton toyed with a wooden crucifix around her neck. The necklace held many rosary beads. As her fingers worked, a silver bracelet on her wrist reflected the early morning light penetrating the poky windows, sending sparks dancing over the walls. Because of the gothic religious nature of the room, Reggie couldn't help but liken the sparks to trapped, restless souls.

She offered him tea, but a graphic painting of the crucifixion had his attention.

'That's Hieronymus Bosch's *Christ Carrying the Cross*,' Becky said, following his gaze.

Reggie swallowed and nodded. The tortured faces in the painting seemed to watch him, their agony frozen in oils and time. His stomach twisted at the sight. He swallowed hard and declined the drink.

'The one next to it was Clive's favourite. *The Temptation of St Anthony*.'

Reggie observed a hellish landscape populated by demons and tortured souls, and his blood ran cold. How could anyone live surrounded by such a visceral depiction of suffering? And where were the Christmas decorations?

Shaken up, he asked her without even thinking, 'You're very religious, Becky. Where's the Christmas tree?'

'The Christmas tree represents spiritual compromise. Have you not read Jeremiah?'

Reggie shook his head.

'"For the customs of the peoples are worthless; they cut a tree out of the forest, and a craftsman shapes it with his chisel. They adorn it with silver and gold; they fasten it with hammer and nails so it will not totter." He wrote this before the popularity of Christmas trees. A divine warning unheeded.'

Reggie gave a slow nod, uncertain of what to make of it. 'I see. So you don't celebrate Christmas?'

'A profound spiritual deception that grieves me deeply. Early Christians didn't celebrate Christ's birth. I discovered in my readings that Roman Emperor Constantine deliberately chose 25 December. Church authorities then used it to help convert pagans by overlapping with their winter solstice festivals – particularly Saturnalia and the birthday celebration of the sun god Sol Invictus.'

'I see.' He really would have preferred Sharon alongside him now, which reminded him... 'I don't suppose I can use your house phone?'

'Disconnected,' she said. 'I didn't pay my bills. So what would you like to know?'

Over her shoulder was the wooden statue of a man riddled with arrows, its agonised expression eerily lifelike in the shifting light. Beside it, a small altar of sorts – a collection of photographs surrounded by flickering candles and withered flowers.

He stepped nearer for a better view.

A chill ran down his spine. A shrine.
To Clive Morton.

She followed his gaze again, her expression unreadable. 'It is better when the flowers are fresh. Candice brings them.'

'Your nurse?'

'Yes. And fresh candles.'

'Can I?' He nodded to show that he'd like a closer look.

Most images showed Clive working in various gardens. He looked enthusiastic, peaceful. His immersion in nature seemed to suit him. Quite a contrast with Riverside College's accounts of intimidation and predatory behaviour.

There was one close-up shot of his face. The candlelight made his face shift. It seemed to move between innocent and sinister, as if unable to settle on a single truth. After a minute, he realised he was becoming hypnotised and forced himself to look away.

'I never let the candles go out,' Becky said. 'And they'll burn until I can no longer light one.' He regarded a box beside the shrine, which was loaded with candles. 'When they are no longer burning, then we shall be together again.'

He noticed a petrol canister near the candles. He pointed at it. 'That can be dangerous.'

'It's empty... I no longer drive. I use it to hold water for the flowers.'

He turned and looked at her. He wanted to regard her face as he delivered the reason for his visit. 'Did you hear about what happened to the old silo near here?'

She shook her head. 'No. Candice could not come for a few days. She is my only source of knowledge.'

'It's been destroyed. Some kids crashed into it.'

'Are they okay?'

'Aye, but the silo will have to be taken down.'

'I see.'

'Well, it's not common knowledge yet, Mrs Morton, but there was a body inside it.'

She twirled her cross as she watched Reggie, unblinking. 'How awful.'

'Yes, they identified the body as Sarah Matthews. Did you know her?'

A shard of light reflected off the silver bracelet and stung Reggie's eyes. 'Not personally. But I know *of* her. I know she disappeared.'

He shielded his eyes. 'Yes, in October 1989.'

'How terrible... and so long ago. She was young.'

'Aye, twenty-two.'

'So very young.'

Reggie nodded, still shielding his eyes from the shards of light.

'"To everything there is a season, and a time to every purpose under heaven: A time to be born, and a time to die; a time to plant, and a time to pluck up that which is planted."'

'Jeremiah again?' Reggie asked.

'No. Ecclesiastes Chapter 3, verse 2.'

He gestured back to the images of Clive in the garden. 'He loved gardening.'

'More than anything. He was always at peace there. Gardens are God's canvas, and we, His humble brushes.'

A particular photograph caught his eye – Clive standing proudly in Riverside College's grounds, his pose somehow both gentle and imposing. He pointed. 'Tell me about his time there.'

'I see where this is going,' Becky said. 'First, we talk about the remains of a girl, and then we talk about the vile lies that were told about him.'

'It's important that we cover all angles,' Reggie said. 'What do you know about the complaints?'

She nodded. 'I just said. Vile. Listen carefully. "There are six things the Lord hates, seven that are detestable to him: haughty eyes, a lying tongue, hands that shed innocent blood, a heart that devises wicked schemes, feet that are quick to rush into evil, a false witness who pours out lies and a person who stirs up conflict in the community." Listen to that proverb, and you have my answer.'

'But why would those girls lie?' Reggie asked. 'Some of them felt intimidated.'

'Because rarely are people so kind... so helpful... so altruistic. When people help, it can unnerve. I assure you he wanted to help... that was all it ever was. And they turned it into hate. Listen to Matthew. "They rely on empty arguments, they utter lies; they conceive trouble and give birth to evil... Their thoughts are evil thoughts; ruin and destruction mark their ways. The way of peace they do not know; there is no justice in their paths. They have turned them into crooked roads; no one who walks along them will know peace."'

Reggie took a deep breath. 'I don't want to upset you, Mrs Morton, but some of what he said was inappropriate. He commented on the lengths of their skirts.'

'Warned them! How can it be inappropriate to steer the young away from fraternisation, to educate them on dignity, not to destroy themselves with fornication?'

Reggie's skin crawled at her matter-of-fact tone. This was one argument he would not win.

'He offered his words with kindness. I knew my husband,' she continued. 'Always. If you think he is involved with this girl's death, you are wrong. He knew the "hands of evil that shed innocent blood" – we both did.

The evil comes from those that stir up the rumours and the lies.'

Reggie nodded. 'Mrs Morton, your husband worked for Dr Hannah Wright between 1989 and 1991. Is that correct?'

She nodded.

'Now, Sarah Matthews was also working there as a nurse in 1989. Their paths will have crossed. Do you know anything about that?'

'He tended to Hannah's garden.'

'Aye, I know, but do you know if there was any relationship between—'

'Relationship! See again! Spilling lies, accusations...'

He inwardly sighed. He was feeling this was rather pointless. Plus, he was winding her up, and she didn't look in the best health. He decided he'd ask another question or two and then call it a day. If Frank wanted to follow it up, he could do.

'How did you feel about your husband dying in Hannah Wright's home?'

'How do you think I felt?'

'Sorry, that wasn't what I meant. Were you angry over what had happened?'

'If you think I am angry over my husband's death, you've not been listening to everything I've been saying.'

Reggie nodded. She was obviously referring to her religious beliefs. 'Why do you think he was within her house?'

'I thought that was obvious. Didn't the investigation conclude the same thing? He was trying to see if she had a gas leak, maybe even fix it... he made the wrong decision, but then, people who help, who are desperate to help and heal no matter the situation, will sometimes do that... I like to think I have helped, but you know, I am tired now, and I feel that if you have any more questions, I would prefer them another day and...' She fiddled with her cross again. 'Maybe, with someone else here? Candice, perhaps? I cannot help but feel that there is pressure here... pressure to condemn...' she looked at her husband's shrine, 'the most precious person I have ever known.'

The room was feeling smaller with each passing moment. The suffering saints in the paintings felt closer to him now, somehow. The last thing he wanted to be doing was dealing with a complaint. He was alone with her, too. Her words would force them to investigate whatever she said. 'I'll get out of your hair, Mrs Morton. Thank you for your time.'

She smiled and twisted her crucifix. The necklace suddenly snapped, and the rosary beads fell. He tracked their descent, watching them scattering and bouncing.

'Let me,' Reggie said, dropping to his knees to gather them.

The silence pressed against his ears as he crawled, collecting each one. Eventually, a metre from her, he looked up and held out his hand full of beads.

She reached out—

He saw the silver bracelet up close.

Reach for the stars.

Cold dread flooded his veins.

He realised his eyes had already widened, and then he realised he'd frozen and stared too long.

Carefully, he placed the beads in her outstretched palm and rose to his feet, steadying himself.

'Thank you,' she said.

She then looked over at her shrine, smiled at Clive, then back up at Reggie.

His mind raced. No mobile phone signal. No house

phone. No Sharon or backup. If he asked her, straight out, how she'd got that bracelet that could have been Sarah's before leaving.

Suicide?

She was old, had little left to lose, and seemed adamant on protecting her husband's memory. Would she finally let those candles burn out?

Best he tried to get away with it. Alert Frank and everyone as soon as he could and have her invited into custody for a conversation. 'Okay... thank you, Mrs Morton. You've been very helpful. Thank you for speaking to me.'

'Thank you.'

Reggie moved towards the door, the painted faces of the damned watching his retreat.

'However, there is something...' she said.

It felt as if his heart had stopped in his chest. 'Yes?'

'Something we haven't talked about.'

He turned slowly. She knew he'd clocked the bracelet.

She was rubbing the rosary beads between her palms, the silver bracelet – *the bracelet that could have once belonged to Sarah Matthews* sliding up and down her wrist, catching the light.

'And this might be your only chance to hear it,' she said.

In that moment, surrounded by images of suffering and lit by dancing candlelight, Reggie realised that this place could just as likely be a shrine to hell as to heaven.

Chapter Seventy-Eight

THE MORNING LIGHT caught Hannah Wright's face. The silence in the room was heavy – like the buildup of ice on branches.

Frank leaned forward in his chair, his joints protesting the movement.

She met his gaze with the steady composure of someone who'd spent a lifetime analysing others' truths while guarding her own. Behind her professional facade, Frank detected something he recognised from countless interviews – the weight of a secret finally ready to be surrendered.

Behind her, he saw the start of more heavy snowfall through the window.

'It was my mistake,' Hannah said. 'I genuinely believed Clive to be harmless. The allegations levelled at him by those students at Riverside just seemed so overblown. He convinced me he'd only been trying to help them. His mother's best friend had been raped and murdered while he was younger, and she'd always drilled it in to her older sister that she needed to be respectable and well-behaved in order to not attract male attention. It was unconventional, yes, warning them about the way they were dressing, and some of their behaviours, claiming it might get them in trouble. It was certainly very inappropriate, and may have come across as threatening, but to me, Clive just seemed to lack a filter due to a multitude of learning difficulties, and seemed to be doing it from an altruistic nature. I saw goodness in him, innocence, vulnerability. I couldn't have been more wrong. I still, for the life of me, can't work out how he pulled the wool over my eyes so effectively. Sometimes, when I look back, I fear it was hubris. That I just couldn't be wrong, and I ignored some signs.' Hannah turned slightly in her chair, her gaze drifting to the window. Her voice took on a distant quality, as if she was reciting a story she'd rehearsed countless times in her mind, even though this could very well be the first time. 'It was a couple of years after her disappearance. '91. John was even more damaged now. He'd lost two of his children and seemed increasingly fragile. In a way, it was better for our relationship. His tendency to vanish on business and 'adventures' with his wandering eye diminished. He relied on me, needed me more, rather like a crutch. No, it wasn't good for him, but it meant I could keep his more self-destructive tendencies at bay. I wanted to believe that we'd a future, even though I knew, deep down, his old habits would return, one day.'

She pressed her perfectly manicured fingers against her temples. 'Clive had been with us just under a year. Again, in all that time, I saw nothing to suggest that he had an insidious nature. Yes, his limited vocabulary and intelligence would often lead to him saying the wrong thing, as I mentioned before, especially when offering advice or commenting on the behaviours and sadness of the young women who came to see me, but we talked about it, and he listened, and I genuinely believed he was improving. God, to think what he'd done on that night in October.'

Frank spotted the first tear running down her face.

'If only I'd known. You should have seen it! He'd be in the garden – loving with the animals, gentle in his day-to-day tasks. He carried a camera and took photographs of wildlife, rabbits, and butterflies. How he loved the bloody butterflies. Some of my patients who came to me would catch a glimpse of him working, and comment on how happy he looked... how gentle. A man in his element. He was instructed not to talk to them and for the most part he followed this rule.' Her voice hardened with self-recrimination. 'What a fool I was.' She turned to Frank, her eyes sharp with a desperate need to be understood.

Frank wanted to reassure her, but not knowing the full outcome, he felt it was too early to judge, so he offered a swift nod for her continue.

Her gaze returned to the window. Outside, the snow was picking up pace. 'One day Clive approached Marie, one of my patients. He told her it was better she fought against the feelings she was having for close, female friends. That it could affect her happiness. Not only was it inappropriate, but how could he have known that? He must have been listening at my door, or examining my files. His literacy was poor so I assumed the former.' A muscle twitched in her jaw. 'You know what he said to Marie? He told her she was like a butterfly who couldn't see its own beautiful colours, mistaking itself for a moth. Such a poetic way to deliver such poison! Obviously, I planned to dismiss him. It was unforgiveable.' She gulped and twisted her fingers in her lap now. 'I never got the chance...'

'What happened?' Frank asked.

Hannah drew a shaky breath. 'Everything. And so

quickly. It was 2 March. John made an early, unexpected return from a trip. He caught Clive pressed against my office door, listening. He waited until my patient had left and then dragged him into me. At first, I was angry with John and told him to take his hands off Clive!

'Yes, I wanted him gone, but I still thought of him as a confused, vulnerable man. I wouldn't tolerate manhandling. John let him go, but then Clive started pacing, muttering – having some kind of meltdown. It seems the rough treatment of him had woken something.' Her hands trembled, the movement catching Frank's eye. She screwed her face up. 'He came apart in front of us. Ranting about nature and purity. Religious rhetoric, we later discovered, possibly from his overly religious wife, Becky, poured from him. Sin and evil, cleansing and salvation. His words became more confused, more desperate. When I told him to leave the property, he seemed to collapse in on himself...' She pressed her fingers to her temples, as if trying to hold the memory at bay. 'In despair, crying, insisting he only wanted to help these "fragile" girls. To clean them. To heal them. He was so pitiable, but at the same time, so sinister. I remember feeling nauseous, panicking. What had I brought into my home? This was my hubris. My unwavering belief that he was misunderstood.' Her voice caught on the words. She stared out the window at the spiralling snow, steadying herself and then said, 'John grabbed him, threw him toward the door. Called him disgusting...'

Tears spilled more freely down her cheeks now, cutting through her perfect makeup. 'I'm sorry.'

'Take your time,' Frank said, although the desire to know the outcome bubbled fiercely within him.

She took some deep breaths.

Beside him, Frank noticed Gerry was frantically taking

notes. 'And then he just lowered his head and froze in front of us. Like his batteries had run out or something. John was grabbing him again, forcing him towards the door, and that's when the photographs spilled from his pocket.'

She stared downwards in horror as if re-enacting the moment.

'Photographs?'

She nodded, tears streaming down her face. 'Thirteen girls. Like trophies. He claimed he could succeed where I'd failed. He said he could purify, and cleanse.'

Oh God, Frank thought. 'Who were the girls?'

'My patients... all my patients. The man wasn't harmless. The man was far from harmless. Of those thirteen, twelve of them were current patients... and they were still alive, thank God... but... the things he'd written on the back of their photographs. Words like: *Licentious, homosexual, profligate, impious, idolatrous, defiant.* He was defining their problems, or identifying the sins he believed were plaguing them – all from the information he'd been getting from listening in to my sessions with these poor girls.'

Frank took a long breath, knowing what he needed to ask and what the answer would be. 'Twelve patients. And the thirteenth photograph?'

She fixed him with a stare. 'You know, already. Sarah.'

Frank felt his insides churn. 'And what had he written on the back of her photograph?'

'*Wayward.*'

Frank lowered his head. His mind wandering back to that moment at the silo when he'd looked at her for the first time, when he'd thought to himself.

I want to know the real you.

And I do, now, Sarah, and it isn't wayward. Lost, perhaps, for a time, aye... needing guidance, which you got, but you were creative, kind and you forged relationships in your life that were meaningful. Clive didn't know the real you. To sum you up with a single word.

Unthinkable.

He looked back up. 'What happened next, Hannah?'

'John shook the photograph at him, and I will never forget the words that monster used: "I tried. I really did. I wanted so much for her to be pure. To be clean." And then John just lost it.' She put a hand to her face and cried.

Hardly surprising, Frank thought, his mind whirring.

Frank decided to give her a moment to compose herself, but Gerry wasn't as patient. 'Did John kill Clive?'

Hannah looked up and stared at Gerry, eyeliner running down her face. 'No, dear...'

Chapter Seventy-Nine

Around him, tortured souls seemed to pry themselves from their frames, hungry for the truth.

Becky's fingers continued to roll the rosary beads between the palms of her hands on top of a knitted blanket. The silver bracelet continued to send sparks of light across the walls. 'I'll show you the truth.'

'Just tell me.'

'A servant cannot be corrected by mere words; though he understands, he will not respond.'

She dropped the rosary beads onto the knitted blanket and wheeled her way past him.

He knew he should leave. He'd have to drive into town to get reception and organise backup.

But there could be direct evidence linking Becky, and Clive, to Sarah's death. If he left now, how much evidence would survive his return? And would she even survive it? Knowing the game was up, she may hasten her exit.

'You need to know that others are coming,' he lied. 'It isn't in your interests to play me for a fool.'

'I'm eighty-five years old,' she hissed as she wheeled out of the room. 'What could I possibly do?'

Sometimes, the truth demanded risks. And to be fair, this one seemed almost minuscule.

'Okay, then, I'll push,' he said, following and taking the handles of the chair.

The wooden floorboards in the hallway creaked beneath them, each step echoing with an ominous, ancient weight, like those brutal, tortured images. 'Just there, beneath the stairs. That door.'

'Okay.'

Age had scarred the wood, its surface bearing the patina of countless hands and secrets.

'Enough,' she said.

He released the handles and stepped back, positioning himself carefully. Despite her age and frailty, he still viewed her as a coiled snake.

She swivelled her chair to face the door, the motion precise despite her apparent weakness, then lifted her trembling fingers to turn a key. The lock's mechanism groaned like something waking from a long sleep. She turned the handle and then wheeled herself backwards with one hand, trying to open the door. She couldn't. She stopped against the hallway wall, catching her breath. 'It's jammed.'

Watching her from the corner of his eye, he leaned over and opened the door. He yanked it open with a groan of rusty hinges. Stale air rushed out.

'You see the light cord?'

He pulled it and shadows danced as a single bulb flickered to life.

He glanced at the worn steps and couldn't help snorting. 'You don't really expect me to go down there?'

Her voice carried that blend of frailty and steel that

made his skin crawl. 'I can walk, with your help. These legs aren't completely useless yet. Help me up, and I'll walk in front of you. You can give me support from behind – how does that sound?'

Ridiculous, he thought. 'This isn't the right approach...'

'Suit yourself.' A smile touched her lips, cold as cemetery frost. 'I always thought detectives were curious folk.'

'I would rather you just tell me.'

'Better that we wait for your friends to come.'

But they weren't coming. Sharon would never get through that snow.

He thought of Christ's agonised face on the wall in the lounge, the arrows protruding from the figure, and those snow-covered angels. So many fragmented, dark images. No wonder every instinct was screaming at him to pack this in...

If not for that bloody bracelet... 'Just tell me how you got the bracelet.'

'No.'

For fuck's sake!

He thought of Frank if he messed this up and she died with the truth. *Bloody hell Reggie. You're brave enough to wear that horrendous moustache, but not have a look at what an eighty-five-year-old woman who can barely walk has to show you!*

He looked down at her again. Would she even have the strength in her arms and hands to use a gun, even if she had the chance to grab one?

Get a grip, he told himself.

'Okay, but you first.' He kept an equal distance between Becky and the steps. She wouldn't have much of a push on her, but best to be cautious. He proffered his hand.

'Thank you.' Her fingers were ice cold.

She groaned as he took her weight, and she rose.

But then, halfway up, the bastard blanket slipped from her lap, and the rosary beads scattered.

Shit!

They sounded like the rattling of brittle bones. He wasn't picking them up again, not in the current situation.

'Wait…' she said, gulping air. 'Stop…'

He released her hand, and she sank back into the chair.

Her breathing came in ragged gasps, her hand pressed against her chest beneath her jacket. 'That was harder than I realised…' She coughed and wheezed for a moment. 'These old bones…'

'Are you okay?'

'Getting there.'

'Shall we leave—'

Her hand shot out again with surprising speed.

'Okay.' Reggie took her hand. 'One last try… okay? Ready…'

He shifted his weight, confident in his strength and that he was in control. He still had one eye on caution, but he'd never been one to be short on pride.

And although pride was the ancient enemy of wisdom – he could handle one frail old lady—

A sudden, sharp pain below his chest made him wince. For a brief second, panic over a heart attack swelled inside him. But then his eyes saw the blade in the hand he wasn't holding.

Shit! She'd had it hidden beneath that blanket!

He released her hand, and the pain quickly intensified. It was just below his ribs at the top of his abdomen.

Instinctively, he moved backwards so she couldn't strike again.

He felt his foot rolling over something.

The rosary beads.

Then, everything was spinning. Jarring and bashing against stone. Pain bloomed throughout his body.

Groaning at the bottom of the steps, he stared up at the silhouette of Becky hunched over in a wheelchair.

The pain was intense.

What had he allowed to happen?

'You won't take me from my home,' she said into the cold cellar. 'I need to be here when those candles burn out. I told you how important that was. When the candles are no more, we can be together again. You shouldn't have come. You'd have left here, spilling more lies. He tried to help Sarah. Cleanse her. And you would have started something new. You are not innocent, DI Moyes. Not innocent at all. And this sacrifice will be a just one. "Then you will trample on the wicked; they will be ashes under the soles of your feet on the day when I act," says the Lord Almighty.'

The door closed.

The lock's mechanism groaned.

He clutched his stomach and looked at the blood on his hands, watched it gleam in the sputtering light.

Ashes under the soles of your feet.

He thought of the candles... and the petrol canister.

Ashes.

Then, he thought of the candles burning out, everything going to darkness.

And then he felt himself moving into that black.

Chapter Eighty

'Like I said,' Hannah continued. 'The bastard was taking pictures of my patients while they waited on my property for their appointments. And with the camera he used for his butterflies, too! It was sinister. It felt... evil. So, to see one of Sarah, in her nurse's uniform, combined with the word, *wayward*, just sent John completely mad. I honestly thought he was going to tear Clive to pieces there and then. Instead...' She swallowed hard, her throat clearly working against the memory.

'But then John suddenly bolted from the room – no reason, no explanation. Just ran. I didn't understand, and I just stood there asking Clive why he'd taken the pictures. And he told me: "To help them, to clean them, to save them."' She stared at Frank and then Gerry. 'What the fucking hell was he?' Her fingers twisted together like pale snakes. 'Then, John came back with a kitchen knife. I could barely recognise him at that moment. His eyes... God, his eyes. He kept jabbing the blade at Clive, testing him.' She swallowed hard. 'Demanding to know where Sarah was. The things John was threatening! *God.* He said he'd cut

Clive into pieces, cut out his eyes. I can see John's face now. Feral, wild. I don't think they were an empty threat.

'But Clive just continued smiling, speaking of Sarah as if she was one of his precious butterflies.'

'Had you ever seen them interacting before? Sarah and Clive?' Gerry asked.

'Of course, she was the nurse at my home! She liked him. Talked to Clive about the garden, about his butterflies. Sarah spoke of him fondly. Maybe she genuinely saw him as a friend. But I doubt he had ever spoken to her like this before.'

'Did he then admit to killing her?'

'In his own way.' Hannah stopped and shuddered. 'His voice seemed to change completely. There was this terrible reverence in his tone. He started quoting scripture, all about cleansing, and the path to purity being a painful one. His eyes... they became fever bright. He explained how she'd come to him one night, seeking help. How he'd listened to her pain and tried to heal her. The way he spoke about her... How he saw it as a sign from God - that she'd been delivered to him for salvation.'

My God, Frank thought, recalling Sean's update regarding Sarah leaving Donna's vehicle by that patch of trees, alongside a dirt path to Morton's isolated farmhouse. In his mind's eye, he saw Sarah walking through the darkness, looking for help, a friend in Clive Morton, completely unaware his intentions may have been insidious.

'Then Clive started reaching out for the photographs – he wanted them back. I'll never shake the image of John slicing straight through Clive's palms. But it didn't deter the monster from reaching out again with his bloody hands. He said, and I remember it so vividly, "I only wanted to help her spread her wings." The way he said it... so serene... so certain. I think at that point, I realised, *understood,* that he must have killed her. And so, too, did John. He pinned Clive against the wall, the blade pressed to his eye, threatening again to dig them out. Demanding to know where Sarah was. I screamed at John to stop. He was on the verge of killing him...' She drew a breath. 'And I got through to him. He slumped backwards. He turned to face me, confused, and the knife slipped from his hand. I grabbed it and went to call the police. It could have ended there if not...' She shook her head. 'If not for what came next. Clive told us about...' Her hands flew to her mouth, as if trying to hold back the words. 'The baby.'

Frank tasted bile.

'He said she'd been so afraid. Pregnant with no one left to turn to, because I'd asked her to leave her job.'

Feeling nauseous, he looked at Gerry. If she was feeling the same, she was hiding it well.

'And that was enough again to set John off,' Hannah continued. The idea of her being pregnant. The idea of us taking away her job to make a point. It was too much for him. He just exploded. He threw Clive into the wall, started punching him, and I thought he would go on to beat him to death... except...'

She stared out of the window for a moment. The snow was picking up pace again.

She took a deep breath and continued. 'Something awoke in Clive. He started fighting back and, before I knew it, Clive was on top of him, strangling him.' She made a gesture with her hands. 'He would've killed him. And, I guess, in my panic, and fear, seeing the man I love about to die, I lost control too...' Her voice dropped to barely a whisper, thick with horror at the memory. 'I grabbed the knife – and I stabbed him in the back.'

Again, she stopped. This time for a short while. Silence filled the room like smoke, broken only by the soft tick of a clock and the whisper of falling snow outside.

Frank set his pen down – he needed a break from writing notes. The story was *so* harrowing.

And then more suspicion reared up in him. If this was true, then why had Hannah run? She wouldn't have got a life sentence for that. Maybe some jail time, but that had been a heated situation, and self-defence could be argued. He readied himself to ask that question, but she got there first.

'Clive was still alive...' she whispered.

Frank took a sharp breath. *Where did this end?*

Hannah's hands trembled as she spoke, her composure completely crumbling now. 'And I don't know why... I thought of Sarah... I thought of what I'd caused, and yes, in that moment, I wanted to kill him. A man taking photos of butterflies, pretending he cared... all the time a vile monster. And Sarah pregnant... oh God... And I stabbed him over and over...'

Frank exhaled. *Good Lord*.

'He was already long gone before John pulled me away,' Hannah concluded.

Chapter Eighty-One

'It's NOT the murder that eats away at me,' Hannah said, her face ashen. 'It's the fact that if I hadn't killed him, we may have found out where he'd put her. Because of me, she remained undiscovered until now... That horrendous old silo. I can't believe it...

'John always blamed himself for everything – so this was nothing new. He wanted to confess, himself. But I couldn't let him. No way. He was insistent. You see, I was pregnant, as well.' She pressed her hands against her stomach, an unconscious echo of the child she'd carried then. 'But this was my failure. My mess. I'd brought him into my house. I'd told Sarah to leave. And then I killed him, taking away our chance of finding her.' Her voice cracked with self-loathing. 'But John was desperate to keep me out of jail. He told me angrily to think of our child.' She looked off into the distance with a bittersweet smile. 'Rosie...

'He suggested burying the body, but I couldn't do it. I couldn't work again as a psychiatrist. How could I? That constant reminder of failure? Together, we caused a gas explosion, placing his body as near to the leak as possible to give the impression he was trying to fix it. Within twenty-four hours, John had obtained a body from a recent car accident, ensuring the face was damaged beyond dental verification. Don't ask me how. John knew people... he was wealthy. When those two things marry up, you can get what you want.

'Burning it all away felt like the right thing to do. How else did we have any chance of starting again? He paid for my new identity, arranged a home – everything. The only thing he said I'd never have was him.

'I know John could never forgive me, deep down, for destroying our chance to find Sarah. But for a long time, he channelled that guilt into protecting our child. He saw it as cosmic balance – having lost one daughter, he could redeem himself by saving another. He could never be with me, but he could be vigilant in the same way he'd been with the other children. Except... he'd failed twice before... and Lewis, his other son, despised him. Monthly deposits, birthday cards with no return address. I retrained as a teacher under my new name, thinking perhaps I could atone by helping others. I tried to keep track of him from afar, but it became harder and harder. He had relationships, continued with his business, developed an alcohol problem which he was treated for. He became more and more withdrawn, becoming a ghost.'

'Did you keep Clive's photos?' Gerry asked.

She nodded slowly. 'They're at my place.'

Frank nodded. 'We can arrange for someone to collect them.'

'Did John ever confront Becky Morton?' Gerry asked.

Hannah's face tightened at the mention of Clive's widow. 'He discovered she'd been working that night at a restaurant in Whitby and wouldn't have been home. One night, he broke in and searched her home top to bottom but found nothing. He stopped himself short of paying someone to go around and threaten her – to find out if she helped... if she even knew. But he decided against it. She was very religious and rumoured to be kind. It was too much of a risk alerting her to the fact that her husband's death might not have been an accident. He tried to believe she had nothing to do with it.'

Gerry apologised and went out to answer a phone call. Frank regarded Hannah – this accomplished woman who had built a second life from the ashes of her crimes – and realised that his pity was in short supply. If they'd come forward, then Sarah could have been found long before now. Plus, how did they know Becky wasn't involved?

Gerry poked her head back in. 'Sir?'

'What's wrong?'

The look on Gerry's face made his stomach clench.

'One moment.' He nodded at Hannah and exited.

'Sharon has been in a car accident,' Gerry said.

Frank's knees nearly buckled, his hand shooting out to steady himself against the wall. 'Is she okay?' He couldn't finish the sentence.

'No, but she'll live.'

Gerry continued. 'It was quite serious – broken ribs, cuts on her face and neck. She'll need some time in the hospital.'

'What happened?'

As Gerry detailed the accident, Frank's mind kept drifting to that treacherous stretch of road, imagining Sharon's car sliding out of control.

'Bloody weather. Is someone with her?'

'Family, apparently.'

'Okay, that's good, because we need to stay here until

she can be taken into custody...' A thought struck him like ice water down his spine. 'Wait a second... she was alone, not with Reggie – what time was this?'

'First thing.' Gerry gave the time.

'So, she didn't make it to Becky Morton's place?'

'Seems not.'

Cold dread settled in his stomach as the implications sank in. He took out his phone and dialled Reggie. Straight to voicemail.

'Shit. I didn't like them going there before when I heard about Donna and the red Fiesta, but after that confession...' His voice trailed off as darker possibilities took shape. 'I certainly don't like it. And now we find that only Reggie is there?'

'She's eighty-five years old and a wheelchair user,' Gerry said. 'I think he could be safe.'

'I know of murders committed by ninety-year-olds.'

'Still, sir, statistically—'

'Not now, Gerry, I'm thinking...'

'Reggie is strong. Fit for his age, too.'

Frank's jaw clenched. 'No need to remind me of that – he does that often enough himself. Wait.' He phoned Sean. 'Let's see if he was warned off.'

Sean confirmed he'd never spoken to Reggie. Only Sharon, who'd assured him she was on her way to join him.

'So maybe Sharon called him?' he asked Sean.

'I doubt it... I couldn't get through to him, so I doubt she could—'

'Okay, get back up there, Sean.'

'Becky Morton is eighty-five years old, boss.'

'Don't you start, young man, just sodding well do it.' He ended the call with more force than necessary.

'Okay, Gerry, please stay here until Hannah Wright is taken into custody.'

'Are you sure that's a good move? You heading to Becky's now?'

Frank's voice carried the weight of over four decades of experiencing humanity's darkest impulses. 'Christ, Gerry, a girl was murdered in that house – or taken from there to die in a silo. Her husband was a killer who stalked vulnerable girls. Are we having this conversation?' He was already moving toward the door.

'Sir—'

Frank didn't hear any more. He was already out into the swirling snow. Somewhere in Ruswarp, Reggie might have walked into a house of horrors, armed only with half the story. The thought chilled Frank more than any winter storm.

Chapter Eighty-Two

Before he reached Ruswarp, Frank saw the dark pillar of smoke twisting against pearl-grey skies.

En route, he pulled over twice to let emergency vehicles pass, each wailing siren making his heart stutter. The second stop was cruelly ironic. It was almost the exact same spot the taxi driver had dropped him off days earlier. The hollow, broken grave still loomed on the horizon.

By the time he'd passed through Ruswarp town and was approaching the wooded area where Sarah Matthews had last been seen alive, the blazing glow was visible alongside the smoke.

When he reached the snow-covered dirt path between the trees, he beheld an inferno at the heart of a frozen world. The snow continued to spiral down, but would have little effect against the raging flames.

Frank's heart sank.

Nobody was walking out of those flames.

The emergency vehicles' lights painted hellish patterns across the snow – the fire engine and ambulance had ventured in, tackling the deep snow. The police vehicles had hung back, closer to where he was now.

Frank sprang into the biting cold and trudged through the deep snow. It took some effort, and he almost slipped over on several occasions, but he didn't care.

If Reggie was gone, he deserved every bruise, every fall.

Hypothermia? So be it.

As he drew closer, heat slapped his face, and the snow thinned out. Two firefighters were currently dragging hoses toward the blaze and would be happy that the snow was melting.

He tried to hear them, but the inferno's roar and crashing timber obliterated their words. Then, when the water finally hit flame, steam rose like escaping spirits.

Through the smoke and chaos, he thought he glimpsed figures in the garden.

Reggie?

Closer still, he saw they were stone angels with spread wings, their faces blackened by ash. They looked more like demons risen to witness the destruction, their blind eyes reflecting firelight.

Then he spotted Reggie's Range Rover Sport, a silent offering to the flames. 'God...' His stomach churned. 'No...'

It was over for sure.

He clenched his fists.

I've lost Reggie.

Everything inside him was turning to lead, and he struggled to free his badge when a police officer intercepted him.

His hand trembled. He didn't look at the officer. He merely watched the fiery grave, wondering how the hell it had come to this.

'DCI Black, you need to stay back. Please... it really isn't safe. The heat's intense. We're lucky there's some distance between the surrounding trees, but it isn't enough to guarantee they won't go up.'

'Tell me you have him,' he demanded.

'Sorry... who?'

Frank showed his desperate, wide eyes. 'DS Reggie Moyes.'

The officer paled. 'I'm sorry.'

'Fuck!' Frank shouted and then glared at him. 'We need to check! Damn it! We need to bloody check!'

The younger officer looked like he was going to burst into tears. 'We can't get close enough to do anything.'

'Then he's buggered, isn't he?'

The officer lowered his eyes.

'Isn't he?' Frank shouted.

The officer shook his head. 'I don't know, sir.'

'Well, he is, because absolutely no one is getting out of that.'

Part of him knew he was being cruel to this kid, but he had very little control now. He turned, stumbled, righted himself, and headed back towards his car.

He thought about Reggie taking the piss out of him days earlier at the crime scene for not being able to keep up with him.

Shit... shit...

He tried his best to keep back the tears, but they were already in his eyes.

When he reached the car, he climbed in, sank into the driver's seat, and spent the next couple of minutes in tears, watching flames devour the house where Sarah Matthews had walked unwittingly to her end.

And now, decades later, the bastard Mortons had claimed another victim.

It would be their last, but that offered little comfort.

He rubbed back tears.

He couldn't help but imagine Reggie smiling over this, stroking that ridiculous fucking moustache.

The guilt rose like bile in his throat. *This is my fault.*

When he got the call from Sean, he'd thought Sharon was with Reggie. But he still should have known better. It still, in retrospect, warranted backup.

My fault.

He'd been so distracted by Margaret's revelation that John White was Sarah's father and, then, subsequently, by Hannah Wright's presence and confession, that he'd not spared a thought for his team, and that elderly woman in a wheelchair.

Countless others may have made the same mistake, but he wouldn't let that exonerate him.

He'd make this his end too.

This is it for you Frank, your final fuck up.

'We need paramedics over here!' The shout cut through his despair like a blade.

Frank lunged from the car, slipping in the snow. It knocked the wind out of him but the snow offered some cushioning. He stumbled back up, watching a firefighter waving frantically at an ambulance.

Heart hammering against his ribs, snow in his hair and all over his clothes, he fell in alongside two paramedics with medical bags and a collapsible stretcher. He could feel the snow he'd picked up from the fall soaking through to his skin.

He must have looked a mess, but he didn't care. And his lungs burned as he tried to keep up with the younger paramedics, but again, he didn't care.

If this is how I go, then this is how I go.

'This way!' The firefighter led them through a small

copse of trees to the right of the burning house, branches heavy with snow cracking overhead.

Twice he stopped to gulp air. The second time he almost vomited.

When he burst from the copse, he saw the paramedics, ahead of him now, charging to someone lying on the snow.

Another firefighter was kneeling beside this person.

Please... God... please... The prayer echoed in his mind with each crunching step through fresh snow. He could hear his desperate lungs. Every wheeze caused by age and smoke. Snowflakes stung his face like tiny needles.

Reggie.

Lying there, one hand pressed against his bloody abdomen, his eyes wide open and, now, focusing on Frank.

'Just watching the show... boss,' Reggie managed through chattering teeth. 'At a safe distance.' His breath hitched with pain.

Frank's eyes fixed on the blood seeping between Reggie's fingers, fear coiling in his gut, but then sought out the familiar cocky smile again for hope.

'Yeah, I see it, Reggie. You made a right bloody mess of that one.'

Reggie laughed and then winced as the paramedics began examining his wound.

'She was as mad as a hatter, but I was an idiot...' Reggie grimaced. 'I saw a bracelet on her wrist – I think it might have been Sarah's.'

A cold chill went down Frank's spine. It wasn't surprising now he knew the truth of what had gone on there. 'I think you need to rest now.'

'I should have got the hell out of there, boss, when I had the chance. Before she did this to me...'

'Aye, you should have.'

Reggie smiled. 'Like you would have, boss?'

He smiled and winked. 'You got me there.'

'She stabbed me and pushed me down into the cellar. Before you say anything... I know she was eighty-five but... don't bloody tell anyone.'

'I had an auntie that lived to ninety that could break bricks with her hands, Reggie. She'd have made mincemeat of us all. Actually, she did one time when I was a wee scrote. Look, books and covers. Give yourself a break, man, and stop bloody talking.'

The paramedics prepared the stretcher.

'Got lucky... after I smelled smoke, I saw a small window... it was barred... but...' He coughed.

'On three,' one paramedic said.

They counted and then lifted him carefully onto the stretcher. Reggie drew a hiss of pain through clenched teeth.

'Hang on in there, fella,' Frank said. 'I'm not replacing you. This will be my last team. You go, I go.'

'You always have a way with words, boss.'

As they moved back through the woods, Frank tracked alongside him.

'Anyway... the bars were set in old bricks, and they were damp and crumbling. I kicked through them, crawled up some steps and' – he closed his eyes, gulped and then opened them – 'through the snow.'

You've been one hell of a lucky bastard, Reggie.

At the ambulance, Frank clasped Reggie's hand, feeling its trembling coldness. 'You want me to come?'

Reggie shook his head. 'No... I want to see if you can salvage any evidence.'

Frank glanced at the inferno but passed on a sarcastic comment.

'You been crying, boss?' Reggie asked.

'Piss off. I fell over in the snow.'

'Your eyes are red.' He smiled.

Prick.

Once Reggie was in the ambulance, Frank nodded up at him from outside. 'Only you'd get caught up in a bloody inferno and not singe a single hair on that god-awful moustache.'

Reggie laughed. 'Don't, boss, it hurts to laugh.'

'Sorry,' Frank said. 'But it wasn't a joke.'

'You do realise that if I pull through I'm keeping the 'tache?' Reggie said.

'We'll see about that,' Frank said as the ambulance doors closed.

He caught the paramedic's arm before he could reach the driver's door. 'Is he going to make it?'

'He's lost blood, obviously, and we don't know the extent of the damage, but I've seen them worse, far more delirious. If no major organ is punctured, I'd be optimistic...'

'Optimistic. I like that word, son,' Frank said as the paramedic climbed in the front seat. 'If that brick holding those bars hadn't been worn, well, we'd have none of that optimism now, would we?'

The paramedic closed the driver's door, smiled at Frank through the window and started the engine.

After the ambulance disappeared, Frank stood witness to the house's last moments. The roof collapsed with an apocalyptic roar, sending a column of sparks spiralling skyward. Burning debris rained down, each fragment hissing as it met snow. The heat had melted the ice on nearby trees, and the branches wept.

The demonic angels in the garden seemed to sneer at him.

Frank thought about the silo, Ruswarp's forgotten grave, and then turned his attention back to the flames.

A second grave. Taking with it the remnants of pure evil.

Good riddance, he thought, and turned away.

Two Days Later

Sharon sat up in the hospital bed. Despite the bandages and cuts marring her face, her smile lit up the sterile room when she unwrapped the Chanel No. 5 perfume. She looked up at her assembled colleagues. 'Thank you, folks. Hopefully, I'll be up and about in the new year to try it out.'

'It's the one you like,' Sean said with the proud enthusiasm of someone who'd clearly chosen it, and wanted that fact known.

Frank looked at him, shaking his head, forcing back a comment.

His cheeks reddened, and he looked down.

'Well,' Sharon said, 'I did have something small for you all, but it's wrapped up at home.'

'We'll look forward to it in the new year,' Frank said.

'Boss? Where's your hat?'

Gerry and Sean's festive headwear made Frank's bare head all the more conspicuous.

Gerry held up Frank's discarded hat, evidence of her failed attempt to spread Christmas cheer.

Frank shook his head. 'Look, I said on the way in. No

point. I can never get the bastard things on.' He'd pointed at his head, drawing attention to what he'd always considered its unfortunate proportions. 'Always been too big for them.' It was a ridiculous lie, of course.

'You saying you got a big head, sir?' Sharon asked.

'Aye... physically, smart arse... you know what I mean.'

The door swung open, and a nurse wheeled Reggie in. He was already wearing a Santa hat, perched at a jaunty angle. Frank couldn't help but notice Reggie's exposed arms as he adjusted himself in the wheelchair – wiry, defined, and muscular.

Bastard. I thought that with you being hospitalised, I'd at least get a few days off from your fitness show. 'Here's the Christmas entertainment,' he said, sneering.

'Ho, ho, ho!' Reggie said.

'The bloody idiot, more like!' Sharon corrected.

It was, however, delivered with an affectionate tone.

'Look, we've been through this,' Reggie said, waving his hand. 'I was never in danger. Nobody can keep a man like me caged.' He flexed his muscles.

Jesus, take me now, Frank thought.

At least everyone else groaned.

That's it, crew, make a point, and let's make it a new year's resolution to shut this bullshit down.

'Bollocks to no danger,' Frank said. 'And if you'd died, me and you would've had a real sodding problem.'

'Ha! What would you have done boss?'

Frank smiled and shrugged. 'I'd have dug you up just to bloody well kill you a second time.'

The laughter that followed felt genuine. It was undoubtedly a release of tension that they'd all been carrying. For the next thirty minutes, they avoided work talk. There was nothing more to say about the case anyway.

Two Days Later

Hannah Wright was in custody, her confession unwavering, the loose ends tied.

Frank had to admit there were positives this Christmas. More than last anyway. For the first time in what felt like forever, he was amongst friends. He had Gerry working with him. She may have driven him nuts, but she made him smile just as much.

The thoughts caught him off guard – when had that happened? When had their peculiarities become endearing as well as irritating?

There was also his blossoming friendship with Evelyn – a lovely walk on Christmas Eve to look forward to.

The only dark clouds were his missing daughter and this mysterious scrote who kept lurking around his house, wanting his ear for some reason.

He took a deep breath, letting the positivity seep into his bones, and made a silent promise: *This year. This year will be the year you find her.*

'Time for some extra presents,' Frank announced, reaching into a plastic carrier bag that had seen better days for two wrapped packages.

'No fair,' Sean said. 'We were buying group gifts remember?'

'I remember. I also remember that I'm the boss and I can do what I want.' He handed one to Reggie first.

Reggie turned the package over in his hands, his eyebrows rising at the unconventional wrapping. 'You wrapped it in masking tape, boss.'

'So... does the same thing, no?'

He unwrapped it. It was clearly a struggle.

'Thought you were strong?'

'I am... ha.' He held up some shaving foam. 'Very bloody funny.'

Two Days Later

'What's funny?' Frank asked.

'Think it's time for you to take the bloody hint, man,' Sharon said.

'Aye,' Frank added. 'There's only so long I can go on being this subtle.'

Everyone laughed.

'I told you it's going nowhere – you'll have to get used to it,' Reggie said, caressing his moustache with the kind of pride usually reserved for firstborn children. 'Because—'

'Don't you bloody dare—'

'I'm rather attached to it.'

The pun made Sharon laugh, while Frank and Sean groaned. Gerry offered one of her precise smiles – the kind that suggested she recognised the social cue for humour without quite feeling it herself.

Frank shook his head with the weary resignation of a man who'd long since given up hope. 'Sharon, because DS Moyes never does a bloody thing I say...' He reached in the bag and handed her a gift. 'I came up with a backup plan.'

She unwrapped it with careful movements, mindful of her injuries, likewise struggling with Frank's creative use of masking tape. She held up a Gillette razor, shaking her head.

'Aye, Sharon, I'm passing the baton...' Frank said. 'Bugger won't listen to me. So, when he least expects it – strike.'

The laughter that filled the room felt like healing – warm and genuine and needed. Frank looked around at his odd bunch. They weren't just colleagues any more, they were something much better than that.

And for the first time in years, Frank Black felt something dangerously close to Christmas spirit.

Christmas Eve

It was a white Christmas!

Especially on Sycamore Close.

He must have been quite a sight, returning home in a Santa costume with a bag of presents over his back on Christmas Eve!

But he didn't care.

Not really.

Peter Watson had spent a great deal of his life anxious and was owed a few days off.

His first stop was number 7.

Jake, bobbing his head, opened the door, releasing a crashing wave of sound.

Jake looked confused. Mind you, he was usually stoned. Judging by the strong odour, that was the case right now. 'Sorry, I... can I help you?'

Peter pulled down the fake beard and winked.

'Man... woah! Peter. Fuck. You know that everyone is looking for you?'

'Why?'

Christmas Eve

'It's well... it's been days, man. They think... they thought... that you, you know...'

'Offed myself?'

Jake nodded. 'That, or died in the snow, I guess.'

Peter smiled, the gesture feeling natural for the first time in years. 'Well, enough of all that.' He reached into his sack and pulled out a gift. 'Merry Christmas, Jake.'

Jake took the package with hands that trembled either from shock or his usual chemical enhancement. He turned it over as if expecting it to disappear. Peter could practically see the thoughts racing behind Jake's bloodshot eyes – wondering if this was some kind of drug-induced hallucination. Something along the lines of: *This can't be... why would the miserable old git from number 9 get me a present?*

He was still turning it over in his hands. 'Thanks, but... yeah, I didn't get you anything.'

'Not about that Jake, now open... sesame...'

Jake tore off the paper to reveal a pair of expensive wireless headphones.

Peter leaned forward and clapped him on the shoulder. 'Now listen. Play as loud as you want till 10 p.m. I was assured that these are top of the range; you should lose none of that bass. Shake your skull until the cows come home!'

His eyes widened, and he looked at Peter in complete disbelief. 'Thank you.'

'Merry Christmas, son.' Peter winked. 'And pass my regards to Lou, lovely lass.'

'Actually, it's Debbie, now.' He shrugged and looked down.

'Debbie then. Merry Christmas!' He turned and crunched through the snow toward number 11. As he passed his home, he noticed the smashed door, and the rudimentary boarding they'd put up.

Christmas Eve

Sandra Chapman answered.

He realised he'd not put his beard back up. He did that now, but the cat was clearly out of the bag. Her eyes were like saucers. 'Peter... thank God...'

'Ho... ho—'

'Are you okay?'

'Never better.'

She nodded and looked around. She reached out to him as if he might disappear in a puff of smoke. 'Quickly... come in...'

'Sandra, I'm fine, but I've a message for your ex-husband. Desmond.'

'Desmond?'

'Aye... yes... we parted on rather frosty terms.'

'Yes, he mentioned it. Look, Peter, can I call someone?'

'Calm down, Sandra, everything is fine. When are you next seeing Desmond?'

'Boxing Day.'

'Okay... I'll try to stop by, but, if I miss him, tell him: "Merry Christmas!" and this will be music to his ears, and yours. My drive is his drive when he visits. Any time he likes. I won't be getting another car, so he can plonk that Bentley gas-guzzler there if he wants.'

Confusion warred with the concern on her face. 'Thank you, but...'

'No, thank you. Merry Christmas!'

Sandra stepped out of her home, but Peter had already turned and was walking away.

And then he saw Lucy, standing in her doorway across the street, one hand pressed to her mouth.

Excited, he made his way over, through the snow.

As he came closer, he saw that her shoulders were shaking while she kept her hands clamped to her mouth.

Christmas Eve

When he was directly opposite her, he saw the tears in her eyes. 'Merry Christmas,' he said. 'And... sorry?'

She threw her arms around him. 'I thought... I thought...'

'I think I know what you thought, eh?' He patted her back. 'Let's leave that for now. To be honest, I feel great. In fact, I haven't felt better in a while.'

She looked over his shoulder at Jake and Sandra. He turned to see that Jake and Sandra were still standing in their doorways, looking bemused.

He turned back. She looked him up and down in his Santa suit and prodded the bag of presents. 'Have you been reading *A Christmas Carol* or something?'

'Did Scrooge dress as Santa?'

'No, but—'

'You surely can't be saying I was as miserly as Scrooge?'

She let out another sob, clapping a hand over her mouth. 'Where the hell have you been?'

'A few places. The cemetery... a little B&B in Staines Donna and I used to love... Went to a few places that I used to hang out with an old friend...' He paused, took a deep breath and thought about Sarah for a moment.

'Peter?'

'Yes... sorry... also, I went to the bench.'

Her eyes widened. 'The bench?'

'You know, *the* bench.' His voice softened.

'Oh.' She looked down.

'Aye. Except there's no bench any more, is there? So, you could say I went back to the place where it happened. Where I lost her. And I sat on a wall for a while – longer than a while, really... nearly a day.' He smiled. 'But it helped.'

She met his gaze. 'I'm glad.'

He rose an eyebrow. 'I took her paper crane, actually. Sat and thought for a long time. Penny was fascinated by the cliffs. Ended up heading there, and letting it fly one last time. It was nice. It went quite a distance before finally falling into the sea.'

'The tablets...' Lucy's eyes searched his face. 'We found the empty bowl.'

'Aye, I took them with me. But, you know, they ended up in the bin.. See, something weird has happened these last days.'

'Weird?'

'Unexpected.'

'Unexpected?'

'Ha! Is there an echo? Something beautiful has happened, actually. Truth be told, it'd already happened, you see. Just took me a few days of reflection for it to sink in.'

'Please, tell me what you mean...'

Mia appeared beside her mum, holding Sophie. Mia's eyes immediately filled up. She handed Sophie to her mum and then hugged Peter. Peter smiled and said, 'You lot only went and happened.'

Reece came down the stairs, his eyes wide.

'Even he's included in that.'

'Peter?' Reece said, smiling. 'Epic!'

Peter's eyes misted over. Mia stood back. He reached out and touched Sophie's face. 'I was surrounded by shadows while I was away. Penny's laugh, Donna's gentle wisdom, Sarah's fierce spirit. But suddenly everything got brighter. It was strange. I didn't understand at first. I thought I had gone mad, but then I realised I was smiling. And I was thinking about your will to fight, Lucy, despite how hard everything has become for you. About you, Mia, and your strong independence. About Sophie's cute face...' He reached out and touched Sophie's cheek and she gurgled. 'I even thought that Reece isn't too bad, he just needs a firm hand...' He clenched his fist in mock threat, the gesture carrying none of his old bitterness. They laughed.

'And that's it, really. I was smiling. Because of you four. And one thing I've learned in my fairly long and troubled life is that you can't take a smile for granted. Especially the real kind. You know? The real smiles.'

He lowered his sack of presents like a man setting down more than just gifts. 'These are for tomorrow, and I wanted to say thank you.' He turned away quickly as his tears started.

He didn't want them to think him sad, because, for the first time, in a long time, he wasn't. They were tears of happiness. 'I'll go and sort my door—'

'You bloody won't.' He felt his arm being gripped. He turned and saw Lucy had given Sophie back to Mia and was holding his arm. 'You're staying right here tonight... I'm not letting you out of my sodding sight again.'

'I should really check the house... someone could break in and steal—'

'That TV?' Mia laughed. 'Reece almost broke his back carrying it over.'

'Piss off.'

'Oi, language,' Lucy said. 'Peter, we took everything we could from your house. It's here. I wasn't prepared for you to lose anything.'

He recalled that Donna's jewellery was stored under a floorboard along with a box of memorabilia of Penny. He expected they would be fine until later. 'But it's Christmas tomorrow?'

'And?' Lucy asked.

Christmas Eve

She pulled him into the warmth of her home, and for the first time since Penny's death, Peter Watson felt like he was walking toward something rather than away from everything.

∼

Lewis White approached Isobelle's door. His heart hammered against his ribs with such force he wondered if the security light's motion sensors might pick up its rhythm before detecting his actual movements.

His ex-wife opened the door before he'd even reached it.

Lewis expected hostility. Spending most of his life in a hostile state meant he'd come to anticipate it everywhere.

But Isobelle wasn't hostile. Just surprised. Her hand flew to her mouth, and then she embraced him.

It was unexpected. They may not have parted on horrendous terms – in fact, it had been rather amicable – but seeing her joy at his return was baffling.

When she pulled away, she had tears in her eyes. 'I didn't know you were out,' she said softly.

'Earlier than expected. Happened for a number of us. Overcrowded prisons.'

'When?'

'A few weeks back. I meant to come and speak to you earlier.' That was a lie, of course. He'd never meant to come and see them again. He'd wanted to disappear beneath the cracks in society – let them get on with their lives. But something had shifted.

More than shifted.

Changed.

'That's a lie.' The admission surprised him.

God, maybe things have changed!

'Sorry?'

'I would've left you be, but I've been with my dad, and, well, he died a couple of days back.'

She pressed her hand to her chest. 'Lewis, I'm sorry. Are you okay?'

'Yes, I think so...'

'I didn't know you were in touch...'

'We weren't. Haven't been for decades. It came out of the blue. His nurse contacted me.'

'And you went? That's kind of you. It must have been hard.'

'It was ... I don't know. Enlightening. In the end, maybe, I saw some different sides to him. It's still hard to forgive him, but it seems he had a different way of viewing things. I guess one size doesn't always fit all, does it?' He felt himself crumble inside, and tears ran down his face. 'I mean, we could say the same about me.'

'Lewis...' She stepped forward without hesitation, her embrace carrying all the familiar comfort of home. He breathed in the scent of her shampoo and closed his eyes.

How had he lost this? How had rage and fear poisoned everything good in his life?

He slipped away from her, although his instincts were to hold on. 'I'm sorry I told you not to bring him to prison. I couldn't at the time. And it just wasn't the right place for him.'

'I agree, but it was what you said...'

I don't want to see either of you again.

'It wasn't right. And it wasn't really what I meant. Or maybe it was.' He rubbed his head. 'I don't know any more, but I was scared, because of what I am or was.'

Christmas Eve

She reached out and put her hand on his upper arm. 'You should have let me in. I would have helped.'

'There was so much hate and resentment, and I wanted to spare you that. But now, suddenly, I'm resolved to not feeling that way any more, and then I just wanted to see you, Isobelle, and I wanted to see—'

'Dad!' His son burst past his mother and embraced him. Lewis kissed his head, barely having to bend now to reach young Felix, named for the uncle he'd never known – here was three years measured in inches of growth and missed moments.

'How was India, Australia...' Felix said. 'So many places...'

The cover story they'd created about international work sat heavy on him, but that was a truth for another day. Lewis swallowed hard. 'I'll tell you all about it, but first...' He slipped off his backpack and pushed it into his son's hands.

Felix unzipped it. His eyes lit up over the wrapped presents inside.

'For *tomorrow* only...' Lewis insisted, ruffling his son's hair. 'You know the score.'

After he'd promised to see him again soon, and Isobelle had sent him to another room, Lewis smiled. 'I want to be in his life. So much. I don't want him experiencing what I did – I want to be there. If that's the only thing I ever give back to the world, then that will be okay. Every second I can see him. Every moment you allow me.'

'It's not about allowing you, Lewis, but we have to be careful.'

He nodded. 'I know. Tell me what to do. I will not fail at this again. I assure you.'

She nodded slowly; she was weighing the authenticity

Christmas Eve

of his words. 'Okay. You know I never wanted anything different, don't you? I always wanted you in his life.'

'I know... thank you.' He took several steps back. 'Can I call?'

'Of course...'

He backed further away, catching sight of Simon – the new man – watching from the lounge. He waved and the man waved back – maintaining neutrality, or at least giving the impression that he was.

'Merry Christmas,' he said to Isobelle and turned away.

'Lewis?'

He turned back.

'Come over at two tomorrow. You can eat Christmas dinner with us. I'll speak to Simon – he'll be okay with it. You can stay for an hour after. Let's see how it goes.'

He smiled and nodded. 'Baby steps... I understand... thank you,' he said.

As he walked away, adrenaline coursed through his veins like electricity. If not for the treacherous ice and snow, he might have broken into a run, shouting his joy to the winter sky. Instead, he allowed himself a swift march, his heart thrashing with the most beautiful surge of adrenaline he'd ever known.

And then he saw his brother, smiling at him from the shadows.

'Felix, I've got this!'

And then he thought of his son, also called Felix, as he had done every day for three years.

Except today his thoughts were filled with hope, and not guilt.

Christmas Day

The warmth of Christmas dinner settled in Frank's belly, accompanied by the soft padding of Rylan's paws across the carpet. His eyes drifted closed, his body sinking deeper into the armchair.

He dreamt of his walk with Evelyn in Pannett Gardens the day before, her laughter carrying on the crisp winter air, the way her eyes had crinkled at the corners when she smiled.

Then he stirred and blinked against the soft glow of Christmas tree lights. Gerry and Tom sat cross-legged by the coffee table, a spread of playing cards between them. Rylan dozed at their feet, one ear cocked in Frank's direction.

'Bloody hell... sorry...' Frank sat up and stretched out. 'How long was I out?'

'Almost an hour,' Tom said, laying down a card with deliberate precision. 'You were snoring like a freight train.'

Gerry's brow furrowed as she studied her cards.

Tom laughed. 'Are you okay?'

'Just a moment,' she said.

Christmas Day

Tom looked at Frank and winked. 'She's retracing her steps, seeing how she lost.'

She put the cards down. 'Okay... I see where I went wrong now.'

'She means I won,' Tom translated with a grin.

Frank watched them packing away the cards, struck by how naturally they moved around each other now. All that anxiety over lists and rules seemed far away.

'You slept through the king's speech,' Gerry said.

Frank clicked his fingers. 'Darn. Another yearly run-through of the problems it's up to us to solve.'

'It was positive – about how well things are going,' Gerry said.

'Eh? That's even worse. A fairy tale. The truth is one thing, being lied to is another.'

'A few messages came through on your phone while you were asleep,' Tom said. 'I didn't want to wake you.'

He checked his phone. Messages from Evelyn.

> Dinner turned into a hostage situation – grandkids refused to leave the table until they got thirds. Janet's threatening to serve sprouts for pudding.

> Don't you dare tell Janet I'm drinking sherry – she thinks this is herbal tea.

He chuckled to himself.

'Evelyn or Henrietta?' Tom asked with exaggerated innocence.

Frank fixed him with a stern look. 'Listen here, you cheeky sod. I'm sixty-five years old. Do you have me pegged for some kind of geriatric Casanova?'

'Well...' Tom drew the word out with a grin.

'Bloody hell, man! I spent most of my life barely

managing one relationship,' Frank continued, 'and now you think I'm part of a harem?'

'That's not what he meant,' Gerry interjected, her tone matter of fact. 'Tom is merely observing that both Evelyn and Henrietta appear to have developed a romantic interest in you, despite your persistent self-deprecation regarding your age and appearance.'

Frank regarded her – he knew it wasn't sarcasm, just her usual blunt accuracy. 'Enough now... I'm grateful for the dinner, but no more references to me as some kind of fancy dandy across town.' He patted his stomach. 'I mean, look at that... if I post a picture of myself online, I'm not getting any. What do you call 'em? Hits? Am I?'

'Don't be down on yourself, Frank,' Gerry said. 'Your weight has come down, and you're male, single and heterosexual. Both Evelyn and Henrietta are both single women of compatible age and social status. These attractions make sense. Statistically.'

Tom had to turn away, shoulders shaking with suppressed laughter.

'Right,' Frank declared, 'that's enough of that. How about I catch up on that king's speech instead? Might as well end the day with a proper fairy tale.'

Gerry reached for the remote, but before she could find the recording, Frank's phone buzzed again. This time it wasn't a message – it was an alert from his brand new video doorbell he'd only fitted yesterday.

He sat up straight in his chair, heart pounding.

It was that scrote. At his door!

He pressed a button to activate the audio feed—only to be informed that his cheaper model didn't have one.

Bollocks!

Christmas Day

'Frank?' Gerry's voice seemed to come from very far away. 'What's wrong?'

He held up a hand for silence, eyes fixed on the screen. The figure was wearing gloves – no prints then. But something about the way they moved... The way they reached for the door...

Then he saw it—a key. His key. Maddie's. 'I have to go,' he said, already moving toward the door. His mind raced ahead – if he took the back streets, avoided the town centre...

'Frank, wait—' Gerry started.

'I'll call you,' he promised, though his thoughts were already at home, calculating times and distances.

The drive passed in a blur of salted roads and Christmas lights. His heart pounded against his ribs as he rewatched the feed on his phone at traffic lights – the figure entering his house, moving with the familiarity of someone who knew the layout.

He barely felt the cold as he rushed up his drive. Inside, the house was silent, but the air felt different somehow. Disturbed.

'Who's here?' he called out, moving from room to room with increasing desperation.

Nothing.

He'd gone.

He spotted something on the kitchen counter. A folded piece of paper.

His hands shook as he opened it:

For 10k, I'll tell you where she is.

A phone number followed.

Christmas Day

He punched in the digits, grip white-knuckled on the phone.

'Yeah?' A young, male voice.

'If you've hurt her, you piece of shit, I'll tear your fucking throat out—'

'She's fine.' The voice was maddeningly calm.

'You've kidnapped my daughter, you little scrote. How do you think this ends?'

'I haven't kidnapped Maddie. I just know where she is. And how much you want to see her.'

Frank's free hand clenched into a fist. 'Where is she?'

'Money first.'

'Money? You won't be able to spend it – I'll be pulling you apart piece by—'

'Ten k. I'll send the bank details. It's not unrealistic. Man your age, healthy savings, retirement plan…'

'You seem to know a lot about me.' Frank forced his voice level, professional instincts kicking in despite the rage and fear coursing through him. 'Who is this?'

'Maddie and I were close once.'

The thought repulsed him. 'How do I know you won't just take the money and run?'

'You don't. But I won't.'

'What guarantee do I have that you even know where she is?'

'I'll send you two images. Then I'm binning this phone.'

The line went dead. Seconds later, two photos arrived.

The first nearly brought Frank to his knees. Maddie, in profile, opening a door. Her hair was longer than he remembered, but that tilt of her chin – pure Mary. His girl. Alive.

The second showed a battered wheelie bin behind what looked like an abandoned house. An address followed, then another message:

Christmas Day

House is empty. Withdraw 2k a day from the 26th. Drop the money in the bin at 3 p.m. on the 31st. You have my word. The line was already dead when he tried calling back.

Frank sank onto the sofa, his whole body trembling. He looked up at Mary's photograph.

'I know what you'd say, love,' he whispered. 'That I should call it in.' He scrubbed a hand over his face. 'But I know how that sometimes goes... Look, if there's even a chance... what's 10k?'

His phone rang – Gerry again. He let it go to voicemail, knowing she'd be worried but unable to form words right now.

Less than a week until he delivered, and he might see his daughter again.

Or until he realised that he'd made the worst mistake of his life by agreeing to it!

He reached for the TV remote with unsteady hands, needing noise, distraction, anything to fill the silence.

The king's speech.

A fairy tale.

God, did he need his own right now.

Three Months Later...

Christie's world had collapsed again. Her hands trembled so violently that she couldn't fit the key into her parents' front door. 'Right-handed.'

Detective Moss's words.

'Right-handed.'

It had become a mantra, pounding through her head.

Right-handed... right-handed...

Frozen in time with her heartbeat, erratic for the last hour. She'd forgiven him. Believed him.

And now, with those words—right-handed—another deception was dissolving her like acid. When she finally managed the door, the house felt hollow, and most of it was dark. Some light spilled from the kitchen.

She found her father preparing tea, squeezing the teabag against the side of the mug with his right hand. That fucking right hand. 'Christie, flower?' His voice carried a familiar note of paternal concern that now made her stomach turn.

Had every moment of concern been an act?

His worry, his love – all part of the performance?

Three Months Later...

'What's wrong?' He asked.

Unable to bear the sight of what might be another mask, and not knowing what to say, she fled back into the darkness of the hallway, and then took the stairs where Georgina Prince had died, two at a time, until she reached her parents' bedroom.

Caroline sat enthroned in her favourite chair by the window, winter light catching her silver hair like a halo. Her nightgown, though pristine, hung on her frame like a shroud. Since the arrest, she'd faded fast. It was hard not to think of a photograph left for too long in the sunlight. Caroline had come home to die. The case would never go to trial.

'Mum?' Christie's voice cracked.

Caroline's gaze drifted toward her without recognition, those once-sharp eyes now clouded like frosted glass.

Christie stared at her mother's left hand, searching for some sign of weakness that might validate the lie she'd told less than an hour ago to Moss. But like everything else in this house, even truth refused to cooperate. Her left hand wasn't curled up like a claw, and difficult to use.

Just like her father, and the governors, and Georgina Prince's parents, she'd joined the realm of the deceitful.

'She's been talking about school all morning,' Stephen said from behind her. 'She was back in the past for a short time. I think I heard genuine happiness in her voice—'

Christie whirled to face her father in the door, rage turning her voice to ice. 'Don't.'

'I don't understand?' He came forward and his hand touched her shoulder. She jerked away as if burned.

'This constant performance! I don't know what's true any more!'

'This makes no sense, flower...' His familiar endearment now felt like a knife twisting in her heart.

Three Months Later...

She led him to another room, away from her mother, before turning on him. 'A detective DC Moss called. About Georgina's death.'

She clocked the stiffening of his spine.

'Her murder,' Christie said. Now, it was her turn to twist the knife.

He flinched. 'Why?'

'He was tidying up the paperwork for filing away. Since it will not go to trial, it needed closing. Something made him curious.'

Right-handed... Right-handed...

She grabbed her skull. Those words. Moss's words. She just couldn't get them out of her fucking head.

She felt his hand on her arm. 'Flower?'

The way he said it, like none of it had ever happened. 'Get your fucking hands off me!'

He complied, but she heard him take a deep breath.

'Right to left... Right to left...' she said, holding up her right hand. 'Face on, the hammer struck Georgina's left temple. So, according to the pathologist, it was more likely the blow came from the right hand of the assailant.'

Stephen took another deep breath. 'I'm not sure what that even means...'

'Mum is left-handed.'

Stephen nodded. 'All sorts of factors influence that, surely... How quickly did she grab the weapon? Maybe the angle when she turned...'

'Maybe... That's why it was easier to lie for you... Dad.'

He took a step back, wide eyed, guffawing. 'What is it you're saying?'

'I'm saying that it was you who hit Georgina with a hammer, not Mum.'

Three Months Later...

He snorted. 'Ridiculous.' He shook his head and stared at Christie angrily. 'Did the detective suggest that?'

'No... he was querying it. And like I said, I lied for you.'

'Okay... let's knock this off now. You haven't lied for anyone.'

'I've... lied... for you...'

'Flower, I—'

Christie narrowed her eyes. 'Fuck you, Dad. Don't you ever call me that again.'

He paled and took another step back.

'I said that because of Mum's condition, she'd been experiencing weakness in her left side. She'd been struggling to hold things. Dropping them. It went some way to explaining why she may have opted to use her right in the heat of the moment.'

The silence stretched between them like a tightrope between cliff edges.

'Let's hope they don't check against her medical records, eh?' she finally said. 'Or we're both fucked.'

He gulped and turned slightly, lowering his head.

He thought for a while, then looked up, fixed her with a stare, and said, 'You shouldn't have lied, Christie, but it's okay now, I'm sure it will be fine. But whatever you think—'

'Bollocks.' Christie spat the word. 'Just stop!' She put her hands over her ears. 'I don't believe anything you say any more.'

He reached out and she evaded his hand.

She circled around him, looking up at the person she'd adored above everyone. The person she'd mirrored her life on.

She could see it in his eyes now. The realisation that he'd lost her. That he was about to lose Caroline. And her

Three Months Later...

brother, well, her brother was never there. Gallivanting off around the world.

Can you sense the loneliness that awaits you, Dad?

She fought back the feelings of pity rising within her. She fought them back with another hard truth. 'You watched your wife, my mother, being led away in a nightgown?'

He snapped his head to one side, and a tear rolled down his cheek. 'What choice did I have? She'd have died alone – without me.'

'She'd have had me, Milo...'

'Not having me would have destroyed her all the more.'

'Instead, you've ruined her reputation – the woman you love. Supposedly. Forever more, those people who looked up to her as a teacher will think she was a killer.'

'They will understand. Rationalise it, because she was sick...'

She pointed. 'No Dad, you're the one who's sick.'

She turned and marched away, down the stairs.

He, of course, chased her. 'Well, if you want it so much... if you believe so adamantly in justice, then phone them... tell them the truth.'

At the bottom of the steps, she turned. 'No... it's too late... I want you to live with what you've done to Mum, to me... and, when I tell him, Milo—'

'Flower...' There were tears in his eyes now.

'My mother will die believing she murdered someone... you cold bastard.'

'She doesn't. She won't. Her memory... it's—'

'Convenient, for you.'

She turned and took the door handle. 'One more thing...' She looked back... 'Georgina Prince. Was that true as well? Did you abuse her?'

Three Months Later...

'No,' he snapped.

'Did you abuse any of them?'

'How could you ask me that?'

'Did you?'

He flinched and looked away. 'Of course not.'

Was that a delay? A suggestion that he was also guilty of that?

'I will call ahead when I visit, so you can be out, Stephen. After the funeral, I never want to see you again.'

And then Christie left, dissolving into darkness beneath the weight of two generations of lies – her father's, and now her own.

The Funeral

Stephen's living room buzzed with former colleagues from Riverside, their voices a low murmur of shared memories.

He moved between them, catching fragments of conversations.

They shared stories – Caroline's fierce dedication to mathematics, her protective instincts toward struggling students, the way her infectious laugh could silence a staff room mid-argument.

He appreciated the gentle murmur of shared memories – echoes of who she was before the illness stripped her dignity.

Nobody had mentioned Georgina. Caroline was being remembered as she deserved to be remembered: brilliant, dedicated, loved.

Christie and Milo had performed their roles perfectly at the funeral, flanking him in the front pew like dutiful children should. The illusion of a family united in grief.

Later, she'd hissed to him in private, 'See how well I fake it? See how well I lie? You must be so proud, Dad.'

Milo hadn't bothered with words at all. He didn't seek

The Funeral

out any explanations, content to ignore him. Now Stephen's children stood together near the buffet table, untouched plates in their hands. Their grief was no longer an act but something raw, something real – grief for their mother, for their lost innocence, for the father they had thought they knew.

The house would go on the market tomorrow. A bungalow would suffice for his remaining years, and his children's accounts would swell with money. A final gift from a father who had genuinely loved them, regardless of what they believed.

Stephen glanced around the room again, noting the faces of those who'd admired him all these years. His reputation had been everything – the cost of maintaining it beyond calculation. In the end, it had cost him his children's love.

He hoped that one day, perhaps when he was gone, they'd find it in their hearts to forgive him.

The doorbell's chime cut through his thoughts.

He moved to answer it, feeling disconnected from his own body, as if watching himself from a great distance.

It was an elderly woman in a wheelchair. She looked frail, almost as if she'd been carved from paper. Alongside her was a young care worker in crisp navy scrubs. Her name badge read 'Sylvie.'

'I'm Margaret Matthews.' Her voice, though thin, carried surprising strength.

A coldness stirred in Stephen's chest, breaking through the numbness of recent days.

'You taught my daughter.'

'I remember.' The words escaped before he could stop them.

I remember like it was yesterday.

The Funeral

I never really forget.
I can't.

'I'm sorry for the loss of your wife,' Margaret said.

'Thank you.' He forced steadiness into his voice. 'And I'm sorry to hear what you went through. Sarah was very talented.' He stood to one side and gestured inside. 'Would you like to come in?'

'No thank you. I just wanted to pay my respects and then give you something.'

Sylvie passed him an envelope.

'I found it when I was finally packing up Sarah's room,' Margaret said. 'I dropped an old horse figurine – it was already broken. It seemed that she'd folded up a poem and slipped it inside. I read it. It's a lovely poem. It had your name on top. "For Stephen." I didn't know of any other. You know, I think it may have been one of her best – I didn't want to give it away, but, you know, it belongs to you. She'd want you to have it.'

He began to open the envelope—

'Not now, please...' Margaret said. 'Alone is better, I feel. She never really connected with any teachers – apart from you.' A ghost of a smile touched her lips. 'You brought something special out in her.'

He suddenly felt the weight of Christie and Milo's stares burning into his back. When he glanced over his shoulder, their faces were twin masks of curiosity and anger.

He turned back.

'I do believe that if not for that monster Clive Morton, Sarah would have been all right... Thanks to people like you, Stephen, people who saw her potential.' She smiled. Her expression was one of the most genuine he'd ever seen. 'Now, I must go... once again, I am sorry about your wife.'

He watched them leave, the care worker expertly navi-

The Funeral

gating the wheelchair down his drive. Only when they'd disappeared from view did he close the door and go quickly upstairs to the bathroom.

In the bathroom mirror, an old man looked back.

Thanks to people like you.

Tears welled in the old man's eyes. *You brought out something special in her.*

The first tear fell, tracking down the old man's lined face.

The poem was heavily creased from being folded and hidden for so long. Margaret had clearly ironed it out as best she could. As he read, the old man saw himself, long ago, on a cold October night in 1989.

Beneath still waters, truth blooms wild and free.

He follows the red Fiesta at a distance, killing his headlights as it turns toward the patch of trees near Clive Morton's place. The Fiesta stops.

He watches, chain-smoking, anxiety coursing through his veins.

Who are you in the car with, Sarah?

A lost soul entwined in a verse none can see.

He watches her run down the dirt path while the Fiesta leaves.

Clive Morton at the door, welcoming her in. Twenty minutes he sits there, chain-smoking, anxiety coursing through his veins.

Why are you there, Sarah?

His watch ticks away the endless minutes until he can't bear it any longer. He reaches for the handle.

From shadowed depths, a flower breaks the light.

Then he sees her, walking toward his car.

He reaches over and opens the passenger door. Tells her to get in.

The Funeral

'No.'

'Get in,' he says, again. His voice hardens.

She slides into the passenger seat, beautiful and tearful. And lying, always lying.

Together, we grew... I grew...

He drives slowly.

'Who was the woman driving the red Fiesta?'

'A friend.'

'Tell me her name.'

'No.'

'You don't get to say no to me.'

'I can and I will. No.'

'Did you tell her?'

'I told her.'

'Everything?'

'No. Just that I was pregnant.'

'How could you?'

'Because she loves me and she's kind.'

'I love you.'

'Yes... but you're not always kind.'

A secret garden, hidden from their sight, but not from the heavens.

So perfect, pure, and true.

He drives faster now. So sick of being pushed out and lied to.

'Why did you go to Clive Morton?'

'Because he was close... I couldn't be in that car any more. I couldn't see her cry like that. See her breaking.'

'You think that she cares?'

'Yes.'

'No one cares about you, like I do. You are my flower, remember?'

'You want me to kill our baby.'

The Funeral

'I want you to do what's right.'

'That's not right.'

He hits the steering wheel. 'And me losing everything is! What about Clive?'

'What about him?'

'He's odd... weird...'

'He's gentle, kind... he listens... he always wants to help...'

'So you told him as well?'

'Yes... just about the baby... not—'

He hits the wheel again. 'You're out of control. Someone could find out.'

'They won't. I've told you. I won't be with you any more. You have to stop following me.'

'Get the abortion and I'll stop.'

'No, I won't do that to a child.'

'It's less than ten weeks.'

'It's a life.'

Fertilise, flourish... hold me close... you gave me the words with which I could tell the truth...

He drives even faster.

'Have you forgotten everything I did?'

'No, of course not.'

'What you were? How I changed you?'

'I was fifteen.'

'Lost.'

'Yes. But I'm twenty-two now.'

'So I don't matter any more? My son. A daughter on the way. I have my position in this community...'

'You should have let me go long before now.'

'I couldn't...'

'Why not?'

'You know I couldn't... where's your bracelet?'

The Funeral

'I gave it to Clive. He said he liked shiny things. I didn't want it any more.'

'You stupid, stupid fucking girl.' He shouts now.

She shouts back. 'I'm not a girl any more.'

'But you're still stupid.'

'Let me go.'

'I can't.'

'Why not?'

'I already told you. You know why."

Now share those words with me.

He stops the car.

'I need to show you something.'

'What?'

He rubs his temples. 'It's out there...'

'What is?'

'What I want to show you.'

'Why are you being like this?'

'Because I love you.'

'And I love you too, but what does that mean?'

'Everything.'

'I wrote you another poem.'

'Really?' His heart rate quickens. 'What's it called?'

'Beneath still waters.'

'Ah... I like that... I really do.'

'It's about being found and growing.'

A tear runs down his face. 'Thank you for writing that.'

'You're welcome, but I'm not getting an abortion, Stephen. I can't.'

He sighs. 'I know.'

'So you understand?'

He nods. 'I have for a while.'

'Will it stop you loving me?'

'No. Nothing could ever do that.' He touches her face,

493

The Funeral

kisses her. 'No. Come, walk with me, tell me more about this poem.'

She wipes away his tear. 'Where are we going?'

He points to the old silo, its dark shape cutting against the starlit sky.

'There.'

Join Frank, Gerry and Rylan on their next adventure when the echoes of past crimes lead them down more winding paths in FORGOTTEN SHADOWS.

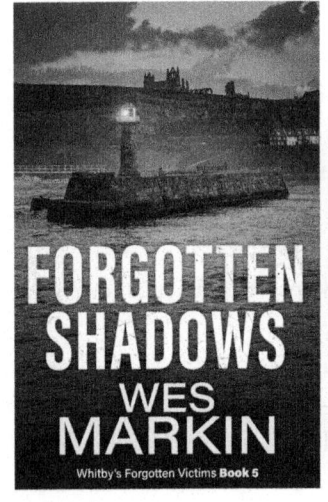

Scan the QR to Pre-order!

Free and Exclusive read

Delve deeper into the world of Wes Markin with the
FREE and **EXCLUSIVE** read, ***A Lesson in Crime***

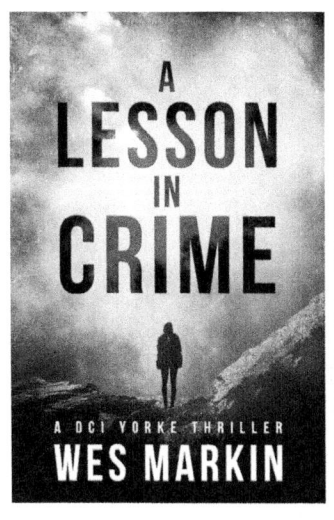

Scan the QR to
READ NOW!

JOIN DCI EMMA GARDNER AS SHE RELOCATES TO KNARESBOROUGH, HARROGATE IN THE NORTH YORKSHIRE MURDERS ...

Still grieving from the tragic death of her colleague, DCI Emma Gardner continues to blame herself and is struggling to focus. So, when she is seconded to the wilds of Yorkshire, Emma hopes she'll be able to get her mind back on the job, doing what she does best - putting killers behind bars.

But when she is immediately thrown into another violent murder, Emma has no time to rest. Desperate to get answers and find the killer, Emma needs all the help she can. But her new partner, DI Paul Riddick, has demons and issues of his own.

And when this new murder reveals links to an old case Riddick was involved with, Emma fears that history might be about to repeat itself...

Don't miss the brand-new gripping crime series by bestselling British crime author Wes Markin!

What people are saying about Wes Markin...

JOIN DCI EMMA GARDNER AS SHE RELOCATES TO KNA...

'Cracking start to an exciting new series. Twist and turns, thrills and kills. I loved it.'

Bestselling author **Ross Greenwood**

'Markin stuns with his latest offering... Mind-bendingly dark and deep, you know it's not for the faint hearted from page one. Intricate plotting, devious twists and excellent characterisation take this tale to a whole new level. Any serious crime fan will love it!'

Bestselling author **Owen Mullen**

Scan the QR to READ NOW!

Also by Wes Markin
ONE LAST PRAYER

"An explosive and visceral debut with the most terrifying of killers. Wes Markin is a new name to watch out for in crime fiction, and I can't wait to see more of Detective Yorke." – *Bestselling Crime Author Stephen Booth*

The disappearance of a young boy. An investigation paved with depravity and death. Can DCI Michael Yorke survive with his body and soul intact?

With Yorke's small town in the grip of a destructive snowstorm, the relentless detective uncovers a missing boy's connection to a deranged family whose history is steeped in violence. But when all seems lost, Yorke refuses to give in, and journeys deep into the heart of this sinister family for the truth.

And what he discovers there will tear his world apart.

The Rays are here. It's time to start praying.

The shocking and exhilarating new crime thriller will have you turning the pages late into the night.

"**A pool of blood, an abduction, swirling blizzards, a haunting mystery, yes, Wes Markin's One Last Prayer for the Rays has all the makings of an absorbing thriller. I recommend that you give it a go.**" – *Alan Gibbons, Bestselling Author*

One Last Prayer is a shocking and compulsive crime thriller.

Scan the QR to READ NOW!

Acknowledgments

Forgotten Graves was a longer and more emotional book than I had anticipated. Bringing together these men in their latter years, standing in judgement over parenthood, led me to reflect on my own journey as a father. Like Frank, it is hard not to wonder if you've always made the right decisions, but I guess we are all learning as we go.

My family remains my anchor. Jo, Hugo, and Bea - your love makes every challenging day worthwhile.

To the readers whose thoughtful reviews inspire me to dig deeper - especially Donna, Kath and Sharon, who have been there since the start.

I owe special thanks to artist and filmmaker David Lynch, who passed this year. From the age of 11, when I first saw Twin Peaks, I knew that I had to tell twisty, complex stories. He profoundly influenced my writing journey and how I approach these narratives of light and darkness.

Soon, Whitby will reveal new secrets, forcing Frank and Gerry to look into the shadows. I look forward to seeing you all then.

Review

If you enjoyed reading **_Forgotten Graves_**, please take a few moments to leave a review on Amazon, Goodreads or BookBub.

Printed in Great Britain
by Amazon